Short Stories, Vignettes & Snippets

CANTINA PSALMS

SAN FRANCISCO NOIR

THOMAS SHESS

THREE PALMS PRESS
SAN DIEGO CA

THREE PALMS PRESS
3245 University Ave, Ste 258
San Diego, CA 92104
threepalmspress@gmail.com

This book is a work of fiction. Names, characters, places, and incidents either are the product of the author's imagination or are used fictitiously. Any resemblance to actual events, conversations or locales or persons living or dead, is entirely coincidental.

Copyright © 2022 by Thomas Shess, Jr.
United States Copyright Office
TXu 2-263-247

All rights reserved. No part of this publication may be reproduced, distributed, or transmitted in any form or by any means, including photocopying, recording, or other electronic or mechanical methods, without the prior written permission of the publisher, except in the case of brief quotations embodied in critical reviews and certain other noncommercial uses permitted by copyright law. For permission requests, email the author, addressed "Permissions Desk"
threepalmspress@gmail.com

Ordering Information:

For details, contact threepalmspress@gmail.com

Print ISBN: 978-1-66784-402-2
eBook ISBN: 978-1-66784-403-9

Author services and printing by BookBaby.com
Cover Design by Kristin Hardy Design.
Manufactured in the United States of America
First Edition

For Phyllis Adkisson Shess, J.D.

CONTENTS

AUTHOR'S NOTE	1
PREFACE	5
1. ART OF THE DEAL	7
2. APPEARANCE OF IMPROPRIETY	63
3. THE DENIZENS	86
4. THE COY POND	104
5. HEMOPHILLIAC OF LOVE	142
6. ROUGH PART OF TOWN	157
7. WHO KNOCKED UP, BABY CAKES?	201
8. ODD DUCK SEASON	229
9. EX, X	243
10. THE PUBLICANS	262
11. SHEET MUSIC	313
12. MEA CULPA HALL OF FAME	336
13. HEAVYWEIGHT CHAMPIONSHIP OF THE WORLD	356
EPILOG	366
ABOUT THE AUTHOR	374

AUTHOR'S NOTE

I love this city. I hate this city. We fell in love when I was sentenced to live there as a daily newspaper reporter and editor of a local magazine. I am equally happy to have escaped. The divorce is final with visiting rights.

Cantina Psalms depicts the high and low ends of San Francisco society, which will not please many. I bend the term *pastiche* to involve the reader in a compression of time: from the past when the city was teeming with original and remarkable characters and neighborhoods, like North Beach, to the future of technological promise.

This work is fiction. It is set in one of the most beautiful and once remarkable cities in North America. For all its beauty, complexities and human cul de sacs, the city also has its gutters.

Much of this work is fanciful. I make no claim to being James Joyce or Lawrence Durrell, but my short stories are presented akin to Joyce's *Dubliners* and in the spirit of the geographic urban noir found in Durrell's Alexandria, Egypt, in *Justine*.

Cantina Psalms (saloons + holy songs) as a work is not meant to champion drug usage or excess alcoholic consumption, but to report on the condition of the natives who do. Only human beings were hurt, most survived, in the creation of this work.

You will note *Cantina Psalms* has a cast of characters and endnotes at the end. The idea to include the above came from a visit to D.G. Wills Books in La Jolla (the closest copy in the United States to Silvia Beach's immortal Shakespeare & Company in Paris). At Dennis Wills' shop, I found a dusty paperback: James Joyce's *Dubliners* by Penguin Classics with annotations. These endnotes were critical in my understanding of James Joyce. I'd struggled with Joyce's works all my life, but I knew if I were to write a novel in the English language I had to come to grips with Joyce. The annotations brought me to writing fiction, otherwise I would have never understood that Joyce flows like the river Liffey.

The *Cantina Psalms* in my work were inspired by a device Lawrence Durrell used at the end of *Justine* (also from Penguin) titled *Consequential Data*. There he wrote character squeezes, the inspiration for the cast of characters in *Cantina Psalms*. Also, Durrell wrote small snippets, which I call psalms. Here is an example of a Durrell endnote:

"Pombal asleep in full evening dress. Beside him on the bed a chamber pot full of banknotes he had won at the casino."

He goes on.

I would never have arrived at Durrell's treatment at the end of his work had I not submitted a short story to a publisher in Arizona. In a thoughtful rejection note, he took the time to be kind and said my Cantinas remind me so much of Durrell in his *Justine*.

I had never read Durrell before. I bought all his works, but I always come back to *Justine*. In *Cantina Psalms,* Annee Kinder is Justine and all the Justine's before her.

My trip to Arizona confirmed what teachers have told us forever:

We must read.

At this point, I offer a reader's alert, which will aid those who took the time to read this preface. Those that do not will be unaware that this work takes place in the near future. Most future concepts will be described as they appear while others, like LOBE, will need the following text:

LOBE ON, LOBE OFF

Late in the twentieth century, Swiss-based Logan Basic Energies developed a dime-sized, snap on the earlobe phone/computer powered by nuclear energy and operated via voice commands. In grandad's terms, it was an iPhone that never needed to be charged.

It never got off the proverbial ground because a device operating that close to the brain demanded long-term testing. No one had the kind of money to fund such a study.

It wasn't until Omni Titanium produced a metal shell, which could contain the micro amounts of nuclear material needed to power Logan's microphone, that Logan and Omni coproduced LOBE, the world's first earring-sized phone.

The only thing keeping the LOBE from being attached to every ear in the world was the incredible retail price of $25,000 new dollars. Only governmental agencies and those citizens willing to pay the per-unit cost had LOBEs. To date, orders from military, law enforcement and techno geeks kept the two companies afloat.

At first, insurance companies refused to insure the devices because opportunistic thieves created a snatch and run black market.

Tech stepped in and gave the LOBE device more sophisticated ID codes, ending the dilemma.

Saudi Arabia was the first nation to subsidize the LOBE for its citizens, bringing down the retail cost to $2,000. Soon the world followed. The LOBE worn by the Feds, local police, and private agents like Art Garcia cost $500 each, with network linkage extra.

NOTED ALUMS

The following San Franciscans founded or attended Sts. Peter and Paul School for Orphan Boys, a boarding school K-12 located across from Washington Square on Filbert Street:

--**Father Ronald MacDonald**, founder, principal emeritus

--**Joseph Martin**, district attorney, mayor of the combined City and County of San Francisco

--**Arthur Garcia**, ex-special agent United States Customs and founder of Art Garcia Investigations.

--**John Wald**, publican and ex-San Francisco Fire Department, paramedic, retired

--**Garrett Ellis**, attorney, solo practitioner, corporate and political advisor

--**Thomas Gresham**, former patrolman, San Francisco Police Department; security detail for Mayor Joe Martin.

--**Wallace "Wally" McGrath**, assigned to the school by his father Thomas McGrath, Jr. after the death of Wally's mother. Thomas McGrath, Jr. was the sole benefactor of the school.

See Epilog for expanded cast of characters.

PREFACE
First Cantina Psalm:

ETHNIC SALAD

On tourist brochures and rent-a-car maps, San Francisco's North Beach neighborhood is labeled as the city's Little Italy. In the old days—the real old days—it was known as the Barbary Coast. Today, it's no different from Boston's Southside, San Diego's India Street or Lower Eastside Manhattan. Ethnic urban neighborhoods are as old as Yankee Doodle. They seldom change, even when suburban flight takes most of the families. Divorced mothers now live atop bakeries, cobblers, and hardware stores. Rents are skyrocketing in North Beach. Poorer families had to share cheaper rentals with sleaze, which began moving in with peep show and Lotto emporium liquor stores as they replaced florists and tailors. Gone are the days when cops on the beat sweated the little stuff. Now, strong-arm artists walk unintimidated, preying on the elderly. Patrolman Ezra Ounce longed for the North Beach of his grandfather, when it was a white Irish and Italian enclave. Now more immigrants cram into what used to be Irish storefronts.

Save ethnic North Beach.

Save the shops. Keep the tourist traps out.

Save Little Ireland. Save Little Italy.

Save your breath.

North Beach is an ethnic blur. It is one giant layer of overlays.

It isn't just Chinese, Irish, or Italian—it's Mexican, Armenian, Arab or Eastern European. Everyone pays rent to Chinese landlords because the Asian mind and wallet invested heavily into land when it was cheap. The Chinese landlords realize tourists are good for business. They're the ones who are buying and maintaining Italian-Irish businesses. They understand boundaries. Chinese and Anglos overlap like some giant overlay map. The Asian is willing to share the same physical space without grandiose displays to acknowledge it's their turf.

All bump into each coming out of T-shirt or pizza-by-the-slice parlors. It's a condominium form of social reality. There can be a Chinese wholesale grocer next to an Irish-American bar like Cortland & James. On the wholesale side, you won't find one gringo—nor will you find an Asian family having an overpriced meal at DeLuca's. Chinese landlords own North Beach and Chinatown, except for the very wealthy homes and condominium buildings on Telegraph and Russian Hill. It used to be only the white kids had the cars. Now, everyone has wheels and guns in a city that has no room for either.

Did I mention everyone in this seven by seven-mile burg is on life support because it is fucking dying as we speak.

1.
ART OF THE DEAL
Snippets

Cantina Psalm:
*The carousel that is also known as San Francisco zips
along on most days at 33-1/3 rpm.
Until someone or something leans on the lever, pushing it to 78 rpm.
When that happens, bodies start flying off.
Others manage to hang on.
Today, someone fucked with the lever, again.*

SOLDIERS OF FORTUNE

Today he was in Stockholm, away from his other presence in San Francisco's Chinatown quarter. His lucrative career as a freelance corporate fixer had him commute between both cities for the past decade.

He had ten minutes to kill.

Six-foot, five inches with a full head of mixed black and gray hair combed back to a ponytail, Art Garcia decided to take advantage of this dawn's mild temperature by stopping for coffee at the

Che Café housed in a nineteenth-century five-level building along Vasterlanggatan There he would read the *International Herald Tribune*, a resurrected print edition of a familiar news brand popular in 20th century and sip on a triple espresso and bite into a *semla*, a pastry filled with almond paste and whipped cream and a taste of cardamom.

To look at him many would compare him with a retired athlete, who kept himself in top shape. Strangers seeking small talk on any of his transits often asked if he were a tight end for a pro team or a power forward in basketball. His athleticism had nothing to do with playing children's games for money. Staying fit at 55 years old meant he could move effortlessly through his life and career.

Cutting to the chase, Garcia dealt in corporate intrigue. As a hired mercenary, he worked to protect his client's interests and if people died as a result, then sobeit. A blunt--though accurate--ID of his role as proprietor of Garcia Investigations. He was a well-paid shadow who was about to embark on one of the biggest treasure heists of his career, an institutional theft that when successful, would force the victim to keep the agonizing loss out of the news. A theft that if made public knowledge would cause a gash in the heart of a powerful nation.

But for now, that action was two days away and he was mired in the classic lull before the storm.

A hired driver was about to meet him at the café and take him to Bromma Airport, Stockholm's executive field eight miles away. He had to be in San Francisco to finalize one important detail. He needed to hire back up for his upcoming assignment.

Garcia prided himself in putting freelance experts together as a team to achieve one goal.

Once completed the assigned team was dispersed and far richer than they had imagined while being recruited. One member of his team had been shot on a recent Garcia assignment. In a decade as owner of Garcia Investigations he had yet to lose an agent.

For now, she needed to be replaced—pronto.

The car arrived and in less than an hour, Art would be comfortable inside a familiar private jet bound for San Francisco International.

ANGEL CITY

San Francisco in the middle of fall was mired in a gray two-week malaise of cold rain. It has stormed more these past weeks than it had in two drought-stricken years, but who could tell what the weather was like inside the tube?

The six-car BART train pulled into the Angel Island Subway Station on time at 8:00 p.m. Tom Gresham, still the head of security for San Francisco Mayor Joe Martin, exited the commuter-filled rear car. He looked forward to an evening of jazz and maybe good company. But he knew the price for that was having to listen to an older friend, a school chum from Sts. Peter and Paul School for Boys who would try to talk him into a piece of freelance dirty work.

Le Jazz Club, a music and dinner venue, was one of the original tenants of Angel City, located on the ground floor of Hotel Juneau. Hotel Juneau, a year-old 10-floor first-class hotel, was the tallest building in what was the instant city, built on five-year-old landfill adjacent to Angel Island. The four-star hotel was part of McGrath Hotel's international chain, which were named after Alaskan cities.

He made his way to a line of electric taxi carts. Cabs with human drivers were allowed as part of maintaining old-time San Francisco, a twentieth century vestige that kept tourists happy. Given the day's storm, Gresham took a ride with one of the flesh and blood hacks instead of hiking uphill along "instant quaint" nouveau cobblestoned streets to the hotel.

En route, Tom read from a "Welcome to Angel City" brochure and map conveniently located in a dispenser behind the driver of the four-seat taxi.

Before entering the hotel, he turned to face the eerie translucent cloud cover that obscured the bay and dimmed the lights of the city's flank of new 150- to 200-story skyrises. Before glancing away, he breathed in the aroma of scented pines replanted as part of the island's reforestation project. He could also smell the distinctive odor of the gargantuan Pacific Ocean to the west.

* * *

If Angel Island were a face, the land mass that Angel City occupied was shaped like a beard along the south end of the island. Its new-found 1,000 acres had been dredged up by subway expansion as an add on to the once pristine island in the middle of San Francisco Bay.

The new purple Bay Area Rapid Transit line now served Angel Island via Yerba Buena (formerly Terminal Island) and before linking with the Richmond Ferry Terminal and existing rails at the Nevin Street BART/AMTRAC terminal in mid-city Richmond, north of Berkeley.

Angel City and the BART line expansion had been designed and rushed into existence after real estate development interests bludgeoned civic officials to set aside environmental and historic limits to create housing for the teeming Bay Area masses begging for million-dollar properties with excellent city and bay views.

Yerba Buena ended up mimicking San Francisco's jammed urban neighborhoods. And all the developers had to promise was to build two supermarket malls and leave room for the new BART station.

The government—both local and feds—sacrificed the last pristine land in the Bay under the guise of creating new jobs after pandemics 19 thru 30.

But there were a few perks.

Angel City to date is about the size of the Principality of Monaco on the Mediterranean coast, with options to become larger with more dredging for a sailboat marina and tourist ferry landing. Each new rooftop on Angel Island was fitted with a retooled DAC machine that sucked carbon molecules out of the air like efficient vacuum cleaners. DAC's (direct air capture systems the size of home air-conditioning units) and much larger mega towers atop all high-rise structures in the U.S. were a step in the right direction.

Gresham, now 40 years old, was ignorant of the nationwide DAC program, but Garcia filled him in ad nauseum before the night was over. Truth be told, Art had a huge investment in several DAC manufacturing operations. Thanks to a massive nationwide investment by the government (and still never touching the $7 trillion in gold stashed at Ft. Knox, Kentucky) carbon dioxide-removing pillars, like the old cell phone towers, sucked the air clean of pollutants. The populace could breathe again now that the coal czars had been economically diverted and become minimized like the Robber Barons of the late 1890s. And the new tech lined Art's pockets as an investor.

* * *

Unlike a nightmare that could be shaken off with a quick shower or a shot of Mexican joy juice, Art Garcia was no specter.

Dressed in gray slacks, Brooks Brothers oxford shirt and a navy Boggi hooded blazer (the coat being the fashion rage au moment), Garcia flashed his famous toothy smile as he stood from the cabaret table inside the lobby bar to greet his school chum from childhoods barely remembered.

They used to be better friends, choirboys at different times in another life. No handshake was offered on this night.

Tom, the epitome of waterfront casual, arrived in denims, a black crew neck sweater shirt, a bomber jacket and black ankle high boots. He eased himself into a cushy chair.

"Tommy, Tommy, Tommy—how have you been?"

Tom shrugged and ordered a soft drink, while Garcia sipped on mezcal with no ice or water to dilute the liquid violence.

"You're not drinking?" Art asked.

"Joe asked me to cut back."

"How's that going?"

"Fucked."

"How long?"

"A month."

"Why is he concerned?"

"I drink too much. Next question."

With men, Tom's standing face, especially with those he was wary of, came off as if brooding were a hobby. Maybe it was an acquired mien from being a street cop ten years earlier, or maybe he was simply a jerk. And the one thing he truly hated was being called Tommy.

"Tommy, you're not smiling. Not happy to see me or is it because I'm not a woman?"

"What's that supposed to mean?"

"You haven't changed. Around women you're the life of the party."

"Maybe it's because I've never been fond of private detectives. Everyone tells me you were more fun when you were a special agent for US Customs."

"Who's everybody?"

"Everybody," Tom almost laughed.

"I'm into corporate security, now."

"There's a difference?"

"It's a matter of sophistication, and corporate pays so much better."

"Whatever, what's on your mind?"

Art picked up the bottle, "What's not to like about me?" Art tilted the bottle to show the label to Tom. "Mexicans still put a worm in the Mezcal."

"I'm not into tequila."

"Mezcal only has the worm. To be called tequila it must be made from 51 percent blue agave. No worms in any bottle labeled *tequila*. Twenty-five years as a special agent for US customs and that's all I can remember from my Latin American stations."

"OK." Tom nodded and changed the subject: "You look pale. Are you still in Stockholm?"

"I've decided to open an office here in San Francisco. Too much work coming out of Silicon Valley for me to ignore." Garcia glanced out of the large plate-glass window into the day-long storm that showed no signs of letting up. "I don't remember any of this. Last time I was in the city, this island was park land and Alcatraz was boring."

"Government needs the money, so it creates jobs to tax the peons," Tom said. "Ordinances fall to the wayside. Once untouchable parks and green space become commercialized. It's all about real estate development for the zillions…we're literally fucking our way to Armageddon, and we need places to house them all."

"That's one way of looking at it, but I didn't invite you over to talk gloom and doom. In fact, I'm tired of bad news, pandemics and assholes who go to jail instead of taking a vaccine. No more," said Garcia, who flicked an invisible gnat off the sleeve of his bespoke blazer. Like so many tall men, especially those like Garcia, he learned early in his life that department stores seldom have anything in his size. By the time he ran around town looking for clothes that fit, he decided it was easier and cheaper in the long run to have his wardrobe custom made.

The waiter arrived with the drinks and a bowl of shelled peanuts. "Will you be dining with us?"

Garcia said, "Give us a few minutes."

Tom sipped his soda and finally smiled, "I seldom go outside of North Beach."

"Pandemics will do that."

"Do what?"

"Keep you close to home. I don't travel unless I have to," Art said.

"Are you still living in that alley?"

"Yes. Same place over the body shop? Chinatown?"

Tom said, "Chinatown baffles me. All those alleys. Jammed buildings."

"That's what I like. If my friends can't find me maybe my enemies will have the same trouble."

"But it's no different than North Beach, is it?" Tom asked.

Art grinned, "you need a guide when you're on Telegraph Hill streets."

The small talk with Art reminded him of the friends he made at grammar school. You can be away from them years and when you reconnect the conversations pick up where they left off. Grade school friends are rare, but not in North Beach. Tom silently counted off buddies that he still sees from Sts. Peter and Paul School for Boys on Filbert Street: Art Garcia, Joe Martin, John Wald, Garrett Ellis and even a soured relationship with Wally McGrath. All were taught by the aging founder and principal Father Mac.

Art asked, "Are you involved with a woman now that you're divorced?"

"I've been divorced forever. I don't talk about that part of my life. Why don't we talk about why you asked me to meet you here?"

Art didn't hesitate, "I want you to work with me. Maybe permanently. We go way back, Tommy. I can trust you and you are fearless. Good stuff for an industrial spy. Besides, you're not getting any younger. You can't be making any money working for Joe Martin. Become a partner with me and I'll guarantee you the money you should be making at your age."

"What should I be making?"

"I'm offering one million new dollars per year as a base doing corporate espionage. That's just to keep you available for assignments each job has its own payout. We're talking game change. I'll keep you busy, but you'll have plenty of time between jobs to knock a few things off your bucket list."

"I don't need a Corvette."

"How about a gorgeous woman?"

"I'm doing, OK."

"Just, OK?" Art asked.

"I have a love life."

"Not from what I hear. I know you're seeing Carly Martin and that relationship is going nowhere."

Garcia touched on something that Tom thought was a bullet-proof secret. "What makes you think I'm seeing Carly Martin? She's above my pay grade."

"People see you with her and they talk."

"For Christ's sake, Art I am the mayor's bodyguard. Of course, I see her."

"Fine, but I'll bet she doesn't want to marry someone that makes pennies on the dollar. I had you vetted. Remember, that's what I do. You're running out of youth. I'm offering you a change to have the things you only dreamed about come true. Earn what you're worth. You are a damn fine cop. You're tough and you're loyal. You always have been."

"Assuming I am interested in your offer what exactly would I be doing?"

"Endure me for a short history lesson: I'm getting older fast. I can't fake it being a one-man show. I'm finding myself up against sheer numbers of people who want me out of the way. I need back up. I need to protect myself on the job and at home. I need you to lead a team I'm rebuilding. And Tommy, the good part is I got more customers than I can take care of. And because we go back such a long way, I can tell you there is no limit to the money I can pay you."

"The money interests me. Not knowing what I have to do for it is what scares me."

"To earn that kind of money takes a certain amount of intelligence and backbone. I'm willing to risk my life by trusting you."

"A million new dollars doesn't seem real to me. I hear red flags."

"Flags don't make noise."

"Don't do that…"

Art interrupted, "the money is good. I have very little overhead, and my clients have no problem paying me. Money is the least of my worries."

"I need the money."

"I know you do. And I need your brains and your muscle. Are we on the same page?"

Tom shifted the conversation, "Joe had you vetted as well. He's thinking of bringing you in to do a job for him. He knows you're the right man but he's a bit concerned."

"OK, I'll ask. What has him nervous?"

"People die on almost every one of your '*assignments*.'"

"I get results. I don't break laws. Yes, I put holes in people but that's self-defense. I don't set out to hurt people for no reason," Art insisted, "I'm not a hitman. Governments, corporations hire me, Tom. They give me a job and I do it and they protect me. I'm not working for cartels of mega thugs. In fact, there are fifteen human smuggling czars who are no longer in business."

Tom finished his drink.

Art asked, "I'm curious why he needs me. He's got an entire police department to work with?"

"Joe told me too much pure cocaine has shown up in the city. ER at St. Augustine hospital is overflowing with ODs. Too many have the same pure cocaine markers in their blood. Joe wants to know where it's coming from; who is bringing it in and to stop the flow by any means, including lethal?"

"Then don't complain if someone gets hurt. You can't have it both ways."

"Just keep the body count low."

Art pointed an index finger at Tom. "That's why I need you. Business is good."

Tom looked in the direction of the bar. A combo with a nice-looking woman as lead singer climbed on the velvet draped stage.

Art wasn't finished with his pitch. But he knew he had Tom. Art's face had that silliness of a gambler whose longshot horse came in the money—or like others who find money when they weren't expecting it. "What if we do a trade out. Tell Joe I'll take on his case if I can borrow you for a weekend job. Tit for tat."

"Nothing's free. If I put my ass on the line, I want to be paid for it."

"Do you know what negotiable bonds are?"

"Financial paper."

"A negotiable bond is a piece of paper that order any bank to pay whoever presents the document the amount that's on the bond.

No questions asked. Put the bond on the table and the banker opens an account for you preferably in Switzerland. Done deal. I'm going to give you a bearer bond for $1 million set up at the Bank of Schliem in Geneva. You can draw on it anytime you wish. The million is a signing bonus. You help me and I help Joe."

"And, if I don't?"

"I'll ask for it back and you won't refuse me. I know Joe wants to be governor. And, if San Francisco has a drug problem that reality will reflect bad on his election chances. That's why he wants us to help him out and at the same time leave no blood stains."

Tom looked away from the jazzmen on stage. "Have you talked to Joe about me helping you?"

"Yes. He said whatever it takes. I'm making a hell of an offer here. Let's do it or am I wasting my time?"

Tom smiled. "I'm in."

Art was relieved he hadn't misjudged a man he had known since high school. "You'll like the singer." He caught the eye of the waiter, who brought over menus. "Let's eat."

"Who is she?"

"Carol Law, an old-fashioned torch singer. Her sidemen are called 'Guilty as Charged.' Classic jazz oldie specialist. Good name, don't you think?"

"She looks familiar," Tom said.

Art said, "Small town. I noticed you're in the same flat. Did you buy it as a condo or still renting?"

"I rent from John Wald. School chums don't raise the rent on each other."

"Let's hear it for Saints Peter and Paul School for Orphan Boys. I never figured how John was able to buy two apartment buildings in the heart of North Beach."

"He inherited it."

Art Garcia laughed. "Tell me, Tommy who does an orphan inherit the cash to buy real estate in San Francisco?"

"I don't want to know," Tom grinned, "Maybe he works for you."

"I recommend the porterhouse steak. Best two-hundred-dollar piece of meat anywhere."

"There was a day when that much money would have bought the entire steer," Tom said.

Art was quick to reply. "Let's forget the past, Tommy. It doesn't exist."

The waiter appeared.

After ordering Tom said. "I'm still Joe's bodyguard at least until next year when his term limits kick in. He can't run for a third term. I can't go full time with you until then."

"Everyone I hire works freelance for me. I have no staff. One assignment at a time. That's why your help is worth the $1 million. How many jobs like this do you need to have a good life? Join me. You can keep your job with Joe. Just help me out when I call."

Art added, "I read somewhere that Joe was thinking about running for Governor. How's that going?"

"Maybe," Tom said.

"How's his health."

Tom stared into Art's eyes. "Joe has cancer. Not the kind that used to kill people, but it slowly sucks you dry. Vaccines and pills knocked the cancer out for five years. Then it came back with vengeance. Joe's feeling the return symptoms."

"Who knows that?"

"You and me and Carly Martin and let's keep it that way."

"That is such sad news," Art grabbed Tom's wrist. "You know that for a fact."

Tom wasn't smiling. He nodded yes.

Art continued, "That changes things. He's looking to save his legacy as Mayor, I figured it was to save his Governor's bid. I hate being wrong."

"He's fighting it and he has kept it under wraps. I know no one outside you me and his wife knows."

"You're close to Carly. Does she know?"

"Maybe."

"Don't be the first to tell her. Give Joe the grace to tell her himself."

"If she knows she hasn't said a word to me about it."

"Then here's what we're going to do," Art said, "I told you I'd help him with his problem after I finish one more assignment. So, that means you and I have a lot to work to do."

"If it's OK with Joe, then I'm ready."

"Something has come up in Europe. Something different for me, a baby-sitting job of sorts, but not something I can't handle. I need you to tail me every step I take while I'm over there. I gotta know you're over my shoulder and you'll be there when I need you."

"Weapons?"

"Of course. Lots of moving parts in this deal. I want you nearby. Do you still ride your motorcycle?"

"Sold it, but I can still ride. What's the time frame?"

"We leave at noon tomorrow."

"So much for advance planning."

"Best to get things like this over quickly. It'll be a nice payday." Art reached in the inside pocket of his jacket. He handed Tom a bearer bond for $1,100,000 in US new dollars. Hundred grand for the Euro assignment and $1 million as agreed to sign on to Garcia Investigations.

Tom read the document; his eyes widened. "How long will this take?"

"By Tuesday?"

"How many die?"

"Depends on the other side. If we do it right, we'll leave Madrid without anyone knowing we were there. If not, then we wing it"

"I'll need a weapon."

"Yes. I'll take care of that. And do you have a LOBE?"

"Yes, I was issued one by city hall, but I don't wear it. I still prefer my cell phone."

Garcia handed over a small LOBE package. "Put it on before tomorrow introduce yourself to Jonna, she's my assistant in Sweden." He also gave Tom a business card belonging to Leon Lee, owner of the Broadway Café. On the back Art scribbled "put it on my tab."

"What's this for?"

"Leon knows a good tailor. Looking good gives you an edge. You're handsome. Use it to your advantage."

Tom opened his mouth to respond.

Art shook his head, "Don't give me shit on this. See the tailor first thing when we get back."

Tom grinned, "Thanks, Dad."

The lights in the bar dimmed. Carla Law on sax and Guilty as Charged opened their first set with a Grant Green instrumental classic, "Idle Moments" from the 1960s.

Later, as they shook hands to leave, Tom looked his friend in the eyes. "I'll do it. This one job, then we'll take it from there."

Art was a happy man. His friend was not as stupid as he looked. Then he laughed to himself "if only it were true."

SAN FRANCISCO TO MADRID

"Buckle up," The steward said, tapping on the side of the cabin door. Tom Gresham obeyed and placed his international edition of Gannett's *World Today* on the empty leather seat next to him. The deluxe first-class cabin, about the size of a bullet train private compartment, offered a large window to view the mechanica of the ageless San Francisco International Airport.

He had never set foot inside the Boeing's hyper Mach jetliner. The 1111 was the darling of world aviation at 300-feet in length powered six engines: two in the tail and four underwings.

Tom gawked in delight at being in such lux accommodations. Garcia Investigations of Stockholm and San Francisco clearly wanted to please its new freelancer.

An escalator hurried him to the top of three levels. First-class had a long hallway that ran the length of the monster jet. Double doors opened into luxury suites. Passenger names in a neon box, the size of a magazine, shone at eye level on the moderne doors.

His suite read Welcome. Garcia was being abundant in his caution. No names.

The suite included a tabletop book highlighting the amenities and history of the American made machine. Tom noticed the lower passenger seating areas resembled honeycombs mimicking how first-class seating appeared in the 20th century.

* * *

Despite Art's hint to dress better, Tom was comfortable flying in Levi's and a plain gray sweatshirt and low top black Nike's.

Most of the one thousand passengers, except Tom Gresham, were waking up. The American listened through a queue of languages offering arrival instructions. "Welcome to Madrid International Airport. Blah, blah, blah.

Flying at Mach 3 got him to Madrid in four hours and tacking on the nine-hour time difference between Spain and California put him at Adolfo Suárez Madrid–Barajas Airport at midnight.

On the flight over, Tom read online that Spain was struggling with its economy. The proud kingdom hung on to its membership in the revisionist first world Holy Roman Empire: United Kingdom, France, Germany, Poland/Czech Republic, United Scandinavia (Norway, Sweden, Finland, Denmark and Belgium), Swiss Union with Italy, Austria and the Slav nations; Spain, the Baltic Confederation, Portugal with Monaco and the Vatican. Spain being the weakest link in the alliance.

Crippled by back-to-back pandemics that stole billions from its citizens during the 2020s Spain showed rents in its national tuxedo but its parliamentary monarchy, to its credit, worked hard to keep Spain afloat with its boundaries intact while smaller countries with weak economies by 2030 had to forego the pride of national independence and merge with other countries to stave off bankruptcy. Also, the bitter Euro banishment of all things Russian and the endless pandemics remade the map of Europe resemble an abstract painting.

But the economic separators between Spain and its wealthier Euro cousins were growing each day. How long could Spain hold out? Landing in the Spain of the middle 21st century was like landing in Berlin in the early 1950s. Spain had a pulse albeit a feeble one.

Creature comforts being what they are impressed Tom. On this flight he didn't have to wake up next to strangers nor would he have to queue in line to throw water on his face or take a pee.

This flying hotel impressed him that he could get used to a new lifestyle. For now, he wouldn't have to worry about leaving his deodorant beneath his seat once he reached the main cabin toilet.

This was deluxe and didn't want the flight to end. En route he drank two flutes of brut Dom Perignon Champagne. The real stuff. He grinned. He justified his broken vow not to drink alcohol by making a new one. From now on he'd only drink outside the borders of the USA. That would work.

* * *

Gresham's royal treatment ended as he stepped into the terminal. No limo. He had to take the public subway into central Madrid. His pre-approved destination was the Hotel Attu. It wasn't near a subway station and the time it took to get from the airport to his comfortable room, he could have flown halfway across the U.S. in his Boeing 1111.

The Attu's uniformed concierge escorted him into the walk in safe. Inside his assigned safety deposit box was a Glock handgun, ammunition for a small war and keys to a Yamaha motorcycle with more horsepower than anything NASA had crawling around downtown Mars. There was also 10,000 in Euros and three burner cellphones. Yes, it helps to have the hotel owner owe you favors but that's a tale for another time.

Tom found the Yamaha parked in the hotel garage. His first test spin took him to the modern décor McDonald's near Atocha train station.

If things went south on the assignment, Tom was to contact Jonna Berk the faceless voice, who represented Art Garcia.

Art insisted that she would fix any loose ends. "And, if she doesn't, you're probably dead anyway."

Tom realized McDonald's spends a lot in Spain to have prime locations and excellent decors—too bad they don't do that in the states. Have you ever seen a line going around the block to get into a McDonalds back home?

* * *

Art Garcia arrived at the Attu, the reconverted office building at the east end of Gran Via at noon. His flight from Moscow was uneventful. He approached the desk manager to check in. He added, "I'm expecting a FedEx package to arrive for me I'd like to check its status."

"Your name, please," asked the desk clerk.

"Fred Pontchatrain," Art said with a straight face.

"Please check with the concierge," the clerk pointed across the lobby.

The woman concierge, a posture perfect 50-something, who did justice to the hotel's haute couture gold and green uniforms greeted him.

Art was never under dressed. He showed up in tan trousers, silk black knit turtleneck and a Brooks Bros. blazer. "Such a beautiful day," he offered.

"Sadly, weather reports are predicting rain all weekend," she replied staring at her computer screen. "How may I help you?"

"I'm a guest of the hotel. He slid a fake passport to her. "I'm expecting a FedEx package on sometime this weekend."

"Yes, we were notified."

"I'd like to get an OK for one of my assistants to pick up the package?"

"Of course, put her name on this form and sign it."

"His name is Fernando Abba."

"Yes, Mr. Abba has already checked in."

"One more thing," he grinned, "how are the steaks in your restaurant?"

"Our bistro is one of the best in Madrid. It specializes in Argentine beef. You'll be pleased," she smiled. "Here's list of others in the downtown area."

They smiled at each other. Argentine steakhouse was the code they both knew meant Art's entire visit was on the house.

The American took the dining guide brochure and tipped her $100. She smiled and placed the bill in a small charity box that sat at the far end of her desk. He opened his wallet and place another c-note in the same box. "For the orphans."

***

At 3 pm Jonna texted Gresham. "Meet the boss at La Pecera Restaurant. It's across the Via from your hotel."

Tom arrived fifteen minutes later and found a seat at the concave bar in the corner of the café facing a rows and rows of multicolored bottles.

Tom glanced at the interior of the restaurant. Three nude art works gained his attention: a painting and an abstract statue. But the one that fascinated him most was the third, a horizontal marble sculpture of a young woman atop a knee-high platform. The middle of the restaurant seemed like an odd place for the sculpture. He would have expected it in a museum.

Tom felt his throw away phone throb in his blazer jacket.

It was Art.

"Order anything off the tapas menu. You'll thank me?"

"Where are you?"

"In my room across the street. I'm going to take a nap. I had to fly coach. Aeroflot sucks."

"I thought we were going to discuss…"

Art interrupted, "Best we are not seen together. Did Jonna explain what why you're in Madrid?"

"Yes."

"Bueno. We're covered. "It's Friday. Enjoy the city but wear your LOBE in case I need you." Art hung up.

***

That evening, the Hotel Attu's quietude evaporated with his entry into the smoky bistro's cocktail lounge. A Friday after hours crowd filled most of the seats. A three-piece combo fought to be heard above the din of conversations.

Moving on to a barstool—farthest from the stage—the American admired jazz but because of the din, he couldn't understand a note.

The lanky bartender approached. He could have been Art Garcia's shorter twin. Both had unruly hair tied back in a short ponytail. Neither shaved closely and they dressed well.

They exchanged small talk. His name was Santiago. He noticed Garcia didn't find anything on the wine list to his liking. "I have a nice red from Priorat. It's from one of the small estates in Catalonia. It is not widely distributed. I have a few bottles."

Art hesitated.

"I see you have excellent taste in wine."

"How can you tell?"

"You ignored the hotel's wine list." The bartender stifled a laugh. "Our owner has excellent taste, except in wine."

Art stared at the platinum-haired cocktail waitress. "But he does have an eye for women."

"Her name is Olivia. Are you staying for dinner?"

"Yes. Send me something that resembles a cabernet sauvignon."

"She will bring the wine to you," the bartender offered.

"Open it and pour yourself a glass," Garcia offered. "You can do that, can't you?"

The bartender drawled: "Claro, this is Spain, my friend." He stopped the passing waitress with one word. "Olivia. Our new friend is joining us for dinner…but first."

The three of them clicked glasses.

The Nordic waitress with high cheekbones and a travel poster face sat the American at table near the stage. She removed the "Reserved" card. As she turned away.

He looked up at the stage. The combo was gone.

Across the room, an older man with a dark, narrow face like a Goya painting, brushed drops of ice water that dripped off his vodka and tonic and on to the sleeve of his Saville Row suit. The jockey-sized man moved slowly across the restaurant toward the American.

Both men wore salt and pepper hair cut short and brushed back at the sides and tied in a knot behind their heads. "May I join you? I have something important to say concerning your stay in my city?" The stranger sat uninvited.

"Do I have a choice?" The American's tone dripped of annoyance.

"You're too kind. My name is Edouard Ayunar. I am an attorney in private practice here in Madrid. I am representing the government. I ask for a few moments of your time."

It was not a question.

His English had classic Castilian accents and trilled r's.

"Which government?" Art asked.

"España."

The American shifted in his small cabaret chair, "Let's make it quick."

"Ah, I see you have a sense of humor," the attorney said, then looked up at the waitress, who arrived with two goblets and the bottle of wine Art had shared at the bar.

The Spaniard waved her off. "Nothing for me, and please put this amount toward my friend's bar tab and keep any change for yourself." He handed her a 100 New Euro note.

She filled Art's glass, placed the bottle on the table and moved on.

The Spaniard's insipid smile was irritating. "I won't be long."

"That would make me happy."

"Wait, please hear me out. All I have to do is snap my fingers and you will be arrested."

Art stared hard at the small man. "You may be mistaking me for someone else."

The Spaniard asked bluntly, "No, but I'll ask anyway, what is your name?"

Garcia grinned, "Fred Pontchatrain."

"You have so many names to choose from and you pick that one. Stick to Art Garcia. That suits you, my friend."

Art put his elbow on the hubcap sized table and pointed his finger at the uninvited man. "I'd like you to leave the table."

"Let's discuss your firm and its reputation for accepting difficult assignments."

The American nodded, "Your point is?"

"It's my job to make sure your visit doesn't cause inconveniences to our government. What brings you to Spain?"

"I'm a tourist nothing more."

"Ah, Is there a convention of spies that I missed?"

"I'm on vacation."

"Are you on assignment here in Madrid?"

"No."

"What is it that you do, Mr. Pontchatrain?"

Garcia smiled. It had become a game. "We like to end the careers of hackers, extortionists, blackmailers, and an occasional high-profile human slave trader. But in Madrid I'm here for the magnificent cuisine, beautiful weather nothing more."

"So many options for a one-man operation."

"I hire as needed."

The Spaniard continued. "Human slavery is an interesting term. It's old as it is new. Name me one of your human slavery cases. Maybe one I recognize?"

The American began to glance around the bar, looking for someone to save him. "The kidnapping of a teenage Follies Maxim dancer in Paris last year. Then finding her on a Saudi yacht in Barcelona. That's one example."

"I would think such a venerable organization as the Follies would make sure they didn't hire children."

"An eighteen-or nineteen-year-old woman is considered an adult in most countries."

"It's so rude for a man to take what doesn't belong to him."

The waitress arrived at the table with menus.

The older man stared down at her legs. "What's your name?"

"Olivia," she nodded.

"How long have you been in the country?"

"I was born in Valencia."

"Join me in a glass?" Garcia asked as the lawyer turned his attention to the bottle. "Finca Lipscomb Tobella Seleccio Especial. I accept," the Spaniard offered, "only because I've never heard of this wine. Where is it from?"

"Near Barcelona."

"How sad. I never seem to have time to leave Madrid."

Art gave him a no-nonsense stare. "You're boring me."

"Of course, to the point. We find it interesting that a businessman like yourself is traveling under an assumed name when there is no reason to do so. Are you in my country to import or export anything that might be dangerous or embarrassing to the monarchy?"

"I'm a tourist, remember?"

"I hear you only take gold for payments."

"What? Gold? You're fishing with bad bait."

"Our source at the Bank of Schliem in Zurich says you have gold on deposit."

"I'll mention that to my banker. She would like to know she has an intelligence leak in her operation."

"Gold fascinates me."

Art sat up in his chair, "Look, given how flaky Euro governments operate, including your own king, I prefer my dollars, pounds, diamonds, negotiable bonds or gold be kept in a Swiss bank."

"You live in Sweden, eh?" The older man smiled. "You're not a Swede but an American, verdad?"

"I have dual citizenship."

"How sad it is to see your American dollar sink to such depths after the pandemics. I've never seen it so weak."

"Bullshit. The new American dollar remains the ruler of all world economies. Once Russian collapsed after the Ukrainian war, the United States led the reorganization of the World Bank. The dollar rules, period."

"You're a nationalist?"

"A realist. The Euro is a second-rate currency."

The Spaniard lifted a finger. "I am a royalist."

Garcia couldn't resist a jab: "Why so intent on protecting a series of fallen kings, who are mired in so many financial scandals? One right after another. You'd think figurehead rulers would be smarter as of today, kings are such a waste of public money and totally useless as leaders. No exception."

"Spoken like a Bolshevik."

"Truth doesn't have political alliances."

"Granted our leadership is resting on thin ice that's why the monarchy doesn't need new scandals to become public. We don't want to fuel legislation to end the Iberian Kingdom even though our royal line stretches farther back than Ferdinand and Isabella."

"I'm confused. Whose side are you on?"

"Like I said, I'm a royalist until I'm told not to be one."

"Finally, an honest answer out of your mouth."

"Speaking of honesty, please tell us the real reason you're in Madrid? You have me curious. What adventure can we expect from you?"

"Not your concern."

"Be careful how you answer. I have jurisdiction."

"I'm here because going through Madrid airport was the easiest connection for me to get home."

"What business were you conducting in Moscow?"

"My business. And please understand my business began and ended outside of Spain. So, this conversation is over, Señor Ayunar."

"Si, si, but please understand there will be serious problems for you if you misbehave while you're here."

"I have no intention of upsetting anyone. Especially you. And there's no need to have me followed."

"Thank you." Ayunar was now holding the wine and examining it by holding it up to the light coming from the bar.

Garcia smiled. He remained relaxed. "I'm impressed, though, with how fast you found me. I haven't been in Spain for more than a few hours and already we're having a conversation."

"I'm good at what I do. When I retire, you may consider me for employment with your firm. Is Garcia Spanish?"

"American. The name is the new Smith in California."

"Why exactly did you select this hotel on this particular weekend?"

"A friend I've had since we were schoolboys owns this hotel. He offered me a discount."

"How nice—please give Mr. McGrath our compliments. Spain is grateful he chose to operate one of his hotels in Madrid. Are you leaving the country, soon?"

"I didn't say."

"I understand your airline ticket to Stockholm leaves Monday?"

"In the meantime, I'll enjoy the weekend."

"I can arrange to have your ticket changed. Perhaps, for the morning?"

"No need. There's no rush for me to go home. I'm ready to be a tourist. Madrid is a beautiful woman. Why rush home?"

"My friends are hopeful you will leave sooner. Me, personally, I find you refreshing. And you are correct Madrid has much to offer a tourist such as yourself."

"I appreciate your royal hospitality," Art mocked.

"I wish you the best of luck. I'm sure we'll meet again. Good night, Mr. Garcia." The man stood up, made a half turn to leave then glanced back toward Art.

"Thank you for the wine. It is young but promising."

"Weren't we all?"

Both men smiled.

"One more thing. Indulge me. I should have brought this up earlier in our conversation. I am full of curiosity how your government arranged the purchase of Baja California this summer from the Mexican government?"

The sudden switch in topics surprised Art. It made him laugh at yet another twist in the rambling conversation. "That's out of my league," he said. "I had very little to do with that."

"Too bad. Our cash-strapped treasury would be interested in selling some of our offshore properties in order to join NATO. We own sixty islands in the Mediterranean and the Atlantic. A few of the remote ones would make interesting military bases. Why lease when you can own?"

"No, one was more surprised than me to see the Baja deal go down."

"A surprising return of unfettered American Imperialism. Your president claimed creating a Baja territory would provide an economic engine for both countries. Money to be made. Speaking as a private citizen, I see it as creating a buffer zone against the hordes attempting to cross illegally. Defending the border from both sides. Very smart. Your most stupid president a while back tried to build a wall. Your latest president is brilliant. Instead of embarrassing your neighbor by repossessing the long-standing debts—she allowed Mexico to clear all debts with a simple land purchase. She understands Mexico is overwhelmed. And the sale will generate cash to improve both economies. Plus, there's money to be made for your Wall Street thieves. And it is all taxable. Your Republican oligarchs like Wally McGrath have struck gold, again. He no doubt has all the rights for new hotels, there. Isn't that so?"

Garcia said nothing.

The Spaniard grinned. "Forgive my conversational wanderings. But you are a very fascinating man. We know your firm eliminated the top drug lords in North Mexico last year. Like your game whack a mole. One head pops up and you cut the next one off. The operation to cleanse Baja of drug cartels has all the markings of the way you do business. A hit man for even the most honorable of nations. Brazen manifest destiny."

"Calling me a hit man is an insult."

"I let your dossier speak for itself."

"Why am I still listening to you? This conversation is over." Garcia turned to look for the waitress.

"You're staying in his hotel tonight, verdad?"

"You're asking me questions you already have answers to. It's weary."

"Of course. Again, my apologies." He handed Art a business card. "It's just friends of mine lost something very valuable while you were in Moscow. We're interviewing all persons on their behalf who have come into Spain. Especially soldiers of fortune like yourself who are capable of high levels of thievery. It was only a few hours ago, it should be fresh on your mind. Do you have any idea of what I'm speaking of?"

"Not the slightest," Art, in turn handed him one of his business cards. "Call me. I have friends who may wish to take your Spanish islands off your hands. And by then you should have a dozen more questions for me."

"Ahh, I knew you would have contacts. For that I thank you, and goodnight."

Art watched the small man walk away from the cabaret table. He realized his firm was not as clandestine as he thought. Something to think about fixing on his flight home.

* * *

Art had barely finished taking a sip of his wine when another unannounced guest arrived at his table. This time a much prettier one. Her tawny complexion with rounded cheekbones and dimpled chin gave her an exotic flair.

Art judged her to be five feet nine inches or taller, lithe with thick auburn hair tied in round bun on the top of her head. In the dim light, he was unsure of her age—mid-thirties? She was wearing a black cocktail dress with a white bolero-style blazer. Between her ample bosom, she wore a sapphire pendant. The brilliant gem was hard to ignore.

"May I bother you for a light?" She held her Gitane in her right hand. He glanced at the bottle of wine she placed on the table. He also noticed no wedding ring.

"Sadly, my cigarette lighter is in my suite upstairs."

"That's too far to go to light my cigarette. I could get one here in the bar."

"But I'm so much more fun and handsome."

"And so modest, Senor! She handed him a book of matches that was inside the ashtray on the table.

"I've learned to speak only the truth to women. Garcia stood. "Then please join me at the table." He held the chair for her.

Exhibiting excellent posture, she made herself comfortable smoothing wrinkles on her little black cocktail dress.

He lit her cigarette then slipped the matches into the side pocket of his blazer.

"You're very kind," she puffed and blew her smoke out of the side of her mouth away from the table.

The smoke left a distinct woodsy aroma in the air, a telltale signature of a Gitane.

He reached for the wine bottle to read the label. *Finca Lipscomb Tobella Seleccio Especial.*

"How odd," Garcia smiled, "Until now I thought this was a rare wine. I've now seen it twice in ten minutes."

"The bartender is a friend," she said. "Santiago is also a fraud. His sister is married to the winemaker so gets a commission from the vineyard for every bottle he sells."

The blonde waitress stopped to pop the cork and poured the wine.

Art raised his glass. "I'm delighted you joined me. Here's to whatever reason brought you to my table."

"Good conversation, I hope."

They clinked wine glasses.

Game on.

Garcia laughed at himself. Her beauty and playful eyes captured his attention. She was a working girl, he judged and was now curious as to how she would play her hand.

His better angels, who according to legend were there to protect him, rolled their eyes. They knew it was going to be a long night.

"American?" she asked.

"What do you think?"

"Very much so. You dress like a Spaniard, but your accent gives you away."

"Are you one of those that can tell where someone is from by their accent?"

"American. Anything after that I'm guessing. California?"

"San Francisco," he said.

She put her cigarette out in the ashtray. "What about my accent?"

"My guess is you learned your English in Moscow." Art opened bluntly.

"I see, do you want me to be a spy? Mysterious Natasha to star in your personal Casablanca?"

Art let his breath out slowly, "I'm just making conversation with a beautiful woman. I'm hoping our meeting happened to by chance and not by some surreptitious design."

"I'm not so sure I understand the meaning of that word?"

"Surreptitious. It means you're acting like you don't know the meaning of that word when all along you know."

She shrugged, "My English is rusty."

"Your English is very good; I forget how hard it is to learn…"

"What? Learn what?"

"Idioms. Never mind, I sound like an English teacher. What I want to say is I'm happy you needed a light for your cigarette."

"Maybe, we're two strangers meeting on a plane?" She reached across the table to touch his hand.

"Yes, that's what I meant."

"It would make me happy if you liked me." She began to dig through her large purse.

Garcia was ready to believe several possibilities:

One, she was a low paid public servant, who earned extra money working hotels that catered to foreign businessmen. Or, two, she was part two of the Spaniard's tag team welcoming him to Spain and perhaps tasked to poison him with a Russian-made chemical. But that would require advance planning. He'd only been gone from Moscow a few hours. Right or wrong, he believed the Kremlin, or its apparatchik could never organize a posse that quickly.

He closed his self-monologue by deciding she might be a freebie tossed to him by the Spaniard. But, for now, he was in the mood to enjoy a sensual oasis between flights.

"Let me be your friend until my friend arrives," she asked. "She usually arrives on time."

Art shrugged.

She glanced toward the bar. "Until then, I can practice my idioms."

He lifted his wine glass, "Here's to idioms."

He felt the toe of her boot against his ankle. "I have a confession," she drew her lips together. "The bottle of wine is from the bartender. He said you needed to be saved from a bore." Santiago likes you. And, I should deliver the bottle and meet a new friend. I hope you didn't think that was too bold of me."

Waitress Olivia reappeared.

Art was now in the presence of the two most attractive women in the bar. The blonde was the image Garcia grew up believing all Scandinavian women must look like. If he got to know her better, he'd learn she was Czech.

"Dinner." Olivia asked. It was not a question.

* * *

The saga continued from dinner into dessert wines: Twenty-dollar glasses of tawny port, Kopke Colheita, 1978 and that combined with her unrelenting eye contact gave him hope for an exhausting tryst sometime no matter the price.

"Your friend didn't show up?" he said.

"I was stand up?"

"Stood up."

She waved off his correction.

Art glanced toward the bar. Olivia lingered at the bar sharing a cigar with Santiago. Only a few tables remained occupied at midnight.

He understood his advantage. He could take as long as he wanted. If she was indeed a working girl or working on someone else's dime, he had no reason to open the bidding.

She enjoyed listening to his escapades framed as a travel agent crafting his adventures to include the best restaurants in the world: from Raffles Hotel in Singapore to the Ritz in Paris.

Noticing a stifled yawn from the bartender made him realize the moment had arrived to either say goodbye or put their proverbial cards on the table.

Who would blink?

* * *

The check came. He paid with his American Express card stamped with Fred Pontchatrain's name.

"How nice of you," she said.

He smiled back, "it's the least I could do for such a good listener."

Without a segue, he stood and pulled the chair out for her. Like a good dance partner, she followed with an encouraging smile. He led her into his fifth-floor penthouse but not before walking by the bar to tip Olivia and Santiago with C-notes. Why go against a time-honored Yankee rudeness to over tip? In the elevator they held hands. She watched him press the button to the penthouse.

The Attu was converted into a hotel from a 1930s office building. The renovators for hotelier Wally McGrath kept the original brass accented elevators and true to form, they operated as slow as a century ago.

As the automatic elevator door opened, he slipped a coin in her hand.

"What is this?"

"A vintage gold coin."

"What do you mean?"

"I collect coins. This one was minted in 1899. I try to collect a gold coin from every country I visit. It's my hobby."

She examined the ten Ruble coin about the size of an American quarter.

"Ten Rubles won't take you far."

"This one will. I'd say it's worth close to a thousand Euro."

"Why so generous?"

"I'm intrigued by you. And I won't be long in Madrid to court you as you deserve. I'm hoping the coin will bring us as much joy as it's worth."

She gave him a knowing look. She was neither happy nor upset. "One condition," she finally said. "I will hold it as insurance." She placed it in her leather shoulder strapped purse.

"That you'll have to explain to me."

"A coin is nothing more than a promise. I will keep it if you turn out to be a louse. If we have a wonderful time, I will return it to you with a kiss. My hobby, n'est-ce-pas," she offered.

They gave each other a first timer's tour of the spacious suite.

"Do you like Martini's?"

"Vodka."

"I'll be right back."

She moved into his bedroom. She glanced through his closet and pulled a starched blue oxford cloth shirt off its hanger,

She let her cocktail dress slip to the floor.

* * *

No one else saw the whirlwind strike Madrid that evening spinning Friday night into Saturday. El tornado consumed all in its path leaving them exhausted.

And Saturday became Sunday morning when they finally peeled themselves from each other.

They were both damp from sex.

He offered, "We certainly don't have much to say, do we?"

"Not in words," she responded.

He watched her move toward the bathroom. She stopped, turned to look over her bare shoulder: "Perhaps we're doing exactly what we both need."

Returning, Art admired her figure—every inch of it. She understood the magic a naked woman has over a man, especially a new lover. She stood still letting him gaze. "Are you happy being with me."

He smiled, "I'm drunk with you. Happy and drunk. And I have no idea who you are? If you walked out of the door right now, I would have no way to find you. That would be a tragedy." He motioned her into his arms.

They kissed.

His hands found the smoothness of her upper arms shoulders.

Her mouth found his ear, "Well, we have something in common. You enjoy my body and our kisses, and I bask in your words they're like songs to me."

"Who are you?"

"Shhhh," She put her hand over his lips. "Be still, Art. Let's live as one for as long as we can."

"So, we can be strangers forever," he mocked.

"Please for a few moments more."

Art excused himself to the toilet.

Once inside his smile turned sour.

She had revealed herself to be more than an enchanting companion.

How did she know his name? Keeping names to themselves was part of the game, yet she knew his?

Reality was a bucket of cold suspicion thrown on his face. It drained him of tenderness. In one instant, he went from a blind fool in love to feeling threatened. If indeed she were a Russian agent, her team could be outside in the hallway.

Paranoia swallowed him.

He tried to calm himself by going to the corner of the spacious bathroom to where, he had tucked his handgun between a stack of white bath towels.

He placed the gun in the pocket of his robe.

He opened the bedroom door quickly.

She sat up on the bed. He smiled at her and that simple gesture made her relax. "Come to bed," she whispered.

He dropped his robe on the floor. The bed was between him and the entrance to the large suite.

She slipped under his body. She directed him inside her and smiled up at him.

"I'm so happy right now," she whispered, "We're in bed like we just learned how to make love."

* * *

Over the old-fashioned house telephone, they ordered room service: two continental breakfasts.

The do not disturb sign has been in place since Friday night. So far, it kept room service trays from being collected inside. They piled on every horizontal surface, with cobb salads and half-eaten ham omelets for late lunch and steaks for dinner.

The gentle knock from the room service attendant made her dive under the heavy comforter to hide her nakedness among the silk sheets.

He donned his robe. Through the small oval spy hole in the door, Art noticed a uniformed hotel waitress. Art directed her inside and to set up the tray on the wrap-around balcony that ran outside from the living room to master bedroom. He signed the bill tipping the teen on her way out.

* * *

"May I smoke out here," she asked and wrapped herself in a sheet from the bed.

"Of course."

The view from the terrace offered a typical Madrid sunny day tempered with a chilly breeze off the surrounding mountains.

She lit her Gitane. "Do you Americans find us barbarians because we smoke so much?"

"Yes," he frowned. "You're freezing."

"No, I'm erected. How do you say my nipples are hard with love? My goosebumps are showing through the sheet, no?"

"Yes," He pulled the sheet away.

"Once again, you have me defenseless," she whispered.

"Come with me when I leave Madrid."

"Such a temptation. I can't leave family?"

"A husband?" he asked directly.

She didn't flinch at his telling remark but her eyes stopped blinking. She offered him a drag off the cigarette. "No, my grandmother. She is very old. I can't leave her without making arrangements."

Art took a long puff. Returning it, he said "I've never fallen in love with a woman before I knew her name."

"Are we in love, are we?"

"I hope so," he offered. "It would be a shame to go to all the trouble to get married if we were not."

"Now, are you proposing marriage? If so, you've made my head spin."

"Tell your grandmother my intentions are pure?"

"I've never been with a man who watches my every move. Your eyes undress me everywhere I go."

"I'm in love, forgive me?"

"Who are you?" she smiled. "Those words coming out of your mouth aren't from an American."

"Yes, they are. We're not all ungrateful egoists."

She pulled the sheet around her torso, "Then I am the luckiest woman in Spain. I found the first honorable American man."

They finished the croissants, pulpy orange juice, and a carafe of coffee. He gazed at his smartphone. She lingered along the balustrade holding a silk sheet against her breasts.

Watching her lean over the railing confirmed what he already knew. What a joy to be with such a beautiful woman. She was full of energy. She waved for him to join her. "Down there." She pointed down seven floors to where the Gran Via spilled into Calle de Alcala. A crowd had gathered in Edifico Metropolis square, where an entire orchestra had been set up. Blue carpeting extended from the maestro's dais to what appeared to be a covered statue.

He also noticed the plaza crawled with security personnel. And if he saw them then they had to notice him. Or maybe they were just gawking through rooftop government-issue binoculars at such an ageless beauty, who kept her figure toned for her trade.

He ducked into the ensuite bathroom where he had previously gathered the book of matches from his blazer pocket, a small adhesive tape dispenser and his smartphone. There, he lifted a fingerprint from the match cover on to a strip of clear adhesive tape.

He transferred the tape on to his investigation grade smartphone before sending it to his assistant in Stockholm.

Once he noticed Jonna Berk of Garcia Investigations had received his text he undid the safety on his handgun and slipped it into his robe pocket.

* * *

While he shaved, she entered the steamy bath to report, "I just saw the King and Queen. We should have dressed up," she laughed.

"What did I miss?"

"It was the fastest ceremony I've ever seen." Without taking another breath, she said, "The orchestra played one tune, then the Queen went to the microphone to thank everyone for joining them on the unveiling of a historical marker: the one hundred thirtieth anniversary of the building of the Gran Via. Soon enough, King

Maximillian, the second and the young Queen returned to the limos and drove away."

He shrugged his shoulders. "Adios, Max."

She let out a deep breath and smiled the biggest smile of the day. "He's gone. Now what do we do?"

"Let's go back to bed," he grinned.

"I wish I could say no to you." It was her turn to satisfy her eyes by touching his warm Latin skin.

She trailed him to bed, an obedient Spanish version of a Japanese kuruwa, who could match his voracious appetite. She was hard to ignore. And it was obvious to her she had not exhausted him. Yes, he might be more suited for a younger woman, perhaps a long-distance runner, she judged, but she was not about to refuse him. She waltzed when it was time to waltz and eagerly samba-ed unquenched in their interminable horizontal ballroom.

She had become Art's Geisha—his yujo.

Their white robes fell on the carpet.

* * *

By early afternoon, it they had finally reached the point both were spent from their weekend of sex. Wrapped in her robe she moved to the terrace to check for the first time her smartphone.

Art sat inside at the small antique secretary desk writing a note on hotel stationery. He felt his phone throb silently in his robe pocket.

Jonna Berk had spent time creating a detailed a dossier on the nameless woman in Garcia's suite.

Although Art could not see her Nordic face topped with short blonde hair that had streaks of gray, Jonna was not pleased.

Jonna's text message reported: DORIA ZITI IS HER NAME. SHE IS A MAGAZINE JOURNALIST AND SHE'S A CAREER AGENT WITH THE SPANISH SECRET SERVICE. SHE IS ASSIGNED TO THE MADRID INTERPOL OFFICE. SHE'S MADE SEVERAL TRIPS TO RUSSIA, INCLUDING MOSCOW THIS YEAR. BE CAREFUL.

* * *

She hovered over at the stationery desk.

He put down his pen and looked up.

Both were still in their robes.

"I've had no clothes on for days. Let me dress. Let's go someplace nice to eat. I want all of Spain to know I'm with such a handsome man."

He sealed the letter before turning to her. "We haven't made love on the terrace."

"No, no," she laughed. "Es una mañana hermosa, no perdamos el día en una cama de hotel!" She escaped him to dress.

Art quickly texted Tom Gresham. RETRIEVE THE FEDEX PACKAGE FROM THE HOTEL ATTU CONCIERGE. IT SHOULD BE THERE BY NOW. USE THE NAME I GAVE YOU. SHIP IT AS PLANNED THEN IN AN HOUR FIND ME ON CALLE MAYOR. IF YOU MISS ME WAIT AT THE SIDE DOOR OF THE HOTEL EUROPA. WE LEAVE TONIGHT.

* * *

From the Attu, the new lovers strolled arm in arm West on Calle de Alcala from Gran Via, however a cloudburst arrived as if on the same daily schedule as the bullet train to Barcelona. The rainstorm easily scattered the tourists from the Calle as they neared Plaza Mayor.

She laughed, catching herself fending off the rain from her hair still wet from her hotel shower. He liked her ponytail. It revealed her long neck and excellent complexion.

Art ducked into a luggage store and purchased a large black umbrella.

Farther along the Calle they veered into a well-stocked newsstand inside the popular Mercado San Miguel.

There she thumbed through a copy of *Il Edifico*, a large sized design magazine before buying a pack of filterless Gitanes.

He had been reading the newspaper headlines.

"Do you like Architecture?"

He turned to see her drop the cigarettes into her purse. "I like practical buildings. I'm tired of seeing garish design."

"You'd make a good Brutalist."

"I said practical not bland."

"You have stunning buildings in your city," she offered.

"What city is that?"

"You said you were from San Francisco."

Art tried to remember if he had mentioned that to her. He didn't recall.

From the newsstand they strolled to a narrow café in an alley away from Mercado San Miguel. On Calle Alcala retracing their steps they found a table to order tapas and pastries. And wine—always wine.

Conversations swayed like the wind. Here. There. But he was now aware of his surroundings.

She asked if he was married.

"No, never."

She raised her eyebrows at his barked answer. "Is that too personal?"

"No more than me asking how you got the scars on your knees?" Out of politeness, he didn't ask about the elongated healed incision across her lower abdomen that he had run his fingers over while in bed.

"Car accident when I was a teenager. My father paid for ballet lessons in St. Petersburg. It was a six-week program, but my luck was bad. My father came with me and was driving a rented car. We were from Valencia—what did we know of Russian blizzards? We skidded, hit a tree. My knees were crushed as the engine came through the dashboard. I never danced again."

He kissed her hand to offer sympathy.

She appreciated the gesture. Her mouth found his.

He broke off the embrace. Then, for long moments they were silent at the café table, occupying themselves by watching the shoppers in the upscale Mercado.

She thought of complications.

His thoughts were on the reason he was in Madrid in the first place. She had become a distraction. Things go wrong when he didn't focus on the assignment.

Until Jonna's text, he would have been content to know he was in bed with a ballerina—yes, a tall, graceful athlete, but the more they made love, his intrigue deepened, until Jonna's report.

The truth shook him. She had him twirling like a top: happy, sad, sentimental, sensual when there was no time for such feelings. He was almost giddy in his thoughts. That was until he walked by the mirror in the suite's dining room. He stared at himself and decided he was looking at a fool.

Jonna's information told him all he needed to know.

Although she had shown no interest in being paid for sex, he realized it was not fate or luck that brought them together on Friday night.

He glanced at his wristwatch. Had he been away from the Attu long enough for Tom to deliver the package.

He wondered if she was working with the Russian FSB? Had the secret police tracked him here? Why not? He flew commercial to Madrid; a private jet would have attracted attention to him. He flew British Airways. He blended in as a tourist.

But did he miscalculate the Russian authorities? Were they wise to the true reason he was in Moscow? He didn't expect the Museum keepers inside the Kremlin to discover their loss until Monday.

"We should go back to the hotel," she said.

He pulled out a Euro note from the wallet in his breast pocket to tip the waiter for monopolizing his table for so long.

"This is Madrid." Her message was clear: It is expected for lovers or liars to whisper in each other's ears and brush lips with slow fingers and linger at restaurant tables. He shook her index finger at his face. "You're in Spain you don't have to tip everyone."

He forced a smile.

She looked sad.

The façade of lovers was unraveling, and they both knew it.

"How will this end?" she asked.

"Who knows?"

"I don't want you to leave?" she said.

"Really?"

"I didn't mean that to be so dramatic." She slipped the gold coin he gave her Friday across the table. "I don't want us to end."

"Keep the coin."

"Maybe, I should leave before we ruin the memory of all our kisses." She smiled.

"Then stop talking about me leaving."

Feeling chastised, she kept quiet.

"Let's not make decisions," he was quick to add. He cupped the sides of her face with his large hands. He pressed her lips with a kiss.

They exited the Mercado district into a soft rain. They picked up their pace back toward Puerta del Sol along Calle Mayor.

Art felt the vibration. Privacy was a downfall of the LOBE units. Art excused himself. "I have to take this call."

Tom Gresham had just texted: YOU HAVE TWO GUYS ON YOUR TAIL, TAN TRENCH COATS. PLEASE ADVISE.

Art Grabbed her hand and led her to a nearby Basilica, just off Calle Mayor.

At this hour, the venerable church was hosting a concert by a string trio playing Beethoven.

They sat with backs to a stone wall near the front door nave. There she slipped her arm into his and rested her cheek against his arm to listen.

The trio performed the sonata to perfection.

He appreciated the calmness of the music to refocus himself. He realized he was in the eye of the hurricane.

He held her close.

He was in love.

* * *

After the last note, they left the venue at once. They stood at the front of the church watching the rain come down in drizzles.

He offered, "will it rain long?"

"No," she said, "it will pass. It's Spring. It always does. Let's walk back to the hotel. Maybe we make love one more time before we say good-bye?"

He said nothing.

They strolled holding hands in the direction of their hotel via Puerta del Sol.

He noticed Sol's extensive plaza had two subway entrances.

She glanced over her shoulder.

He stared ahead at the entrance of the Hotel Europa.

Once inside, he led her away from the lobby into the cafeteria with the long coffee bar.

She followed him to a small table inside the expansive café. They moved a small table in the rear, away from the block long counter and avoiding a direct view into the lobby.

"Please order me a double espresso," he asked and excused himself, pointing in the direction of the toilets.

Once out of sight, he used his LOBE to reach Gresham. WHERE ARE YOU?

* * *

Tom sat astride the parked Yamaha at the edge Plaza del Sol. Via his LOBE he heard Art: "If they get too close to me distract them. Then go to the side entrance of the hotel. Watch for me there."

Tom lowered the black helmet's plastic shield. The men were the only ones in sight wearing business suits made. No trouble to spot them.

The duo kept a block behind.

Tom followed slowly not wishing to create a roar, given the bike's huge engine.

But once Art had entered the Europa, the clowns began to chase after them. Only stupid men and government agents run while wearing leather shoes in the rain.

Tom gunned the Yamaha. A bit rusty from his police motorcycle days, he almost lost it when the machine lurched forward. A big jolt of adrenalin refocused him. He bore down on his targets.

They never turned to see where the roar was coming from. That's the moment Gresham veered between them, the blowby sent them flailing to the sidewalk. One slid headfirst into the cement base of a three-story light post. The other hit the curbing of a circular island that once was a fountain.

Exiting the plaza, weaving through the bystanders, who howled profanities at him, Gresham braked at the far end of the Europa.

The agents were strewn on the plaza pavement like puppets who had lost strings propping them up. They were damaged but not mortally.

Where was Art? Tom asked himself.

* * *

Doria Ziti by now snapped on her LOBE device from her handbag. She planned to arrest Art when he returned from the Europa's lobby toilets. She expected her agents would burst into the cafe as back up.

She slapped the Europa's café table with the flat of her hand. He was taking too long to return.

The arriving aproned waiter blocked her view of the lobby.

He flirted with her while placing the cortados on the small table.

She stood and moved away from the table. She yelled "Interpol" for LOBE to connect with her office. "I may have lost him," she reported.

She wouldn't remember moving back to the small table to slap a 20 Euro bill on the table or how fast she ran into the lobby and into the men's room. But while there she focused on pushing open the stall doors searching for the man, who hours ago had been her lover.

The stalls were vacant.

Still holding her weapon at her side, she raced through the lobby and out into the plaza. "I can't see him," she shouted to her Interpol contact.

"Señorita, Señorita!"

She spun around. The waiter was running toward her holding up an envelope.

She yelled at him, "I don't need the change."

The voice on her LOBE asked, "Do you see your back up?"

"I don't see them. Where are they?" she moaned in frustration. "Get someone to his hotel. If he grabbed a taxi, he should be there soon. No one has arrived here."

She turned back to the barista and slapped on an impatient disappointed smile.

"Señorita, this fell from your purse," the young man waved a small envelope toward her.

She grabbed it from his hand.

"It was on the ground," he pointed.

She refused to open it until she scanned the Sol one more time. It was then that she noticed both entrances to the Metro and the simple truth: The Puerta del Sol was on the subway line to the airport.

* * *

Earlier when Art first texted Tom from the Attu, he immediately headed to his hotel.

Once there, he approached the concierge desk with the claim chit Garcia had given him for the double-sized briefcase left for him in the hotel safe.

The woman concierge returned with the large valise. She had been rewarded handsomely by Jonna Berk for simply guarding and transferring the locked valise to Fernando Abba. Given the nice fee, the concierge was not a curious woman and she followed Art's instructions to a tee.

From the Attu, Tom hurried along Gran Via to a 24-hour Amazon overnight express office. There was no line. In five minutes, the shipping transaction was complete.

From the express office, he climbed back on board his Yamaha and headed back to look for Art along the Calle Mayor.

He patrolled along the narrow street until he saw Art hand in hand with Doria Ziti.

That was when he alerted Art he was being followed.

When Tom noticed the agents start to sprint that's when mowed them down.

Art stood in the alley across from the Europa's side door.

But when he saw Tom arrive, Art jumped from behind a construction dumpster and hopped aboard the Yamaha.

They disappeared around the curve of the street as a bewildered Doria Ziti ran out into the plaza—followed by a waiter from the hotel café on her heels.

* * *

By midnight, Tom was on a red-eye British Airways Mach 5 carrier back to San Francisco. Art boarded the waiting private jet that Jonna Berk had arranged before Art left Moscow. He returned to Stockholm an hour before Tom's Boeing 1111 throttled down on approach to San Francisco International.

* * *

That evening, Doria Ziti finished watching television news with her husband Zorenzo after her twin boys had been put to sleep. She remained adrenalin wired from her weekend adventure. Her mind was 1,600 miles to the north in Stockholm.

The live-in maid left them alone and returned to her quarters after cleaning up after a late dinner.

Doria gave her husband a brief kiss. He excused himself back to his study.

He was used to her assignments away from home, the ones that she could not share with him.

She knew her husband was a good man. He knew to keep away from her professional secrets. One secret she didn't share with her husband was how she obtained that expensive gold coin that she placed inside a small music box on her vanity.

Tomorrow would be a day of bureaucracy for Doria filled with expected meetings, debriefings, explanations, and then the agony of composing reports. If she was lucky, a new assignment would land on her desk like a bright new shiny new coin.

And if they ever met Mr. Pontchatrain again, she would ask him whether he had truly fallen in love with her.

She hoped she knew the answer. In a way if they were in love then their on-the-job adultery could be rationalized. "It's my job," she whispered. Her new mantra.

Another thought bothered her. How did he slip through her fingers? What gave her away? How unexpected when all along she believed she had him curled around her little finger. She had read him wrong. Such a failure. And she was so close to making the biggest international arrest of her career.

Who was the bigger fraud? she mumbled.

The note she sent him had been destroyed but she remembered each word:

I ACCEPT THAT YOU ARE A SPY, BUT I CAN'T FORGIVE THE ACTRESS WHO BETRAYED HER HUSBAND, HER FAMILY AND ME.

"God damnit, you pompous ass," she whispered, "who's the bigger whore?" Her words were bitter but they didn't come from the heart.

* * *

Midweek, she was called into the top Spanish agent's office. A Russian investigator joined them. Moscow was livid.

She had assured the men that she had gone through Art Garcia's possessions in the hotel while he showered, and he did not find anything worth reporting. She spoke in Russian, "Perhaps, if I was told up front what to look for…"

"Shut up." The Russian grunted. He waved her away.

The smaller man rose and walked to his office window and peered out. "Doria, the crown no longer needs your services," Eduardo Ayunar said while looking out of a large window. "Go home. I'll call you if I need you, again."

2.
APPEARANCE OF IMPROPRIETY

Sketches and Short Stories

Cantina Psalm:

Shhh, it's probably a secret

THE MARTINS

A few days before St. Valentine's, North Beach basked in a false spring morning, typical for a Bay Area winter.

Sunshine streaked through the clouds for the first time in two weeks, accompanied by a bone-chilling wind from off the ocean.

The young couple still in bed ignored the sunrise until a loud ear-jarring metal-against-metal grinding woke them.

Both recognized the noise. It came from a city bus that came uncoupled from its overhead electric lines and stalled in the intersection below Tom Gresham's bedroom window.

After compact energy pods made overhead electric lines obsolete, the city kept the number 30 bus line from downtown to North Beach in operation, along with the Market Street trolleys, as a historic throwback. They remained the only lines with human drivers.

But when you are trying to sleep late to nurse away a hangover, he cared less that the most complex public entities take the longest to change. That is why they look and operate the same way for decades or even centuries. San Francisco is no different. It took forever to convert the electric bus and trolley system to run on forever batteries.

Thanks to Anthony Guereca, a University of California, San Diego-trained power grid engineer, who came up with the fusion pod that captured the power of safe nuclear energy in a bread box-sized unit, world transportation systems on Earth, the Moon and fledgling efforts on Mars changed forever.

Think of how the world changed after Edison, Tesla, Ford, and the Wright Bros. Guereca's pod allowed cars, trucks, buses, and planes to be powered only once from the factory. No more overhead electric lines, batteries or fossil fuels were needed to move the masses.

Guereca's team told all the fossil fuel kingdoms and corporations to go fuck themselves. And, what endeared him with so many was that he dispersed his knowledge to anyone that asked. He became as wealthy as Wally McGrath, whose McGrath International built the pods for Guereca and the world.

Tom tried to fall back to sleep, but a blaring horn from an impatient driver aimed at the unhinged orange and white Muni bus ruined his chance to sleep late.

Carly Martin's vibrant green eyes fixed on him. "Nothing's changed," she said. "All you did was get me drunk and talk me back into bed with you."

He yawned.

A curly bedhead of blonde and gray hair sat up. "You're right, nothing has changed. How many times have we done this dance?" He gently put his hand on her black hair, cut pixie style.

The evening before, they had bandied over the act of separation. Back and forth she insisted it was time to break it off, again. End a clandestine romance that was now in its fifth year. And every time she brought it up, again, he would say, "fine." She would reinforce, "I mean it this time."

He knew Carly was raging at her inability to halt advancing old age.

Carly, now an assistant DA aping her father's career path, had been complaining for the past week that she was about to turn thirty.

Distasteful as it was, she was not about to let the milestone day pass without a celebration.

She dropped her head back down on her pillow. "Garrett has booked me for a birthday lunch day after tomorrow."

"Ah, the ever-opportunistic Mr. Ellis, your Black God."

"He doesn't know we're seeing each other. Give him a break. Maybe he's being polite. I hope."

"You'd think he'd get the hint."

"I like him. He's attractive and has a great sense of humor. And he loves going out on the town."

"Well, if you and I were allowed to show our faces as a loving couple, I too could be a gadabout."

She continued. "Leave him alone. At least, he asked me. And, no, he's not sleeping with me."

"Yet," Tom added.

"Look, the sun's out," she said.

"When is your birthday exactly."

"Monday. That gives you all weekend to buy me a lavish present."

"I'm on duty later this morning. Your father is playing golf at the Olympic Country Club. Maybe we can do something this afternoon."

"Why don't you call him and tell him LOBE news has been reporting a gale is on its way. Save you a trip. Save you a day out of your life."

"No, it doesn't work that way. He might want to go somewhere else."

You're such a good slave, Tommy Gresham," she said.

He walked out of the bedroom to shower.

She realized her remark probably offended him.

Carly dropped her head back on her pillow in frustration reminding herself of his most agonizing personality trait—his passive acceptance of their relationship no matter which direction it took.

She listened to him in the shower until she let her thoughts drift away. She inventoried his bachelor's bedroom. It hadn't changed since the first time they made love on his lumpy double bed. Has he ever made his bed? Changed the sheets? Seldom. Or has he put on the new pillowcases or the sheer curtains that she bought for him?

She put her hands over her eyes. It didn't really bother her the bed wasn't made but the thought nauseated her if he brought other women to his flat.

Carly sat up in bed. She realized she was trying to find reasons to leave him, again.

In the shower, Tom sensed she was about to make another exit. It had been the third or so time she mentioned Garrett in passing. He felt it and he wasn't happy, but he was going to argue with her. How do you argue with a woman that makes a living debating life and death situations for a living? And, if there was anything true about himself, he was never going to win an argument. He could hear her say: *Yes, the sky is blue but there is evidence that it can be gray or orange. We have a lot of variables here, your honor.*

But trusted her to return. So far, she always has. He asked no questions when she returned because he understood she was in charge, and he had few choices. He felt blessed to be with such a dynamic woman, who left little to chance. She pushed hard in life as she did in the courtroom. Hers was a Terrier personality while his was a St. Bernard. He knew he was a lucky man. He melted in the presence of her beauty and smarts. Not because he was gutless but because he had little money. His hands were tied. And it made him bitter that she paid for almost everything. One day, he knew she might not come back. How could he keep her on a cop's salary? End of story.

Carly sat up. She looked in his dresser for a clean t-shirt to pull over her nakedness. She shook her head at how such a physically strong, fearless, and good-looking man could be so passive when it came to their relationship. She yearned for him to be fed up with her. Save her from her ending the romance.

She walked in on him because she had to pee before she burst.

He was shaving. The room was a sauna.

They didn't speak.

The carousel kept spinning. Ad nauseam.

That was yesterday, on and on and on and on.

* * *

Tom went directly to the kitchen from the shower. He pulled on a pair of gray sweats. As he brewed a pot of coffee, he walked over and opened his kitchen window. He pushed Carly from his thoughts by asking himself if he should buy his flat by using the money, he made on Garcia's Madrid assignment.

It would be the smart thing to do. Time to invest in the future. He figured he could live until eighty unless someone put bullets into him: one in his upper torso and another in his ribs. For now, he could use a tax shelter. Call it a mid-life crisis or a nod to the bourgeois.

But he stopped himself. He sipped on the hot coffee. Did he want the burden of owning his own place? He dreaded the bureaucracy of it all. He always returned to the thought of buying the vintage Ford Mustang that his friend John Wald offered to sell him countless times. John threatened to junk the 2x2 fastback. It was a dinosaur with a banned gasoline engine forever housed behind his friend's saloon, a block west of Tom's flat. Wald wanted the garage space for needed storage to run his Powell's Saloon.

That would be great for John, but Tom would have to find a parking space on the street. And that would be an added parking hassle considering he drives the 40-year-old Chrysler sedan, Joe Martin uses as his Mayoral limousine. The gray ghost averages five parking citations in North Beach alone per month, a dilemma he charges off to the city.

But if he owned the Mustang, he wouldn't have the fiscal protection of being head of Mayor Martin's security detail, a team of one.

San Francisco did not suffer auto withdrawals like other fossil fuel guzzling cities up and down the West Coast. Reason is because its narrow seven miles by seven miles city limits that meant it had always been a walking and biking city. And the expense of finding black market gasoline at $20 new dollars a gallon was not worth the squeezed juice from an old lemon. Gasoline-fed cars were too costly and too much trouble.

He dismissed the idea of buying John's Mustang. Everything was too much trouble. That and including Carly Martin.

Bureaucratic red tape aside, Tom never thought he'd be able to own his own apartment. San Francisco lacks housing. It is on record being the only city in the country with no homes less than $2 million available to buy.

Then it hit him. Why so gloomy? Brighter lights went on inside his gray flat.

Thanks to Art Garcia putting Tom on retainer with his detective agency he could unchain himself from living paycheck to paycheck. He could buy his flat!

He could rent a garage to house John's Mustang. Being able to convert it to a cheaper pod fuel engine would give him a splashy road car. It had been his dream to convince Carly to marry him and then move to San Diego away from the blue blood naysayers who would cluck that she married way below her station in life.

If that ever happened, Southern California was nice for the simple reason it never rained. He could get used to sunshine. And, he'd already have a car to cope with San Diego's urban sprawl. Plus, Carly could join the San Diego DA's office and be away from the shadow of her father's tenure as District Attorney.

The burden of no longer living paycheck to paycheck brightened his spirits more.

He heard the bathroom door open and shut and a few seconds later the shower came on. She screamed on cue when the hot water disappeared.

* * *

Those framed windowpanes in his kitchen were the windshield of his airship. From there he could disappear into the clouds. Brilliant Van Gogh clouds swirling and twisting from billowing white to shades of gray to black full of more rain.

Across the street from Gresham's second floor aerie, he noticed Washington Square Park was empty. At the far corner of the park near the bed and breakfast, he heard a French horn being played by someone hidden by the trees. Tom found the music soothing. It was something bittersweet by Duke Ellington but he was no musician and the name of the tune escaped him. Nonetheless, it haunted him all day.

Gone was the priest who sat on the same bench day after day reading his newspaper. Absent were the Asian couple gently twisting, breathing, living, and practicing an ancient exercise.

A rush of cold air entered from the opened window bringing in the aromas he loved: garlic rising out of restaurant roof vents; coffee beans being roasted at Graffeo's down the block; the smell of new rain, familiar streets and of the paved asphalt of Saints Peter & Paul's school playground on Filbert Street.

Tom made enough toast and a pour-over dark espresso for two from the ground Graffeo beans and day-old sourdough baguette from Stella's Bakery, which was just a block away.

He lathered his with blueberry jam he bought from Lee's Grocery across Columbus Avenue, the Leon Lee owned store that was on the same block long building as Coit Liquor and Powell's saloon.

She insisted her toast be lightly buttered—real butter and she'd only accept a light spread of lingonberry jam processed in Malmo, Sweden.

Yawning, blinking her emerald-colored eyes, she had wrapped herself in the finest silk robe, his second most prized possession given to him by the maharajah of hyperbole.

She sipped on the coffee and ignored the toast. He had run out of her jam.

She refused to let him give her a morning kiss. "We can't see each other ever again."

"How can we do that? I work for your father. We see each other every day. You've heard him, he considers me family."

"Don't force me to say mean things. Why can't you see the obvious? I can't be in a relationship that I have to hide. I can't have you in bed and Garrett out in public. It's not fair to you or him."

"Then choose," he said. "I can handle your decision."

"OK, I choose Garrett."

"Fine."

"Doesn't that make you mad?"

"I've enjoyed every minute with you. If it comes to an end—so be it," he said, not fearing she would pack up and leave that moment.

"That's my point," she said, pushing her index finger into his shoulder.

Tom grabbed her hand. "The point is you don't want to let the world know we are in a relationship—a serious one. What do you want me to do when you're the one who is making the rules?"

"You're right. I wish you had some other job."

"I'm working on that."

"See it to believe it." Carly stared at a stack of papers on the dinette. Her curiosity overcame her. "Real estate papers?" she asked, raising her eyebrows. She picked up the top document. "Are you finally going to buy this unit?"

"I'm thinking about it."

"What's stopping you this time?"

"I always think about buying it when you announce you're walking out on me."

She rolled her eyes.

"Then when you come back in the middle of the night, I remind myself that the place will be too small if we get married and have a kid."

"Cheap shot, Gresham." A tear rolled down her cheek. It was a sweet thought. But the reality was they would never marry, much less move into this flat—not when she lived on Russian Hill in a townhouse that her parents turned over to her when Mr. and Mrs. Joseph Martin moved into the mayoral mansion out on the Westside.

"Buy it as an investment," she offered. She placed the papers back on the stack. She looked pleased.

He decided to buy the flat. He'd show her the deed the next time she knocked on his door unannounced.

"Did you hear the music from the park?"

The know-it-all smiled: "Don't get around much anymore."

"Beautiful, huh?" he asked.

She was on other thoughts and didn't answer him.

* * *

Golf was out. Pouring rain or the fact it was the weekend didn't stop Joe Martin from asking Tom to drive him to the office of the chief medical examiner located southeast of the city at India Basin. Doc Martin had informed Joe over morning coffee that the remains of six unrelated drug overdose deaths had arrived at Med-Ex overnight.

Carly had taken the number 41 self-propelled bus six blocks up Russian Hill.

Tom approached the gray ghost. Thanks to divine intervention, it was parked legally below his kitchen window and at the side entrance of Mario's Café.

"Tom," a man's voice called. It was Pauley Carbone, who waved at Tom to join him inside Mario's.

Tom sat at the counter stool nearest to the front door.

Pauley Carbone said, "The other day, two cops were in here having lunch."

"Let me guess," Tom interrupted. "Ezra Ounce and Mike Kinder."

"Yes, I heard them calling you all kind of names. They come in here all the time and all they talk about is you and how you're such a fuck. What's with that?"

"I used to be Ezra's partner when we walked a beat here in North Beach. But when Joe asked me to be on his security detail, it went against the unwritten rules that plum jobs need to go to those with the most seniority. Joe said he didn't want Ezra. So that was that and Ezra has been badmouthing me ever since."

"Listening to them talk, I can't blame Joe. But it sounded like something more."

Tom paused to think. "Johnny Wald told me Father MacDonald complained to him that Ezra, while on his nightly patrolman rounds, stops in the middle of the park to piss on the statue of Benjamin Franklin. I think Father Mac complained to Charley Nye at North Beach precinct."

"That would do it," Pauley laughed. "Even the village priest hates Ezra.

Tom nodded. "I know something like that would bother him. All those years being headmaster of the school, he has little regard for rudeness."

"Maybe so, but it sounded serious enough for me to tell you," Pauley said.

"Thanks for that and do like everyone else in the world does—ignore them."

Pauley smiled, then changed the subject. "Father Mac comes in here a lot. He thinks the world of you."

Tom glanced through the café window to Saints Peter and Paul school and church on the other side of Washington Square. "He says that about all his alums."

"But we love the old fraud, don't we?" said Pauley.

"Never a doubt."

* * *

Twenty minutes later, after leaving Mario's Café, Tom pulled the city hall-issue Chrysler into the driveway of Mayor Martin's two-story Tudor-style compound. The grounds were first rate but no different than his neighbors' cluster of multi-million-dollar estates on West Washington Street in the northwest part of the city.

Seven years earlier, in a *San Francisco Monthly* interview, a writer asked him what the biggest change in his life had been since being elected mayor. "For the first time in my life, I had to move out of North Beach," Joe Martin answered.

Who can blame him? San Francisco's Westside, for the most part from Twin Peaks to the ocean, is called the Avenues. Clouds butt up against the two mid-city mountains and stay all day. When the gray sets in, 8 am looks like 4 pm. Kids grow up in the Sunset District never seeing the sun. San Francisco, for all its forty-nine square miles, has several distinct climates. The unifying weather theme is that it gets damn cold in the shade. Bone-chilling cold—a graveyard cold and that is different from the cute mittens and sweater cold at those Nevada-border Lake Tahoe ski resorts.

Today's downpour continued as a full-on gale, living up to BOT weather predictions on his LOBE smartphone. He barely made it into the Martins' foyer before the huge droplets turned to hail.

Tom entered the empty kitchen. He knew the drill: inside the twelve-by-twelve pantry he would find an older but still functional capsule coffee maker. Somehow the coffee always tasted better at Joe and Victoria's.

"Hi, Tommy," a feminine voice surprised him from behind.

"Hi, Carly," he lied a wide-eyed lie without turning around. "Is your dad ready to hit the links?"

"It's holy fuck raining, and besides, I'm not Carly. That's two brain dead things you've come up with and you just got here." She did not get the fact that Tom was teasing her about her dad's non-existent golf agenda—not about the rain.

Turning toward the barefooted six-foot teen, Tom faked a double take that made her smile. He put his hands over his eyes to avoid staring at Melissa "Missy" Martin's stack of hair curlers, neon-colored robe, tightly stretched dental braces and a whiny facial expression. Only a researcher of teenage angst could comprehend what and how she was feeling.

"I knew that was you, I'm yanking your chain," he tried.

"Nope. You blew it. You like Carly better than me. Everybody likes her better than me, including my own parents and all their friends."

"How can that be—you're cuter?" he said. "Besides, I'm a family friend and I like you better than Carly, and your beauty defies all limitations Greek Gods placed you to rule mere mortals. And I like the slope of your nose. To me, you're the perfect white girl."

The seventeen-year-old smiled, revealing additional state-of-the-art orthodontistry. "I suppose you want a hug for all that B.S.?"

"I'm family," he said. "Hugs are part of the deal, but only a little hug. Touching a female under 18 is punishable by death in this part of town."

The lithe high school volleyball bench warmer moved awkwardly inside his arms, where her peach-fuzz complexion met his bad shave.

She stepped back.

"My God, Gresh, you reek. It's Carly's perfume. Did you spend the night with her? God, I bet you did. Didn't you shower?"

"It's Saturday," he smiled, "Besides a lot of people wear that perfume. In fact, I had fashion models from Amazon/Macy's over to my place last night and they all wore that same perfume. Who would believe that coincidence?"

"Crap, crap, crap. Are you dating her behind everybody's back? I'm so jealous. You promised me when you forgot to bring me a present for my first holy communion that you'd marry me. I'm still holding you to that."

"I can afford to buy you a present now can we forget what I said?"

"Nope, I'll never forget. A deal is a deal."

"I'm perfectly happy to wait for you," he beamed.

"Hah, not if you're sleeping with Carly. I know you are," she bluffed.

"How's your mother?"

Missy's smile faded. She wanted to tease him more, but he wasn't playing. "She's working too hard. Told dad she's seeing a lot of drug ODs come into her ER. I mean a lot."

"If I needed an ER experience, I'd make sure your mom was on duty," he said.

"Mom looked beat up—not physically but way too tired when she came home this morning." Missy frowned.

Tom shook his head. "It's her own fault. She runs the whole ER wing. She was begged to take over St. Augustine Hospital's new facility; why does she work the graveyard shift? She doesn't need to do that?"

"Because that's where the action is," Missy insisted.

He wanted coffee. He held an empty cup in her direction. "Aren't you supposed to make the coffee? It's your only responsibility in this entire family."

"Are you sleeping with Carly? Tell me."

"Tell me, what?" a tall silver-haired woman in a wildly colored kimono entered the kitchen.

Caught with her hand in the cookie jar, Missy recovered quickly. "I was just asking Tom to drive me to my prom in Dad's limo, and if he didn't, I was going to complain to you."

"I'm not a chauffeur," Tom said.

"I didn't think you wanted to go to the prom because it was too 'unadult.'"

Tom laughed.

"It is. Proms are so ancient, but everyone else is going and none of us have dates."

"Take Tom to the prom. I'm sure he'd love to take you on his day off."

"Thanks, Mom, but he'd just try to do nasty things with me in the back of the gray ghost."

"Tom," Victoria mocked concern. "Would you let Missy do that to you?"

"She's too young for me," he offered. "And it's so hard to make out with brace face."

"Tommy, is the coffee ready?" Doc asked.

He glanced sideways to Missy, "Mr. Lincoln didn't free all the slaves."

"I'll do it since I've obviously been bred to do so," Missy said and took over making the bullet coffee come to life. Then she whispered a quick aside, "Tell me about Carly and you or I'll hate you forever."

The ponytailed medico asked Tom, "What? No good morning hug?"

Missy's eyes widened. "Don't touch him, he has cooties."

"Has what?" Tom asked.

"Tom told me he was fighting a cold," Missy lied.

"When was the last time you heard the word cooties? And remember, I'm a doctor."

"She's your daughter."

Doc Martin stared at Tom. She realized why he was standing in her kitchen. "Oh, Tom I'm so sorry. You drove all the way over here. We should have called you. My apologies on that. I'm groggy. The hail woke me up. Joe is almost ready. He'll be dragging since I kept him up talking about work. I've never seen so many drug overdoses in my ER ever." She reached up and touched his forehead with the back of the palm of her hand. "He doesn't have cooties."

Missy said nothing. She poured her mother a cup of very noir coffee.

Victoria said, "Your great-grandmother used to say cooties. It has been ages since I've heard the word."

"It's a fatal disease, Mom."

Victoria shook her head and started to remember her grandmother Millie. Maybe memories are a genetic thing, she thought.

"Are we ready for school this morning?"

It sounded odd to Tom, to hear Victoria nag Missy to get dressed for school when the school room since her freshman year was down the hall in the library of the mayor's mansion. Nevertheless, Victoria insisted Missy dress properly even for Zoom classes.

Missy came up to Tom and whispered, "I almost forgot to tell you? I got tits."

Tom closed his eyes. "Let's alert the media."

"No shit," she teased. "This is big news for me. It was like last night I was flat chested and now I have thirty-two Bs. Wanna see 'em?"

"Missy! No," he insisted.

"Better now," she teased, "because for you there won't be a tomorrow."

"Go away," he said. "And besides, woman's breasts don't appear overnight."

"How would you know, Mr. Virgin America? Why are you still single? Are you trans with a donkey?"

* * *

Driving toward the coroner's office on Newhall Street, Tom's sense of humor kicked in. He wondered which corpse was posing a danger to His Honor to the point he needed a bodyguard. But no one asked him.

The deaths came via ER at St. Augustine Hospital, where Victoria Martin signed off on the toe tags.

St. Augustine, the hospital, was built as a twenty-first century version of the 1930s Works Project Administration (WPA), where the Feds stimulated a broken economy by creating new jobs and new public works. Joe Martin contributed his idea to the WPA that came to be built underneath the Oakland Bay Bridge's western terminus.

Joe's dream was to create housing and medical facilities for downtrodden military veterans, especially those who were homeless, and drug afflicted. Joe had local laws pushed through. These laws mandated that on a citizen's second drunk or drugged in public offense that the wino/druggie be committed and housed in the bowels of St. Augustine's new floating medical center and rehab unit.

Defense attorneys checking out the back alleys of the law looking for work felt outraged that habeas corpus writs had been violated. They filed very creative lawsuits aimed at the US Supreme Court. The problem for the shark attorneys was that the Supreme Court was too busy deciding if bullets or abortions killed more babies.

Given he put one mothballed aircraft carrier to work for humanity instead of destroying it, Martin was sensitive to any spikes in drug use in the city, especially since ER drug abuse recidivism has dropped in the city by 75 percent.

"Are these ER deaths a coincidence or we're seeing a new cartel operating in the city?" Joe asked.

SLAB CITY

Carla Boris, the assistant medical examiner in her forties, handed Joe Martin an unstapled inch-thick stack of printed data. Tom liked her New England accept and her preppy wardrobe. She was on record being the oldest woman in San Francisco to wear parochial girl plaid skirts with penny loafers.

"What do you have?" he asked.

"We tested the blood on the new arrivals. We haven't seen coke this pure in a long, long time. I've sent samples to the Feds to let them determine what part of the planet the powder came from. They can do that quicker than my team."

"Anything else you can tell me about the victims?"

"Undernourished. They're veteran drug users. That's why I'm curious why they were caught off guard with more potent cocaine?"

"A new source," Joe said.

"Want me to guess?" she asked.

"Sure."

"One of the citizens had recently come back from a business trip to South America, according to his family. They swore he had never done drugs."

"One-off tourist," Tom said from the back of the lab.

"Where in South America?" His Honor asked.

"Peru," she said.

"And that Peru citizen," Joe asked carefully, "had similar cocaine in his system."

"Yes sir."

"What about the others?"

"Card-carrying druggies, all of them."

"Where were they picked up from?"

"I can have staff give you geographic data. Give me a week."

"I need a favor," Joe asked. "Stall any press calls on this if you can."

"I'm a bureaucrat. I'm one of you. I can stall with the best of them."

Tom followed Joe out of the lab. He handed her his business card.

"What's this for?"

"Dinner. I'd like to take you out to dinner—sometime. It's a weekend. You work hard and as a citizen I'd like to thank you in a small way." He laughed and realized he was attracted to her. The plaid skirt worked. "And I know I've seen you before. I just can't place it."

"I'm married, slick."

Tom snapped the card away. "Since when did a nice offer for dinner turn out to mean I want to screw you on the metal slab over there."

"I wasn't born yesterday. I know what you want?"

"OK, tell me what I want?"

"I know your type. Fuck, fuck, fuck that's all that's on your mind."

"I'm offended."

She mocked, "Go ahead call HR and stand in line to complain."

"Not that offended."

"Look, I'm maybe ten years older than you. I'm good looking. I still have the stuff men like you have been drooling over since I was 14. You'll be nice to me just to get me in bed. That's dishonest. It's lying. Guys like you think I'll be grateful to get laid because I'm older than you. And I know all you want is to screw me. You aren't interested in a relationship or even a friendship. Tell me I'm wrong?"

"What's evil about a one off?" Tom frowned. "I never thought about your age. You're terrific looking but now that you've made a deal about it how old are you?"

"Good side of dead. Don't mess with me on dead jokes," Carla said.

"Dinner is dinner. I'm a single guy. No relationships. We don't have to have sex."

"I didn't say I didn't want sex. I just said I know what you're up to so don't sweet talk me."

"Let's get to know each other. What do we have to lose?"

"I may take you up on that," she took his business card back.

"Where?" he asked, wondering what restaurant she'd pick.

"How about the metal slab right behind you."

Tom snapped the card back.

"You started it," she laughed, as the closing swinging doors made Tom Gresham disappear.

Tom's thoughts were scrambled, So far it has been quite a morning. The woman in his bed wanted to dump him; his boss's seventeen-year-old daughter called him a virgin; now a woman ten years older messed with over asking her out on what he thought was an innocent enough dinner invitation. In the good old days, asking a woman out to dinner wasn't so God damned complicated. "When did that change," he mumbled.

* * *

Driving back from Joe's mansion to North Beach to catch up with the rest of his weekend, Tom received a call on his LOBE from Carly.

"Are you still at my flat?"

"I came back, I forgot my iPhone 33. Since I'm here I want to make us breakfast."

"Do you need anything from the store?"

She rattled off a long list ending with, "Grape juice. I have this craving."

"You're craving more wine. We finished off two bottles of your grandfather's pinot noir last night." They had eaten at Tim's Place, an Italian restaurant in Pleasant Hill, a suburb thirty-five miles east, where they felt save dining in public.

"Don't remind me, and hurry, I'm hungry. And…" she paused, "I'm sorry I was mean to you this morning."

"Hungover."

"Why won't you be mean to me? Tell me I'm spoiled…I deserve it."

"You're spoiled."

"I know. I'm sorry."

"Let's continue this over the kitchen table."

"And see if you can find some Italian sausage, and did I say orange juice?"

"Grape juice," Tom corrected. He stared up at the rain. He had not seen it rain this hard in a long time. Water, water, everywhere.

He liked seeing the hillsides stay green all year long, but rain had become a nuisance now that there were new federal pipelines in play from the Arctic to bring needed water to drought areas in the West; rain was no longer worshipped as it had been in the last century.

3.

THE DENIZENS
Sketches

Cantina Psalm:

"... Come by on Halloween, St. Paddy's Day or Cinco de Drinko if you want to take home a drunk co-ed or a salesman down on his luck. But know this the real drinkers stay home..."

--John Wald, owner, Powell's Saloon

AMATEUR HOUR

The cat and the rabbit sat in Powell's middle of three window tables that viewed Washington Square and the massive church beyond the green. The fully costumed late twenty-somethings were taking a few moments before the start of the lower school's annual costume carnival to fortify themselves. It was 11 am.

The floppy eared rabbit fidgeted as if she were late for a meeting. She kept glancing at the empty school yard next to Sts. Peter and Paul and its tall twin spires.

Bar owner John Wald recognized the pair as North Beachers; they were regulars in his pub arriving with the last call shift. Powell's was a popular hangout with night owl waiters, bartenders, cabbies, off-duty cops and strippers, the latter trekking up from Broadway after dancing their last set. The wee hours where when those bar and strip workers with sleeping tots at home could kick back and enjoy a little free time.

The rabbit had the best costume a figure-hugging white jumpsuit, tall ears, a large cotton tail and matching bunny slippers. She was drinking a bloody Mary.

The cat was simply cute. She wore cat make up and exaggerated whiskers with black and pink cat ears pointing at odd angles. Matching baggy sweater and black yoga tights completed the look. Pussycat drank her Irish Coffee and fought the whipped cream off her whiskers

Mrs. Rabbit kept making eye contact with the bartender while sipping her drink. Then she'd double up on the chatter as if a moment of silence would spoil the day.

John looked around his otherwise empty bar. It was rare for Powell's to have only two customers at this hour. Wald had expected a slow lunch crowd and his prediction came true. Being Halloween meant amateur drinkers and regulars would come out to howl after work not before. The influx of name-the-holiday drinkers disrupted his regular crowd. These outta-the-hood drinkers affected a swagger as if the pseudo holiday gave them license to be the assholes they really were, especially the married ones.

North Beach regulars kept quiet. They avoided the hustle bars. The locals hated that part about their neighborhood's boozy reputation. No one liked hearing shopworn bullshit from the young suits aimed at the arriving co-eds from Frisco State.

On the other side, John liked college girls better. They were the most honest of his clientele. On fake holiday nights, they had set aside the night's prowl in advance to have fun, get drunk and let the most handsome feel them up in the dark stairwell leading to Powell's basement. They didn't need masks, but the other guys did:

"What if we get together for lunch at Tadich Grill?"

"What about dinner? I can be there by 8 p.m.?"

"Nah, that's too late, I gotta be in the office early."

"Come on, Mr. Lucky, you can get a pass from wifey for one night?"

By 10 pm, having their fill of older men, the college age women collected their troupe and headed back to the dorms. Coeds in packs were good for business and John never checked IDs.

But it was still morning when the cat and the rabbit showed up. North Beach was quiet for now. Later by 4 pm a few denizens new to North Beach bars, would show up with faces dull as pencils. That is until the co-eds show up and silly juice starts making the rounds. Soon, the sad get sadder the silly get sillier and the bitter souls begin to steam like a hot caldron covered with a loose-fitting tin lid. Happy hour has arrived to take the denizens in whatever direction life pushed them.

John saw it all.

Who needs Halloween?

He sees it every day.

Cat-face and her buddy finished their drinks. "I'll pick up the tab," she said to her friend the bunny. "Go on to the carnival—save me a seat for the parade. I've got to talk to John."

At the bar, whiskers leaned closer to John. "Hi, handsome, remember me?"

It was a line out of a bad movie, but he loved it. "Give me 100 years and I'll remember your name."

"One-night last summer you and I played kissy face your office downstairs. Ring a bell?"

His face brightened. "You're Shannon."

Surprised, he remembered, she laughed, how do you do that?" The tall brunette hit her fist on the bar. "If you remembered my name, why didn't you ever call me?"

"Because every time I see you—you're with a different man."

"Occupational hazard," she laughed. Her blue eyes were riveted on him.

"So, what were you girls gabbing about so seriously?"

"Nothing important. We found out one of our stage door Johnnies was trying to date both of us."

"I thought the term was stage door bozos."

"I get it." She lowered her voice "But most of all I was trying to get the courage to ask you if you had any hours for me? I need the work. I'd be so much better to do cocktails here than dance at Clementine's."

"Are you a dancer?"

"Thank you for not calling me a stripper."

"I heard dancers bring in great tips. My crowd real shy when it comes to leaving tips."

"Tips are great but working for Junior DeLuca wears thin. Know what I mean?"

He let her comment slide. "You know I've always been meaning to come see you dance," he grinned.

"Stop it, you're the only decent man on the planet."

John, surprised by her request was happy she asked. Business had been good lately and he'd been meaning to put a help wanted sign in the window for a cocktail waitress.

But the bureaucracy of it all kept him from acting on it. Always too busy.

Standing in front of him in her whiskers he couldn't picture her stepping out of a G-string on stage. Clementine's on Broadway was the sleaziest club on that two-block long stretch of Broadway. She looked too wholesome, a Miss Nebraska Junior Teen Queen. He recalled in the few times he gabbed with her across the bar, she didn't come across as a druggie or a bimbo. If she had told him she worked at a bank he would have believed her.

To his credit John didn't say *what's a nice girl like you stripping in a place like that?*

Early in his bartending career he did ask a drunk girl from one of the strip joints that the same question.

"I suck cock backstage. It pays better."

He never asked that question, again.

John said, "I got a couple of shifts open. Halloween. Tonight, 4 to midnight. Can you make it? I know it's short notice?"

"Yes."

"If it works for you--you can have as many shifts as you like."

"What should I wear?"

"Same as Clementine's. Hell you'd rake in the tips."

"Seriously?" A frown replaced a smile.

"Lousy joke. Wear what you want?

"Jeans and a top."

"Perfect."

She reached across the bar and gave him a kiss while smearing her painted on cat whiskers. "You won't be sorry."

John didn't know it at the time, but it was the first job she had since arriving in San Francisco that she could wear clothes.

MISTER METER MAID

Leaving Joe, the Assistant Medical Examiner and six dead bodies in his rear-view mirror, Tom had driven from Med-Ex complex via His Honor's trendy Westside digs then to North Beach. He circled the block twice before he gave up trying to find a legal parking space. He finally pulled the four-door gray ghost into the red bus zone in front of Powell's Saloon. From there he dashed around the corner to Lee's Grocery. Both the grocery and Coit Liquor next door on the corner were among the oldest businesses in North Beach. A hundred years from now, he figured they would still be there, unless the building burned down. There was a lot of comfort in knowing that.

Tom filled the hard plastic hand basket with Carly's order. He included a two-foot-long baguette baked at Stella's Bakery across Columbus. He bought thin sliced prosciutto, Spanish olives with the pit, lettuce, a wedge of provolone and a tin of oregano. For a chaser, he added a six pack of San Pellegrino orange soda.

Stepping out of the store, he glanced across the divided avenue to the corner window of his flat. He was surprised she let herself back in. It gave him a warm feeling that she was waiting for him.

Tom turned the corner—headed west half a block on Union to Powell Street, where he had parked the museum piece on wheels a few minutes earlier. He needed to move it to a legal parking spot. Tom realized a squall had come and gone while he was shopping. He picked up on the aroma from the new rain: a distinctive smell of asphalt mixed with wafts of roasting coffee from Graffeo's Wholesale Coffee two blocks north on Columbus at Filbert Street. Times like this made him happy to live in North Beach.

The erstwhile limo (paid from the fund trust Joe set up for his solo practice law while he was in elected office: DA and mayor) roared to a start on the first try. The oversized wipers splashed water off the windshield like a shaking dog.

Gresham clunked it into gear.

It made a lot of noise, but it didn't move. He was lodged against the curb. He put it in reverse. Nothing.

Before he could figure what was blocking the car, he heard a knuckle wrap on his driver's side window.

One of the city's finest traffic enforcement scooters had rolled up next to him. Mr. Meter Maid, dressed in a yellow slicker, was motioning for Gresham to roll his window down. "You're parked in a red zone, pal. You got a boot slapped on your right rear wheel." The Santa Claus-sized bureaucrat had a very smug look on his face.

"You're kidding. No one boots the mayor's car."

"Well, I did. Go look for yourself," the meterman smirked.

Tom didn't have to. Fellow citizens at the bus stop nearby were nodding sympathetically.

"Is that funny to you?" Tom screamed at the meterman. "What the hell did you do that for?"

"Shit happens, pal, especially when you park in a red zone and your ugly bus has outstanding warrants."

"You're no beauty. What's your name?" he barked. Tom had never seen the traffic agent before.

"Eddie Peabody. And just so you won't forget, you'll see my signature on the ticket."

"What ticket, Pea brain? There was no ticket on my windshield," Gresham hollered. He was red-faced.

"Must have blown off in the storm. Trust me, you got one. I'll see that you get a copy mailed to you, pal."

"Don't call me 'pal.' And this happens to be a city vehicle. And it happens to be Mayor Joe Martin's limo."

"It could be King Tut's chariot for all I care. It still gets a ticket and a boot for being in a red zone."

"You're an idiot," Gresham realized. "I'm sorry, that's not accurate—you're a fuckin' idiot!"

"I'm not the fuckin' idiot that parked in a red zone. You're lucky I didn't have it towed."

"So, this is better?"

"Have a nice day, pal."

"I told you not to pal me. Screw you. Get back here and undo the god-damned boot—you fat ass!"

Mr. Meter Maid shut off the scooter's engine. "What did you call me?"

"You heard me. This is the mayor' car. I need to pick him up and take him to the office. You're interfering with a city official and impeding his ability to conduct his duties."

"That's not what I heard?"

"You probably heard me say fuck you, Eddie *Pea*body."

"Yeah, that's the part you're going to have to explain to the patrolman I'm going to call."

"Save your breath, dipshit, I'm a cop and you're the last call I would respond to on a day like this."

"You sonofabitch," Eddie said and jumped off the scooter seat. "Get out of the fucking car so I can level you."

"You got shoe leather for brains, pea head. I think you better unlock that wheel if you know what's good for your career."

"Go to hell! The lock stays. You figure it out, pal. Start by paying your tickets on time."

"Look, you fat-ass scooter moron. I don't have time for this—unlock the wheel."

"I should slap you around," the badged scooter jockey said.

"What kind of jerk are you?"

Mr. Meter Maid bent over and shouted: "Show me where it says anywhere on this car that it's the mayor's limo. I don't see any special plates. You show me?"

Gresham leaned up off his seat: "This car is part of a security detail; what kind of security do you think we'd have if we plastered Joe Martin's name all over it? You tell me, scooter boy?"

"Looks like you're gonna have to do some explaining to His Honor, and that's what that ferret faced, bleeding heart liberal gets for hiring you—ain't that right, hot shot?"

Gresham yanked for the door handle.

Eddie Peabody leaned into the door.

Gresham was stuck behind the wheel. "I'm not explaining shit."

"Tell your sad story to the tow truck driver because you're gonna have to wait for her, and when she gets here, you're gonna have to pay her or we start this silly dance all over again."

Both peace officers were close enough to smell each other— Mr. Meter Maid's stale coffee and Gresham's toothpaste.

"Fuck you."

"Fuck you."

"You are the stupidest man alive," Gresham shouted.

"I'm not the asshole who parked this car in a red zone. The sign is printed in English just for you--you Irish sonofabitch. And the curb is red as your neck."

"What are you a limey?" Gresham's forefinger was half an inch from the meter maid's face.

"So, what's it to you, Mick?"

Gresham pounded on the steering wheel. "This is truly fucked," he mumbled to himself as he reached for his wallet to show his ID that identified him as a special city hall security agent.

As he opened it, four tickets fell into his hand. The ducats were to the first ever meeting between the new National Football League's expansion team the San Jose Silicon's vs. San Francisco 49ers game on Sunday.

He stuck the tickets Joe Martin gave him last week into Mr. Meter Maid's face.

"Eddie, you prick, I'm asking you for the last time. Unlock the goddamn boot."

The meter agent yanked the tickets from Gresham's hand. "These better not be cheap seats."

"Top of the line seats. Mayor's box on the fifty-yard-line."

Eddie Peabody feigned surprise and shouted loud enough for the bystanders to hear him, "JESUS, WHY DIDN'T YOU TELL ME SOONER IT WAS A FUCKING CITY EMERGENCY?" He bent down and unlocked the red boot off the Gray Ghost.

"Next time, you Irish dickhead, you ain't gonna get off so easy."

Gresham did notice a couple of thumbs ups flashed in his direction from the bus stop crowd as he pulled the limo out into traffic. In his rear-view mirror, Mr. Meter Maid was putting the yellow boot into the trunk of his scooter.

STATUE OF LIMITATIONS

The new storm lasted through until Monday morning. A loud pre-dawn banging startled Father Ronald MacDonald, the white-haired headmaster of Saints Peter and Paul School for Boys. His blue eyes darted until he realized the noise came from his bedroom window. Blown open by the stubborn storm, he mumbled toward the open casement, "Come in, Jehovah, are you my new alarm clock?"

The thin septuagenarian had fallen asleep in his leather recliner. As he sat up, his wire-rim glasses atop of a mystery novel written by a distant ancestor slipped to the floor.

Without his glasses, life became a Claude Monet painting. Lights in his beloved North Beach neighborhood kaleidoscoped into garish streaks of bold color. Streetlamps became round balloons of amber and street puddles—like tonight—become mirrors.

While relatching the rectory's second-story window, Father Mac noticed in the park below the squatty figure of a fifty-year-old patrolman splashing his piss onto the 120-year-old statue of Benjamin Franklin.

The nightly pissing scene had become a foul habit. But shouting at the cop to stop on those too numerous to remember nights had brought only one-finger salutes. Tonight, Father Mac was not in the mood to live and let live.

* * *

Dawn chased the storm. A fiery sky outlined Telegraph Hill with tangerine hues. Soon an AWOL sun crept over the famous hill, casting a warm light on the two-hundred-year-old wooden buildings in the eclectic valley between Telegraph and Russian Hills. Seeing blue sky in North Beach was a relief after a month of gray clouds and cold annoying drizzle.

North Beach denizens could tell when it was 8 a.m. by either listening to the spire bells at the church clock on the left twin spire or by seeing Father Mac enjoying his golden retirement years at Mario's Cafe reading his mailed weekly copies of the politically remodled right wing version of the International Herald Tribune and The same old, same old left wing leanings of the Paris Review.

On the metal cabaret table near his knee that he had crossed over his other bony leg was a tall cup of noir espresso, which had been enhanced with Vov, a mysterious potion, an elixir second only to Holy Water in its ability to calm the soul. And it is known to bestow imbibers the ability to see sunshine where none exists.

Also, 8 a.m. meant Father Mac would be a few minutes late for his meeting with the top cop at North Beach Precinct. Walking to the stationhouse on Vallejo made Father Mac wistful for what used to be. He recalled venerable North Beach businesses like North Star Café, Cole Hardware and Green Street Mortuary that had disappeared faster than decades off his life.

On Green Street, toward Powell Street, Capps Corner, an old-school gingham plaid red table-clothed Italian restaurant, would serve meals family-style. Everyone shared the large tables. Great for lunch and early dinners, but a too loud place to try and talk your date out of her panties. Not that a young priest would think of such a thing.

Sadly, Capps is gone. Replaced by a take-out only pizza joint.

Then, there was the stately albeit remodeled Club Fugasi, a pocket-sized theater, a ninety-nine-seater made for small non-equity shows that needed a home at a fair price.

Father Mac remembered the burlesque house switched from risqué to performing "A Christmas Carol" for three weeks each December.

That was when the school treated the students, staff and friends to performances. Father Mac never tired of the play. Venerated alums like Joe Martin, Garrett Ellis, Wally McGrath, John Wald and Tom Gresham would rather yank out nasal hair one by one than sit through another performance of the Dickensian classic.

Father Mac left Green Street and arrived at the station house on Vallejo. He walked straight to the captain's office bypassing the sinners sitting in the lobby. Dressed as civilians, Mike Kinder and Ezra Ounce were a pair of six-footers who arrived an hour earlier expecting the worst. As Father Mac often said, the pair were in deep soup.

The newly suspended cops entered the stationhouse standing six feet tall and left by the side door a mere five feet two.

Modern-day animators would have a comic hero in Charley Nye. The precinct captain was rangy, quiet, and possessed the face of a gentle giraffe. He did not exude swiftness, but in his deliberate way, he was efficient and a worthy public servant. He wore the blue/black uniform of the San Francisco Police Department with pride and neatness. He was an honorable cop.

When Father Mac left the meeting with Nye, he still refused to forgive the two in the lobby. The priest walked back to Mario's Cafe to continue his morning.

After a quick meeting with the cleric, Captain Nye had fired patrolmen Ezra Ounce and Michael Kinder. The duo were on previous disciplinary probation for playing poker in Dante's bar while on duty. Also, they also had been ratted out for stealing two police storeroom shotguns and attempting to sell them to undercover ATF agents. Nye had to rid himself and the department of two clueless assholes. Too many others worked too hard to allow such a minority of stupidity to exist among the rank and file.

Once outside on the precinct steps facing Vallejo Street, Kinder screamed. The dead a block away at the mortuary sat up from their coffins wondering what the hell was that?

* * *

The newly sacked, Kinder and Ounce were beside themselves with shock turning quickly to anger. Their fuming trek back to their flats took them along Columbus, where they paused at the traffic light at

Union Street. Their dismissal had been a shock. "Nobody gets fired on St. Patrick's Day moaned Ezra Ounce.

"At least we can drink to that," Kinder said. It would be the last pleasant words coming out of either ex-cop's mouth for a while.

The duo stopped cold at the traffic light at Columbus and Union Streets. Ounce pointed across the intersection at Mario's Café. "That's him. The bozo priest who reported us."

Once Kinder realized his partner was right, the ex-cop charged ran against the red light toward Father Mac.

"HEY FUCKHEAD!" Kinder screamed, "Your big mouth got us shitcanned. You happy 'bout that, you pompous jerk?"

The priest, who sat in the middle of five outdoor tables, lowered the newspaper he was reading. He didn't recognize Kinder out of uniform.

Shouts from the charging maniac put customers and passersby on edge. Kinder sounded like a distressed mule. To get to Father Mac, Kinder hurled himself into the café crowd consisting of an Asian couple with a baby in a stroller, who were giving their order to café owner, Pauley Carbone; two Israeli journalists, who were asking directions from goth teens, a Black and Hispanic, who were holding hands; the café's bus boy, a college wrestling champion; a cabbie in a cowboy hat who had just stopped for the traffic light.

Kinder proceeded to slap the newspaper out of the priest's hands.

"Are you mistaking me for someone else?" Father Mac bent to retrieve his newspaper.

"Bullshit, you know what I'm talking about." Kinder pushed Father Mac off his chair.

The older priest fell on his side, his forearm kept head from bouncing off the sidewalk. Kinder kicked the priest twice. And, for two seconds the Earth stood still. Silent as wide-eyed patrons froze to access the attack.

Two seconds passed.

"WHAT ARE YOU DOING?!" came the Asian mom's shout, plus an unholy chorus of yells, crashing tables, glass breaking, grunts and screamed epithets echoed off nearby walls.

First to react to the attack was the wrestling champ in a letter's jacket from Merrimack College. She jammed the spear tip of her umbrella into Kinder's left leg. "Get away from him you crazy sonofabitch!" she roared.

Next, the purple-haired goths, who were screaming just to be screaming jumped on Kinder's back, scratching his neck and the arm he used to swat them away. One Goth chomped on an ear.

Owner Pauley grabbed his cellphone and dialed 911 for police assistance.

One Israeli tourist grabbed and held on to Kinder's arm as he was about to punch the Black goth. The other lifted Father Mac by his armpits and pulled him away from the fray. Two years of mandatory Israeli military training paid off. They ushered Father Mac to a chair away from ground zero.

The Asian dad used his body to shield his baby as the melee was in full tilt around his stroller. The beefy Mario's bus boy slammed a Melmac tray on Kinder's head.

The ex-cop, who was desperate to repel the goth from chewing more of his ear began shouting, "Stop it, I'm police!"

Most ignored Kinder. They were staring at how much blood a cut from an ear could produce.

"No cop kicks a defenseless priest," shouted the 300-pound cabbie with a "peace" tattoo on his forearm as he grabbed a handful of hair, forcing Kinder's chin into an upward angle. It was a perfect pose for the cabbie to deliver a hard right cross to the side of the ex-cop's face.

The last thing Kinder saw for the next half hour was the blur of the Cabbie's face and other denizens as he collapsed face first on the sidewalk into an overturned pepperoni pizza.

The two goth girls, now on their knees, peered through purple forelocks into his face. "He's out, he's out."

One Goth asked, "Check his ear, I'm missing one of my nails."

Pauley Carbone retrieved half a dozen bar towels to attended to the Goth's face fresh with Kinder's blood.

Father Mac quietly returned. He stepped on Kinder's ankle, a trick he learned to inflict pain to those caught fighting on the playground. No one noticed so he stepped harder.

Kinder was moaning face down into the sidewalk to the delight of Mario's Café coffee klatch.

The melee ended as fast as it started. The silence that permeated the battlefield broke into unexpected laughter when the baby tossed her plastic rattle from the stroller, hitting Kinder as he staggered, attempting to stand.

Pauley, who had tears of anger and laughter in his eyes as he brushed off Father Mac's tunic and adjusted his collar, turned and shouted to Ezra Ounce, who remained frozen in place across the intersection, "Anyone else want to put a finger on this man has to come through me!"

Pauley shouted loud enough that the bodies back down at the Green Street Mortuary, a block away, lay back down in their coffins where it was safer.

4.
THE COY POND
A Short Story

Cantina Psalm:
"When it comes to sex crimes, especially those involving children, the perv perpetrator is known to the families of the victims."
--Snippet from a past media interview with Carly Martin, who obtained a conviction against a sicko who kidnapped his twin niece and only released them when he was tired of raping them.

HIGH RENT DISTRICT

The date on the embossed invitation celebrating Joe and Victoria's thirty-fifth anniversary read April 25, 2:00 p.m.

Carly Martin, whose house she rented from her grandfather Eugene Carling at the family discount became party central, a four-level 1930s streamline moderne in the international style, was built smack in the middle of the high-rent district.

Today's hostess was hard to miss wearing a white slit-at-the-thigh pearl colored hajib, which covered a white bikini. The hajib's hoodie was perfect to deflect the rays from her untannable white skin.

The Martin's oldest daughter led the newest arrivals to the top level of the *Architectural Digest* approved urban villa that jutted from a tall copse of fir trees, where Green Street made a cul-de-sac at the highest point of Russian Hill. A double staircase led up to the pool deck, where Joe and Victoria Martin were standing along the top-level circumference railing. The railing gave the sleek look of a white ocean liner protruding out from a cliff. Although, it was several miles from the shore, the urban forest surrounding the Martin's splendid abode made it appear as if it were chicly tucked away on a bluff along the Amalfi coast.

* * *

Party day turned out to be sunny and clear. The city was enjoying a three-day window of sunshine and fogless mornings. With Alcatraz Island and North San Francisco Bay in the distance, Carly proudly showed off her part of the world to her parent's guests, Zorenzo and Doria Ziti of Barcelona, Spain. "When I was a little girl, Alcatraz Island looked like a tramp steamer coming into the bay," she said told the noted design journalists.

But it was the sailboats on the bay that attracted the guests.

"I'd love to be on the water." Zorenzo offered. "We have a schooner we keep in Ibiza."

Carly pointed to the bay. "Sail it to San Francisco. Glide under the Golden Gate Bridges. That's always a thrill."

Earlier last year, the Ziti's asked to visit the Martin's Russian Hill aerie for a possible magazine photo spread. The call came from out of the blue. They insisted on a visit to research a possible article. New information about the streamline's unknown architect had surfaced. The coeditors of *Il Edifico*, Europe's leading architectural journal, were surprised that the mayor was no longer living there.

They were not privy to a tradition that once elected, mayors move into the city-issue brick Georgian mansion on the Westside. Once Joe explained that the Bauhaus-style prize was still in the family, a date was set for this day. The visit coincided with the Martins' thirty-fifth anniversary date, making it easy for His Honor to toss a cocktail reception for themselves under the guise that Carly was in charge. The journalist's visit was a personal perk. The Martins footed the bill, although it could have gone on the city books as an official salute to the visiting journalists.

* * *

Rising over the cool water of the aqua-colored swimming pool, designed in the shape of Botticelli's *Birth of Venus* seashell, Missy Martin lifted her head above the pool's heated and steaming waterline. The seventeen-year-old was bored and well into her high-maintenance bitch mode. No matter who paid for the soiree, it was just another of an endless drumbeat of parental events. And for now, she figured she could do three things: get drunk at the patio bar; ask the Fairbanks Hotel catering assistants if they had any more cocaine to share, and then jump in the pool so the chlorine would redden her eyes to mask the cocaine she had been ingesting all morning, a trick she learned from her social studies teacher at the Ware Academy for Women, a four-year high school located on the cusp between Chinatown and Nob Hill. The teacher ran an extracurricular class on hands on Lesbianism. After trying to seduce Missy, the teacher realized her mistake. Missy sensed an opportunity. "I want straight A's in your class—got it."

The crestfallen teacher whispered, "thank you."

Moving on, Carly set a goal to spend the rest of her senior year with Carly instead of continuing to reside with her parents in the mayoral mansion out on the West side where the sun never shines. Missy seethed at Carly's rejection of the idea. "I like it the way it is," Carly told her mother. "Let's keep it with the adults."

Missy had overheard that conversation and threatened not to come to the anniversary party. Her grandfather Eugene Carling saved the day by inviting her to a Sausalito shopping spree before driving her to his winery for Christmas break. Pure economic enabling by an expert. It worked.

Stepping from the pool in a blue bikini, Missy was intrigued by an older couple who had arrived rather late to her parents' party. They looked European.

Doria Ziti chose a Donna Koran suit accessorized with a multi-print halter blouse and flowing white harem pants. Her shoes were vintage high heels by Charles Jourdan.

Zorenzo was straight from a Fellini movie bespoke in his summer blue Brunello Cuccinelli suit that fit easy with a silky white shirt and collar with overcool tourmaline cufflinks. His Berluti shoes were in light brown leather snakeskin.

Missy, now pulling her sandy-blonde hair back in a ponytail, dismissed the arrival as another cliché of a much older man with a younger "thing" on his arm. He was probably a lobbyist, a term not popular in the Martin household over the years.

Then, Missy corrected herself. Her father would not have invited a lobbyist to a family party, so it had to be an ancient lawyer with a fading starlet or a once upon a time fashion model.

The rest of the party saw a handsome fiftyish man with an infectious smile and a gregarious thirty-five-year-old woman, who was his wife, judging from her mega-carat wedding ring that Missy did not pick up on.

A man's voice from behind said, "Missy, I'm here."

Thank goodness, she thought, her other coke connection had arrived. She laughed at the older man, who sartorially channeled Tom Wolfe, the magazine writer turned author from the last century. Knowing that the man was the duly elected District Attorney for the City and County of San Francisco made it even more weird—in her eyes. He was trying to be cool to impress Missy but seeing him in gold rimmed purple tinted sunglasses with a white suit, shirt, shoes, and Panama-made hat only made him more cringe worthy.

* * *

Also, noticing the glorious, white-suited arrival was Ben Adams, a neighbor, who Mayor Martin had known since the time the Martins lived in the party house. He and Joe were golf pals (not much else) making small talk "Did I tell you Patsy and I have decided *not* to sell our house? We were sick of San Francisco; too many bums living on the street. I was thinking of taking an early retirement by selling my half of my cloud business and move to Ireland."

"What changed your mind?"

Ben leaped at the chance to praise Joe Martin, "You did, Joe. Your leadership by taking the addicted off the streets and helping them rehab themselves was eye-opening. I think you deserve the

Nobel Prize. I've decided not to give up on San Francisco, thanks to you. I believe you will put the city back on the right path."

Joe had been sipping on too-sour margarita from the bar at which they both stood. "That's awfully nice of you, Ben, but I had a lot of help. Do you know Wally McGrath?"

"I know of him for sure. I voted for him to be on the Board of Supervisors, but I've not met him personally."

"Without his vote and without the billion dollars he invested in the project, St. Augustine's Hospital would never have seen the light of day. I'll introduce you when he arrives. He promised to drop by."

Both men turned to the pool when they saw a man dressed in a white suit, white shirt, purple tie, Panama hat and crepe-soled white Speedo deck shoes offer a hand to Missy.

She lifted herself out of the pool and just as quickly wrapped herself in an oversized pool towel.

"That's quite a garish look," Ben Adams offered. He tried to avert his eyes from the blue-eyed swimmer but failed.

"That's none other than our district attorney, Harre Ling. Around here we call him Uncle Harre. He's fond of our daughters."

"That's nice, but I didn't vote for him. Now I'm glad, seeing his outfit this afternoon. He's a bit old for the look. What do you call it?"

The Martins at one time were closer to Harre Ling. He was the best man at their wedding—hence the invitation to the party. But the friendship chilled over the years. The DA was a sloppy drunk, especially at alum events held for Sts. Peter and Paul School for Boys.

"Now that you ask," Joe said, "I'd say it was akin to putting a miniskirt on great grandmother.

They had a good laugh and watched the DA and Missy walk down the staircase from the pool deck.

"What's down there?" Ben asked.

"Family room, kitchen, guest rooms, weight room, where I keep my golf gear and more food and the restrooms if you need them."

Ben smirked, "I hate to bring this up, but a year ago at the boys school golf tournament you promised me a new set of golf clubs. You said a lobbyist gave them to you and you couldn't accept them."

"Of course. Damn, Ben those clubs are sitting in a closet at my office. You should have reminded me sooner."

"You're a busy guy."

"I'm going to take care of that." Joe pointed to Tom Gresham who was across the pool deck at a portable bar set up between the pool and the large Jacuzzi spa. "See the blonde kid in the tan shorts and the open Hawaiian shirt showing off a flat stomach you and I wish we had?"

"Yes, I'll have Tom bring them from the office that's the least I could do."

Neighbor Ben was all smiles. "I can't wait. By the way, who is he."

"Head of my security team. Actually, he is the security team," Joe said. "Sadly, sometimes I treat him like my chauffeur and caddie."

"No, I mean the man standing next to him."

Joe Martin's head swiveled back to the bar. "That's Garrett Ellis."

"The Garrett Ellis?"

"Yes. All-American Second Team NCAA basketball campus czar at Cal."

"I met him at a fundraiser at John Bruce's penthouse. He and I were the only men of color attending."

"What was John peddling this time?"

"The high rise that got voted down last year. He wanted the city to pay for it then put his name on the lower floors as a cultural center."

"John and I don't see eye to eye," Martin said, "he's always giving money to my opponents."

"Bruce is a ferret and an asshole." Ben shook his head. "But I like Garrett Ellis's reputation. I liked what he had to say in the small time I had with him. He's a liberal but I'd vote for him if he ran to fill your seat at City Hall now that you can't run again."

"He likes being a civil attorney but what I'm not fond of is his interest in dating my daughter all the way to the altar."

Adams stiffened.

Joe's face turned red, "And before you raise your eyebrows the reason I'm not keen on him as a possible son-in-law is simply because I want my daughter to date men that aren't my best friends. There's a city full of good men out there that she could date that aren't older than me."

"There's a city full of good men out there that she could date."

"Including me."

"Yes, even you if you weren't older than Methuselah's grandfather and you're married to neighbor Karen."

"I agree Carly is special. There should be a long list of men that would love to ask her out."

Joe flashed a quick, let's change the subject smile and said, "So, when I bring over your new clubs we'll have to play some golf."

Ben Adams watched Joe work the party. He also glanced at Harre Ling. "Bastard." Ben caught up to Joe. He decided to tell his neighbor what he witnessed a month ago.

Too late. Joe moved into a conversation Police Chief Andy Roehr was having with Father MacDonald.

Ben walked over to the hors d'oeuvres. It wasn't a good time to bring up that he came home early from his law practice. It was a month ago. He looked out of his kitchen window. Ben's house was higher on Russian Hill than Carly's. He looked down to his neighbor's pool deck and spied Harre Ling swimming with Missy. She should have been in school and she shouldn't have been alone with him naked.

* * *

The welcomed now cloudless skies brought up the heat. The Martins were hoping for a sunny day without rain or heavy overcast. They did not expect temperatures at the 2 p.m. party time to exceed eighty-five degrees. Staying in the shade to beat the heat was a good idea for Tom. He had to keep his blazer on to hide his holstered 9mm Glock from guests.

Next to him, family friend Garrett Ellis was stretched out on a chaise under the temporary party tent. The slim, 6'-6" family friend wore Bermuda-length black surfer shorts, black flip flops and a slightly open white silk shirt. He looked damn good for a fifty-year-old man.

Tom gestured with his plastic tumbler toward the guest of honor, the newly arrived Italian redhead speaking with Victoria Martin. "Who's she?"

Ellis replied, "She's editor of an architecture magazine in Barcelona."

"Really, how do you know all this?"

"I helped Carly with the invitations. You forget I'm doing all I can to become Mr. Carly Martin."

"How's that project going?"

"One day I'm encouraged and the next day she says I'm older than dirt."

Tom stared off toward Harre Ling walking downstairs with Missy arm in arm. "I don't like our white suit lothario taking Missy downstairs."

"Relax, he's the DA for Christ's sake."

"I don't like it."

"I think you're taking your job a bit too seriously. This is a family event."

"Maybe so."

Garrett, who had been admiring the compelling bosom of Mrs. Ziti, asked his friend, "how old do you think that woman is?"

"Doria Ziti?"

"Yes. She's beautiful. She and Carly have the same figure—ten years apart."

"She's no match for Carly."

"I want to marry her someday," Garrett said catching Tom by surprise with his comment.

"You mean Carly?"

Ellis wasn't laughing.

Tom said, "I'd love to marry Carly, too. Maybe we could flip a coin?"

Garrett grinned, "I want to marry her *today*."

"Nah, you don't have a chance."

The lawyer stopped smiling. "Why, because I'm Black?"

Stunned by the remark, Tom's face was a picture of confusion. "Are you serious?"

"Answer my question."

"Garrett, I'm just foolin' around with you. I thought we were joking around."

Garrett looked away. Silent.

Tom walked around to get in Garrett's face. "Man, all those years we went to school together it was never Black or white; it was us—you and me—friends. Don't tell me that's changed?"

"Stop it, Tom. I misspoke…"

"Hear me out. You're my big brother. My hero, the jock that put our orphanage on the map. You always treated me square. What, are we nine years apart? Damnit, Garrett you ain't Black and I ain't white."

"Tommy, Tommy. It's just she's got into my head. I've never wanted anything more in my life. I want Carly to marry me. That's all. I don't need to be the first Black Senator from California. I don't give a damn…that's Joe Martin's dream. I want to marry his daughter…that's my dream."

"Christ," Tom said, "Have you asked her out?"

"We go to lunch a lot but it's nowhere near anything romantic."

"Have you told her how you feel?"

"Yes. I told her I wanted to date her."

"Dating? You're fifty years old, counselor. No one dates beyond college. You want a relationship, period."

"Whatever, I'm a mess. I see women all the time and have for years but when it comes to Carly I feel like a schoolboy."

"What did she say when you asked her that you wanted to be more serious?"

Garrett smiled, "At first I thought it was the Black, white deal, but she said she doesn't want her father to know she's dating one of his friends."

Tom thought. *Doesn't that sound familiar.*

In truth, Tom was wise to Garrett because Carly told him she went out with the lawyer.

But did Garrett know about her affair with Tom?

Tom didn't think so.

Garrett was clueless, Tom thought, Carly was good at keeping secrets.

He always treated Carly's insistence that they stop seeing each other with a cavalier air. He figured if he was patient, she'd end up calling him. But after his conversation with Garrett, he felt a pang of jealousy. He didn't like it one bit.

Both heard voices coming from the pool.

Missy had slipped back into the pool. This time nude.

Tom grinned. "Can you believe her? Why don't we marry her, instead?"

"Yes, she's starting to fill out."

"Most do at this age," Tom added.

Garrett only shook his head. "I'm sorry, Tom."

"You're right, we're too old for her."

"No, I meant I'm sorry…"

"I know, I know what you mean," Tom said, then walked to the wet bar where Victoria Martin was in conversation with the magazine editor.

Garrett, seeing where Tom was heading, jumped to his feet, and caught up. "Tommy, all this about Carly is between you and me, OK?"

"Of course."

Garrett gave his friend a solid embrace.

* * *

Victoria Martin noticed the arrival of Father R. MacDonald, the white-haired priest who was about to retire from the North Beach orphanage school that four of the party's male attendees had attended at one time or another. The thin, almost gaunt cleric, who kept his gray hair parted in the middle, had a police escort. He had arrived with Chief of Police Andrew Roehr, an African American civic leader, who was not an alum of Father MacDonald's Filbert Street all boys school. One of the few in this crowd.

"Father Mac still looks good," Tom said, approaching the bar.

Smiling, Victoria Martin reached for Tom's arm to pull him closer, "It's not fair you men get better looking with age."

Tom decided not to respond.

Victoria said, "I'd like you to meet a colleague."

He greeted a lithe middle-aged woman attractively dressed in light-colored suit.

Victoria was beaming. "This man works with my husband in security. Lucky me, I get to see him every day."

"Lucky us," the shorter woman said.

"Tom, this is Amanda Ruiz, MD, my new best friend. She's chief of staff at Jenner-by-the-Sea Rehabilitation Hospital in Sonoma."

Tom shook her hand warmly. "And I get to see this wonderful woman every day."

"Look you made Victoria's face red," the visiting medico said, grabbing Tom's arm. "We're hoping to convince this excellent doctor to join our staff. We consider her one of the best emergency trauma surgeons in the country."

Tom asked, "Is this a news flash?"

Victoria put an index finger up to her lips. "Shhh. Amanda is very kind, but I'm contracted to St. Augie's at least until I retire."

"We've done some research and we know you're eligible to retire next year. Maybe sooner if we can come to a buyout agreement."

"She's one of the souls of this city because she saves so many of them," Tom said a bit more grandiose than he intended. "Maybe we don't want to part with her."

"Tom, I'm not going anywhere, and Dr. Ruiz is just doing her job to bring qualified doctors to her facility. It's by far the best rehab hospital in the West for physical, mental, and recovering chemical abuse patients. Thanks to her."

"It's my turn to blush."

"Doesn't Jenner Hospital have an elitist reputation?" Tom asked.

Amanda glanced at Victoria. "He obviously does not want you to leave your hospital."

Victoria widened her eyes, "Tom, we're having a conversation, not a job interview. Normally, he's not so blunt."

Amanda moved her hand in a calming manner toward Victoria. "No, he has a point. We like to think Jenner is elite for our medical expertise, but in some circles, we're considered a hospital for the rich. But we're trying to change that. We admire what Joe Martin's administration has done to create a solution to homelessness and veteran's drug abuse. We'd like to get into prevention instead of only rehabilitation. We want to steal a public success story and privatize it in other coastal cities. In fact, if we could partner with cities and states to add services for low-income families, and seniors. It's a brilliant concept."

Tom said, "Are you talking about St. Augustine's?"

"Exactly. Our board of directors like the fact that you took a mothballed aircraft carrier from another century and turned it into a huge homeless village and state-of-the-art hospital dedicated to preventing and curing drug abuse."

"Have you met, Joe?" Victoria asked.

"No, I live in Sea Ranch on the Sonoma coast. I'm not in the city as much as I'd like. I've seen him on TV so many times I feel I know him."

"Perhaps he can join your board. Secretly, I'd like Joe to retire from politics 100 percent and take on a few boards and take it easy. The media is making a big deal of Joe running for governor next year. That's an idea I'm not fond of. So, don't give up hope, Amanda, you may land both of us."

"What a dream come true that would be. But do you really think such a hard driving man like your husband is ready to retire.

Dr. Ruiz noticed a sadness in her new friend's eyes.

"Tom, your lips are sealed," Victoria said to change her thoughts away from her husband.

Tom held back a laugh. "In other words, he hasn't asked your permission to run."

She put her arm around Tom's shoulder. "Such a smart cookie."

Victoria noticed Missy jump in the pool. She only saw the splash and didn't notice her daughter was nude until Tom asked:

"Do you want me to help her find her bathing suit?"

"She did the same thing as a toddler. I'll take care of it if I need to step in."

Tom smiled professionally. "I will excuse myself and it was nice meeting you, Dr. Ruiz."

"Oh, Tom, please go retrieve Father Mac," Victoria asked. "I want to introduce him to our distinguished guest." She turned to Amanda, "Father Mac has retired as a priest, but he still runs a highly praised school for parentless boys. He has saved more souls than I'll ever hope to serve."

Amanda leaned back and stared off in the direction of the light glinting off the pool. "Is that your daughter swimming? Stunning figure, how old is she?"

"Seventeen."

"I thought she was a college girl."

* * *

Now on a mission to find Father Mac and to keep a self-appointed watchful eye on the young catering staff, Tom proceeded to patrol the pool deck.

He came up on a waiter dressed in green lifeguard-styled trunks and a Gatsby era gold and white tank with Fairbanks Hotel Catering printed on the front. The young man was bent to one knee presenting Missy with hors d'oeuvres off his tray.

Missy rewarded the young waiter by reaching up for two canapes. In doing so, she revealed what were no longer toddler-sized breasts.

Another male waiter approached carrying a tray of crystal Ajika flutes filled with Carly's favorite Schramsberg sparkling wine.

"Hey, morons," Tom said as he walked by. "Don't serve drinks in glass flutes. Didn't your catering manager know this was an outdoor pool deck party? Plastic flutes would have worked fine." Tom thumbed the arriving waiter to leave. "Take care of the rest of our guests after you switch to plastic."

Missy gulped the first glass flute she had been offered and blithely tossed it over her shoulder into the deep end. She gave Tom her best *fuck you* smile.

Tom bent down to the teen server and grabbed him by the back collar of his shirt. In one swoop, Tom yanked him away from the pool. "Put the fucking tray down."

The catering assistant obeyed.

Tom said, calmly, "Go fish out the glass she just tossed into the pool, and while you're down there, see if you can find her swimsuit. Also, tell your manager she's off limits. No more alcohol for her. She's a minor. Got it?"

The older of the caterer's agreed. "Yes, sir. I'll handle it."

The younger attendant dove into the deep end of the pool.

Tom followed by grabbing a dry towel off a chaise and tossing it, hitting Missy in her face. "Get out of the pool and put your swimsuit back on. This isn't the Missy Martin strip show."

Missy was outraged.

Joe Martin followed Tom to the edge of the pool.

She glared at her father.

Joe Martin nodded. He gave her a familiar fatherly stare to do what Tom said *now*.

Seeking a second opinion, Missy turned toward her mother.

Victoria dismissed the impromptu scene with a shake of her head.

Missy stormed away from the pool and ran to the bar populated at the time with Harre Ling and Ben Adams.

Missy ran up to Harre and grabbed him by the hand. She was on a mission as the pair disappeared downstairs.

* * *

The visiting editors caught up with Joe Martin, Carly Martin, and Chief Andy Roehr, who surfaced from the kitchen, where Chief Roehr offered to supervise the desserts.

After short introductions, Carly tugged at Doria Ziti's bare arm to escort her to the catered buffet. The gesture was what Victoria did infrequently, but when she chose to take part, she did enjoy being first lady to Joe being mayor. The house tour began with Wally, Andy and Victoria in tow.

Victoria was intrigued by the pendant Doria was wearing, a Russian Ruble coin in a white gold setting and necklace.

"I picked it up in an antique shop in Madrid," Doria lied. "Do you like it?"

"It's creative," Doc Martin replied.

*　*　*

Chief Roehr excused himself midway through the tour. He slipped into a deck chair at the far corner of the party deck to listen to Payne Ensemble, a Bach quartet about to play. He found a seat next to Father Mac, who'd snuck into the party to enjoy the music.

Next to arrive was Wally McGrath. The 6'-8" politico/industrialist arrived tieless in cream-colored trousers, a blue Brooks Brothers oxford shirt and a silk blue blazer. Kennedyesque in his good looks and waves of red hair. McGrath was dressed in a summer suit for the occasion. The billionaire stopped at the bar for gin and tonic. He obeyed the wave Victoria gave him from across the pool to join her.

"You have such a beautiful city, and your home is an architectural jewel," Doria said, squeezing Victoria Martin's hand. "My husband has discovered some interesting history about your home." They smiled as McGrath walked toward them.

"Good history I hope," Victoria asked.

"I'll let my husband tell you."

"Good, in the meantime I want you to meet Wally McGrath. He's the angel of our hospital project."

Doria offered, "Victoria was telling me about your generosity in helping create the St. Augustine aircraft carrier medical facility."

He bowed slightly. "Anything for Victoria. She told me you were coming. I'm a fan of *Il Edifico* magazine." He stared at Doria's figure.

The Spaniard bowed, "Thank you so much. I've been an admirer of your hotels. All of them are remarkable architecture, especially the one in Madrid. But since I have your attention why did you name it the Attu?"

"My grandfather started the chain at the same time he began focusing on mega engineering projects. His father, my great grandfather started the family fortune by delivering merchandise to miners during the Alaskan Gold Rush back in the 1890s. Alaska was near and dear to the family fortune. So, when the hotel chain was purchased all the properties were named for Alaskan cities or locations. That's a long way to say Attu is an Alaskan island."

Doria giggled at his windy explanation. She added more wind by asking "How is your Paris hotel coming along?"

"Next month will be our grand opening. You're invited to attend."

"We will be there," said Doria.

"I think it's time we heard Zorenzo speak. We're primed and ready to listen," Victoria insisted.

"Yes, he's been waiting for his moment in the spotlight," Doria added.

Wally said, "I do know my grandfather, Tom McGrath, Sr. was the builder of this home. It had to have been one of his first projects. Back then, McGrath businesses were switching mercantile goods to dam building and to airport construction. But the one residence they built happens to be the one we're standing in."

"Wally, then do you know who the architect of this house was?"

"It's all so foggy. When my father, who was Tom McGrath, Jr. sold this place to the Martin's I never knew who drew up the plans," McGrath said, "I'm sure all of that is buried in some company files. You're welcome to dig into our history."

Doria smiled. "We may take you up on that, especially when you complete the high rise I hear you're planning to build."

Wally shrugged. He was impressed, "No, I don't recall ever hearing who the architect was. You two seem to know more about my ancestors than I do."

"It's all on the Internet, if you know where to look," Victoria said.

Doria added, "But the good news is a woman designed this home in 1933 right after Hitler took power in Germany."

"A woman, Wally," Carly teased. "Who would have thought?"

Doria was on a roll. She sounded like the audio track of a documentary. "And to think we might have never known her if it weren't for contemporary Germans discovering and dealing with their daunting past. And we wish to publish this story in our magazine sometime next year."

Victoria was beaming. She put her arm around Carly. "Who will write it?"

"I will, of course," Doria said.

"Who was the woman architect?" Carly persisted.

"I have no clue," Wally said. "Doria is being coy by dropping hints like rose pedals at lesbian wedding."

The women within earshot of Wally's comment raised their eyebrows.

"Where's your wife?" Carly pulled Wally aside for a brief word. "Or is this a scouting trip for you?"

"She decided to rest today. We're in the middle of a big misunderstanding. And besides, she doesn't like your father's politics, remember?"

"Wally don't tell tales. Jennifer and Joe are quite civil to each other," Carly insisted.

"I love my wife, but she chooses politics over friendships. I am the opposite."

"I hear she's pregnant," Carly said bluntly.

"Yes. She's starting to show."

"How do you feel about that? Fatherhood might change your lifestyle."

Wally offered a wry grin, "Do you really think so?"

Carly walked back to the collection of women surrounding Victoria Martin. "Ladies, I'm going to take Wally to the bar. Will you excuse us?"

* * *

Harre Ling approached Garrett Ellis and Missy under one of the party tents. "Missy, could you point me to the nearest restroom?"

Missy sat up, wobbled until honorary Uncle Harre grabbed her elbow. "I'll be happy to show you. Follow me," she said.

Garrett figured the strip show was over; young Martin had returned to wearing her bikini and a terry cloth robe to keep off the hot sun.

He did notice she was beginning to slur her words and grind her teeth.

* * *

A waitress in full Fairbanks Hotel green and black regalia, who continued to serve *hors d'ouevres* from a tray she carried, noticed a man in a white suit lead a much younger woman into the men's toilet.

* * *

Coming down the stairs from the pool deck, Tom stopped Carly and Doria as they continued the tour. He whispered into Carly's ear. "In case you're interested, Missy has downed at least six flutes of bubbly so far…and she and Harre Ling are AWOL."

"I didn't invite her. Someone else will have to babysit. Would that be you?"

"Well, if someone sticks a dick into baby cakes, then somehow that will be my fault."

"How's that?" she asked.

"I provide security, remember. She's part of the assignment."

"And you're well paid, I trust."

"Don't be catty," he said.

"Not my problem. And, on that note, talk to her mother," Carly meowed.

"Have you seen Wally?"

"Upstairs at the bar. He's waiting for Ziti to speak before he leaves."

* * *

Garrett noticed Joe Martin wave at him to join the conversation with the editor. Greetings and handshakes followed, with Joe cutting to the conversational chase.

"Garrett, I want you to hear this: I was telling Zorenzo about your team's efforts in creating the Golden Gate Compassion City Recovery Act."

"It's Joe's brainchild. I'm helping him put all the pieces together as an outside consultant."

"I think it is a wonderful idea," said Ziti. "It shows compassion and at the same time removes decaying ships from polluting in rivers and ports. Absolutely brilliant."

Garrett nodded. "We have a lot of work to do. We have to get Congress to order the Department of Defense to release more mothballed ships for our use."

"I'm shocked no one has done this before," Ziti said.

"Like I said it's all Joe Martin's vision. We lost a big chance to save the conventional aircraft carrier Kitty Hawk before it was scrapped but there are still almost 20 helicopter carriers in mothball fleets. Aircraft carriers are horizontal skyscrapers. They are already built with hospital facilities, huge kitchens and bunking areas for thousands; we're merely salvaging and repurposing resources to help homelessness, drug addicts and those who can't afford basic medical services in general. I hope to God someday he's president," Garrett said.

Ziti took out a notepad and pencil from inside his blazer. He began writing while asking, "Where are you getting the ships?"

"Navy mothball fleets. The government has more ships than they are admitting to but the big moorage areas have been Bremerton, Washington, Philadelphia, Pearl Harbor and the Sacramento River. The Navy has dozens of inactive non-nuclear submarines that could be converted into important clinics. We outbid several major scrapyards to grab the Saint Augustine helicopter carrier from thirty-five miles up in the Sacramento River estuary. Have you been given a tour? It's impressive."

"Not yet. It's on our list before we leave. But I do want to ask where the money is coming from?"

"To date we have convinced several major corporations to fund us. Locally, McGrath International donated the most," Garrett said.

"Where are going to keep these ships?"

"The state of California is on record saying they will donate waterfront space if all the rest of the project comes into play. We have our eyes on two supercarriers and two helicopter assault carriers. We will bid on them or take them as government handovers once they see how effective our conversion program has become."

Joe interjected, "We don't need carriers to make the program work. Smaller mothball ships can be retrofitted to become medical centers, job center and homeless housing village."

"But the carriers are best because they're floating cities," Joe added. "They have bed, medical, food and storage facilities on board that can be expanded. Decks can be made into public parks," Garrett added.

"I will write about this. I want to help. I have some ideas," Ziti said, "Maybe we can raise the entire Italian Navy from the bottom of the sea."

* * *

Joe Martin stood at a borrowed hotel convention table covered in a white tablecloth. A wooden dais had been placed in front of him bearing the mayor's seal.

His Honor went through a lengthy litany of quips, toasts, and introductions before bringing the Ziti's up to the podium.

Doria had put on her white blazer. First thing, she pointed at Wally. "Mr. McGrath," Doria said coyly, "you know who built this beautiful home we have the pleasure of visiting today?"

"Yes, my grandfather Walter McGrath."

"True," Doria nodded.

"Your honor, do you know the name of the architect of your family home?"

"Before I answer, I'd like to mention that Eugene Carling, my father-in-law, who is the deeded owner of this home, has just arrived. He sends his regrets for being late he was stuck in traffic on the Golden Gate Bridge. He's also Carly's landlord and Missy's favorite grandfather. Carly, please go find him I want to introduce him.

Carly beamed and acknowledged the applause. "Maybe you have all tasted the Salazar Vineyards wine we're serving. My grandfather owns the winery."

More applause greeted her announcement.

Joe spoke up. "But getting back to Doria Ziti's question—no, I do not know who the architect of this home is."

* * *

Doria continued "Let's let Zorenzo tell everyone."

Zorenzo was a man of average height with a full head of dark hair. He was overweight but was movie star handsome. He was comfortable standing and speaking without notes, "This house was commissioned in 1933 by Germany for Ambassador Joaquin von der Maaten, who was the top German official in America at that time. While the house was being built, von der Maaten lived in one of the two top penthouses at the Fairbanks Hotel. That's where he met Walter McGrath. The two men became good friends, and soon after, Walter had the contract to build the ambassador's home…right here where we're seated. But my excitement is learning that this house was the first home designed by Ille Druck, a German Jew who studied with the founders of the Bauhaus architectural style in Weimar,

Germany. It was the last project she designed as a free woman. She was arrested after 1933 during the Jewish purges led by Hitler. Her talent spared her life, and many Nazi buildings were designed by her slave labor. Is this new to you, Mrs. Martin?"

Victoria was stunned. "We had no idea. What a remarkable story."

Doria said, "We thought you'd be pleased. We want to publish it in *Il Edifico*, but we need your permission."

"What more do you know about Ille Druck?" Victoria Martin asked.

Zorenzo continued, "Sadly, she died in a bombing raid in Dresden, where she lived while under house arrest. She was closely guarded because she designed so many sensitive buildings for the Nazi regime. We only recently were able to dig into the Arosen Archives. The archives were sitting in a warehouse since the war— all fifty million documents. In recent years, historians and political scientists have been sorting through the political files. Now, the architectural and building files have been opened. This is all new to us, too. "We do have her architectural sketches of your home. We framed one of the more significant images, but we did not receive it in time to bring it here on our trip." Zorenzo paused. "You must come to Barcelona to pick it up."

The rapt audience laughed.

"No, really, it should be couriered here any day. Our apologies for the delay."

* * *

Basking in the audience's warm applause, Doria tried to make eye contact with as many as she could to thank them for their attention and warm welcome to the city.

There was a new arrival, a man reddish brown hair pulled back in a short pony, who stood in the back by himself.

Then it hit her. She recognized him. A pang of surprise sent an unexpected jolt of adrenalin through her body.

Art Garcia smiled at her.

There was no doubt in her mind. She returned a nervous smile. She didn't know what to do with her hands. She chided herself for that. *Training*, she whispered, *training*. Show no outward signs of weakness or guilt.

She approached him at the bar. "We meet, again."

"Yes, it has been a year." He took her hand and kissed it. "Doria, is it?"

She pulled him close, kissed both cheeks. "Yes. Yes, I want to speak with you but not here," she whispered.

Both realized they were standing at the keystone between two different worlds.

"Now, I know your name. Are you here on business for your magazine or your country?"

"Do you find it interesting our roles have reversed since we last saw each other?

I'm the tourist now," she said.

"You were magnificent in bed."

Her face turned red. "Please. Let me have my secret, especially while we're here."

"Of course. Did you come to find me or is this coincidence?"

"Coincidence, yes. Zo and I met the Martins at a reception for a delegation of California politicians and trade ministers. I was assigned to show them Barcelona and they courteously invited us to visit America. He jumped at the chance. He loves art deco, streamline, you name it, especially those designed to old-world standards."

"Let me fly you to Stockholm. This evening. Now."

Her head turned across the pool deck to where her husband was talking with Joe Martin. "I'll admit I have no defenses when it comes to you. But all I can offer is lunch, perhaps, while Zo is touring the hospital ship with your mayor."

"I'll be at the Le Central Restaurant at noon. Meet me there."

"No, no. My heart is beating through my chest," she said. "No matter the reason we left each other I confess the passion was real. Too real. But for now, please see me as a magazine editor."

"And a wife," he said.

"The magazine is my new career thanks to my husband adding me to his staff. The Spanish government is no longer impressed with my clandestine talents."

"Better to be the trophy wife."

"Hardly, a trophy, we've been together since he was my professor at the university."

"Maybe I could hire you. I hire freelance talent all the time."

"What did you think of Zorenzo's report on the Martin's house?"

"It was very informative, especially the part about the Nazis."

"We all have secrets. How do you know the Martins?"

"I was in the wedding."

"May I count on your discretion? My husband…"

"Yes," Art interrupted. "I will not mention you tried to get me killed."

"Please, no need to be so dramatic. You were wanted for questioning by my country. I was doing my job."

"If you say so, Doria," He tipped two forefingers to his forehead.

"My children thank you…"

"Actually, I admire you for being able to keep your other career a secret."

"I'm very good at what I do and he's a trusting man by nature."

"That's convenient."

"Art, please let me hear it from you that we were in love that afternoon."

"How many men would love to hear what you just said and from such a remarkable beauty."

"I'm so sorry we never met when we were single."

"Or spies."

"Was it love, tell me?"

He smiled. "It was love."

She let out a sigh. "Then it was worth it. I had to listen to the Ambassador to Russia yell at me for what seemed hours. I was grateful for being a Spaniard and it was only an internet video link, otherwise I would have been taken out into the courtyard and shot. They know you did it."

"Did what?"

"Stole from them."

"I trust for the sake of your young sons you will not reveal you saw me."

She blanched. "Is that a threat."

"Of course it is," he took her hand and pressed it to his lips.

* * *

Carly noticed the man who had phantomized—no one saw him arrive. She hurried to her parents. "Art Garcia is here."

"Oh, that's terrific." Victoria clapped her hands together.

Joe's big smile noted to all that the new arrival was most welcome.

For the next ten minutes, the Martins and Father Mac joined Art and Doria.

* * *

Zorenzo Ziti, however, was more eager to corner Wally McGrath to discuss McGrath Industries' 201-story skyrise now being built on Hunter's Point, where Candlestick Stadium, home to the Major League baseball Giants, used to stand. "I hope you don't mind, but we're in league with your competitor, Tony Guereca for an article in our magazine."

Wally gave him a big smile, "No, not at all, Tony Guereca is a potential client not a competitor. His monster went up first. Now, I'm building mine on spec. Anyone who partners with me can have their name on the damn thing."

"Good no hard feelings. I was concerned because tomorrow night, Doria and I have tickets for the elevator to the top of Tony's BOT for the laser show."

The Guereca financed Bay Origins Tower, the only completed and operational two hundred-floor office, commercial and residential building in California offered the popular Moon Laser Show, a monthly light show featuring a high-energy laser beam that was fired from atop BOT at a moon-based reflector shield. From the moon, the lasers split up into different colors and were directed at other corporate satellites forming a speed of light zig zag pattern in the sky.

The show was free to all, however, posh penthouse sky view seating at $400 new dollars per also offered a deep voiced narration mixed with space age music and open bar.

Nothing gave Madison Avenue execs a bigger stiffy than to see client logos being "thrown" onto the face of the full moon in ten-second, thirty-second or one-minute time frames—depending on the ad budget. The most expensive show being the Super Bowl Flash during half time.

If low clouds hampered the monthly show, huge Samsung space-vision TV screens linked with other BOT kiosk facilities around the world so that the San Francisco viewers would not miss the extravaganza.

Zorenzo asked. "Do you have plans for your new building to come up with something equally spectacular?"

"Of course, the game is on with every mega high rise being built. We'll have a few tricks up our sleeve to wow you. When it's completed, you'll be my guests. I wish I could say what the surprise will be, but I'm sworn to secrecy by my marketing department."

Zorenzo couldn't resist what he believed was exclusive information. "My spies tell me your proposed skyrise will devote the entire top five floors for America's first hovercraft transit station.

And you've hired Guereca Organization to handle the Bay Area network of hovercraft—flying taxicab stations if you will."

The editor continued, Fueled by GO Pods, the hovercraft would operate Uber style to ease commuter congestion on the ground. Guereca Organization partnered with the coal industry by giving the dirty energy industry a face-saving opportunity to switch to clean energy by retooling to build hovercraft with cheap GO fuel pods, Ziti paused.

"You have excellent intelligence. You're not far off."

"Am I still invited for a tour of your blueprints?"

"Yes, of course, I obviously have no secrets."

"I hope you are giving me a scoop?" Zorenzo asked.

"I'm offering you naming rights to my new skyrise airport."

"Too rich for a humble magazine."

"Not if I'm on the cover of your magazine when the construction begins." Wally let out a large fake laugh.

Doria Ziti came up behind Wally McGrath and linked arms. "What are you two hatching up, or are you only interested in the naked teenager in the pool?"

"We're talking about the future," her husband said.

Zorenzo felt a tug on his arm. She whisked away toward the poolside bar.

When out of earshot, Wally said, "I saw you speaking with Art Garcia. Be careful I know what he wants from a stunning woman."

Doria replied, "You have a lot in common with him."

Then he moved closer to Doria, "I'm more interested whisking you off to one of my hotels. The one in San Diego is stunning."

"Is that what you really want," she demurred.

"Since you asked, what I want is to see you naked on silk sheet. I don't care where," Wally whispered in her ear.

"That will be expensive view," she whispered back.

"What's the cost?"

"Your life, Senor."

* * *

Eugene Carling, the tall family patriarch, Victoria's Swedish American father, had arrived at the party in his 1950 Ford station wagon. His woody was a hit with the valet parking team. If you saw him from a distance, the lack of any gray hair made him look like a perennial beach boy. He bonded instantly with the young car parkers.

But he had no time to gab about the woody. He needed a pit stop. And soon.

He hiked—not too slow, not too fast up the stairs from the lower-level parking area to the bathroom and family room level below the expansive top terrace.

Puffing from his arrival, he turned quickly into the men's room.

The 78-year-old man stopped in his tracks. The shock of what he saw in front of him buckled his knees. "WHAT ARE YOU DOING?" Eugene shouted.

Carling saw his granddaughter in a toilet stall. She was on her knees in front of a man sitting on the toilet. She had let the terrycloth robe fall from her shoulders.

Surprised, then horrified, Missy screamed. She clambered off the man and stumbled to the filthy floor of the stall. "Oh, Poppa don't look," she pleaded before bursting into a wail of tears. She wiped her mouth with her hand.

Carling, now spitting mad, rushed toward the man, who was zipping his cream-colored trousers and attempting to sidestep Missy while trying to hide his face behind his shoulder.

Carling slapped the white hat off the man's head but still couldn't see his face. He reached for the lothario but was deftly brushed aside with a painful straight arm blow. He fell on to the floor next to Missy.

Now livid, Eugene grabbed the man's ankle, tripping him to the tile floor.

Carling scrambled after him, punching him with his fist.

"Stop it, stop it!" Missy pulled at her grandfather, who had managed to land on top of the white-suited man.

Carling's fist glanced off the man's ear.

"Poppa, stop!"

Harre faced Missy and started to laugh. "He doesn't recognize me."

Another fist landed on Harre's nose. It hurt. Harre stopped smiling. "I'm leaving, I'm leaving."

Eugene swung at him again, but Harre ducked. "I don't want to fight!"

Harre didn't see the next blow coming. It hit him hard on the chin. Stunned, he slipped to the floor face first. "No more, God damnit! Don't worry, I'm so fucking coked up I couldn't get it up. I didn't rape her."

Eugene Carling stood over the DA and took one more swing. Harre's nose exploded in blood. It washed all over his suit.

Harre was on his knees. His forehead rested against the floor. "Oh, Gene, just kill me. Put me out of my misery!"

He yanked Harre to his feet and bum-rushed him out of the compound. He yelled for the parking valets to call a cab. "He's too fucked up to drive." As the taxi arrived, it was then Eugene Carling recognized Harre Ling.

COLLATERAL DAMAGE

By dusk, after the guests had departed, Art Garcia and Tom Gresham were sitting in Carly's kitchen. The caterers had wrapped up loading the party equipment rentals into their trucks. Now it was time for the cleaning crew.

Art was holding a plastic wine glass. "Her grandfather makes very good wine."

They toasted plastic to plastic water to wine.

Garcia was smiling—cutting short a laugh.

"What's so funny?"

"I was thinking back to Madrid when you drove the Yamaha onto the Plaza del Sol—"

"To save your ass."

"I ran into a little surprise from that job today. The woman who came out of the hotel with a gun in her hand looking for me was here at the party."

"You're kidding. Did you two love birds reconnect?"

"Yes, we did. She looks even better than I remember," Art said.

"Is she working? Should we be nervous?"

"I don't think so. It may be a coincidence."

"What are the chances of that?"

"I really don't know—fifty-fifty?"

"She's on our turf now," Tom said. "Should we be worried?"

"I think I scared her. Her hands were shaking. She's here with her husband's magazine. This house will be featured in the Ziti's publication."

"Well, if you say so. But until she gets on the jet, I'd be careful."

'No one saw you, Tom. You had that biker helmet on all the time."

"And I should—"

"Follow them until they fly away."

"Is this an assignment?"

"Of course."

"Remind me again, who does she work for?"

"Spanish secret police."

"You do get around."

"I need you for another assignment. I talked to Joe at the bar, and he said I could borrow you for a few days. What I have in mind is also in Joe's best interest as mayor."

"Doing what?"

"My firm has been retained to find Alan Carter, the heir to Carter Pharmaceuticals. He was paroled from Bonita Valley Correctional Farm in San Diego County three months ago for smuggling cocaine. He hasn't been seen since. His family gave me a blank check."

"Where do you want to meet?"

"Tomorrow morning at the Broadway Café. Nine a.m."

"Let's make it noon. I'm staying here tonight."

Art looked confused.

"Carly asked me to stay over tonight. Missy has passed out. I'll have to drive the little princess back to her mansion in the morning."

"She was a handful at the party." Art smirked.

"Sisters couldn't be more different."

"Maybe," Art said. "You didn't know Victoria Carling when she was single, did you? She was my idea of perfection. Still is, but on a higher plane," he added.

5.
HEMOPHILLIAC OF LOVE
A Short Story and a few Snippets

Cantina Psalm:

"If you live a sad ass life in East Jesu, New Jersey you can always catch the next shame train west to the next city and start over. Pretty soon you run out of towns. San Francisco is the last stop. And, if you fuck it up in Frisco there's always the bridge."
--Graffiti found inside the brains of the Lemming Sisters, the world's last vaudeville act, who jumped hand in hand into eternity.

DEFECTIVE GENE

By morning, Carly's grandfather called and made his apologies to Carly for his late arrival to yesterday's party she tossed for her parent's anniversary. Eugene Carling asked to speak with Missy.

"Poppa, she's still asleep," Carly said via LOBE. "No, wait, the dead have risen."

Luck was with Carling. No family had spoken to Missy since he put her to bed in Carly's guest bedroom during the party. And better yet for tender reputations, no one but granddad witnessed the untimely blowjob interruptus she had with Harre Ling.

Gene Carling thought that was important as he listened to the tiny voice in his ear. The retired editor was in full crisis mode. "Has anyone mentioned me and Harre Ling?" he asked, "Did anyone else see you and Harre making out in the toilet before I saw you two?"

"No, Poppa," she said into the phone.

"Good. But I need to know one thing. Did Harre rape you?"

She hesitated. "I'm going to cry."

"No, don't do that. Please, I don't want anyone asking why you're crying."

Given this was the most difficult conversation she had so far in her life, Missy rose to the occasion. She cleared her throat and listened.

"Missy, this is critical. Did he hurt you, did he drag you into the toilet stall and force you to—"

"Poppa, we didn't have sex. He didn't. I was drunk and I was mad that Carly and mom were treating me like a child. I decided I wasn't a child, and I did what I did with him. It was my stupid idea—"

"Did he have his cock in your mouth?"

"Yes, Poppa, I'm so sorry." Tears flooded her face, "Call me this evening when I'm in my room."

"Be strong here, Missy. The man is Carly's boss and he is the district attorney? If I tell what happened to you, our lives—all our lives—will change for the worse. Have they yelled at you yet?"

"No, Poppa. You're scaring me."

"Let's hope they don't bring it up. And by God, don't tell them. No time for true confessions. And, if someone saw you and Harre go into the bathroom, tell them he was making sure you didn't fall because you were so drunk. Yes, tell them he helped lead you to the toilet in case you threw up."

"I did throw up…after…"

"Missy, you must never say anything to anyone about what happened in the toilet between you and Harre. NOT ONE WORD. Hear me out. What Harre did to you was wrong. Very, very wrong. He may have mental problems. But we are in a delicate situation. As bad as what happened to you we have to hide the fact that it did happen. Listen to me. Here's why. Your father is thinking about running for governor. Once the media learns that a man as important as the district attorney raped you--the media will twist things around. People will defend Harre. And that alone is terrible. They will say you were the one that started it. They'll say you are a tramp. Your father's enemies will maximize it. You will be called names. It will become a media horror show. It will ruin our family. Do you understand what I'm saying?"

"Yes, yes—"

"Missy, you must be strong for me, for the family and for you. Keep it all quiet. And call me immediately if anyone starts questioning you too closely about what happened. I will handle this. I will talk to your mom and dad on how to handle this but for now keep quiet."

Gene ended the call. He walked into his living room. He was going to turn off the television that he left on all morning. His eyes widened. He saw a scene of the Golden Gate Bridge. The headline at the bottom of the TV screen read: **Breaking News police action on the Golden Gate Bridge.**

IT'S THE SUDDEN STOP THAT KILLS YOU

Overnight, another storm rolled in off the Marin Headlands. The storm was accompanied by a low wind and cold irritating rain that spit sand into faces and windshields. One of the faces belonged to the Golden Gate's next jumper.

DA Harre Ling, the 50-something Anglo with the Asian name was ready to die rather than face his family, the victims' family and all those who voted for him and especially those who didn't. He was in the back seat of a cab heading for the bridge not giving a crap that the bridge was by far the most popular suicide spot of the 2,000 jumpers since it was built in 1937 with only 300 known to survivors. Reason is the bridge is over water and the distance doesn't achieve terminal velocity required for 100% lethality.

Professional high divers know it's best to dive in toes first.

Point being if anyone in town needed a mulligan it was Harre. He spent a sleepless night search his fog addled brain for a solution and only found one: jump 220 feet off the fucking bridge.

How does a DA get himself into a fix where he's too drugged to work and on his day off he goes out and forces the mayor's underage daughter to mouth fuck him at a family party? He was giving scum a bad name. The answer in two words. He's an asshole. OK, two words: cocaine addiction with a booze chaser.

"FOR CHRIST'S SAKE," Harre shouted into the air. His brain was pounding inside out. "Make it all go away!"

Harre was in agony. If addiction is a disease, he needed drugs to ease the pain—now!

Shit bricks kept stacking in front of him with each thought. Brick number 99: If anyone knew better it would be a career do-gooder like Harre. Hell, his office is supposed to provide leadership in rehab and mental reform. And he's the boss.

Harre had jammed more cocaine into his nose. "Stop here," he shouted to the cabbie. His hand moved to the 9mm in the right pocket of his white suit jacket.

The third-worlder that drove him onto the northbound side of the recently expanded Golden Gate Bridge refused to pull over at mid-span.

Harre shot his SIG through the roof of the taxi.

The cabbie braked hard, swerved toward the pedestrian walkway, and came to a grinding fender-mashing halt along the railing. The tall refugee bolted from the car, screaming in agony, slapping at himself trying to find where he'd been shot.

* * *

Meanwhile, at 500 feet above San Francisco Bay: "Copy that! I got a name on that bozo who's dangling his ass off the Golden Gate," screamed C. Frank "Chris" Barrett, the KNUZ-TV helicopter pilot to news anchor Jennifer McGrath, who sat in the co-pilot's seat with a pair of binoculars pressed against her eyes. She was barely able to stretch the seat belt extender around her pregnancy.

"There are five jumpers a month. What's so special about this one?" Barrett glanced over the top of his amber tinted aviator style sunglasses.

"Because it's Harre Fucking Ling, that's why!"

"That'll do!" he said.

She dropped her binoculars to her lap. "Tell me we'll be the first chopper there."

"Have I ever let you down?" Barrett asked and coaxed the ex-Coast Guard chopper turned news bird for all it was worth. He was now in the process of dropping nose down to skim lower across the choppy bay.

"There. Dead ahead." The thirty-nine-forever blonde reporter focused on a whirling burlesque of blue, white, and red emergency lights flashing mid-span. "That's him in the white suit."

"Marin Tower to KNUZ chopper one…you are proceeding into a FAA no-fly emergency area—please reroute away from the Golden Gate Bridge area…acknowledge—"

The TV reporter grinned. "Can you turn that down, C.J.? I can't hear myself think."

The pilot turned off the radio. He could only shake his head and smile. It was never dull with Jennifer McGrath riding shotgun.

* * *

Since the Feds Works Projects completed a six-lane adjacent bridge to the Golden Gate, the California Highway Patrol could divert traffic as needed to the other span in case of a traffic accident or suicide threat.

Thanks to advances in bridge construction, the west-side bridge did not need the huge towers to support the new one-way southbound six-lane road. Built adjacent and almost invisible to the original span, the new side nearest to the ocean was painted black as to appear in the shadows of the old Golden Gate. The side facing the city was painted in the usual rusty colors that were all too familiar to generations of saps willing to pay the $20 toll. Saps because there were no tolls for the state's other large bridges, the Vincent

Thomas in Long Beach, and the Coronado Bay Bridge in San Diego. But the taxpayers were sold that a 100 percent increase in toll fees were needed to pay for its construction. The two bridges went by the Golden Gate Bridge moniker.

Harre was in luck. The suicide guard rails were being replaced because the originals were made with inferior Communist made steel.

When San Francisco Police Chief Andrew Roehr approached, Harre leaned back from the rail—holding on with one hand. "Stop right there, Andy. Don't be the one to screw up the rescue!"

A nameless Marin County Deputy Sheriff, who was assisting to block northbound traffic, shouted from his position behind a squad car: "Jump you, sonofabitch, so we can all go home."

Harre heard the insult. His temper flashed, "Thanks to you, pal, I'm going to string this out for another couple of hours." Harre fired several shots into the low clouds and fog above.

Everyone on the bridge flinched.

"NOBODY SHOOT!" Chief Roehr shouted and waved his hands over his head in a classic football time-out motion.

"How many shots was that?" Chief asked.

"Four," said a policewoman within earshot.

"Someone find out how many shots he fired at the cabbie. What's he holding?"

"One" came a reply.

The policewoman in full SFPD sniper gear answered, "We had eyes on it and it's a .357 SIG P229 and not standard issue for DAs. It carries twelve bullets."

Chief Roehr frowned. "Hell, he can still shoot himself silly with that many rounds."

"Said like a man, who is thinking of running for DA after this is over?"

He stared at the rank and filer. "Don't spread that around—even if it's a good line."

* * *

Carly Martin sat in the administrative lobby of the CalTrans building next to the tollbooths on the San Francisco side of the bridge. She had been ordered to the bridge by Chief Roehr.

The top cop burst into the lobby. "Carly, Harre's not listening to me. He wants you out there to hear him moan and groan."

"If he won't listen to you, then there's nothing I can do," she said.

"Go out there. Talk to him," Roehr said.

"Where's his wife?" the young deputy DA asked.

"Not an option. She refused to come out here—even with a police escort."

"Her reason being?"

"She said he was all yours. You can have him."

"What?"

"She said you were having an affair with him."

"No, I'm not! Why would she say something like that?"

The chief closed his eyes in exasperation. "Look, I'm telling you what she told me. Let's work on getting him off the railing."

"Let's get this clear. I'm not screwing Harre Ling."

"Fine. Fine. Help me out here. He's asking for you."

"Christ, Andy. I don't want to do this. The media will screw this up. Trust me."

"No one will hear you two. The wind's howling so bad."

"No way."

"Please, Carly. Do what you can to make this end."

"Chief, if he's talking smack about me, I'm all for him jumping."

Young Martin cinched her trench coat and walked to the door of the office. She stopped and turned to Roehr. "How close can I get to him?"

"Close enough so you can use the bull horn," he said. "If anyone gets closer, he puts the SIG to his head."

The pair walked out of the CalTrans lobby. A glint of light caught her attention from above the bridge. A yellow and blue helicopter was trying to hold its hovering position.

"Moron," Roehr shouted. "Somebody radio that fool to get out of here. Jesus, I now wish Harre had shot that bastard out of the sky."

Within seconds, the KNUZ news chopper pulled out of sight under the roadway.

A blast of salt air slapped their faces with bits of sand. Chief pulled Carly closer to shield her. "Say what you can—"

"I'll do my best, Andy."

* * *

Once seeing him on the railing, she stopped walking. "Oh, my God, Harre," she whispered before clearing her throat.

Disheveled, unshaven, with his hair wild in the wind, he was still wearing the white suit he'd worn yesterday to her parent's anniversary party.

Carly tried to remember anything that happened at the party that could have triggered Harre's outburst of *non-compos mentis*.

Carly pressed the bullhorn button. It squawked. She flinched but held it firm. "Harre, this is Carly Martin." She gave her full name because the world was listening, and she wanted to come off as a professional. Plus, given the gossip that Chief Roehr had hit her with, she did not want to sound familiar with him in any way.

Harre's eyes rose. He stared at her with a faded smile. "Come to save me, Car?"

"Please listen to me," She continued. "Please come off the rail. Think of your family, Harre. Think of your daughters. Think how scared you have them. You can always start a new life—so can they, but you can't ever shake the terror from them if you die this way."

"I'm gonna die someday," he shouted back.

Carly shook her head. She was not listening to the words coming out of her mouth. "Harre, I don't want to lose a friend."

Ling raised his hand to shield his eyes from the biting wind. The same hand he had wiped his nose with. "That's why I'm here, Carly. You demoted me to friend status. I really can't handle that. You know and I know we're more than that. But I know I fucked up. Big time."

"We're friends, Harre. I've known you all my life."

"Nice try, sweetheart. The only thing that will pull me off this rail is for you to live up to your promise to marry me. But after the stunt I pulled at your parents, I know being together will never be an option."

Carly's face flushed. "You're not making sense, Harre. I never promised I'd marry you. I never said that."

"Now, you're lying to me. But I can't blame you."

Her mouth opened. No words came out.

"I changed my life for you." He began to cry.

"Harre, what are you talking about? Why are you acting this way?"

"You and me—what the hell do you think I'm talking about?"

"There was never you and me. Why are you doing this?" she asked the man, who was thirty years her senior. "Are you drunk?"

He jammed the barrel of the gun to his head.

Thinking there might be one more round in Harre's gun, she screamed, "No, Harre—don't! I'm sorry, please Harre. We all need you at the office. You need some time off. No one wants to lose you. Harre, drop the gun so they can come get you. We all need to get warm. It'll be fine. We can talk. I promise I will listen. We can get you help. If you let us help you a year from now no one will remember what happened here."

He looked up. "All I ever wanted was for you to listen to me. What I did at the party was because you refused to talk to me—to let me explain how it can work between us."

Carly lowered the bullhorn. She was confused. What did she miss? What did Harre do at the party?

Harre Ling's face contorted into tears. He shouted. His words disappeared in the roar of the storm. He waved her away.

She gasped as the wind pushed Harre backward.

Fumbling between his legs, he grabbed for a railing. As he did, his SIG slipped from his hand. It clunked on the sidewalk and bounced under the railing and over the side.

A yelp went through the assembled crowd of rescue workers and law enforcement.

Chief Roehr rushed to Carly. "Good work, good work. Now ask him to step off the railing and lie down on the roadway."

"Harre, please come off the railing. Harre, please. We can work this out. It'll be OK."

Harre nodded. "I'll come off the rail, if you promise you'll talk to me before they haul me away."

"Yes. I will."

Carly's heart raced. She saw him mouth: *OK, I'm coming down.*

At that moment, a grinding, swishing roar from beneath the bridge grew inexplicitly louder. The piston-throbbing roar came behind and below Harre. WUP-WUP, WUP-WUP, WUP-WUP THUD, THUD, THUD, THUD, THUD, THUD, THUD!

No one on the bridge within earshot of Harre had a clue where the huge sound was coming from.

A heartbeat later, everyone had the answer.

Carly's eyes widened in amazement.

The bright yellow KNUZ News chopper rose from beneath the bridge: SSSSSSSwwooooOOOOP! THUD, THUD, THUD, THUD, THUD!

It faced the bridge broadside no more than twenty yards behind and directly at level with Harre.

* * *

Back at the station, KNUZ Hourly News broke off its commercials.

It was now top of the hour. Showtime.

* * *

A megawatt spotlight from the chopper flipped on and flooded Harre.

Startled, he twisted to see what was going on.

The prop wash flapped against Harre's rain-soaked white suit.

Still perched on the railing, Harre struggled to sit up.

A moment later, he turned to look at the chopper. As he did, a blast of wind whipped across the roadway and struck Harre square in the chest.

The dominos began to crumble one upon the other.

The same heavy air current shot the helicopter high over the bridge roadway.

Now positioned above Harre, the downdraft from the massive chopper blades slammed against him like a burst of water from an invisible fire cannon.

At no time did the megawatt spotlight from the chopper move off Harre, causing an eerie glow to bathe the scene in a surreal yellow.

His clothes flapped in the turbulence.

Carly saw his distress. "HARRE, HOLD ON!"

Desperate, Harre flailed for the railing. His wet hands slipped off the wet metal barrier. Harre tumbled backward.

The last thing Carly saw were the soles of his white shoes.

She screamed.

A dozen voices behind her screamed.

Chief Roehr shouted, "No way is this happening!"

The KNUZ team caught the entire scenario live for all local stations and a patched in worldwide feed via CNN.

Harre plunged, his arms flailing.

The wind in his face made him gasp for air.

Falling.

He closed his eyes and gritted his teeth and prayed—he didn't want to die.

Other people had survived the fall. Water, he reasoned, was not like falling on cement.

He had a chance.

As he cut through the nothingness between the bridge and the saltwater, he stiffened his body, pointing his toes downward. His last thoughts were not noble.

"Oh, fuck get it over with—"

Harre hit the water proving once again it's not the fall that kills you—it's the sudden stop.

For an infinitesimal moment, District Attorney Harre Ling recognized gurgling water rush past his ears.

Then, there was nothing.

His prayer was answered.

He entered the forever void.

* * *

"No, this can't be real!" Jennifer yelled from the cockpit. Then it hit her. She bit hard on her lower lip, now realizing this would be her first national story. And for KNUZ's fourth place standing in a four TV station ratings marketplace, the tragedy couldn't have come at a better time: two weeks before ratings sweep.

6.
ROUGH PART OF TOWN
A Flashback and Low Rent Sketches

Cantina Psalm:
"It never ceases to amaze me the stupid things men will do for a few bucks, a snort of coke or a piece of ass."
--Judge Bailey Crawford

NEARLY NORMAL NORMAN

Before the turn of the century, when Juicy Lucy, the longtime girlfriend of Nearly Normal Norman Oklahoma, the founder of Clementine's, one of North Beach's oldest strip joints, finished her last dance set on a chilly night, she literally struck gold.

That lucrative moment happened on a rainy night when Lucy left the stage to a scattered applause, entered the apartment that she shared with Nearly Normal, her 80-year-old lover, and found him dead.

The shock caused her to drop her costume on top of the three-inch heels she was wearing Immediately, she shut and locked the door to the vault-like bedroom Norman had built off the basement of the then 100-year-old strip club.

For those new to San Francisco, Clementine's faces Broadway, a few doors down from Columbus Avenue along a tawdry stretch of North Beach called the Barbary Coast.

During Norm's heyday, the media took turns calling him the eccentric sultan of skin, the poohbah of pulchritude, the sheik of sleaze. What they didn't expect to call him was missing in action.

Had Norm's fatal heart attack occurred anywhere else, it would have been a slow day news epic. But since his body hadn't been found a year later, the media softened its name calling. He went from sleaze bag to becoming a cultural pioneer harkening to the years he owned and operated Clementine's, a throwback men's club to the heady 1960s when topless/bottomless dancing became the legal rage. Community standards had not recovered from that plumet.

So, what happened to Nearly Normal's skin and bones? Let's go back to Juicy Lucy finding his body sprawled face down on his waterbed, the size of Oakland's Lake Merritt. But before she checked for a pulse, she set eyes on the open refrigerator-sized bank vault next to the bed and spent the next hour adding up the $50,000 cash that was bundled in the safe. But what excited her more were the fifty standard-size gold bricks at the bottom of the safe that she later discovered weighed twenty-seven pounds (about 430 ounces, which translated into 1973 [Norm's death] gold prices into $2.1 million).

Being closer to fifty than forty, she still had solid abs and great legs. Fuzzy blue stage lighting and silicon injections took care of the rest. Not being a 20-year-old bimbo like the other dancers in house, she quickly understood that what was in the safe would be the only inheritance she'd ever see.

To get to Norm Oklahoma's on-site bedroom—what he called the Garden of Eatin'—you had to enter the misogynist's locked door off the club's basement-level dressing room. Lucy had one of the two keys to the bedroom door. Norm had the other.

Lucy figured she had a week to move the cash and fifty gold bars, along with Norm's remains, before tongues would start to wag and Norm's aroma would be noticed.

* * *

Because North Beach back in the late 1880s or earlier was a beachfront property, the businesses south and west of Telegraph Hill were built on landfill. Most of the buildings on the east side of Columbus Avenue (from Broadway to Washington Square) were constructed on very tall stilts.

That left space underneath Clementine's, where Nearly Normal had hired cheap labor on the sly to construct his pad. He had it built with double cinderblock walls and a solid steel door that led under the ancient wood buildings to who knows where.

Lucy, 5'-9" with long bamboo poles for legs and breasts (known among wags as the original Silicon Valley), was not all T&A; she had an instinctive entrepreneurial streak that went back to junior high when she would charge any boy interested ten bucks to take a quick peek at her gender differences under her parochial school plaid skirt.

Unlike many of her peers, Lucy understood the possibilities of the future—and that to leave a Kansas town she hated, she had to save her money. And that's what she did. When the time came, it was through her savings that she was able to skip graduation from Topeka's Immaculate Deception High and instead Go West, Young Lady to dance naked in San Francisco.

For Norm, it was love at first sight. When Lucy applied for work at Clementine's, she was a honey blonde, decades Norman's junior. Me too-ers of the next century would have scoffed at her mores, but Lucy used all her charms to woo and win over the 5'-5" bowling-ball-shaped impresario.

After discovering the safe full of Ft. Knox-sized gold bricks, she did not pull the *gracious me oh my* when the squatty club owner met his maker and Lucy found her reward.

She hatched a plan on the spot. First things first. She needed to get rid of the body without letting anyone know what she was up to.

She knew the never-used door in the ensuite bathroom led to a sandy beach beneath Clementine's and DeLuca's restaurant.

If you check a map of the Northeast corner of San Francisco, you'll see Columbus Avenue runs diagonally through the heart of the neighborhood called North Beach. That's because Columbus was roughly the shoreline of San Francisco Bay back in the middle 1800s.

From a point north and east of Columbus and Francisco streets is landfill. Half of today's North Beach—all those jammed-together homes, businesses, warehouses, fisherman's wharves, and Embarcadero docks—were built on the new shoreline filled with construction rubble and decades of collected trash.

Lucy loaded Norm onto a fluffy comforter off the bed and dragged him through the bathroom and out on the pristine sandy beach next to a flowing sewer. Storms would have backed and flooded the buildings except for the fact that a six-foot diameter underground cement pipe swallowed the gutter water like some gargling leviathan.

At open sewer's edge, she paused. If she dumped the body into the rapids, it would jettison into the sewer flume that ran from under

Broadway, down Telegraph Hill's steep grade, and emptied into the bay. She didn't want to chance his body being discovered too quickly, as she needed time to empty the safe and hide the contents away from Clementine's without being seen.

As mentioned, Lucy's figure and regular exercise from dancing every day kept her in shape. Being toned kept her employed at Clementine's. But that didn't stop her from populating a little black book with names of men who appreciated trysts with exotic dancers. She had her regulars, and she kept all names confidential. She had a long list of favors due her.

One of her best side actions was Leon Lee, who was about the same age as the dearly departed Normy. Except Leon didn't personally have sex with Lucy. He acquired gift certificates from her so Leon could use them as he wished. Sex made an interesting birthday or Christmas present to someone Leon liked.

Leon was also generous and discreet. They were fellow travelers.

Leon, the enforcer, who rose to become the big deal head of all Chinatown Tongs, assisted in creating a gold account for Lucy at the Bank of Schliem, a long-standing Swiss banking entity in Zurich.

There, the interest earned off the gold bars gave Lucy a nice income once she retired from her stage work. As one hand washed each other's money, Leon and Lucy became fast friends. She moved to Sausalito and opened a modern-day brothel for all known genders who appreciated discreet services from a professional woman.

Meanwhile, what happened to Nearly Norman?

Lucy started visiting the Broadway Café for breakfast, lunch, and dinner until she personally delivered every gold brick to Leon.

Once the safe was empty, Lucy returned to the open sewer and pushed Norm into eternity.

Every so often, she'd wonder what happened to his corpse. It was never found in the bay.

Curious, she asked Leon, who mused that because Nearly Normal was dumped during a very stormy time and the sewer acted like a waterfall, the strong current probably carried the body into the middle of the shipping channel.

He wasn't far from reality. The body was trapped in a sunken fishing net that eventually was hooked onto a passing freighter. The cargo ship towed Nearly out beyond Hawaii enroute to Hong Kong, when heavier seas detached his now fish-food carcass one bone at a time to filter down to the bottom of a deep Pacific trench. The skull landed not too far from the 1930s era wreckage of a Lockheed model 10 all-metal Electra twin-engine monoplane.

Another of mankind's mysteries.

DID SHE, OR DIDN'T SHE?

"This is Scott Keating, your host for this Memorial Day weekend media round-up here at KQED, San Francisco public television. Our guests this afternoon are Max Wax, an ex-reporter with *San Francisco Daily News;* Ray Potter, managing editor of the *Daily News*; and civil attorney Garrett Ellis.

"We appreciate you gentlemen being here tonight, and as a side note, I wish to assure our listeners we did ask a woman to appear tonight, however, Jennifer McGrath, the anchor at KNUZ-TV and co-defendant in Mr. Garrett's monster lawsuit, declined our invitation as she is on deadline for her evening broadcast.

"Let's start with Garrett Ellis, one of San Francisco's leading civil attorneys, who as recently as last week filed a monster multi-million-dollar libel lawsuit against Bruce Communications Chairman

John Bruce, owner, and publisher of the *San Francisco Daily News;* The Bruce Foundation and our guests this evening, former *Daily News* reporter Max Wax and current *Daily News* Managing Editor Ray Potter. First, I'd like to ask Garrett Ellis is the mayor's daughter Carling Martin your client on the lawsuit? And, next I'd like to ask Ray Potter why Max Wax was terminated by your newspaper? Does it have anything to do with the lawsuit? First, Mr. Potter:

Potter: Call me, Ray. Thank you for having our side join you this evening. It is no secret the *Daily News* is reorganizing to avoid bankruptcy. We are an ongoing business and we made decisions based on moving forward to improve our fiscal position. We can't wait for lawsuits to be resolved before making workplace decisions. The leadership of this newspaper decided we had to make changes. We had to let go more than 30 persons in our editorial department as part of our reorganization. We regret we had to do this. Mr. Wax was among the most junior employees let go. His leaving the *Daily News* was based on seniority or the lack of it not on the lawsuit we are discussing here."

Keating: "Nonetheless, the timing is suspicious."

Wax: "Of course, it is. They rushed to make these firings as an excuse to get rid of me."

Potter: "It was a sad day for all we had to let go. No one was singled out."

Keating: "Tell us, Garrett how you plan to win?"

Ellis: "I will let the truth emerge. Sadly, my client was libeled when she was accused of having a sexual affair with the late District Attorney Harre Ling. The jury will believe Miss Martin and won't believe the fabrications written by Mr. Wax and published by the *Daily News* and the broadcast by Jennifer McGrath and KNUZ. The jury will make it clear publishing lies without supporting evidence will not be tolerated."

Keating: "Some will say Miss Martin is a public figure and that she can't be sued because she is also a public official, as she works as a deputy district attorney in and for the city and county of San Francisco."

Ellis: "That's not the law. On the facts of the case, the jury will agree. The other side lied when they knew all along that they were publishing a false article. Miss Martin never had a sexual affair with the deceased. No proof exists. It was hurtful to her and equally horrific for the family of Harre Ling."

Keating: "Will John Bruce settle this case?"

Potter: "My feeling is it will be resolved before there is a trial, but I don't speak for the legal team."

Keating: "For the record, lead defense attorney on the case, Martin Van Buren the seventh, declined to be on our show tonight."

Potter: "If I may interrupt, Mr. Van Buren passed away two weeks ago. I hope you were on vacation or maybe you should read our newspaper or fire your producer."

Keating: "How unfortunate…"

Potter: "Certainly for Mr. Van Buren.

Keating: "Let's move on, our time is limited…"

Wax: "If I may Scott, I'd like your listeners to know we had evidence proving Miss Martin did have a sexual affair with Mr. Ling. As a reporter, I have the right to inform the public of shenanigans involving our elected officials and public servants—"

Ellis: "Our side looks forward to seeing your evidence."

Wax: "My apartment was broken into and the tape recording that backed my article fully was stolen along with several file folders of my notes for the article. Convenient burglary, don't you think?"

Keating: "Was the theft reported to the police?"

Wax: "Yes, and I took a polygraph test."

Ellis: "Which was inconclusive."

Wax: "I was robbed. And the city was robbed of the truth."

Keating: "Did you ever recover your evidence?"

Wax: "Not yet. We are investigating."

Keating: "What do you say to that Mr. Ellis?"

Ellis: "We will patiently let the system reward justice and the truth. The jury's verdict will speak for us."

Keating: "There is a rumor that a two hundred-million-dollar judgment will be the end of Bruce Communications, given that it is on record already undergoing Chapter 11 bankruptcy proceedings. Would you care to comment on that, Mr. Potter?"

Potter: "Again, Scott, I am not on the legal team, but two hundred million doesn't fall out of trees."

Wax: "It's not too late for Miss Martin to have the decency to admit the truth. I beg her to do so. My sources acknowledge she did have an affair with Mr. Ling. My article was the truth. I've lost my job because of it. I simply wish to clear my name. I am an honest journalist. I did not have malice toward her or Mr. Ling."

Keating: 'Your firing isn't exactly a vote of confidence from the Bruce team. Care to comment on that?"

Potter: "Scott, didn't you listen when I just addressed that issue?"

Wax: "It's simple. If I hadn't written the article I wouldn't have been fired."

Potter: "For the third time, the dismissal had nothing to do with the case in question."

Wax: "No one believes that."

Ellis: "I do, Mr. Wax. That should put a torch to your generality."

Potter: "I'm not going to comment beyond what I've said tonight. It is an internal company matter. We are a privately held corporation and we are not required to be transparent on a long list of subjects."

Keating: "Let me add, when cases go to trial, each side has an equal chance to win or lose. Sometimes it's best to compromise."

Ellis: "We're not going to compromise the truth. We are not going to settle, but I look forward to your offer. It will speak loud and clear."

Wax: "Sue all you want. If I win, fuck you; if I lose, I have no way to pay the judgment. As a result, no one will hire me in this city. No job, no money. My reputation has been damaged.

Keating: "We don't have on record any job applications you have submitted to KQED. How hard have you looked for work?"

Wax: "I'm not going to sit here and be a clay pigeon for everyone's pot shots. I have better use for my time than sitting here. I need to find who robbed me of my evidence."

Keating: "For those of you listening to our simulcast on radio, Max has unhooked the microphone on his sweater and walked off the set."

Ellis: "That speaks for Mr. Martin's maturity. It's the same rash attitude he took in writing and publishing a false story about two important citizens of this City and County."

Keating: "Miss Martin has taken a leave of absence from the district attorney's office."

Ellis: "Old news."

Keating: "It has been...what, several weeks so far?"

Ellis: "Maybe."

Keating: "Would you elaborate? I'm sure our taxpayers in our audience would like to know."

Ellis: "Miss Martin is currently on an unpaid vacation leave. It's a private family matter. We're all entitled to some family time when it is important."

Keating: "Was the leave stress related because of Harre Ling's suicide?"

Ellis: "In the five years she has been with the DA's office, Miss Martin has not taken any vacation time. There was a lull in her schedule, and she took the opportunity to take some of the time she earned as a county employee to do what she wishes."

Keating: "Counselor, let's cut to the proverbial chase, did Carling Martin have a sexual relationship with Harre Ling?"

Ellis: "Scott, you know better. She can't comment on that will the suit is pending."

Keating: "Then, let's call it a night."

Wax: "Wait, I got some things to say…"

STUNTS THAT GET YOU KILLED

The late spring two-day gale that blew into early June ebbed, but it never stopped drizzling, the kind of rain that spits in your face. Cold. Gray. Windy. Dreary.

A fishing trawler, slowly motoring under the century-old Golden Gate Bridge and into the now calmer waters of the vast bay, was coming home like some feral alley cat who was in the middle of a slashing, hissing catfight.

Like endless one-two punches in the ring, the storm pummeled the 60-foot *Angelina* shaking three experienced Vietnamese fishermen including pilot Don Vanchester.

The older, crewcut Anglo was also head of security for the Fairbanks Hotel. Wally McGrath viewed the moonlighting as a favor to this restaurant pal Larry DeLuca. Fishing boat pilots are hard to find, and Vanchester, an ex-Navy officer, fit in as a retired PT-boat operator.

Storms were not new to the crew, but the weather gurus had misjudged. They crystal balled light rain—not the wave-churning monster that sent the boat's gyroscope on a joyride.

* * *

Ashore, Alan Carter, a recently hired part-time truck driver and wharf handyman, sat in the passenger seat of a two-ton refrigerated Kenworth truck. He opened his hard-plastic lunch pail for another hit from a large stash of cocaine he had been given as a bonus for the past week's good work: driving and delivering *Angelina's* ice-packed catch to Los Angeles seafood wholesalers.

Gaunt with dirty blonde stringy hair Alan had watched the seiner tie up to the aging pier he was parked on. The old redwood planking, turned gray then black over the years, was one of the few remaining fishing piers along the northeast Embarcadero.

Tonight, the *Angelina's* crew were in no mood to unload its catch into the waiting truck. But they had been paid to do so before dawn. And they could see the Junior DeLuca was there pacing the planking to make sure they did. The younger DeLuca ran the fishing operation that was owned by his dad father, who also owned DeLuca's restaurant located on the east side of Grant and Columbus Avenues.

It was 2 am. *Angelina* was seven hours late.

* * *

Clanging directly below an abandoned flat on dead-end Romolo Alley, the Kenworth entered from Broadway and backed until it groaned to a halt by the rear door of DeLuca's restaurant. Its weekly pre-dawn arrival from Fisherman's Wharf woke the deaf, dead, drunk, or drugged for blocks around that run down part of North Beach.

Truck noise woke Max Wax, the Ex-*Daily News* reporter, who has not worked since he was canned for the investigative article claiming the late Harre Ling and Assistant DA Carly Martin were lovers, a claim still not proven.

Now he was a squatter in an abandoned broken-window flat at the rear of Kerouac's Bookstore across the alley from DeLuca's rear entrance. Max glanced at the old windup clock on his nightstand. It was 3 a.m. The two-day storm had picked up, splattering hard against the cracked window next to his bed.

The noise out in the alley was not new. It came from the men unloading the restaurant's share of the weekly catch and preparing to truck the rest to wholesalers as far down the coast to Santa Barbara and Los Angeles.

The racket across the alley was the big reason the small studio was unrentable over the years, except on occasion to down and outers like Max.

And, if it was not the DeLuca trucks making clangorous mayhem, it came from honking cabbies on Broadway, drunks fist fighting off the main sidewalk or junkies screaming when they burst a vein with cheap heroin.

Max endured the ragtag room because he traded working a couple of weekend shifts at the bookstore for his garret. It was a new living arrangement, but at least he could finance his growing alcoholism without worrying about rent.

The studio had electricity but no heat, which caused him to see his breath now that the mornings ebbed closer to winter. It was too cold to go back to sleep—even while wrapped in his navy-style peacoat under a wool blanket that came with the flat.

Max rubbed his eyes. He lay back down hoping the heavy rain pattering on the flat's flimsy roof would put him to sleep.

A sudden crash of metal against pavement startled him awake. Looking around at the dilapidated walls and the busted-out window behind him that had been nailed shut with soggy cardboard, he decided he had had enough. Time to move on. Staying here was a new low in his life. He would rather be a dead man than spend another night in a squatter's hellhole.

It was that thought that forced him to climb out of the swamp. No more broken flat. No more North Beach. No more San Francisco. He decided to swallow his pride and head downtown to the Tenderloin district's St. Anthony's Homeless Rescue. He would have no privacy, but he would be warm and dry. Once he got a free meal in him, he'd leave town.

On the verge of tears, Max jammed all he owned into his hiker's backpack. Now, if he could borrow fare money to take the aging shame-train Greyhound, he could be in LA by tonight.

He knew his friend Lyn, the midnight shift counter waitress across the street at the Broadway Café, would be on duty. He'd hadn't asked her for a handout before. Some cash. Anything. A cup of coffee would do. Should he ask for twenty dollars hoping he would get five? Life is a crap shoot. Maybe he could do that? Why not? *Or plan B*, he thought, *why not dive off the curb into the slow lane and let any oncoming truck end it for me.*

Time for a farewell piss into the stained toilet bowl before hitting the road. "Outta fuck city," he mumbled. Finishing his pee, he peered through the only window of his studio that faced the alley.

A large Kenworth that he had seen before was parked directly below his window. A light over DeLuca's rear door shone on a cooler sitting unattended in the truck's cabin. Whatever the trucker fixed to eat would be fine with him. He waited until the alley was empty of workers before moving down the wood stairs to the truck on the sly.

Bingo, the passenger side door was unlocked.

Max was no longer embarrassed to be pilfering someone else's lunch. It was now part of his lifestyle.

Grabbing the blue and white Coleman cooler, Max cut through a passageway between the rear of the bookstore and a line of garages in the alley. Now on the opposite side of the building he'd called home, he looked at several dumpsters that were puddling rainwater. There he could toss the cooler and dash across Broadway, where he could eat the evidence at the Broadway Café with a cup of hot coffee.

Max opened the cooler. He could not have been more surprised. He believed he would find fixings for lunch, maybe a chicken salad sandwich, a pickle and maybe an apple. Instead, he picked up what felt like a pound of white powder wrapped in clear heavy-duty cellophane. Cocaine? He jammed his forefinger into the wrapping to pull out a taste.

Cocaine! It had to be a fucking pound of cocaine along with an operating cell phone. His luck was beginning to turn.

* * *

He hustled across Broadway to the sidewalk in front of the diner's large plate-glass window. Yellow light from the cafe was the only sign of life along the four-block stretch of honky tonks, liquor stores, hock shops and a ragtag used bookstore.

He peered inside and let out a sigh of relief seeing Lyn Lee, the owner's niece, who effortlessly poured coffee for a pair of cabbies sitting at her counter. She was his only friend in a city of half a million.

As Max entered, a wave of stove heat slapped him. It smelled of stale coffee and onions. Only half of the six fans overhead were circulating. Each spun with the speed of a glacier, and none contributed to anyone's comfort.

The lack of air conditioning kept the place unbearably hot all year round. Like the waves out at Ocean Beach, the Broadway Café never shut down.

Max sat on the far side of the cabbies.

Lyn sensed his nervousness.

"What's with the cooler?" she asked.

Max offered a weak smile. "I need a favor. If anyone asks if you've seen me, tell 'em you heard I was in Reno for the last couple of days. But between you and me, I'm heading to San Diego. My folks are there. I gotta dry out and clean up."

"Good idea, but what scared you straight this time?"

"Long story. You haven't seen me, OK?"

"Hate to break it to you, but you're not exactly the main topic of conversation around here."

"And especially you never saw me with this cooler." He patted the plastic container.

"You are one mysterious dude."

"Is that a promise?" he asked.

"Whatever."

When she went to the register to cash out the cabbies, he waited until she turned her back before sticking a small saltshaker and a regular teaspoon from off the counter into the pocket of his rain-soaked coat.

He grabbed his new cooler and headed to the toilets. Glancing around, he was happy the diner would be empty once the cabbies left.

Normally, gothic North Beach--those denizens with nowhere to go at night but with a little money to spend--ended up at the Broadway Café. They would be perched like crows on a farmer's fence. But not tonight. Blame the rain. Blame the fact that the Fed-backed welfare checks hadn't arrived, yet—whatever the reason, the Cinderella trade was slow.

WHAT SHANNON SAW

Junior DeLuca caught up with Alan Carter inside Clementine's half block long bar, which ran from the velour curtain entrance on the south to the brick wall property line with DeLuca's restaurant on the north.

The bar stools were empty. The Asian crew had finished moving the coke from the Kenworth to a storage room below Clementine's wobbly stage.

Junior had paid and released the crew. He climbed up from the basement via a staircase that entered the dancer's backstage dressing room.

He had cut across the shiny stage flooring and pushed through the closed velour curtain.

Already morose by having to wait seven hours for the *Angelina* to arrive with the bales of cocaine that were inside the Kenworth, Junior was incensed at Carter for losing a pound of coke—and now to see him pouring himself a glass of house wine. "That ain't your liquor."

Alan smirked. "I'm thirsty."

"Drink water, fool."

Junior marched up to Carter and held the point of his switchblade a foot from Alan Carter's gaunt face.

He put the blade down when he saw his morning shift bartender come through the front door.

Junior yelled without looking at her. "Sweetie, why don't you go get some breakfast. Come back in an hour."

Shannon Reading nodded in agreement. She was wearing a gray hoodie sweatshirt and denims. "I got to get my raincoat backstage—it's pouring out there."

Junior turned back to Carter and flipped open his switchblade.

"Hey, hey, no rough stuff," Carter yelped, pushing Junior's hand away.

"Have you found the coke you lost?"

"It had to be stolen. It was in the truck right where I left it," Carter pleaded and reached inside his jacket pocket to unlatch the safety on his Saturday Night Special .38.

"Whatever, you fuck…it's gone. Find it before the trucks head to LA or pay me for a pound of snow. Cash money. You got till noon."

"I got no idea where it went. Put the knife away; I'm no thief."

Junior shook his head. "Where was the last time you saw it?

"In the cooler that you gave me. In the van."

"Did you lock it, you stupid stooge?"

Carter could only shrug. "What's the problem? It's my coke. Not yours. And don't call me stooge. Fuck you, Junior. I quit. You can't pull knives on people and expect them to work for you."

Ticked, Junior shot back. "Look, *stooge*, I gave you the powder because you're doing good work. Losing the coke means someone we don't know has it and now they know where to find it. Pounds of coke don't fall out of fuckin' trees. No loose ends. And because you didn't lock the stupid truck, we got problems. Someone was snooping around the truck. Maybe they saw what we brought in from the *Angelina*. That's why I'm pissed! None of us want to do federal time because you're stupid!"

Carter wasn't a scholar, but he realized where his talk with Junior was headed.

"Hey, I'm not the stooge here. Somebody stole from me," he repeated. I didn't—"

"Shut the fuck up." Junior swung and missed with his switchblade.

The tow head leaped back and reached for his Smith & Wesson.

Junior was quicker. He plunged the knife blade into Carter's heart.

* * *

Shannon did not quite make it to her raincoat in her backstage dressing area. She heard a man scream in pain. It had to be the truck driver, who was arguing with Junior.

She peeked around the red velour stage curtain to see if they were just roughhousing.

What saved her life was her not screaming or gasping at what Junior had done. He was wiping blood off his knife using the struggling man's shirt.

Shannon retreated quickly through the backstage door that connected Clementine's to Deluca's private Club Car room. From there, she hurried through the empty restaurant and out the front door. She was now at Columbus and Grant. Now that it was raining no one would pay attention to her run the four blocks to the back door of Powell's Saloon. The door was always open. It led upstairs to the apartments that ran the length of the block long brick building.

She pounded on John Wald's door.

* * *

Wald drove her to the airport. "John, please don't tell anyone what I just told you, especially the police. You've been around North Beach long enough to know that if I come forward, I'll be killed. I don't want to die."

John couldn't disagree. He knew that when a citizen witnesses a cold-blooded murder, they become a victim that is forced to endure the mental cruelty of knowing they too could be slaughtered for being at the wrong place at the wrong time.

John felt a chill for Shannon. Being forced to testify against Junior DeLuca would be stupid even if convicted and jailed. His thugs would find her and make her disappear.

She was right to leave town. No one in their right mind wants to be looking over shoulders for some goon to kill you. Shannon said nothing the rest of the ride to the airport what could they say?

Junior didn't remember who was working at Clementine's the day Alan Carter was stabbed to death. No police came to question Junior because no one reported the crime or the fact he was missing.

Soon after, Junior had gone to sea with the *Angelina*. When he returned only then did, he learn Shannon was gone. He didn't put two and two together. Why should he?

* * *

On those other nights, when he clung to his job at the *Daily News*, balding, bespeckled Max Wax was an easy target for a laugh. He dressed like a cartoon: scraggly, a taller Toulouse Lautrec who hung out with dancehall girls from Clementine's across the street.

By nature, strippers are playful, especially in a crowd. Max fit right in. He was a "class A" flirt. He had little use for men as pals. Women were less judgmental and could care less if he did not ooze macho. He dove right in to be among them—the more the merrier. They were, after all, neighbors.

Even when he was penniless, that did not stop him from joining their table. One would eventually buy him a drink.

He ran paycheck to paycheck. His reporter's salary should have been enough to pay the rent, but not if one would rather bar hop. On those lonely stretches, no money meant no food. Then, on those most glorious of days—paydays—he shone like the moon. Then the moon went dark after he got fired.

But in today's wee hours, he crossed the line. He became a thief. And he knew it. He could not shake his father's face or his voice—that voice we hear at night when we fuck up. *I won't always be around, Maxwell, to bail you out.*

Max put his hands over his ears. *We're all raised with certain values in life. Values are the guardrails that keep us from losing all self-respect and the will to make things square again. No values, no hope.* Max couldn't remember the last time he'd thought of his father. At least being dead kept the old man from knowing his son had committed grand larceny—even if it was a slime-on-slime crime.

Max splashed water on his face. And dried his hands with Leon's paper towels.

The quietude of the toilet stall gave him a chance to plan.

* * *

Max offered a cheery "good morning" over his shoulder as owner Leon Lee shuffled by him. Old Leon entered via the same hallway that led to the basement and the toilets of his vintage diner. Leon grunted and kept walking to his window seat, but not before telling Max in perfect English: "Make sure you pay for the coffee you're drinking. I'm not running a soup kitchen." It was followed by a shouted order in Mandarin not to serve him.

Max looked at Lyn and shook his head at Leon's insult. "Did I deserve that?"

"He tells me you've skipped paying quite a few checks."

"Have I ever not paid you? When did I stiff you on a check?"

"I'm not here all the time. I'm repeating what Leon says about you."

Max was not in the mood to defend himself, especially since Leon was right.

Lyn felt sorry for him and asked if he wanted breakfast.

"Yes. I'm good for it."

"No, you're not." She slipped a wadded up twenty-dollar bill into his hand. "Order some food," she said.

* * *

Taking his last bite of toast after a plateful of scrambled eggs, Max saw Xandy Williams, who danced the 6:00 a.m. to 10:00 a.m. shift alone, hurrying from her cab toward the diner. Her daily routine began with breakfast at Leon's before checking into the strip joint.

Xandy, who was totally black skinned, closed her red umbrella, shook the rain off, and dropped it into the bin next to the front door. Her grand entrance was a sight few had witnessed along the Barbary Coast, the ancient name for that stripper stretch of Broadway. The 35-year-old kept alive a garish tradition on the street: be gaudy or be gone.

The lime-green robe she had on under her raincoat was loud enough to require sunglasses. The shiny faux satin garment was something a prize fighter would wear entering the ring. "Flaunt it, baby," Max said way too loud and embarrassed Lyn.

Xandy waved to her admirers. "It's so me," she gave Max a hug.

"We gotta talk," he whispered.

"Not now, honey, I'm starved."

Max had been quick to bond with the black stripper, who he'd met when she danced at the Condor Club a few years back.

Max shared coffee and street gossip with her when he could. She let him fondle her thighs at those dark back booths up and down Broadway. If there was a song that would follow her around, it would be, "I Don't Want Anything to Change" by songwriters Maia Sharp/ Stephanie Chapman/Elisabeth Wagner Rose. Like the song says, *I like it lonely, I like it strange. I don't want anything to change.*

Everybody loved her. Nothing did change.

Xandy swooped on to the counter stool nearest to the front door.

Max slipped in next to her. "Let's go to a back table. I have a business deal for you," he said.

First, she ordered and paid for a cup of coffee and a bowl of clam chowder.

"You good?"

"Coffee, black," he said. "I just ate. I'll bring it over to you." He watched Xandy move to a table in the back.

At the counter, Lyn scribbled his order on her small pad. "Anything else?"

"Nothing else other than I really want to fuck Xandy. I've never had a black chick."

Lyn looked up from her pad. "Have the decency to keep your baser thoughts to yourself. I don't want to hear it."

"So much for freedom of speech."

"It is crude. You're nicer than that. You're coming off like a teenage goon with no manners or sophistication."

"Is it sexist to speak the truth? I can't help myself. I know what's underneath that robe."

"You might do yourself some good hearing how you sound from a woman's viewpoint. How would you feel having someone who gives you the creeps constantly drool over you? Why do that? It's stupid, annoying, and crass. I'm trying to be your friend, but if you talk like that in front of me again, I'll stop trying."

"I didn't think it was offensive to say she turns me on. Can't friends be honest with each other?"

"Max, let's drop it."

"I'm sorry you were offended. I'm sorry I can't be frank with you and speak what's on my mind."

"It's not my place to filter your thoughts. I simply don't want to hear what gives you an erection."

Max spun around on the worn red vinyl stool and walked over to Xandy.

The dancer pointed a finger within an inch of his nose. "I heard what you said to Lyn. You're a jerk. I don't want to hear any crap from you. In fact, I don't want you sitting next to me."

"I'm sorry, X. I've already apologized to Lyn. I'm in trouble. I need a favor."

"You have an asshole way of asking. Don't call me X."

Max looked at her.

"What, what?" She could see it in his eyes that he was serious.

"I completed a writing assignment for a friend who is starting a PR firm in town, but the problem is he paid me in coke. I need the money, not the powder. Is there any way I can sell you some, so I can make expenses? You know I got fired from the *Daily News*. I'm tapped out."

As offended as Xandy's face appeared, the demon started whispering in her ears. "How much you got?"

Max did not blink. He was now into his bullshit wheeler-dealer mode. "I got five grams. I'm keeping one and hoping to sell the rest."

She reached into her robe pocket and pulled out a wad of bills. "Here's three hundred. That's all I got on me."

"OK, it's all yours," he pulled out the saltshaker he'd lifted from the counter earlier. "Careful, remember the lid has holes."

X-woman handed over the money.

Max sat back and sighed. "You're a lifesaver. And don't tell anyone, especially at Clementine's or DeLuca's, that you got it from me. Tell 'em you got this from a cabbie."

"Relax, Max. I'm on your side."

The conversation took a pause.

She took it up again. "You stole this coke, didn't you?"

"It wasn't me, beautiful."

"Where have I heard that tune before?"

"I gotta get cash to get out of this town. If I stay here, I'm a dead man."

"Pulling a stunt like that will get you killed in any city."

"I got to get to LA. I got something lined up there."

"Like what?"

"Writing jobs. I got some pals down there that are into screenplays. I can do that."

"Are you serious about leaving Frisco?"

"Now I am. Thanks to this cash."

"That won't take you far."

Lyn waved from the counter. The stripper's order was up. Max retrieved it.

* * *

Max had an eerie feeling that sooner or later Xandy may let it slip that she bought coke from him. Knowing that about his friend scared Max. It was time to leave town. He held Lyn's hand while he said goodbye. It was one of those farewells when both understood this was probably the last time, they would ever see each other.

Not wanting to show his face on Broadway, Max asked Lyn if he could use the diner's basement elevator to Leon Lee's below-level twenty-four-hour underground mall. From there he could use the mall's Kearny Street exit and walk to the city's only CalTube intrastate station.

IF WALMART HAD A CASINO

Max Wax climbed down the worn wooden steps that led from the Broadway Café to a basement level.

The basement was a storage room for the 24/7 diner. He moved to a modern elevator at the rear wall. After pushing the button, the door parted with a crisp-sounding bell. He stepped inside the private elevator that connected the four levels of eighty-year-old "Leon" Lee's Bazaar de Bizarre.

Level 1 was a square block underground shopping mall, a Walmart of Asian shops, services, and food counters.

The public could enter Asia Mall from a lobby on Kearny Street next to an entrance to Level 2, which was a public garage.

Level 3 housed a full-sized casino. Open to club members only. Membership to the casino club was guarded as any of the leading private clubs in San Francisco.

Level 4 was a private marketplace only known as the *vault* to the clandestine society of high-end weapons traffickers.

Built to U.S. Army bunker standards, Leon had, the same need-to-know multinational contractor that built the Cheyenne Mountain facility for the Air Force to build his Byzantine mall. The top two levels were public; however, the lower two were built on the sly for obvious reasons.

Because Leon owned the entire block, it was easy to excavate beneath his properties without raising suspicions.

Leon, thanks to his gaming and gun-running interests, was a billionaire in Switzerland, Macao and the Ria Islands near Portugal. In the United States his sole legit enterprise being the Broadway Café.

The various Tongs in Chinatown took turns owning a piece of the mall. Leon liked to keep convoluted as simple as possible.

As a result, Leon's web of accountants were first rate. He was current in his taxes with the IRS. They had to be as the old man's fingers were in every cash register till in Chinatown.

* * *

The elevator stopped on Level 3. Max stepped out at the casino level to pick up a bus boy. If one pictured a Las Vegas hotel gaming room stripped to its shorts—no fancy neon or two-inch deep carpeting or any trappings of a pricy interior designer—then you would have the twenty thousand square foot cement-walled gaming emporium that was the economic engine of Leon's empire. Tonight, casino attendance went wall to wall. This underground gaming enterprise made Garcia shake his head and smile in wonderment, even though gambling in Chinatown's back rooms has been a longtime staple of Leon's empire.

Despite its warehouse appearance, the "house" was fully equipped with high-end gaming tables, slots, and gambling furnishings. It smelled and sounded like any Reno or Lake Tahoe casino and operated 24/7, 365 days a year on a wink and a nod.

Max walked into the casino. The teen bus boy gave Max a "whew."

The wet wool hoodie Max had lifted off a hat rack at Dante's Saloon a few weeks back didn't pass the sniff test. The bus boy was right to be offended.

Ahead were the roulette tables. All were filled with players. Max decided to put half of his money on noir once he got a chance to move to the table. Noir would give him more cash to make the trip to LA.

He could also ride the escalators back up to the first level, where he could buy a new coat or maybe the 24-hour dry cleaners could do a rush job for him.

The roulette tables beckoned as if he were in some alien force field that magnetized him toward the white bouncing, rolling ball. Sirens howling for his soul.

What if he lost?

Max was sober. Had he been drunk there would be no debate. He would have dived into playing the wheel. But the better angels in his make-up forced him to pause.

He glanced to his left and saw the casino pit boss talking on the phone. Soon, the man in the tux, a handsome Samoan who most likely tripled Max's weight, moved toward him.

Sweat flooded Max's entire body.

Did Junior call ahead to alert the pit boss to be on the lookout for him?

Did Xandy already spill the beans?

Max moved between the slot machines and made it to the glass exit doors facing Kearny Street.

A loud buzzer went off as he reached the door.

Locked.

The fucker locked him in.

Max spun his head around, looking for an escape route.

The Samoan grabbed his shoulder. "Mr. Wax. Miss Lee just called and asked me to escort you out of the casino. You are not to return, understand?"

"I got lost, I'm looking for the dry cleaners. This coat needs it."

The bulky Samoan walked Max up two levels to all-day and all-night cleaners. Turns out the shop belonged to his family. "Take off your coat. No, go into the room over there, take off all your clothes, put them in a basket and sit there until they're done. Got it?" Max was slipped a clingy terrycloth robe.

A very round woman hugged her son. "We do our best job for your friend. Thank you, Phillip."

"Phillip?" Max grinned.

"You got a problem with my name?"

* * *

For an hour, Max sat in the dry cleaner's fitting room. His clothes arrived still warm from being pressed. He offered to pay.

"Miss Lee will pay for you," a teenage girl said.

From North Beach, Max moved quickly through the Jackson Square's colorful brick buildings and quaint narrow cul de sacs filled with merchant shops.

At a four way stop at Jackson and Montgomery, he flagged down a passing cab. Amazing what clean clothes do for an image. Cabbies stop to pick you up.

He felt like a million bucks in his clean clothes as he arrived at the CalTube station.

* * *

CalTube, built on empty land on Hunter's Point section of the city, was another post-pandemic public works project, but this time by the state. Boeing Corporation handled the design and construction. California financed the magnetic, nuclear pod fission train that connected San Diego, San Francisco, and Los Angeles.

Oregon and Washington states paid for the atomic pneumatic passenger tube trains from San Francisco to Seattle via Portland. Once the two north states agreed, California agreed to pay its share from San Francisco to the Oregon border.

In a brilliant stroke, the federal government subsidized the fares by 75 percent until the country fully recovered from the series of pandemics.

Another genius idea that came to pass occurred when it was decided that CalTube would be built above ground. It was genius because the CanAm water pipe system that brought water from the Arctic to Southern California had an adjacent tube that easily fit the rapid train. No more drought and finally a fast surface train linking LA and the Bay Area.

Max wrote several articles about CalTube and the water delivery project describing the green tubes as a double-barreled shotgun hurdling water and people as far as the eye could see.

Today, he purchased a one-way $100 ticket to San Diego, and it was the first time he had been aboard the sleek bullet-shaped train—much less in first class.

Four hours later, he was at the CalTube station in San Diego's Balboa Park, a magnificent structure in twentieth-century Spanish revival architecture style that was erected on methane laced empty land that once was a landfill.

Waiting for his SuperUber, he closed his eyes and stared up at the warm sun.

Max's parents were stunned to see their boy on the front steps of their North Park home. He had his first good meal in months that evening.

Max may not have been living a scholar's life, but he was smart enough, like Shannon Reading, to know when to get the hell out of Dodge City.

PIER PRESSURE

The original commercial piers along Fisherman's Wharf were redwood roadways made from logs nailed together with railroad spikes. The wooden lane surrounded aging warehouses also made from first growth early twentieth-century timber that faded gray.

While most San Francisco docks had gone to maritime museums or tourist traps, a few wharves still clung to fishing operations.

This gray day turned black by mid-morning, and Junior DeLuca backed his restaurant's white delivery van onto Pier 47, a commercial fishing dock one mile south across the strait from Alcatraz Island.

A pounding rain, which continued to sweep in off the bay from the Marin Headlands to the northwest, rendered his back-door windows and side mirrors useless.

Had he stood on the west side of the warehouse pier, he would have heard grumbling in the sky over the ocean. Then, a few seconds later, a huge bolt of lightning tore through the sky, illuminating the Golden Gate Bridge as a ghost ship creeping into the harbor.

Because he made this trip so many times over the years, Junior used from memory the warehouse siding as a landmark. Eventually, the old Dodge van pulled astride the gangway leading to an equally non-descript trawler berthed across from Giacalone's Fisherman's Wharf restaurant. The *Angelina* had docked earlier in the wee hours to transfer its catch into the bigger refrigerated truck still parked by DeLuca Restaurant's rear door.

Jumping from the van, Junior saw Don Vanchester in the pilot house. The crewcut fifty-five-year-old stayed behind to do what he could to have the boat ready in advance for the next voyage.

Junior came in from the heavy rain.

Vanchester was replacing a faulty gauge in the pilot house.

"Can you lend me a hand?" Junior asked.

"I got a day job. I signed on to pilot and take care of your fishing boat. That's it. I'm not part of your organization. You figure out the snafus." Vanchester was a foot taller; he looked down at young DeLuca.

"All I'm asking you to do is take what I got in the laundry bin and dump it into the fishing tank. I gotta get back to the restaurant to drive the two-tonner to LA. I don't think it's too much to ask."

Vanchester groused, pulled his navy-colored pea coat, and watch cap from the nearby hook. He hurried to the bin Junior left behind on the dock.

* * *

Alan Carter's body was covered with a red and white checkered tablecloth from the restaurant's dirty linen pile. Junior had retrieved a wheeled fish bin from the alley and loaded the still-bleeding man into the canvas-sided container. Once the bin landed on the pier planking, Vanchester pulled the cloth away. "Jesus, he's still twitching."

He grimaced in disgust, let out a breath, then leaned into the bin for a grisly coup de grâce with his switchblade, ripping Carter's discolored throat with two violent back and forth slashes.

He heard a heartless last gurgle emit from the newly dead.

Vanchester wheeled the laundry bin up the ramp and onto the boat deck.

From there he hustled to remove the four-by-six-foot aluminum cover over the raised bait tank amidships.

A blinding flash crossed the black sky above the *Angelina*. For full two seconds, the jagged bolt illuminated all of Fisherman's Wharf, from Pier 39 to the Maritime Museum.

He froze. Vanchester counted, waiting for the rolling molto basso that trails all flashes.

The thunder crackled before it blasted full tilt into a weapons-grade explosion. He squatted, covering his ears with the palms of his hands. Vanchester couldn't recall such a loud boom outside of the equatorial seas south of Vietnam. It was the satyr's unholy howl: Satan bursting from the depths of hell.

*　*　*

No longer asleep, Jerry Longstreet, now career homeless, who had been run out of more bars than a cockroach, screamed "incoming" at the top of his lungs. He jumped out from a shanty of wood pallets and discarded plywood. Wide-eyed and scared, he began to shiver in the rain.

He heard voices aboard the *Angelina*, but as he neared the boarding ramp it was quiet all up and down the wharf.

Old Jerry was filthy and hungry, yet somewhat clearheaded. He had been sober two days because the unending storm had put a crimp in his public panhandling earnings. As a result, he had been too broke to buy the sugar wine that made his puffy skin reddish purple and his liver mush.

Jerry noticed a man working in the pilot house. He had seen him before. Maybe a year ago he would have remembered Vanchester's name. But now the cheap alcohol had taken its toll on his brain cells.

Jerry walked sideways, facing away from the eye-irritating spits of gritty rain. Coatless, he braved the chilling cold to make the solo crewman his last panhandle of the night.

The approach of unexpected company startled Vanchester, who immediately slipped his hand around a small .22 handgun inside the pocket of his rain duty hoodie.

The older man spoke first. He stared toward Vanchester, who had one round scar on each cheek. "Aren't you the fella that works at DeLuca's? I know you."

Vanchester grumbled. "I'm new in town. It must have been someone else."

"Can you help a fella out? I could use some spare change for food. I'm really hungry."

A long silence followed.

"Wait here."

The tall pilot returned from the below-deck galley with a plastic container of chicken salad and a plastic fork.

The hard timer devoured the offering.

Smacking his lips, Old Jerry continued offering his best Humphrey Bogart grin. "I know you, don't I?" He did not have a clue what he was saying. He was pulling out all stops to be sociable. Then he stepped on his dick. "I've seen you doin' some funny shit on this pier. I know what you're up to. I've seen what you're unloading," Jerry bluffed.

"You know nothing," Vanchester said. His stare was evil, calculating how to deal with what had become more than a beggar's plea.

Jerry kept smiling, now more of a plea than a gesture of friendliness. "For a couple of bucks, I'll keep quiet. In fact, I'll warn you if I see the cops coming your way. I'm good at that."

Finally, the driver responded: "I need you to pick up trash around the boat. Help me do that and I'll give you a couple of bucks."

"That's a deal, buddy." Jerry noticed round scars on his face—one on each cheek. He had seen that face before, but right now could not remember where.

"Help me take the lid off the bait tank. I gotta see if they left me any bait."

Jerry obeyed.

The driver offered no help.

Jerry took forever to pull off the heavy lid. The smell was outrageous and made him gag. It was only bearable due to the blowing wind. "Well, I'd say you got lot of bait telling by the smell."

Vanchester grabbed him in a headlock.

Jerry struggled. He was no match for the burly captain.

Death was swift as Vanchester snapped the old man's neck. There was no scream, no moan or torrent of blood to splash on the deck. The only sound the pilot heard was the monotonous slapping of waves against the trawler's hull.

Vanchester dumped him into the tank with the rotting chum and maggots. He knew that in forty-eight hours the old man's body and that of Alan Carter would be flushed out to sea when the seiner returned to open sea to flush its bait tank.

Vanchester climbed back up into the pilot house. He heard only the wind and the rain pelting the lid of the bait tank.

- He saw more lightning to the east. The wind masked the thunder.

- He relaxed, poured himself some lukewarm coffee and felt confident *no one saw nothin'* except for the pair of ancient eyes positioned between the crates where Jerry had been sleeping.

DON'T GET AROUND MUCH, ANYMORE

Lousy, cold, and repetitious, the thunder and lightning that came with the current storm, had been lighting up the Bay Area to the point that all the TV crews were out aiming cameras at the heavens for another slow day news story.

Californians can be weird about any deviation in weather patterns. And more weirdness was predicted for the week ahead.

If Jazzy had a cell phone, she would have heard rain was on the way and made the agonizing trek to the homeless shelters in the Tenderloin. It was a painful hike for old bones.

No money. No home. Jazzy Montgomery, once the belle of San Francisco, who through chemical abuse had become the Queen of the used-to-be's cried in torrents. The man she'd known for most of her life—her companion in the last agonizing times of her life—had been snuffed and dumped in the maggot bin.

Unable to wait for a break in the downpour, the small woman crawled from the makeshift shelter on Pier 47 to find a cop. She was desperate.

Feverish and now drenched, she shuffled toward the 24-hour Denny's across the street from Fisherman's Wharf between Piers 45 and 47 for help.

Her pallor under the wool navy watchman's cap was a yellowish purple. A cold sore scar in the shape of a jagged star hung on her upper lip beneath her still delicately shaped nose.

Despite her ragged appearance, Jazzy Montgomery had Nob Hill eyes, a stone-cold blue that had seen her share of the good times. Now they were a pool surrounded in a red sea.

All her possessions were tucked inside a weathered high school letterman's jacket misplaced years ago by a Midwest tourist. Under the red and gold jacket with soiled white leather sleeves, she wore a gray long-sleeved sweatshirt with an attached hood.

Three unmatched sweatpants—soaked to the skin—completed the ensemble.

As a kid growing up in Sonoma County, Jazzy never wore shoes. Even at her zenith when she sang blues with the Alexander MacArthur Orchestra at the Mark Hopkins Hotel, Jazzy performed barefoot. "Barefoot in MacArthur Park," was the title of her often dreamed of but never made record deal. Now her feet pained her as she trod on the wet hardwood.

Piano player Jerry Longstreet remembered when Jazzy ran off to LA with the saxophone player in the orchestra. She left a note on the bathroom mirror for her husband on how to mix the baby's formula. The kid grew up to be a stockbroker in San Diego. Baby and his dad never saw Jazzy again.

Jerry had his own love affair. He kick-started with marijuana and fried his wiring with crack cocaine and heroin when he got lucky.

Jerry and Jazzy met at St. Anthony's Kitchen, a homeless shelter and rehab unit. They sang for their supper. Jerry on Piano and Jazzy on vocals.

For a while, they cleaned up. They made it to the venerable now-dead Washington Square Bar & Grill, a popular North Beach media restaurant where owners Ed Moose and Sam Dietsch let them play the house piano for meals.

Customers kept buying the couple drinks.

It did not take long before they were back to Fisherman's Wharf living off tourist handouts.

* * *

Jazzy did not find a cop in Denny's. The manager stopped her at the door, but she had time to notice no cops were inside.

She scanned the cars driving by, hoping to see a patrol car.

She needed a cop, now.

Jazzy doubted she could make it up the hill to Green Street and North Beach Precinct. But she had to, for Jerry's sake. The fucker killed Jerry. She had to tell a cop.

The midnight-colored van belonging to St. Augustine Hospital's Rescue Mission, the Bum Mobile as it was called in the newspaper gossip columns, swept in and pulled Jazzy off the street.

The new restaurant manager took pity on her and called the mission to report Jazzy. Given the crappy weather, he was happy the van only took minutes to arrive.

"I got to get to the North Beach precinct. You can't take me to St. Auggie's unless I want to go."

"It's raining," said the social services volunteer driver.

"I don't need a weather report, I need a cop."

He ignored her and drove her to the Embarcadero and to the homeless shelter aboard the *USS St. Augie,* the fun name given by wags to the new homeless shelter and medical center. The small van drove up the "up" ramp that had been built on the north side of the ship to move ER and other vehicles from pier to flight deck, 56-feet, or about the height of a six-story building. An entire social services community, including the ER, had been designed and built on the massive carrier's flight deck. The rehab and homeless facilities occupied four decks below the hanger deck. Those not needing ER services could use the heavy-duty vehicle elevator on the south side.

Awake and warmer, Jazzy looked out of the rear door glass of the van. Moving up the ramp, she had a wonderful view of San Francisco at night and in the rain. It was a beautiful view—almost heaven—except she knew better. "Goodbye," she whispered and licked her chapped lips.

* * *

Father MacDonald had been up since dawn. It was his turn to volunteer as "Priest of the Night" aboard the Augie. Both the carrier and the old priest had one thing in common. They were both over the hill but still kicking as servants to man and God.

Augie was one of a dozen mothballed carriers set to be repurposed as hospital ships in ports like St. Louis on the Mississippi River; Baltimore; Seattle; National City, CA (San Diego); and New Orleans. The project, first created by Joe Martin's administration, was designed to take care of homeless, veterans and the citizenry for the next two centuries. For the cost of one new aircraft carrier in new dollars, the medical carrier consortium could rebuild half the current fleet.

The uniformed security guard that looked like a Black Homer Simpson stuck his head inside the small chapel. "A nurse in geriatrics sent me to find you. A patient wants to see you, Father Mac."

The good father, who never used his given name of Ronald, walked into the geriatric ward, where Jazzy had ended up after her patch job at the ER. The Geri Ward, the human warehouse—once the carrier's hanger deck—filled up by midnight. That is when the winos, young or old, fall on their heads, the punks OD and the drug deals go very bad.

Father Mac labeled drunks that were homeless as winos, as did his longshoreman father. Drunks were weak souls, and it still took everything he had to force himself to be compassionate. It was not always like that with him, he thought. Is losing his social filters a curse of growing old? Otherwise, he was careful to be *au courant* with trendy PC phrases and labels. He still called Asians Orientals.

* * *

The priest followed nurse Cilla Davis, a Filipino nurse who had married a retired Space Force officer she met at Space Port Philippines on the eastern coast from Manilla. The so-called Geri Ward was a quarter full, filled with sad eyes. Some coherent. Some happy to be warm. Some happy to be alive. Some about to be dead.

Cilla pointed to a bed in the corner.

Father Mac approached with care. "Yes, she is from the neighborhood," he mumbled to himself. On rainy days, a few homeless would enter Saints Peter and Paul and sit in the rear pews.

She looked into the eyes of the priest, one pair of ancient eyes to another. She wasn't pleading. She was an honest messenger. He had seen so many eyes before that he could tell apart the cheaters, the convicts, and the convenience liars. Eyes of the dead tell no tales. Jazzy whispered into the priest's ear: "A tall sonofabitch killed Jerry and stuffed him down a hole in a boat." She gagged on a mouthful of phlegm.

"Did you tell the police?"

"No time. No time. I'll tell you."

"Of course. Did you see the man's face?"

"Yes, I've seen him before on the pier. He works on the fishing boat." Jazzy coughed and shook her head side to side.

"Let me go get the policeman."

The next spasm of coughing brought up a flood of blood.

Frightened, the padre ran for the nurse.

When he returned to her bedside with the nurse, both could tell Jazzy had passed.

* * *

Father Mac closed his eyes while repeating the prayer for the departed. This visit with Jazzy was not new. For a couple of years, she would arrive in the ER breathless, agitated and with her eyes scared, and she would tell anyone that listened that her Jerry had been murdered "or worse" on the docks. She repeated her story with each visit. This time it was true.

And on this morning, in the wee hours, Jazzy joined the cosmos where the clouds didn't hurt her feet. It was time for her to get busy. She had to find Jerry, her husband, because no one else missed him.

No cops.

Another perfect crime.

7.
WHO KNOCKED UP, BABY CAKES?

Two Short Stories

Cantina Psalm:

Don't ask, it's complicated

NARCISSISM BEGINS AT HOME

When you are twelve years old and spoiled rotten, the pronoun "me" is spelled with mega-sized letters worthy of a seven-story Times Square electronic billboard. But when you are seventeen and in the throes of a not-so-immaculate conception, new words take on a special meaning. For example, "they" as in, "I was drunk, and *they* don't understand" and "we" as in Madonna and child for infinity.

Melissa Martin, now six months pregnant, was not happy as she stood next to her grandfather on Cruise Line Pier 2, south of the Bay Bridge along the Embarcadero.

She did not join him in waving goodbye to her parents, who were somewhere aboard *Luxembourg*, a state-of-the-art NASA-constructed nuclear-powered ship designed to mimic a gigantic space community.

"I don't see them," said Carling.

Missy yawned. "I'm hungry."

"It should be quite an adventure," he added, "If I were ten years younger you couldn't have kept me off that ship."

The Lux, or Deluxe as it was advertised, was not a run of the mill commercial ocean liner. Passengers were required to help run the largest vessel ever constructed. Everyone accepted had a task to perform. It was named at random for a nation with a reputation for peace.

Gene Carling had written about the then under-construction Lux ten years earlier as editor of the San Francisco *Daily News*. This was the first time he had seen the completed ship. The NASA project was an entire floating city (with alleys and parks): an on-Earth experiment for the first planned domed community in outer space.

Built in a San Diego shipyard, the *Luxembourg* (the first NASA ship commissioned), completed its sea trials earlier in the year and was making a final stop in San Francisco before heading on its world tour. Next stop: Hawaii.

The project—called Fort Hope—was a final year-long test of the basic human essentials needed to construct the first city on Mars. The new city (to be called Metropolis), the first self-contained frontier post on another moon or planet, would (when completed) dwarf in size the current 20-person Interplanetary Space Station dome now in operation on the red planet. Being on the NASA ship was a good way to test all the non-human apparatuses for quality and need. Isolation had already been tested aboard the previous international space stations still in orbit around the Earth.

The Martins signed on for a month. Joe agreed to assist in any way he could—working on legal documents ranging from passenger wills to double-checking NASA commodities contracts. Victoria was assigned to the on-board hospital.

Joe Martin, who was revered by many NASA scientists for his floating hospital concept, was granted sea plane fly-off privileges to return home, a gesture not granted to other non-emergency passengers. Timing was set for them to be back in San Francisco well ahead of Missy's June due date.

* * *

"Why are we here?" Missy asked. "They can't see us."

"I'll bet they can," Gene said. "Besides, bonding with your widower grandfather can be a new tradition."

"What tradition? I see you all the time."

"We're going to have a terrific time together," he said and continued to exaggerate his wave. "Besides, I had to come into the city to pick you up."

Missy's maternal grandfather, a lanky first-generation American of Swedish parents, blondish, was seventy something and wore a baseball cap but still put his hand across his eyebrows in a frozen salute to catch sight of the Martins.

To Missy it was a futile effort: one pile of ants waving at another. "What if it hits an iceberg and sinks? Possible," she teased half-heartedly.

"No one has ever seen an iceberg off of Honolulu...much less the entire Pacific Ocean."

"You think?" Missy loved her poppa, but truth be told she had lobbied long and hard to stay with her society darling sister Carly, who, according to *San Francisco Magazine*, was one of the city's most eligible young public lawyers.

Missy knew that if she stayed with Carly at her Russian Hill townhouse that she would experience *laissez les bon temps rouler* while she could.

Truth be told, Carly would leave her alone and not ask so many questions. Missy didn't want to discuss the baby or its father because she knew she was going to give the child away. She expected a tsunami of questions, comments, and planning sessions if she spent the remainder of her pregnancy with Joe and Victoria and her only grandparent.

Cold. Harsh. Missy understood there would be no fairy-tale ending. Uniting father and mother of the new baby was not going to happen. On that she was firm.

But to the rest of the world, Missy didn't announce that fact.

Everyone assumed she would keep the child and raise it with or without its father.

To date and much to the chagrin of family, she had not announced who the father happened to be. Privacy on her part. Unyielding stubbornness according to her parents.

Joe and Victoria were beside themselves. How could a teen keep such a secret for so long, and why?

The first of two long blasts from the ship's horn startled Missy. She stiffened at hearing the manmade *basso profundo* that blared for miles around.

She grabbed her grandfather's hand. "Whoa, what was that?"

"That's the captain telling the world that this monster is about to leave the dock."

"That WAS loud," she laughed.

The ship's horn along with a lungful of cool salt air cleansed her mood.

"If we hurry, we can drive over the Golden Gate while your folks sail under the Golden Gate Bridge," he said. "It has to go out to sea at low tide, otherwise she won't clear the bottom of the bridge. It's the tallest vessel in the world."

Missy, or DisMissy as he'd called her since she was born, shook her head. "Why are ships girls?"

For once, the former editor of a metropolitan daily newspaper was ready with an answer. He always said being an editor was akin to being a garage sale of information. "It's a long-standing tradition going back to when ships would go off on long voyages. We're talking ancient Greek times naming a ship after a goddess, so she'd guide and protect the crew. And to foster teamwork because the ship was a sailor's wife or mother when out on the bounding main."

"What's bounding main?"

"The ocean. Any ocean. Now, I thought you were hungry?"

"Let's eat."

"Breakfast, lunch, supper?" he asked.

"Food will do." She pointed to Giacalone's Seafood Restaurant across the Embarcadero from where the Lux was docked.

"Why did you pick this place?" he asked as they approached the hostess.

"It rhymes with abalone and baloney. So, it has to be good."

Missy picked at her favorite menu dish—fish and chips.

* * *

Gene drove his 1950 Ford Woodie station wagon along Lombard Street toward the Golden Gate bridge, Missy blurted, "Poppa, how many of your woodies were made?"

"Almost twenty-three thousand. Ford had to make them in a separate location. They weren't mass produced."

She turned stared up at the towers of the massive bridge. "It's red not gold. Why do they call it the Golden Gate?"

It was another kid question. It was also a bittersweet moment for him. It was not that long ago he had answered a similar question to his daughter. *Where do the years go?* He whispered. "The geographical space between the ends of the bridge is called the Golden Gate. That's the strait gold miners back in the eighteen forties and fifties sailed through to land in San Francisco."

"Wow," she mocked. "Someone missed a big clue. They should have painted it gold."

"It could have been worse," he smiled. "The Navy wanted to paint it yellow so it would be easier to see. But it's not really named after the color."

"How?"

"What color is it?"

"I did a story on the bridge painters, and they said it was a custom color named International Orange?" he said. "What do you call it."

"Burnt Sienna or maybe vermillion," she said.

"You wouldn't be wrong. Back when it was built the color was very controversial. What style is the bridge?"

"Art Deco."

"Very good."

"You made us read it at Thanksgiving dinner. I was 10."

"It'll be 100 years old in a couple of months," he said.

"Before I wrote the piece, I thought red rust was probably the only paint color that the bridge builders had because of the Depression. All the other colors were taken so they had plenty of red rust available."

Missy smiled, "So, it could have been blue if that was the only color they had?"

"Just like Cuba," Gene added.

"What's Cuba have to do with anything?"

She fell for one of Gene's quirks. He made silent segues in his head as he changed subjects. That was a trait her older sister loved about Poppa. Missy, however, found it confusing and plain gooney.

"In Cuba, paint is a luxury, and the government rations it. People must wait for the day printed on the ration ticket to buy paint. Too often, the color desired is out of stock when it comes your turn to buy it. That's why you will see entire neighborhoods and old cars painted all different colors: pink, yellow, green...in other words, they take the colors available that day."

"Good to know." She wondered once again what her ex-newspaper editor grandfather didn't know. She remembered his favorite line:

What I don't know is news.

"I love you, Poppa."

* * *

Missy fell asleep in the passenger seat of the woody.

He lifted the white Styrofoam container filled with uneaten fish and chips off her lap.

Her soft features reminded him of his only daughter at a similar age. Missy in many ways was still a girl, while Victoria at the same age already possessed the demeanor of a woman ten years older.

Both were beautiful and had gentle no-nonsense souls. He knew this visit might be the last vestige of her childhood. But who was he kidding? That day had passed. His thoughts switched to predicting what he was in for the next few weeks. Angst, aggravation, or a Zen bonding with a visitor from the future?

* * *

The next morning, Missy arrived in the kitchen a few minutes past 11 a.m. wearing a backward green baseball cap with no logo and a white XXL size men's crew neck tee shirt. Already 5' 11", Gene wondered if she would grow much taller. He was 6' 5" and Victoria was 5' 10".

He had to think hard to remember his, Brit-born wife Sarah's height. He felt a twinge of sadness realizing how much she was fading from his memory. She died five years ago of breast cancer. Then he blurted "Five feet eight inches" while standing at the kitchen sink.

Missy, thinking it was a question, answered, "I'm almost six feet tall. Why did you ask?"

He gave her a confused smile.

"You just said out loud that I was five foot eight. I'm taller?"

He didn't want to bring up that he was thinking of his dead wife. Instead, he diverted to the first thing that came into his mind. "I was thinking about you going to college. Having a baby doesn't mean you can't go to college. Not everyone earns a scholarship to Mills College for grades and volleyball."

"Poppa, in case you haven't noticed, my life has changed. I'm not thinking about college."

"If we bring in a nanny you could do it. I'll help you pay for one."

Missy went silent. She chose to stare out of the kitchen window at everything and nothing.

He placed a cup of coffee in front of her at the rustic table. "Two sweeteners and two gallons of cream. Did I get it right?"

She looked up and smiled.

"Hooray," Gene cheered, "I got a smile."

Missy reached for her grandfather's hand. "Can we talk?"

"Are you going to tell me who the father is?"

"No."

"I'm listening."

"Remember when you found me in the toilet with Harre Ling?"

"Tough thing to forget. He was a bastard to—"

She squeezed his hand. "But we never told anyone, did we? It is still our secret, isn't it?"

"Yes, it is for the best."

"I will answer all your questions truthfully, but you have to promise me. Swear that everything I tell you is a secret. No exceptions. You have to choose. Me or mom. You can't have it both ways."

"Go on," he gestured with his hand. "I promise."

She said, "I remember once when you and dad were arguing over sources of information. You said client privilege for a lawyer was the same thing as a journalist protecting his news source."

Gene nodded. "There are exceptions."

"Your dad is a lawyer. He'll argue blue is black. Not with me. Not between us," he said.

Missy's eyes darted, "That's the way it has to be between us. Nothing I say about the baby, or the father can be repeated to anyone on this planet. Got it?"

"Why all the secrecy?"

"I'm not going to keep the baby. Garrett Ellis is helping me with the paperwork. It's a done deal. I won't get to see it. An unplanned child deserves to be raised by a family—someone other than a teenage mother."

"Have you thought this out?"

"Thinking? If I had half a brain, I wouldn't be in this soap opera."

"Missy don't be like me—everything is not a joke. No one in the family will approve of you giving away the baby. I don't approve."

"It's my choice."

"That's selfish. That baby is family whether you like it or not. My great grandchild and Joe and Victoria's grandbaby. At least discuss it with them."

"OK, we're discussing it. What would you do?"

"Keep it. You and I can raise it until you find a husband."

"Are you serious?"

"Yes. That baby belongs to our family. You can't give away a human being like it was a nineteen fifty-one Ford. I want it to stay with my family. You have no way of knowing, but families do adjust. You're not the first person in history to have an unwed child."

"I don't want to be a mother."

"Too late, Baby Cakes. That bump under your T-shirt should be your first clue."

"Poppa, I don't want to spend my visit with you talking about me being pregnant. I know I am, and I am frustrated because I can't do anything about it."

"When are you going to tell them?"

"I haven't decided, and I didn't want to worry them on the cruise."

"They're actually happy. It's not the best of circumstance but that is their grandchild. You'll hurt them deeply."

"You don't seem hurt."

"I wasn't raised Catholic."

"Have they said anything to you?"

"Lots of things but not one mention of you giving up the child."

"Maybe if they discussed things with me instead of assuming—maybe if they did that nobody would get hurt feelings. No, one discusses things with me in this family."

"Why's that? It's because you pull that teenage shit—stonewall what you don't want to talk about. This is real life. You have just as much responsibility to talk about this situation as your family."

"I'm talking to you. You are family."

"Being pregnant is also about having to grow up ten years sooner than you should. You must stop thinking like a child—like it or not. You can't wait for the world to fix it. You must talk to your parents. You must plan."

"Poppa, enough, can we please not talk about it."

"One last thing. This baby is just as much about Harre's family as it is ours."

"No, it's not! No."

"How can you say that? I didn't see anyone else in that toilet stall at the party."

Seeing the horror on Missy's face was enough for him to stop questioning her.

His voice was almost a whisper. "You know in the eyes of the law—you weren't at fault. What he did to you is a sex crime and it's totally egregious. I can't believe a man of his position and family would do something so stupid and illegal."

"Poppa, I was being stupid. I was running around naked—"

"That doesn't give anyone a right to do what he did. No right."

"Then why didn't we go to the police?"

"That is all on me. My fault. I should have told Joe and Victoria. I thought I'd have at least a day to think it over before I approached your parents with what Harre did to you. I didn't figure on him falling from the goddamned bridge."

"Too late. You can't tell them anything, you promised me. Poppa, I'm begging you, let's leave it alone. I don't want people to know *how* I got pregnant, especially my parents. Let the world guess all they want. It isn't any of their business. And Harre doesn't deserve to be punished."

At that point, Gene's face turned red with anger and frustration. "In the eyes of the law, our high and mighty district attorney raped you. He is responsible. He had a moral responsibility to protect and serve. Raping you is not protection. He needs to be strung up."

"He can't be punished anymore." Tears fell down her face. "He never put his dick inside me. It wasn't him. It's not his baby!" Missy ran to her bedroom.

* * *

Gene Carling moved his hands over his face. His mind was racing. It was like a rapid-fire time-lapse scenario of jigsaw pieces falling from the sky into place onto a family room table without rhyme or reason.

His face turned white. He'd believed Harre raped Missy. He'd figured the oral sex he witnessed had been part of their lovemaking—their affair—not the extent of it. Until now he thought he knew the truth. Seeing is believing. That sonofabitch Harre was the villain all along. But now? Now, he realized, he knows nothing.

* * *

It was mid-afternoon before Missy left her bedroom and joined him at the kitchen table. He was watching TV news on the small set next to the counter toaster.

His granddaughter moved next to him and gave him a long embrace. Sometimes it was hard to believe she was only seventeen. Today was one of those times.

Missy whispered into his ear. "Poppa, I will explain everything. I promise. We'll talk over dinner. But right now, I want to eat."

Gene reacted to the conversational switch like a drowning man being tossed a life ring. "Lunch?"

"I still want breakfast."

"Oatmeal, toast, grapes, and I can scramble eggs if you like?"

"Breakfast and orange juice and a cheeseburger."

He wiped a tear from his face and chuckled. "Juicer is under the buffet countertop. Oranges are in a basket out on the back porch. Knock yourself out."

"We're in the middle of a vineyard—can we be like the French and have wine with every meal?"

"No alcohol, mom."

"Yes, of course." She pursed her lips. "An ocean of vines and I can't have a sip."

"Go ahead, have wine if you want your kid to look like—"

"Like what?" she interrupted.

"I'm sorry that was uncalled for... I was trying to be funny."

"I know I'm pregnant. I wasn't thinking of polishing off a jeroboam."

"How do you even know a word like that?"

"What word?"

"Jeroboam."

"You can thank your wine snob daughter, who buys it by the jeroboam."

"Really? That much. What's a jeroboam hold these days?"

"Six regular sized wine bottles."

"Who's her connection?"

Missy answered, "Your buddy Ted Salazar. He ships her a wooden crate with four jeroboams inside."

"Fine, we can have a glass with dinner."

"What's for dinner?" she insisted.

"We haven't decided on breakfast."

"Poppa, I'm thinking about what kind of wine we'll have for dinner. Since I'm getting rationed, I'd like to pick a red wine I like."

"You choose."

"Good. After breakfast, let's walk down to the winery shop so we can bond *some more* buying wine." She smirked and put her arm around her grandfather. "Besides the guy behind the counter is cute—a lot like you," she added for effect.

"Can you handle walking a mile?" he asked.

"Can you?"

The Salazar wine shop was on the side of Healdsburg Road at the beginning of the vineyard's dirt road that ran from the highway to the river.

* * *

It would be hard to distinguish the rows of Salazar Vineyards wine stock from other wineries in Sonoma County. Except Eugene Carling's bungalow sat in the center of a huge tract of grape stock laid out in north/south rows. In general, most of the vineyards around the world run north to south to receive morning sun on one side and afternoon sun on the other.

Once his craftsman had been the Salazar family's main home, but now it was his after they built a new complex a decade earlier. The few sheds and a large barn around the house remained in Ted Salazar's control. All were filled with the machines and fertilizers needed to grow the grapes.

The hard-packed dirt road straight as a string ran the length of the winery. North was the Healdsburg Road. South beyond the forest of trees growing tall on the banks of the Russian River was the new main winery operation.

* * *

At 3 p.m., when the pair began the trek to the highway, the sky was clear. Now, thanks to a low cloud marine layer that arrived with the regularity of a commuter train schedule, temperatures were dropping fast.

Once the sun had disappeared, Missy put on her cardigan sweater that she had been carrying around her shoulders. Gene glanced at a copse of ubiquitous coastal valley oaks ahead. He feigned a pebble in his shoe to sit on a grayed wood bench under the trio of trees. He was the one needing a breather. From his vest pocket, he produced a plastic bottle of water.

She drank half and stopped to be polite.

"No, finish it," he said.

He stood, grimaced, and walked out of earshot. "I have to make a call," he said and took a deep breath.

"Are you alright?" Missy tilted her head and pushed her eyebrows together.

The call did not last long before he returned to the bench.

She handed him the still half full bottle.

He sipped it and took another deep breath. "Ready to finish our march?"

Halfway to the wine shop, Missy realized in all the years she visited him she'd never asked, "How did you end up living here?"

"When I was editor of the *Daily News*, Ted's dad Frank invited me to a harvest feast. When the grape picking season is over, they celebrate with a family and friends dinner out in the winery. We became friends, and a couple of years later he asked if I'd be willing to buy the house. It was Frank's way of making sure the original family home stayed intact. He didn't want his son or anyone to tear it down, sell it or remove when they enlarged the operation."

"They must have been good friends."

"It was a bit odd at first. I rented the house to Ted and his wife even though it was right in the middle of their winery. He lived there until I retired from the newspaper and Ted moved to his wonderful new home next to the river."

"So, anyone buying the winery will have to deal with you."

"That's exactly what Frank had in mind. He couldn't bear the thought of having the land fall out of family ownership. I never got to ask him before he died."

"Do you get along with Ted?"

"Yes. The winery is in good hands. His wife is as solid as they come."

"Carly and grandmother will be very happy to hear that her wine connection won't be going away anytime soon."

* * *

Inside the wine store, the clerk was in the middle of the busy work that needed to be done before he closed the shop for the day.

Gene held two bottles of Cabernet Sauvignon grown from California grapes. One from Napa's Ric Forman Winery and the other a bottle of Messier Central Valley Cabernet Sauvignon. The labels reminded him of a day long ago when he covered the grand openings of both labels for one of the magazines for which he freelanced wine articles.

Missy came up to him and they linked arms. "Don't hate me," she said. "I can't remember great granddad's name?"

"Rupert Carling, and your great-grandmother, Emma, was a World War II war bride from London."

"I knew that—maybe. What kind of a name is Rupert?"

"British. If you'd like, after dinner we can go on my computer and check out our family Ancestry.com file."

"Mom warned me that you've traced the family tree to Adam and Eve."

"It's not a family joke. On your mother's side, a great, great, great grandparent set had first names Adam and Eve."

Missy frowned. She stared down at her feet. "You're joking. I can never tell sometimes."

"Upside of you being pregnant is I get to tinker with the family tree or at least half of it."

She handed him a bottle of vintage California chardonnay by Husch Vineyards off the wineshop shelf. Husch, she learned was fifty miles north in Mendocino County.

"Young but impressive," he said, "and expensive."

"Like me." Her cheek pushed against his shoulder. "Can we catch a cab back to your place?"

"No cabs out here."

"I was kidding."

"But I called the Salazar's for one of them to come get us." Gene put his arm around her shoulder, "I've been meaning to talk to you about your dad...about his cancer."

"Please no more bad news."

"We should talk about it."

"Yes, mom said he's getting better, right? Mom's the doctor in the family."

"He's in remission, but that doesn't mean he's cured."

"You'd tell me if it was more serious," she asked.

Missy's sad eyes stared into her grandfather's. "I love him so much."

* * *

Gene's call had been to Sebastian Salazar, Ted's youngest son, who arrived at the wine shop. The young man pulled up in a well-used 1955 Ford pickup truck. The fifteen-year-old was already accomplished driving a stick shift. He didn't know quite what to make of seeing a pregnant teen near his age move next to him on the truck's bench-style seat between him and Mr. Carling.

"What are you going to name the baby?" the boy asked.

"Sebastian," Missy said, making Gene laugh.

Gene joined in. "What if it's a girl?"

"I don't know Sebastian's just as good a name for a girl."

Gene laughed. "Her name will be Stella."

"Why Stella?" Sebastian asked. "Are you a cousin?"

"I'm not your cousin. Stella means star, and no one in our family is named Stella, so I won't be hurting anyone's feelings if I don't name the baby after them."

"Too late," Sebastian said. "My mom's name is Stella."

"Opps," she offered.

He ground the gears going from first to second and laughed. "Anybody else want to drive?"

"Beats walking," she said.

Sebastian stared at Missy. Her face was radiant. Her cheeks rosy from the cold air. "What's your husband do for a living?"

Wasting no time, she turned toward the teen. "He's a spy. I can't tell you more."

* * *

Earlier, when Gene made a call on his cellphone, he also made arrangements for the Salazar family housekeeper Maria Fierro and her daughter Rosa to fix dinner. Gene was generous and paid the willing Fierro women for their help.

When Missy followed her grandfather into the bungalow, Maria and daughter were busy peeling avocados, onions and cilantro and chopping a sheet of flank steak for the carne asada burrito dinner. The dish was Missy's favorite, especially when it was home made. The table was set, and a bottle of Salazar red wine was open and breathing.

Missy was pleasantly surprised. She liked the idea of having dinner prepared for them. It gave her a little extra time to think whether she'd tell her grandfather, who was the father of her baby.

Maria, a gentle-faced woman close to 60, chased them from the kitchen in a thick Hispanic accent. Rosa giggled and said in a totally gringo accent, "Mom, this isn't your kitchen."

In Spanish, the slim woman responded, "Es cuando estoy cocinando."

Rosa was older than Missy by maybe a year or two. They glanced at each other with a smiled that hinted a friendship could blossom in the weeks ahead.

Before leaving the kitchen, Missy noticed several maternity smocks neatly pressed on hangers the doorknob leading outside.

Maria caught Missy looking toward the garments. "Por favor, llévate cualquiera de las batas premamá si te gustan."

Missy held up the four smocks.

Rosa offered, "My mom says you may have them if you like them."

Missy held them close. "I love them. They're not so frilly." The mono-colored tops were dark colors: burgundy, navy, dark green and a Scots plaid. "Thank you so much."

"Nuestra famila es muy fertile," Maria said.

"If you like I can drive you into town. There's a mom's shop that is with it—style wise," Rosa said and explained that it would be no trouble because she was a student at the nearby community college and drove into Healdsburg three times a week.

Gene walked over to Maria and quietly put his hand around her shoulder.

"These are all fine," Missy said. "Perfect."

* * *

Gene thanked the Fierro women for a great dinner, consisting of the Asada burritos, refried beans, rice cooked Mexican style and a rich flan pudding for dessert.

"You've done enough," Gene said. "I will do the dishes."

Maria objected until Rosa whispered into her mother's ear.

As soon as they were alone, Missy's face slowly became sadder.

"You made a friend in young Rosa," Gene said.

"She's nice," Missy offered.

Gene didn't waste time. "Can we talk about the baby?"

"Yes, but not about the father."

"Is there any chance I can convince you to keep the baby?"

"I don't want to raise a baby without a father." Missy didn't think about what she had just said until she saw her grandfather's face.

"Have you talked about the baby with him."

"He's out of the picture so why talk about him."

"Do you hate him."

"No. Not really. It just happened."

"Who else did you make love with before, during or after the party?"

Hearing his question, Missy, who had been looking away, quickly turned to face him. "Does it matter?"

"Maybe. Maybe Harre wouldn't have killed himself if he knew the truth."

"You're saying that knowing he had to face my parents that I'd been sucking him off might have put him on that bridge."

"Don't use ugly words with me."

"Was there anyone else that night? Who was he, Missy?"

"If I tell you, I'm convinced you'll do something stupid." Missy squeezed her lower lip, biting it harder than she intended. "Poppa, I got pregnant. You've got to stop asking me. No more water torture. We agreed to keep quiet. So, stop with the questions."

Gene let out a deep breath. "You said you'd tell me everything."

"If you don't know then you can't blab about it to anyone. No one."

Eugene Carling shut up. He decided since they'd be together all summer than he didn't need to push her. He decided to let her tell him. Both could live with that.

Then unexpectedly she moved into his arms and whispered in his ear. She softly mouthed a name that only they could hear. She followed with how and where they conceived her baby.

Gene turned away from her. He stumbled through the front door and out on to the veranda. Emotionally, he felt the same shock and disbelief that came over him the day he heard the news broadcast that Harre Ling was dead. "O, my God, Missy are you sure? Tell me, you're sure!"

MALVINA'S

Cosmopolitan habitues of San Francisco, Chicago, Boston, and Manhattan, who cheat a few years off their real ages by dressing well. A lithe woman like Carla Boris, who colored away any gray hair, could claim being 35 instead of pushing 50. Her professional style had Tom Gresham fooled. He didn't dwell on it, but he figured she was close to his age. In Tom's world, Art Garcia dressed from ads out of *Gentleman's Quarterly* while his pal John Wald was a t-shirt and jeans guy, who looked ten years older than Garcia. In truth their ages were reversed.

The assistant coroner fought off aging by focusing on taking care of herself by applying good nutrition, exercise, and a sophisticated wardrobe appropriate for being forty-five years old. Her make-up was subtle, and she avoided plunging into the Botox trap that ruins so many middle-aged women. Puffy lips do not make anyone look younger. They make you look like a circus clown. But what set her apart was her smarts and solid sense of humor, traits that made Tom Gresham look forward to meeting her.

A driverless SuperUber dropped her off at the front door of Malvina's Coffee House at Stockton and Union Streets. She was dressed in her best business look. Her face was radiant and her make up applied flawlessly. She was a credit to all she learned at Goodwin College in East Hartford, CT.

She had called the meeting and told Tom that she would make it worth his while on several counts. He accepted with pleasure and hearing his happy tone made her less nervous.

To him it was a business lunch with a business pro, where he could use the mayor's office credit card and order anything he wanted. He had dozens of meetings like this over the span of his seven years as Joe Martin's bodyguard cum administrative assistant.

She had been sexually attracted with Gresham's faded blonde hair and green eyes. But maneuvering him into bed she found herself on uncharted ground because she was married and a bit rusty on the boy girl dating patois. But she also knew nothing ventured nothing gained. If she was going to cheat for the first time with another man she'd do it in a nanosecond with a man, who looked like Tom. As she would learn, Gresham was a bit more complicated.

Tom was waiting at the window table facing west into Washington Square and his flat one block away. The weather was turning sour fast.

Malvina's had always defined to him what San Francisco coffee houses should be like. Owners over the years kept the brick walls to support high transom windows that in turn always allow dusty light to penetrate inside, even on the gloomiest days.

The venerable café in North Beach was jammed and noisy. It was named for the century-ago beat generation poet, singer, and songwriter Malvina Reynolds, who became best known for writing "Little Boxes" back in the 1960s.

Sadly, Malvina did not survive into the twenty-first century, but her homemade songs, "What have they done to the rain?" "Morning Town Ride" will go on as long as North Beach stays bohemian.

The duo gave each other perfunctory hugs at the café table. He helped her slip off her wet trench coat. He walked over to the coat rack to hang it when up a jagged bolt of white and gold flashed across the park, engulfing the coffee house in brilliant light

"Wow," a collective shout rose. All conversation ceased.

An imperceptible slice of time later, the thunder blasted and cracked overhead.

Gasps of surprise rather than fear came and went from the filled room. "Climate change," she offered. "We never used to get so many thunderstorms. I can deal with the rain but being struck by lightning isn't something I want to worry about."

The hanging khaki-colored light globes dimmed ever so slightly.

"That *was* close," Gresham offered.

A round of laughs and increased chatter filled Malvina's.

"The Gods are not pleased." Tom smirked. "Have you ever worked on a lightning victim?"

"No. Next question."

"Menu?"

"Thank you."

Both ordered Super Latte's, the universal name for soy-based fake coffee that for years had successfully replaced natural beans. Independent coffee houses like Malvina's couldn't compete with skyrocketing demand for real beans and eventually embraced the mass-produced brown powder. At least the indies kept prices of faux flavored coffee at half of what the big chains charged.

Coffee drinkers did not mind paying $5 new dollars for a latte but not the $15 RePeet's charged per cup for real coffee.

After a decade, few remembered the old coffee bean taste except those connoisseurs who could discern the taste between Arabica (Starbucks et al) and Robusta (instant coffee) beans.

Before they could even get close to discussing business, torrents of rain splashed hard against the large plate-glass window. Tom placed the back of his hand on the pane. It was ice cold.

Tom had been looking at her in the window reflection. "You look terrific."

"Thank you. I was hoping I'd see you in anything other than a lab coat. Sadly, they don't make designer lab coats."

"You looked great in white. What did you bring me?"

She reached inside her purse and handed Tom a blank toe tag that she used to identify bodies. SOP.

Tom had asked to let him know if bodies of interest ever showed up on one of her slabs.

She was eager to help the mayor.

What she didn't know that it was Art Garcia doing the asking via Tom Gresham. Art's firm had been hired by the Carter family to locate Alan, whose last known address was in the Bay Area. Tom was on Art's payroll for the Carter case.

"The Coast Guard delivered two bodies first thing this morning. You're the first outside of my office to know one was an older man—maybe 70 with no visible wounds and the other—maybe 35 was stabbed in the heart." She showed him iPhone images of the dead men.

"Send the images to my phone," he said.

"Of course."

"We appreciate the heads up."

She stared at him with a mischievous smile. "Maybe dinner, tonight?"

"I'll need a note from your husband."

"I was hoping you wouldn't remember."

"The second you're not married, call me." Tom smiled. Carla Boris was among the best-looking bureaucrats in the city. She would have no problem finding men to make some sheet music with her on the side. But Gresham wasn't going to be the first to cross that line.

"Are you really that noble or is it that I'm forty-five years old?"

"Don't make me the bad guy that busts up the marriage. If things go south, you'll always blame me. I'm not in good shape right now. A woman I happen to love very much is leaving me. It hurts. The thought of starting up new with someone this very moment wouldn't be fair to either one of us."

Carla Boris nodded. She patted Tom's hands. "Too bad, I had such plans for you this afternoon."

"How about a raincheck? I mean that sincerely. Let me know who the young guy turns out to be."

"Happy to help. Don't be surprised if I take you up on the raincheck."

"Done deal."

8.
ODD DUCK SEASON
Sketches

Cantina Psalm:

The whole city is one cel overlay over another.

ONE WOMAN TOUGH CROWD

The ponytailed strawberry blonde with a gap in her upper front teeth, a dental anomaly that her parents never fixed because they thought it looked cute, arrived at a narrow, two-level wooden Edwardian era house with a garage occupying half of the street level.

Dressed in comfortable jeans and a neatly pressed sweatshirt over a white-collared blouse, the thin woman with a milky way of freckles across her cheekbones knocked on 750 Filbert. While waiting for the door to open, she checked the back of a business card to make sure she had the right address. She did.

She judged this part of Filbert to be a typical working class neighborhood. Glancing to her right across busy noisy Columbus

Avenue, big chain link fence surrounded the playground to Sts. Peter & Paul School for Boys. To her left, Filbert and Mason Streets intersected. One of the famous cable car lines used Mason to get to Fisherman's Wharf.

A flat-nosed 30-something man with uncombed black hair and an ugly black eye answered the door. Loud TV football chatter blared from inside. Unshaven, thick chested and wearing sweatpants and a wrinkled undershirt, he asked in a sleepy voice "What's up bueyful?"

"Are you Mike Kinder?"

"That's me?"

"I'm Annee. The rental agency sent me. It's spelled with two n's and two e's."

"What is?" The man was sincerely dumbfounded.

"My name is Ann*ee* not Ann*ie*."

"If you say so. Got a last name?"

"I'm one of those one namers…like Tee R.A.S.H."

"What?"

"Tee R.A.S.H., the singer…never mind." In a city of bright lights, she realized this man had a few bulbs burned out.

"Come on in, ignore the Tee R.A.S.H on the sofa—hiz name is Ezra. You got luggage or something?"

She looked at the scratches around his face and a large bandage on his right ear.

"Luggage?" he repeated.

"Problem. —I paid the cabbie. I went to the trunk to get my backpack and computer, but he drove off, leaving me standing there."

"That is such an old con. What color was the cab?"

"Gray and red."

"That's Alien Cabs. They hire anyone that ain't blind and if they have a rap sheet the mo' bettah."

She watched him squeeze an oval metallic earring the size of a dime. "Yeah, gimme Alien Cabs." He smiled at her while the LOBE bot connected the call. "After the second pandemic, no one would take taxi jobs except the undocumented—"

Kinder interrupted himself. "Listen, this is Mike Kinder over at North Beach precinct. One of your stooges took off with my friend's luggage in the back of his cab. I want it back. I want it now. You know where I live. I don't give a shit that you're busy. And if it ain't on my doorstep in ten minutes I'm coming down there with cuffs and tire locks, understand? Yeah, yeah, you'll recognize me. I'm the cop that busted your face last time you pulled this stunt."

Annee's eyes diverted to Kinder's ear cellular, the only earphone with Internet connections. Squeeze and talk anywhere in the world. She was impressed he had one considering they were $3,500 *a pop*.

Her LOBE was in her pilfered suitcase. That was the big scare she had in having her luggage ripped off.

Ezra Ounce, an older man and much better dressed. His clothes were wrinkled but looked clean. He was slouched on the sofa watching a half-wall-sized TV. "Who's winning"? she asked

He sat up. "Niners are way behind, but what's new."

"I'm Annee." She smiled and revealed the space in her front teeth to the older roommate.

"Ezra. Ezra Ounce. I hope to God you're Kinder's new tenant. He owes me money," Ezra said, his voice rasped like actor Humphrey Bogart.

"I will be until I find a place of my own."

"It ain't glamours; it makes up by being convenient. Buses on Columbus Avenue twenty-four seven and the cable car is a block up the hill on Mason Street. It'll take yuz downtown—that is if yuz like tourists."

Annee was trying not to laugh. "I don't recognize your accent, where are you from?"

"Pittsburgh. Polack Dutch. Mikey's from Philly."

"Damn, I should have known."

Mike returned from the kitchen holding three cans of cold beer.

He tossed one to Ezra and handed one to Annee.

She popped it open and guzzled the can.

Kinder was impressed.

Ezra more so with her figure.

Talking as they went along; the trio began a tour of the two-level flat. "Where you from?" Ezra asked.

"Too many questions, "Kinder replied, annoyed at his roomie.

"Are you both cops?"

"How can you tell?" Kinder smiled, revealing bad teeth.

"The rental agent told me."

"Yeah, yeah, we wuz until we got shitcanned for rousting with civilians." Ezra's voice jumped several octaves. "Citizens, bullshit, the old priest deserved it—fucking goodie-goodie."

"She don't care, Ez. Drop it," Kinder said.

"So, what are you guys doing now?"

"Bartending—little of this, little of that," Kinder said.

"What do you do, skinny? Ezra asked.

"Looking for a job..."

"Lemme guess," Kinder said, "you're a model, ain't ya?"

"I've done that. But I'm looking for bar work. I'm a good cocktail waitress."

The trio stood in what would be her room. "This is one of the bigger old-fashioned houses, Kinder said, "Old, but you can see the bedroom is big. Walk-in closet has plenty of room. Bathroom is across the hall but it's private. Ez and I have separate rooms upstairs with toilets."

There were no curtains in the window that faced Filbert.

"So," Mike began, "you want the room?"

"I'm still looking around. I'd like to find something more permanent, so I don't have to move, again."

Ezra spoke up, "Yous have to fucking wait in line for a place of your own. Unless you're bucks up. You got that kind of dough, sweetie?"

"Annee," Mike interrupted. "Your door key is on the pillow there and if you lose your key there are extras in the bowl by the front door. Like I said, Ez and I live upstairs; we got opposite flats in the back by the laundry room. You got downstairs. We all share the living room and kitchen. Linens in one of the closets. The maid was here yesterday. She comes once every ten years."

The doorbell rang.

Kinder opened the door and glanced down at a brown suitcase with leather straps and brass buckles and a green backpack.

"Yours?"

"Yes. That's what it looks like," Annee said, peering around Kinder's burly frame. "Thank God."

"It better be." Mike closed the front door. "So, do you want the place?"

"Maybe? Is this a cop hangout? If I work cocktails, I don't want a lot of noise in the morning," she said opening the suitcase snaps.

"We're church mice." Ezra offered. "Nobody moves around here in the morning."

Kinder added, "Look, if you take the room pay me what you think it's worth. I trust you."

Annee opened her purse and handed Kinder four c-notes. "That's each month, right?" The LOBE was where she left it.

"Of course. Ezra, do something to earn your beer. Take her bag her room."

The older cop obeyed. "He's all talk, especially when he has an audience," Ezra said as he brushed by her with her suitcase.

"Are you married?" Kinder asked.

"Not while I'm in San Francisco."

"I get it."

"No, you don't."

"Well, if you have any more hassles, let me know. No extra charge for the personal security. And, if you like, since you're here more than a week, you can say yous my fiancé—Annee Kinder. If the jerks catch Kinder is your last name, you'll be left alone. I'm still the law on the streets around here. And, you don't have a last name anyhows, right, miss one-name?"

She grinned. "OK, that works. I'm Annee Kinder."

Mike handed her keys to her room and continued the tour. "One of those keys opens the laundry room in the back by the kitchen. If we do have company, we stay in the living room and kitchen. Keep your door shut no one will bug you. And one more thing: I hope you're not a goodie-goodie because we get noisy, especially if there's four or five of us playing poker. And, uh, we do coke. Don't let that be a shock to you. Lotsa of people do snorts here. Just don't flaunt it."

Annee stopped midway up the stairs. "Tell me where I can pick up some coke?"

"I got some, how much you want?"

"An ounce."

"Seriously, a whole ounce?"

"I got the cash."

"OK, I'll have an ounce delivered."

"I took you for a local dealer. You don't have an ounce?"

"Look, we're both unemployed," Kinder said. "No credit. You got to be good for the cash. Junior doesn't like welchers."

"Who's Junior?"

"You didn't hear that and don't ask ever again."

She walked back down the stairs. She sat on the bottom step, unzipped her brown ankle boot, and pulled out a 1,000 new dollar bill. "Get me what this will buy?"

"Plenty."

"And one more thing," he said, "and please don't be pissed at me for asking, but are you a working girl?"

Annee turned and walked up the stairs, not answering him. "Do you know the difference between a hooker and a call girl?"

"One is big bucks the other one ain't."

"I'm a call girl, Mikey. Can you handle that? I get two grand a pop to "do" middle aged computer geeks in the back seat of their Tesla's or get driven there by their chauffeurs."

"Expensive broad. OK, if I save up my money I'll come knocking on your door."

"We understand each other. I don't do freebies."

* * *

Annee had been out most of the night since late afternoon. She returned to her new digs at 11 p.m. with a bottle of wine as Kinder was getting ready to open his last beer from the refrigerator. He was well on his way to having an irreversible pot belly.

"You find any coke?" he asked.

"Couple of college boys had a few lines. Bad stuff," she said.

"Where did you go?"

"Met a friend out at Perry's in Cow Hollow."

"That's an old name. Who called it Cow Hollow?"

"Uber driver."

"He must have been an old fart."

"Where's Ezra?"

"Out trying to get laid."

"Have you got my ounce?"

"In your room. I put it under your pillow."

"OK, but that's the last time you enter my room without asking. Got it?"

"Yes, ma'am."

* * *

It must have been two a.m. when newly named Annee Kinder walked slowly down the squeaking wooden steps holding a bottle of wine.

"Jesus Christ," Kinder shouted. "You can't walk around here dressed like that!"

She was in a pair of black panties and a white Salt Lake City Lakes t-shirt, the new Major League Baseball franchise.

"Mike, it's only skin," she said. "I didn't bring many clothes. You've seen women's legs before."

"Not that long or good looking. You'll trip over my hard on."

"That was good stuff you bought me," she said. "I'd even say it was amazing. You didn't step on it, did you?"

"Nope. It's pure shit. One hundred percent."

"Yes, it is. I can't sleep."

"Maybe I can help." He walked up to her.

She could smell the oily herring he had for dinner.

She moved around the old coffee table and went into the kitchen to open her wine.

"I mean it, that coke was worth the price," she said over her shoulder.

Mike stopped at the door. His eyes were on every move she made.

"I'd like to buy another ounce."

"Whoa, I had to look all day to find what I got you."

"I want to cut it up for some friends."

"Don't blab where you got it."

He came over and took the bottle from her and found his opener. He leaned closer, pretending to read the label. His rough chin whiskers brushed the back of her neck. "Is dat wine? Looks like expensive frog shit."

"It is. Two hundred a bottle at Coit Liquor."

"Looks like red wine, I hope you're sharing," he said, after removing the cork.

"Help yourself."

They clinked jelly jars.

"Maybe tonight I can collect on my newlywed thing. What do you think?"

"Man, you don't give up, do you?"

"You're so good looking you make my teeth hurt. I think you're the best-looking woman I seen in this town."

"I'm nothing special, Mike, lots of women look like me. Just give me some space or I'm out of here."

"We're cool."

Annie opened her backpack, which was wet from walking in the rain. She pulled out a twenty-five-caliber handgun.

"Why are you showing me that?"

"In case you or Ezra don't knock on my door before you enter."

"You're a regular one-woman tough crowd."

"Guys like you make me that way."

"Come on, we're jus' messin' wit' you."

"I'll be gone in a month. But I'm going to use your last name? Do you really think wise guys like you will leave me alone if I'm Annee Kinder?"

"Yep. For sure. Done deal."

"Why don't we say we're brother and sister?"

"Nah, I told a lot of people where I bought your coke that you're my new wife. Tol' 'em we got married in Reno last week."

She took back the image and handed him another $1,000 in big bills. "One more ounce."

"That's a lot of cash I seen you with already. Why you staying wit' us? You could be staying at one of those hotels down by Union Square?"

"I won't find coke down there."

Ezra Ounce put his *Racing Form* down. "Yous can walk around the place in those panties any time, we won't bug you."

"Thank you, Ezra." She stared at Mike. "Such a gentleman."

Kinder poured himself some more of her 2010 Chateau Cos d'Estournel, a modest blend of Bordeaux red wines from St. Estephe, France into his jelly jar and headed upstairs to his room. Alone.

ABOARD THE LUX

Victoria Martin stood at the rail of the massive cruise ship. Her thoughts were of Joe, who was too tired to enjoy breakfast because he slept until noon. She remembered breakfast was his main meal.

She believed the ocean voyage would distract her from the reality that Joe's pancreatic cancer was faster moving than the highly curable prostrate. The opposite was true.

Given Joe's deterioration, she never once thought that her father would outlive her husband.

We humans so deceive ourselves about death.

We must, otherwise the sadness of leaving all that you cherish behind is nature at her cruelest.

A tear rolled off her smooth cheek, rolled away from the corner of her mouth and fell into the sea.

* * *

The wide Caloosahatchee River as it drawled its way toward the Gulf of Mexico seldom raised a ruckus, except once a generation when a hurricane would blow through.

Along the south shore of that river, Victoria Carling was raised in a two-story antebellum estate in Fort Myers, Florida. Her father, Eugene, was editor in chief of the *Lee County Traveler*, the Ft. Myers-based daily, and her mother a registered traveling nurse. They raised their only child among the neighboring Ford, Carter, and Edison ancestral summer homes near McGregor Boulevard. The Carters got rich by selling pharmaceuticals. Carter Industries invented the doctor-to-doctor detail salesmen that went door to door pushing pills. Some of them actually saved lives. Of course, everyone knows what the Fords and Edisons were up to over the decades.

Victoria was bright, independent, and beautiful. She found out in her early teens that if a woman doesn't respond blushingly to male teasing, she'll be forever labeled tight kneed or worse. It didn't bother Victoria (never Vicky) that the bubbas in town didn't think kindly of her attitude that she'd prefer to enter a nunnery before she'd let one of the good ol' boys touch her porcelain skin. But she loved making fools of them with jokes the boys didn't get.

With a combination of saved up cash, scholarships and favors owned her father, she got into Stanford University School of Medicine, where she met law student Joseph Martin. The young doctor and lawyer were wed as soon as their Stanford diplomas were signed. Joe was her anti-bubba tonic.

Fort Myers became that place where her parents lived. Nothing more, nothing less. And while she thought she lost her southern lilt by moving to California, the rest of the world knew exactly where her roots lay. *I've been fixin' to tell y'all I ain't gonna die in the South.*

But she did give her daughters southern names—in a way, although it was nothing given much thought. First daughter was Carling, and ten years later Melissa was born. The girls preferred Carly and Missy.

Joe's family background was limited. His grocer dad and stay-at home mom were killed in a traffic accident along Highway One. They died tragically when a bus they had boarded for Big Sur blew a tire and rolled off a rainy mountain road near Santa Cruz. They left Joe, then a three-month-old, behind with neighbors while they enjoyed a brief respite from young parenthood.

Joe was raised with foster families. His education began at St. Peter and Paul's School before it was a boarding facility for orphan boys. He went on to public high school, where he landed an academic scholarship to Stanford. For living costs, he landed a job as a physical education instructor at Saints Peter and Paul after it became a boarding school.

After law school in Berkeley, he joined the San Francisco district attorney's office and she joined St. Vincent's Hospital in the Tenderloin. It wasn't until Joe's second term as mayor that St. Vinnie's became the floating St. Augustine Hospital. There she became head of the trauma unit and held a seat on the board of directors.

Victoria felt a chill as the sun was about to touch the horizon. "That's when it happened. That's where she got pregnant," Victoria said aloud.

Now, more than anything she wanted Joe to see his grand baby before it was too late. That was what made her cry today.

9.
EX, X
Short Story

Cantina Psalm:

If given a choice naïve or lucky, pick lucky.

DELUCA'S UNDERBELLY

Ebony Williams a.k.a. Xandy "the latest Black goddess of whoopee," the barmaid at Clementine's who replaced the recently skipped Shannon Reading, clunked the bar phone back on its hook. Like Shannon, who left town faster than a proverbial bullet, Xandy worked naked behind the bar except for a pair of boxer shorts hiding a black G-string and a pair of cheap sneakers. Wiping her hands on a small towel, she motioned to one of Clementine's strippers sitting at the customer side of the crowded bar.

Xandy, 29, longed to be a front-line dancer instead of tending bar. She made it clear that she'd grab any slot in the dance line that became available. Turnover was such that she didn't have to wait long.

"I gotta pee. Cover for me, please," Xandy said as she reached under the bar and pulled on an oversized white T-shirt covering most of her to mid-thigh. The shirt had a distinct aroma of beer foam.

From the bar, she hurried into dancer's dressing room behind the stage.

In the next vanity stall, a woman's voice with a smoky Brooklyn accent named Melody D'Amour asked, "Dat you, X?"

"In a hurry."

Melody grabbed Xandy's arm. "That new blondie with all the freckles is in the Club Car room with Big Bucks. I thought he was your John?"

"Wally?"

"Bingo."

"She's a bitch. I'm gonna punch her."

Xandy pulled open a door that led into a private twenty- by twenty-foot room wallpapered in faux red velvet. A large red velour drape covered the entry. A huge ceiling-to-floor one-way mirror separated the restaurant's banquet room from the back of Clementine's main stage.

Xandy glanced at the circular table was surrounded by twelve red leather chairs. Victorian-era sconces lined the empty room.

A tall red headed man sat in one of the plush chairs with his back to Xandy. It didn't take much imagination to recognize he was being serviced by the new girl. No one knew her name.

Wally McGrath shouted down the interruption, "Get the hell out of here. And close the fucking door."

Xandy obeyed.

Larry and Junior DeLuca, the father and son owners of DeLuca's and Clementine's, created the Club Car room with a wall sized two-way mirror. These special guests preferred to dine in private and catch a few sets of nude female dancing without anyone seeing them stare into seedy Clementine's.

Xandy took the hallway that led passed DeLuca's kitchen and spilled into the Grant Avenue side of the no star restaurant.

She walked up to the bar, where Larry DeLuca was sitting alone at the restaurant's four-stool bar, sipping Alka Seltzer neat.

Xandy approached the 300-pound Italian immigrant by tapping him on the shoulder of his silk three-piece suit. "Larry, someone asked for a bottle of Cabernet Sauvignon next door."

"Really? Give them a bottle of our Dago red and tell them it's French,"

Xandy walked around the back of the bar. She was greeted by Mambo Moretti, the head waiter. DeLuca was too cheap to hire a full-time bartender. He made the waiters mix cocktails.

"What do you need?" Moretti asked and put his hand on her waist.

"A bottle of rot gut red."

He reached under the bar and pulled out a label-less bottle of wine.

"Thanks," she said, matter of factly.

Larry asked, "Who ordered the Cabernet?"

"An older foreign dude with a nice suit and a ponytail."

Mambo turned sideways. "Must be a tourist. Who'd order that in this dive?"

"A gentleman of taste," she said, batting her eyelashes at Fat Larry.

Junior came out of the restaurant kitchen. He blocked Xandy from ducking back into the Club Car room. "Don't go in there. It's busy."

"I know I just walked through."

"What the fuck for?" asked the 5-7 string bean, whose face was marred by a forever scowl and acne scars.

"A customer at my bar asked for a bottle of wine." She held the bottle in his face. "And, why the hell is blondie messing with Wally. He's my John. Has been since I got here."

"She's new. Started today. I'm upgrading the kennel," Junior was amused with his line. "You're in second place now."

"Not after I have a little talk with her."

"You don't touch her. If you do your black ass is out the door and you'll be sitting in gutter."

"OK. How the fuck do I get this bottle back into Clementine's without going through the Club Car?"

"Use your head. Go through the restaurant and out the front door. Make a left on Grant; another left on Columbus and another left on Broadway. I hope you know the way back to the bar from there."

"It's raining out there." Xandy stuck a middle finger at young DeLuca.

"Don't point that at me." He grabbed the offending finger and twisted it hard.

Xandy didn't give him the satisfaction that it was causing her a lot of pain.

"Now go grab an umbrella from behind the hostess desk and get out of my face, woman." He released her finger.

Junior turned and walked back to the Club Car door. The red bulb over the Club Car's door turned off. That meant Wally had finished his dessert and exited through the DeLuca's kitchen and into the alley.

There the Vice Mayor and Supervisor in and for the City and County of San Francisco stepped into the black Chevy Suburban that was parked behind DeLuca's delivery trucks. The car and the chauffeur belonged to McGrath's hotel. He preferred not depending on the city/county's bureaucracy to manage his comings and goings.

Don Vanchester, the hotel chauffeur, who also doubled as Wally's bodyguard, drove him back to the Fairbanks on California between Taylor and Mason Streets.

Junior entered the private room that linked the restaurant to Clementine's backstage. Thinking back to his spat with Xandy, he did have some territorial sympathy for her. When the bartenders and cocktail waitresses and dancers were doing tricks, they shared tips. If a customer didn't ask for a specific girl there was a pecking order. The new blonde was supposed to be at the bottom of the barrel not at the top.

Junior was about to explain that to the new girl, whose real name he couldn't remember. Turns out it didn't matter the Club Car was empty.

Now curious, Junior peered through a break in the velour curtain separating the two-way mirrored wall to see who had ordered a bottle of wine at a strip club? He saw Xandy burst through the stinky, front door curtain separating Clementine's from the worst weather in half a century. She was dripping from the rain.

Junior noticed his father was following him.

Larry came up behind his son and peered over his shoulder into the dark strip bar. "who's the ponytail talking to Ezra?"

Junior shrugged, "Don't know."

"Tell Xandy not to serve Ezra. He's not a cop anymore. He pays now like everybody else. As for the other guy," Larry said, "find out who he is? Remind her to make sure he tips. Talk at my bar isn't cheap. He looks like a foreign asshole. Remind the new girl to ask for tips. Euros don't think they have to."

Xandy hopped back behind the bar and quickly returned to her official bartender's uniform, a G-string, and a smile. She placed the bottle and a high ball glass in front of him. "That's a hundred, plus tip."

She looked around Ezra Pound was finished talking to his friend at the bar.

Moreover, she was surprised the Euro dude didn't flinch at the price but did so when he tasted it. He put two c-notes on the bar and told her to keep the change. "I hope this is a rare vintage?"

"OK, I'll bite. Why?"

"So fewer people will be poisoned by it." His laugh was gruff.

She didn't laugh out loud but offered, "That's funny. Where are you from?"

"Come closer I'll tell you."

She leaned forward.

The old man pinched the nipple of her right breast.

Xandy yelped and hit him hard with a left hook. She was right-handed otherwise Mr. Spain would have been knocked off the barstool.

"Get the fuck out of my bar, old man," she said through clamped shut teeth.

"Wait, I have a question before I leave." Eduardo Ayunar took his hand off his cheek. He put another c-note on the bar.

"Make it two, fucker," she insisted. Her hands covered breasts.

He obeyed, from inside his suit jacket he put a grainy photo of a man coming out of an airport. He tapped it with his index finger. "I'm trying to find a business associate. I know he lives in North Beach."

Xandy glanced at the photo laid out on the bar top, "Maybe I seen him. Maybe not."

"I will pay you one thousand new dollars if you help me find him."

"Really?" She glanced at the grainy photo. Her attitude changed, "Well, honey pot, get those twenties on the bar, right now because I know where he is."

He pulled out a thick wad of bills.

"That's cool, but I get off duty at midnight. Can you wait that long? And keep your hands off me. That shit don't play in my bar."

"Show me the Benjamins."

He took two five hundred new dollar notes from the top of his folded bills and placed it next to the photo.

She snapped up the bills and tucked them into her office. "Yeah, I seen him. I didn't know his name, but that's him in the picture. He hangs out at the Broadway Café. And this time of night—if he's there--he sits in the front window with the owner and he has a ponytail like yours. Maybe you guys have the same mother?" she chuckled.

"What's the owner look like?"

"Small dude. Chinese. Older than dirt."

The older man sipped the wine, then pushed it away. "That's what I needed to know. Thank you, Miss Williams."

She was surprised he knew her name, but he'd probably asked around when she left to get the bottle of wine. "Still interested in meeting me after work?"

"Next time I'm in town." He smiled, bowed, and walked out of club.

* * *

Xandy didn't have to wait long for her turn to get on the stage. Junior told her to get ready because Little Oral Annie took off with Wally McGrath. And, without saying good-bye.

Xandy was ready for the extra work. She in great shape and wasn't shy or coy. The boys came to see her naked and understood she was there to please them right from the start. It was that sense of defiance when she danced that made her so alluring.

Xandy's three song set was the last of the night. "Last call, boys," a woman's voice over the PA system cracked with static. Judging from the tips tossed on stage and the howls from the sailors, Xandy was a hit.

X couldn't leave right away because the sailors swamped the bar for a closer look. They bought more drinks and were leaving big tips. She reveled in the attention. Her smile was infectious. There was nothing phony about her: she knew her role and was having fun with the fleet.

One sailor impatient for her attention pushed through his buddies at the bar and tossed his glass of beer on her chest. "I like mine wet," he hollered.

"What's wrong with you," one sailor shouted. Three of his cronies turned on him and roughed him up as the flung him into the flooded gutter in front of Clementine's.

Xandy made the most of it. She popped open a Budweiser and poured it over her breasts. "Let me taste that beer, honey," one sailor leaned across the bar.

Working her way down the bar, she collected more cash tossed her way as sailor after sailor was allowed a brief taste of her nipples now hardened by the cold beer.

Emboldened, the fleet began grabbing at every inch of her flesh they could reach. Junior DeLuca had to come behind the bar to rescue her. He was laughing all the way to the dressing room. Xandy *indeed* was a hit. Clementine's had a new star. It was a no brainer for Junior Xandy was moved from daytime to nighttime. He wondered why he didn't do that sooner?

Her shift was over. After showering off the suds, Xandy began to dress.

Melody D'Amour came backstage to hand her friend a business card." The foreigner tipped me a c-note to deliver this. Make sure he keeps coming around. We can use the money."

The card read: *take a coffee break and go over to the Broadway Café to see if Art Garcia is there. If he is come tell me. I'll be waiting in a cab in front of the bookstore next door.*

After a quick trip backstage, Xandy dressed and put on a black NFL Raiders jacket with silver leather sleeves and tight stovepipe black denims, she sat down at the Broadway Café's long counter. She blew Leon a kiss. The ancient one was seated with Tom Gresham and Art Garcia.

Leon's gopher teeth made a smiling appearance before Groundhog Day.

Art, who had been watching the tall beauty cross Broadway's four lanes, noticed her leave just as fast as she had arrived. She beelined toward a cab that was waiting in front of Kerouac's Book Store.

Art looked at Leon. "Ask Lyn to come over."

Waitress Lyn Lee saw her boss wave for her to join the table.

The vinyl booth dynamic was such that Tom and Leon faced each other closest to the plate-glass window. Art faced Leon.

Lyn slipped in opposite Art.

"What did she want?" Art asked.

"She wanted to know how long you've been here."

Art looked at Tom. "Did she ask for me by name?"

"Yes."

"Anything else?"

"She seemed nervous," Lyn said.

"Do you know her?"

"Remember John Wald's girlfriend?"

Tom nodded. "Shannon Reading."

"This Black chick took her place when Shannon quit," Lyn said, "She comes in here a lot."

"Why would she want to know how long I've been here? What do you know about her?"

"Not much other than she's gorgeous. She came by last night."

"Alone?"

"No, she was with Junior DeLuca and Ezra Ounce."

"Odd couple," Art said.

"Junior likes to be seen with his girls, but that's the first time I've seen Ezra since summer or longer."

Tom looked at Art. "Why Ezra? He's a social retard. He has no friends other than Mike Kinder."

Lyn shrugged. "Ezra's looking for work since he got fired by Charley Nye."

Art asked, "seen anyone else new come in here?"

"With Xandy?"

"Her or anyone else."

"Older man. Looked Italian. He had a ponytail and was very well dressed."

"Art looked at Tom. "Guess who that might be? First, we see Doria Ziti arrive in town and now we see our old friend Eduardo from Madrid. Coincidence?"

"No coincidence," Tom said.

* * *

Back-to-back, two jagged cracks of thunder came from then direction of Broadway Café's large plate-glass window. The foursome sitting at Leon's booth froze for one second staring at the spiderweb cracks in the glass that had formed.

"WHOA! SHOTS FIRED! EVERYBODY DOWN!" Art shouted. The high velocity bullets made flower shapes on the glass. It was like a pickax hit a frozen lake, shattering the smooth sheen. The treated glass stopped the slugs.

Lyn grabbed Leon and shielded him with her body.

Leon managed a smile. "Bulletproof glass."

Tom pulled his service piece from his holster. He was braced on the floor leaning against the vinyl seat. He gripped his Glock with both hands. His arms extended toward the front door in case whoever shot at them might come rushing through.

Tom, Art, and Lyn cautiously rose from the floor next to the vinyl booth.

Art shouted. "Tommy, the cab in front of the bookstore is driving toward us. Get to the door."

Tom bolted through to the door. "Door's not bulletproof," Lyn shouted.

Tom kneeled on the wet sidewalk

The blue and white taxi completed a wide U-turn in front of the café. Two more shots rang out from the taxi's rear window. Shots went wide of Tom hitting the sidewalk ten feet away from him.

BAM, BAM, BAM, BAM Tom fired into the cab that was now squealing its tires in a 180 turn East on Broadway. He had heard glass shatter. The cab was hit but it bore away in control down the hill toward the Embarcadero.

* * *

"Tommy, go to the Spanish consulate," Art directed. "Sutter and Franklin Streets."

Lyn jockeyed the Yamaha from its parking spot in the cement walled Mall beneath the Broadway Café. Art jumped on behind her. She pulled on her helmet while Art rode bareheaded. Seconds later they roared out of the mall via the Kearny Street parking garage entry.

Because the cab went East on Broadway, Art figured, the shooter's cab most likely would 180 from Broadway and the Embarcadero and head back to the Russian or Spanish Consulates via Fisherman's Wharf. If the cab went elsewhere, they'd have a tough time chasing it down.

Garcia knew Eduardo Ayunar could get diplomatic immunity consulate in either consulate. If he did, it was a good bet it was Ayunar who shot at them and that meant the consulate knew what the short man was up to.

Tom ran the five blocks from the Broadway Café to where he had parked the gray ghost on Union Street.

The din from the Yamaha inside the Broadway traffic tunnel blasted into Art's ears. In no time, Lyn was speeding through Pacific Heights heading west to Divisadero. A zig and a zag later they pulled up to the seven-story consulate at the corner of Baker and Green streets.

No one was kidding anybody. Everyone inside the Russian consulate is a spy. Period. It's a fact for as long as Russians operated in San Francisco. But on this night, Art and Lyn sat on the motorcycle and waited—all was quiet.

If Art was the hare, Gresham was the tortoise motoring south on Van Ness from Broadway.

The pandemics drove a lot of storefronts in that commercial part of town out of business. For lease signs dotted so many windows.

The Spanish consulate was far smaller than the Russian and for all appearances had joined the other shuttered neighbors.

He parked the Chrysler in the yellow zone in front of the café/liquor store opposite the consulate. He waited.

All was quiet. Tom thoughts turned to Lyn. In the split seconds following the shots hitting Leon's plate glass windows, Lyn had gone from Leon's café manager to Art's moll de guere. The way they went into action showed Gresham tonight wasn't the couple's first fox trot.

He wondered what else he didn't know.

While Tom Gresham. Lyn Lee and Art Garcia staked out their consulate targets, first responders were arriving at the scene of a one car accident.

A speeding taxi roaring down Broadway never made an attempt turn onto the Embarcadero Roadway or to stop before it exploded headlong into the front door of the wharf side Molly's Café.

Leon was still examining the damage to his plate glass window. From its station next to the Chinatown entry to the Broadway Tunnel, two of SFFD's biggest fire trucks roared by Leon toward the waterfront.

Leon stepped out on the sidewalk in the rain. Before ducking back inside, he saw an orange hue against the darkness of the clouds.

The owner motioned for a bus boy to join him. He wanted to alert Lyn to the fire. The bus boy made the call as Leon hadn't figured out how to use Alexander Graham Bell's invention much less operate any newer incarnations.

TOAST

When Dennis Rath received the late-night call from SFFD, the County's Chief Medical Examiner immediately called Carla Boris back to work. The fire department had control of the fiery crash scene on the Embarcadero. They had given Dr. Rath a heads up that toast was heading his way.

Boris was a pro. She rolled out of bed, pulled on her brown sweatshirt and an old pair of denims. She knew to dress warmly knowing the MedEx lab was always colder at night. In truth, it was no colder than the refrigerator-like temperatures during the daytime shift. It was a mental thing.

Rath once again was thankful for Carla's dedication and expertise. She was among the best in the nation when it came to identifying charred remains and meticulously identifying clues that might lead to what the hell happened.

Two gurneys of remains were delivered.

Carla and two assistants went to work.

In the course of her work, she discovered both bodies belonged to African American citizens. Boris refused to ID them as victims. The dead were her clients. They were citizens.

Sadly, the crash and fire were routine for vehicle crashes. Fires were less frequent as electric cars replaced internal combustion engines run on gasoline. But, in the case of the hard pressed local "human" run cab industry gas guzzlers were still being operated.

Carla distracted herself from the gore of her job by filling her mind with "official" thoughts. She figured, this crash, because of its spectacular fire and location was high profile thanks to every available media covering the incident most likely meant the end of gasoline cabs. Driverless taxis would soon rule the streets of San Francisco.

She blinked hard. A more official discovery came to light. The larger remains had a bullet lodged in his neck.

It was dawn, when Tom Gresham arrived with a backpack filled with Asian dim sum treats for a welcome breakfast for Carla and her staff.

After her work was completed, she had removed her protective lab coat and entered her office to begin the laborious detailing of her findings. She had to do it immediately no matter how tired she was because it had to be done. Midway through her computer work, she glanced at her cellphone. Tom Gresham left her a message.

"Of course," she mumbled and immediately thought of the bullet she found. "The mayor's office was never the first to call her. It was always the media and then after she delivered her report would the authorities check in. "What's with him?" she asked aloud.

"Let's go into my office," she said.

He obeyed.

"Sit down," she said and shut the venetian blinds making her office as private as she could, "lock the door." Her share of breakfast sat on her desk.

She put her arms around Tom's neck. "Good to see you. I got good news bad news. You pick."

"Bad news," he said.

"Things got away from me. I forgot to call you. We ID-ed the bodies we fished out of the ocean last week. The old guy is Jerry Montgomery. Homeless. The other is Alan Carter. Here's where it gets interesting. His family owns Carter Pharmaceuticals."

"Who have you told about Carter?"

"His family. The police."

"The media?"

"No."

"Don't tell the media before I tell Joe Martin."

"That will cost you," she grinned.

"What's the good news?"

Carla locked her lips on his. They stumbled to the small sofa opposite her desk.

* * *

The sexual storm passed as quickly as it arrived. It was as if it never happened. She sat at her desk and began to explain her new findings to Tom.

She ID-ed the cabbie by the unburned contents of his wallet. So far, she had no clue as to who the woman was.

"I might be able to help." Tom said. He knew full well it was Xandy Williams, who Leon Lee recognized earlier in the morning just before the bullets struck his plate glass windows."

"I don't want to be the source," he said.

Carla flipped her pencil off her desk in his direction. "Help me out then."

"Show me the photos."

Carla handed him a stack of computer printout of her phone camera shots.

"See around the cuffs," Tom said, "that's a letterman's jacket. I know a dancer in North Beach, who works at Clementine's. She always wears that jacket after she finishes her sets for the night."

"Did you see her, tonight."

"Ask Leon Lee at the Broadway Café. The dancers always go there on coffee breaks."

"What would Leon say when I ask him."

"Her name is Xandy Williams."

Carla looked down at the computer printout of her preliminary report. "Well, since I normally don't get IDs done until we do dental checks. I'll give you a pass asking you more questions. That's a big help."

"Only if Leon can confirm."

"Yes."

"Tom, I'm skirting the city limits here. I think you should leave."

"Raincheck on seeing you, again."

"Only if you mean it."

"I mean it."

She turned away. "Long night. Oh, one more thing. Do you think I'll find the gun that belongs to the bullet in the man's neck?"

"Probably in a sewer or it was tossed off the Oakland bridge."

"The gun wouldn't be in this room right now?"

Tom smiled, "Should have checked while you had my pants down."

She laughed and pointed to the door. "I was too busy doing other things."

"Like eating dim sum?" he added.

"Like eating dim sum. Thanks for that."

Tom stared at her at the door to the lab. "I still haven't figured out where I've seen you before."

"I used to work at the Déjà vu Museum on Ellis Street."

"Funny woman."

* * *

Tom returned to the Broadway Café. Art, Lyn, and Leon were sitting in the booth. A team of commercial glass workers had replaced the damaged window next to them.

"That was quick," Tom said as he slid into the booth next to Lyn Lee.

Lyn said, "Finding one of Leon's nephews to do glass work was a piece of cake. That's why he's an oligarch."

Tom wasn't paying attention to Lyn. Instead, he was feeling sorry for the cabbie that perished along with Xandy. It's a tragedy, he thought, dying just because you were trying to make a living. Sucks.

"It's all over the news." She said and pointed to the TV hanging in the back of the café above the long counter.

Tom refocused, "Who did they ID."

"Jennifer McGrath was reading the news. She looked too God damned perky for that early in the morning. Anyway, she said it was Xandy."

"Did they say who ID-ed her?"

"First responders recognized her—evidently she was a legend among males under 30 in this city."

"Under 80," Leon said.

"Was he hit with one of your shots?" Art asked.

"Same caliber," he said, "but that was only an eyeball by the MedEx."

"Give it to me. I'll get you a new one," Leon said.

Art waited until the waitress left after refilling his green cup with coffee. "Was the other body our friend from Spain?"

"No. The cabbie was almost your height," Tom said looking at Art.

"The fuck's still out there. Let's find him."

Leon asked, "how'd he get out of the cab before it crashed."

Art said, "we have no way on knowing if he stayed in the cab after firing at us or if he had the cabbie let him out on the way down the hill."

"Well, he wasn't at the consulates," Tom said.

"You're wrong. He's there. I've hired some people to watch for him. If he steps outside consul building, he'll be dead," Art said. "It's him or us."

10.
THE PUBLICANS
Imbiber's guide to North Beach saloons

Cantina Psalm:

One helluva night..

LITTLE WHITE COCKTAIL DRESS

She opened her eyes.

Reflected in her bathroom vanity mirror, Carly twisted her head back and forth, staring at her newly coiffed feathered haircut that her film buff mother called a Jean Seberg bob cut, a look that the French film star stamped on the 1950s.

But Carly had only seen vintage black and white photos of the film star.

An impish grin crossed the Assistant DA's face: *I'm prettier than Jean Seberg,* she mumbled before taking a last drag from her Lucky Strike and blowing the smoke into the mirror.

Carefully, she studied her recently applied make-up and practiced a few smiles as she checked her teeth for lipstick for one last time. She checked her fingernails. Too red? Would anyone notice the shade didn't quite match her lipstick?

So what?

Life was finally back to normal. The press in the time since Harre's death had not been able to prove that she and the dead District Attorney were lovers. Led by the *Daily News*, where Max Wax the growling terrier at her ankle, kept asking what Carly Martin was hiding. Did the affair lead to Harre's death? Few media refused to paint her as a black widow, but they did notice a spike in the *Daily News* circulation each time a story ran. Of course, it had little to do with the course of justice.

She was glad to hear the pest had left town. And equally elated that Max had disappeared.

Rumors had it that Max was in drug rehab somewhere in the Mojave Desert.

Others say he was murdered. Few media followed up after his breaking news disappearance fell onto page 20. That's what happens anyone cries wolf. Readers and the media shrug and move on.

Carly's denials if nothing else were consistent. "I went to the bridge to see if I could help Harre. I did what dozens of fellow assistant DAs would have done. Also, I've known Harre Ling all my life. He and my father were close friends at one time. I categorically deny all spoken or published reports that DA Ling and I were romantically linked. I will be filing a lawsuit. I've been libeled."

She ended up being sad that the newspaper her grandfather spent so many years at as a decent editor had turned into a Brit tabloid.

Lately, the only media questions had been when would the lawsuit go to trial? It was a foregone conclusion that Carly Martin would not settle the case. And how much longer would the young prosecutor stay out on her leave of absence.

Given that her father's illness kept vacillating from remission to aggressive, she asked herself the same question. Would her time be better served taking a staff position in his office?

Her zeal to be the best prosecutor in the city also was waning, as was her inability to find a relationship with a man that truly inspired her. Her world in the last few weeks seemed dull and gray. She had been thinking of asking Acting DA Bailey Crawford, a retired Superior Court judge to grant her a leave of absence to be with her father.

* * *

Tonight, however, she made a stylish effort to put a positive spin on a night out on the town. Why not? She was tired of being tired with her life. What was wrong? Really? She felt comfortable with her looks, and, in truth, she had a great family, a public law career that she could return to in an instant, plus she was free and far from living paycheck to paycheck. Living well is the best revenge; therefore, *fuck you, Max Wax.*

Yes, it was time to jump back on the carousel. Go back to work and curb her keeping busy social rounds, fashion shows, chamber music events, restaurant openings and charity galas. The bitch was back. Cue the music.

Carly tossed the cigarette butt into the toilet.

Turning back to the mirror, she watched as if by third-person eyes letting the robe fall off her shoulders and form a semi-circle around her ankles.

Carly slipped into her sizzling take-no-prisoners, white cowl neck cocktail dress in white satin from Bergdorf Goodman. It clung to her body like fresh paint and chicly ran out of material five inches above her knee. It was a dress that dared eyes not to stare at the tiny plaza of white skin that ran from under her chin and between her full breasts.

She also slipped into her thoughts. Tonight, was the third "official" date this week with Garrett Ellis.

Twice, they'd dined at C&Js. Twice, he'd dropped her off at her Russian Hill moderne. And twice, he'd gone home alone—each time saying goodnight at the door of her upper Green Street address.

Third dates made her nervous, especially in the same week. She fell back on thoughts going back to her college dating years when a third date meant it was decision time on whether to have sex or move it on down the road solo.

But she figured to play Garrett Ellis a bit longer before intimacy. He was her father's longtime friend. And he was her friend too. She went to the same law school in Berkeley but fifteen years apart. He fast-tracked into corporate law and was on Joe Martin's wish list to join his staff if he ran for governor next year.

Until this week, the friends never really dated. They always mingled at family or friend events.

As delicious as the thought of being undressed by Garrett happened to be, she needed to carefully end her other romantic relationship that supposedly no one knew about before she began another.

And having Garrett Ellis representing her Martin v. *Daily News* lawsuit was problematic. Her practical side pushed for her continued abstinence from a deeper relationship until after the case was resolved. She smiled at her chances of staying out of Garrett's bed tonight. Slim and none.

Carly envisioned her grand entrance into Sonata Restaurant, the new Nob Hill bistro where she and Garrett would be on theme and contra theme: her whiteness and his blackness. He would be in his blacker than black bespoke tuxedo and she would show off her whiteness in her basic little white cocktail dress.

Each had flawless skin, yet so opposite in color.

To keep the chill away, she accessorized it with a blue gray plaid blazer also from Bergdorf Goodman.

Shortly, she heard the distinctive William Tell Overture announcing an incoming LOBE call.

Garrett pleaded, "Complications with the case I'm working on can I meet you at Sonata in an hour. I'm really jammed…"

Carly was gracious. *Shit happens.* She removed her high heels and went to her kitchen to pour a glass of Salazar's pinot noir. The wine would be in place of lighting another Lucky Strike.

She had not been to The Sonata since the Martin family celebration of Carly's thirtieth birthday. She remembered, that well into his wine, grandfather Carling toasted, "Anyone conceived while shagging during any Beethoven's sonata will be born a musical genius."

At the same dinner, Victoria Martin, hearing her father's toast, rolled her eyes and turned to her younger daughter. "And what is your favorite Beethoven sonata?"

Missy, sucking on an ice cube, replied, "When they end."

Carly would have said, "Pathetique, Movement Three."

Joe Martin was listening to ESPN on his LOBE.

Tonight, the birthday girl arrived a few minutes late for her thirty-first birthday dinner.

And tonight, like a year ago, she looked forward to making tongue's wag. *Who is that woman in the plunging white dress? God, I hope she has strong nipples because that is all that is holding that bodice up.*

And tonight, if all went well, someone *was in for a treat. Something one-on-one. Skin on skin.* "How delicious," she smirked aloud. Her cockiness was operating at full tilt. She was ready for a fun evening.

* * *

Carly had taken a driverless limo to Sonata's, a quasi-private restaurant located on the ground floor of the newish thirty-story residential edifice, offered mahogany paneled interior walls and red leather upholstery. It was designed by Ronald Ruscha for McGrath International's commercial building division.

The entire building was paid for by a quartet of young princes, to house the then new Saudi Arabian Embassy's bloated staff and their father's aging harem. The Brutalist structure wiped out four side-by-side Edwardian era apartment buildings.

What was appealing to residents, however, was the clever design of a porte cochere that united Powell Street with Miller Place, the alley at the far end of the corner lots. Now residents could share the double lanes through the building. Cabbies, chauffeurs, and drivers like Gresham could now enter Sacramento and exit via Powell. It ended dealing with a tiresome dead end.

Major Domo Alexandre Duvee made a big deal over Carly's arrival by swinging out from behind the reception podium, grabbing her hand and kissing it delicately. His flamboyance was reminisant of a quote he gave San Francisco *Monthly* in an interview last year: "A mere brush of lips to flawless beauty." If nothing else he was predictable, which made him a harmless fan favorite.

Chef Guy Montpelier, who never lost his rural Normandy mien left his display kitchen only for a handful of Sonata's stock and trade. The Martin's were on that list. He gave Carly an awkward hug. His black apron was still sticky from having spilled an oyster mushroom sauce on it moments before. "Bon soir, ca va? We are safe from crime, n'est-ce-pas?"

"Crime never sleeps," Carly repeated a hack line that she swore to shelve soon. "Is Garrett Ellis here?"

Duvee said, "No. We haven't seen him."

"Did he make a reservation?" she wondered.

"No, not this evening."

Carly closed her eyes and shut her lips. She grabbed his arm and whispered, "I hate all men except you."

"Come to the table. I'm sure he won't be long. And I have a Champagne for you that I know you will cherish. Compliments of Mr. Ellis."

"Don't cover for him. Put this on his bill. He's late and I want to punish him."

En route to the only empty table in the twenty-table restaurant, she slipped by four men in business suits, who turned in her direction. If their eyes were searchlight beams, Carly would have been flooded in light from head to toe.

Carly eased into a leather banquette with her back to a mirrored wall.

"How is your mother and His Honor?"

"They're in Hawaii on a NASA cruise. Of course, that leaves me here babysitting my sister."

At that moment, Carly noticed the front door open.

It wasn't Garrett. It wasn't anyone she knew. Another suit joined the table, the same one that was going overboard staring at Carly.

GRAY DAY SUNDAY

Dusk on his day off, Tom Gresham had slept in until late afternoon.

He woke up on his living room sofa, where he had stumbled on stone drunk the night before.

Opening his kitchen casement window, the cold air flowed across his face. It flushed the stale smell from his apartment.

He breathed in the aroma of wet rain and listened to the steady traffic noise on the street below.

Tom treated being alone in his flat as a house arrest. He called it being bored, but lonely would better describe his mood. Someone once told him drunks hate staying home alone. Probably someone who criticized his drinking and someone he chose never to see again.

His next thoughts moved on to Carly. She hadn't called him in three weeks. If he phoned her now to invite her over, it would be the first time in their non-affair that he was the one to rekindle the romance after one of her tantrums.

He mumbled: *Yes. No. Call? No call? Do it!*

No.

Instead, he closed the window and turned to open refrigerator door. One lonely bottle Heineken beer greeted him. That's when he heard his cellphone ring. He smirked. He was pleased with himself. Right on time. Carly was nothing if not predictable.

Problem.

It wasn't Carly who was on the other end of the call.

"What's up, Art?"

"You sound terrible."

"I helped John bartend at Powell's last night. I've barely recovered."

"You drink too much."

"Thanks for that, what do you want?"

"You called me," Art said.

Tom's attitude changed from irritation to serious. "I just learned from the MedEx that they fished a body out of the ocean and it's Alan Carter."

"For sure?" Art asked.

"The Assistant Medical Examiner says she'll keep it out of the media as long as she can."

"Doesn't matter. We were hired to find him. We just did.

Nice work," Art said. "Check your bank account in the morning."

THE CHAMPAGNE DRINKERS

Carly was in her second flute of Sonata's house Champagne Perrier Jouet Belle Epoque when restaurateur Duvee approached her with a different bottle. He showed her the label. "In my humble opinion this vintage is the last great one from le fin de siècle." he trumpeted.

"Beautiful women should only drink French Champagne," he laid it on. "This is my favorite Louis Roederer Cristal Vinotheque Edition Brut Millesime 1993. I'm so proud to serve this to the most beautiful woman in San Francisco—perhaps le monde."

Carly blinked at his grandstanding. "Thank you, Alexandre. This should be for my dad. I can't drink all this by myself. I'm serious. Save it for him."

"Of course. It will be an honor to serve it to him. May I add something more?"

"Yes, Alex."

"The gentleman I just seated has joined a table with his friends. They want to send over a cocktail."

Without turning to look, "are they worthy of my company?"

He could not tell if she was joking or not.

"Nouveau riche. They're having a good time. In my opinion: harmless."

"No man is harmless."

"Personal or professional opinion, Miss DA?"

"I talk too much."

So far, Garrett was not doing well in keeping dates that he had arranged with Carly. The pattern was familiar. They planned to meet at a restaurant, and he would be delayed before joining her an hour later or not at all. She was beginning to have doubts. "No one is that busy," she mumbled to her mother when asked if she were dating Garrett.

Last year, he stood her up four times, and that was when she'd stopped making any plans with him until recently. Harre's suicide brought them close once more.

Yes, he apologized. He was the leading cause of dead flowers in the city.

After dinner, a fine cassoulet with roasted vegetables, plus glass of house Bordeaux, a modest white with a buttery afterglow, Carly bolted down a shot of espresso neat and began catching up on messages. There were none. She put the phone down on the white tablecloth in time to hear:

"Hi," may I interrupt for a moment?" It was a man's voice.

She shifted in her chair to look up at him.

"I'm Horace Smith from the table across the room. We're hoping you'd join us?"

"Are you from the gang of five?"

"I see you've been warned."

Her first instinct was to shut the man down and send him on his way, especially when his goon squad at his table were into big grins, cute waves. Nothing worse than married men out on the town trying to be cool: *college sophomores no matter what college,* she thought.

"In town for a convention, are we?"

"We're here on a conference and we're bored with each other. We thought we could have a few laughs with the locals. You made our radar—lucky you"

She hesitated.

Her silence was making him nervous. He glanced back at his buddies. "Are you a San Franciscan?"

"Yes."

"Good, we were hoping to meet someone not from our convention or Missouri, what do you say?"

"Well, you get points for being honest. You've got quite a pickup routine going for you."

"We don't have a lot of practice."

"Well, I have a lot of practice being stood up."

Horace had the sense not to ask a follow up question."

"In that case, please join us."

"No, this isn't a table-hopping place. Sit down," she said.

"Thank you." He grinned. It took everything that his mother taught him about etiquette not to turn to his buddies and offer a thumbs up.

"So, let me guess. All of you are in the same line of work and you're in the sales department. All of you are married except you, and you're all in town for a corporate conference."

"Not bad." He almost whistled at her accuracy but realized he wasn't on his father's farm in Nebraska. Beatrice, Nebraska, for the curious.

"We're engineers for McGrath International. We're the guys that designed the ice pack pipeline from Nome, Alaska, to San Diego. No more droughts in the Southwest thanks to us."

"Yes, I've noticed, and you did this over the dead bodies of thousands of environmentalists."

"War is hell, ma'am. We solved two major human dilemmas. Ended drought conditions that had been plaguing farmers in the west for decades, and it put to work a lot of people that lost their jobs to Covid-19, Covid-22 and Covid-25. I think it was a genius idea by ex-President Harris. And people can water their lawns and fill their swimming pools."

"Congratulations. I know your boss and I'm surprised he isn't in the restaurant tonight."

"Who would that be?"

"Wally McGrath."

"Him?"

"Yes, we're close friends," Carly said.

"He wasn't the one coming to have dinner with you?"

"No, you're safe."

"It's our first time to headquarters here in San Francisco. We hope to meet Mr. McGrath before we leave."

"Well, you came to a fantastic restaurant. I'll bet you're ready to hit the town?"

"Depends. I am but my buddies are a bit stodgy."

"Whatever, but you won't find action in this place. Let me recommend you take a cab to North Beach. Start at Powell's, where the drinks are cheaper. Then go to C&Js across the street for the girls. Tell bartender Seamus Doonan that Carly sent you."

Horace Smith stuck his hand out. "Thanks, Carly, we might do that."

"In fact, I'll might meet you there," she offered. "Give me an hour. Powell's in North Beach."

"What do you do, Carly?"

"Don't ask," she said and looked Horace's friends. Although the next thought didn't show up in her consciousness, an old-fashioned demon tucked away in her libido was urging her to go for it. *Take 'em on all. Give 'em something to talk about on the flight home.*

The demon would have won if her mother hadn't installed in Carly's brain a blessed St. Rita's anti-slut app when she turned 13

"North Beach is where you want to be," Carly's app said instead.

* * *

Tom survived one of the world's biggest boozer cities by holding his liquor well. Looking at him at closing time, bartenders like John Wald, Mike Cortland, Neil Polishname, or a dozen others would go on any witness stand swearing Gresham was near sober when he walked out of their saloon.

The veteran cop made himself a promise never to be a sloppy drunk. Falling down drunks like his dead father had drinking problems. He also could go a month without alcohol, a San Francisco version of a camel.

No one called Gresham a drunk, but he was.

No one slept for 12 hours if they weren't.

Another secret in town well kept.

* * *

Tom went back to his kitchen window. He watched the sidewalks filled with umbrella carriers dodging in an out of restaurants and bars. He recalled hearing Joe Martin keynote the recent San Francisco Historical Society's annual meeting. During a question-and-answer session after his talk, he was asked what makes San Francisco fun.

He went on to say San Francisco is a city of small living spaces for the poor as well as the rich. Most are apartment dwellers. Only the truly well to do have homes with lawns and garages. As a result, most folks socialize in restaurants, especially the popular power pubs and grills along Union, Clement, and Castro, in the Financial District, North Beach and the trendy enclaves on Treasure and Angel Islands. It is easier to maintain your power broker status if *the hoi polloi* doesn't see how and where you live. When the restaurants are filled and there are lines to get it—that gives any city a sense of vibrancy. "I love our cabaret society," Martin said. "That makes the city fun. Nightlife."

Tom caught a whiff of coffee being ground. Most likely from Graffeo's Coffee Grinders two blocks away on Columbus, who were preparing for its next morning trade.

Another charm of the city, Joe had pointed out, that many establishments keep the same name as the founders. The owners of the original coffee grinders were no longer the Graffeo family. They were the Michelle Xie Family, who were the current owners.

Tom's mind wandered like the needle of a Richter scale machine during an earthquake by admitting how dull the office is when Joe Martin is away. Like yesterday while Joe was on his cruise, Gresham's main duties were to stay near the office and be available if acting Mayor Wally McGrath needed city hall security services. Wally, however, was self-contained; being a billionaire, he already had bodyguards in place wherever he went; two agents from his hotel security staff shadowed him. They were so good at their job that Tom Gresham didn't realize they were on duty until they introduced themselves. They pointed out McGrath's version of a secret service contingency was so well staffed that he had protection around the clock.

Gresham and McGrath's chief agent, Don Vanchester, an unnerving man with deep facial scars who also ran the Fairbanks

Hotel's security apparatus, cut a deal after Joe and Victoria Martin took off on their voyage. Tom hung around city hall while the McGrath agents watched Wally and Jennifer McGrath 24/7.

Tom heard his cellphone chirp once more.

This time it had to be Carly.

He turned away from his curtainless casement window.

John Wald asked. "What are you doing, I need a big favor."

POWELL'S BAR & GRILL

Gresham skipped over to Powell's Saloon keeping close to the tan brick building to avoid the rain. He had on gray sweatpants, sweatshirt, loafers, and a navy-blue wool cap.

Powell's was Tom's neighborhood clubhouse. In San Francisco, every block has such a bar and the affection the locals have for their waterhole is impossible to describe unless you hang out there. It's one of those bonds like the grip that keeps grandchildren rooting for the same sports teams as their grandparents.

John Wald, for example, was left as a baby on the steps of Saints Peter and Paul church, but to this day he roots for all the Minneapolis teams despite never visiting there. How can that be? He swore that if he ever tried to trace his biological parents he'd start in the Dakotas or Minnesota.

Wald invested his San Francisco Fire Department retirement funds to launch his bar and decided to name Powell's after the intersection it sits on. Why get more complicated? Wald hated trendy shit. But he came to appreciate his public house's reputation as a no-frills shot and beer joint, a throwback 60s kind of place devoid of quiche mentalities, ferns, or fancy mineral waters. It was a guy's place and a magnet for college girls. John was protective of his female clientele.

He knew when the girls dropped by the place would soon be wall to wall. If he saw a goon go too far in showing off his peacock feathers, John would toss him over the curb and into Union Street.

Older women liked Powell's during the day. A great place for a foursome of Attila, the hens to have lunch. At night, women, who enjoyed a cocktail or two with friends found nighttime Powell's having too many co-eds and rubbing shoulders with anyone in a softball uniform wasn't in their society blue book. Who could argue?

Cortland & James, however, was widely preferred by the 30-something Ann Taylor, St. John Knits wine drinking crowd, while the shot and a beer swillers packed Powell's, especially during John's happy hours every Thursday, Friday, and Saturday at dusk.

Unofficially called the anti-Christian Science Reading Room, Powell's since day one has been a rank-and-file media bar. It's where local wags, pundits and unpublished literary sages came to salve the frustrations brought on by a tough day's living in what they called one of the most overrated cities in the world.

If Powell's was midway between a high society bar and the dregs. The dregs were only a few blocks away at Dante's. Tom swore if he ever stepped in Dante's because it was the only place he could afford to drink in—he'd shoot himself with his own service piece.

When Wald took over, he made his corner bar even more popular by taking bad checks from poorly paid cops and newspaper hacks with bum balances. He brought in street musicians and symphony-bred piano players to work for food and drinks. These solo entertainers gave Powell's an eclectic reputation for being a chamber music salon one evening and a honky tonk the next.

And as newspaper wag Max Wax said in print, *"Powell's new owner steadfastly refuses to turn his place into a neighborhood cribbage* den or a PR-hyped watering hole for tourists or self-important, low-watt literary luminaries who scribble romance novels for supermarket book stalls."

On the culinary side, John began a once monthly "Hundred Penne Dinner" on the last Wednesday of the month. Everyone ate pasta and red meat sauce with garlic bread for a dollar between 5 and 6 p.m.

When the bums and winos showed up for their meals, John had tables set up behind Powell's to serve the riff raff. If you didn't past the sniff test you were pointed to the al fresco dining in the parking lot.

A wiseacre attorney, a bozo who sniffed the back alleys of the law, filed a complaint on behalf of the mostly homeless crew, who felt snubbed. Several local attorneys friendly to John Wald countered with pro bono services.

The San Francisco Bar Association surreptitiously funded John's hundred penne night until the suit was tossed out by a judge, who asked who was harmed. And from the bench, he praised Powell's calling the establishment a business with a soul.

John stopped the dinners as the publicity put Powell's on the map. His kitchen no longer had any down time. For weeks after the dinner program ceased, several homeless men turned on the complaining attorney each time they recognized him accusing him he ruined Powell's free dinner program.

* * *

The tall owner waved from the other end of the bar. It amused Tom to see his friend twirl an end of his handlebar mustache each time he recognized a friend come into his bar. But today John looked different.

He ambled down the wood planks on the floor behind the bar and stood in front of his friend. "Tommy, Tommy, you look so good when you dress up."

"What's up?"

"I need a favor something's up in the basement."

"Call a plumber. I got things to do, tonight."

John laughed. "Dressed for a night on the town, are we?"

"Why me?"

"I thought of you first because you have a five-foot-long bar tab here."

Tom understood. He focused on John's face. Tonight, something was different. "No mustache?"

"Decided to get rid of it. Too gray."

"What are all your women saying about that?"

"Too soon to tell."

"You do look different."

"Is that good or bad?" John asked.

Tom recognized an opening. "Too soon to tell."

"Funny man."

John was like most East Coast smart asses who when they hear a truly funny joke they never laugh. They simply nod their heads and say, "That's funny...that's funny."

"I'm going on the wagon for a while," Tom interjected a whole new direction to the conversation.

John looked at him. "Are you sure?"

"I'm positive."

"Why waste all that energy? You know damn well that's going to be an unfunded mandate." John popped open a Heineken and slid the green bottle in front of his friend. "On the house."

"Thank you, reverend, for seeing the evil of my ways," Tom beamed and took a sip of the Euro beer with the big red star on the label.

Their conversation zigged. "Like I said, I need a big favor," John said.

"Name it."

"There's a lovely down in the basement that I'd like to audition and the next Mrs. Wald, but I can't have her sitting down there until I close the bar tonight. Besides Shannon's in town, remember her?"

"Shannon Reading, of course. What happened to her? I thought you guys were dead."

"She's back in town and going to stay with me and I expect to show up any minute. Help me out here."

Tom's head swiveled in the direction of the toilets. Between the loos was a staircase leading to John's basement office.

"It's not her turf?" Wald continued, reading his friend's expression. "I've been so busy up here I didn't close my safe. I got a lot of cash in it. I don't want her to tempt—" He didn't finish his comment.

"You want me to just close it."

"Slam it—spin the combination. Thanks, Tommy."

"What's her name?"

"Something like Amy?" John knew his friend well enough that his questioning look was begging for more details. He relented. "She could very well be gone and my safe cleared out. I can't believe I let her do that."

Gresham looked surprised. "She's probably taking a pee in your toilet downstairs."

John sighed, "She came in wearing nothing but a trench coat five sizes too big for her. That and her hair stringing in her face made her look like a wet cat. I told her to go downstairs to see if she could find a dry towel or if there was anything in my barrel of lost and found clothes. She's been down there half an hour…"

"You do have the best lost and found bin in the city." Tom grinned. "Half of my wardrobe comes from there."

John frowned.

"What do you want me to do with her?"

"Stop yammering with me. Go get her. Take her someplace else. Tell her I'll call her. Some shit like that. You're good at that."

* * *

Powell's used to be a corner pharmacy. The narcotics safe was built into the basement masonry. Wald used it for cash receipts and various ledgers and computer disks.

Gresham spotted a curly haired strawberry blonde sitting halfway down the stairs. The basement smelled like stale booze and wet cardboard. She sat there like a chromatic flower issuing out of a long-corrupted log.

"How's it going down there?" Gresham raised his voice. He caught her snorting coke from a small packet.

Startled, the woman, who appeared to be in her mid-20s, looked up over her shoulder and gave him a coy smile, "Powdering my nose." She was draped in the oversized coat that John described.

Instantly, Tom understood why John might have been smitten because he certainly was. Tall and very pretty, he took her to be another cocktail waitress that came in looking for work. And for one, he liked the gap in her front teeth and her wall-to-wall freckles. To him she had a Euro mystique. John was right to try to connect with her.

"John thought you might be job hunting, how's that going?"

"No, I'm trying to find something dry to wear."

"Why the big raincoat?"

"Maybe because it is raining outside?" She returned to searching through the clothes bin"

"London Fog's are terrific. Next time buy one that's your size."

She ignored him.

"My flat's across the street. It has a dryer. Why don't we go there to dry your clothes?"

She lifted a wrinkled light blue gingham seersucker raincoat. "My God," she said this is made by Solbiati."

"Whatever it is let's toss it in the trash, otherwise you're giving lost and found a bad name."

"It's so bad it's perfect." She let the trench coat fall off her shoulders.

"Christ, you're naked."

"Wow, you oughta be an eye surgeon." She pulled on the new-found gingham coat and began buttoning it. She stuffed the huge trench coat in the lost and found box.

"Whatever, John wants us out of here. He wants to keep it a tourist free zone."

"Thanks for delivering the message."

"Whatever, let's go." Tom noticed she picked up a plastic bag with pull ties. The logo said Fairbanks Hotel. "What's in the bag?"

"My uniform. I'm a cocktail waitress at the Klondike Room."

"So how did you end up here?"

"You only get the story if you or John buys me dinner."

"Dinner's fine."

"But not here," he announced.

"Why someplace else."

"For whatever it's worth his girlfriend is coming here any second. He didn't want to explain why a naked woman was in the basement of his bar. And I think it's nice of him to let you rummage through the lost and found bin and popping for dinner."

"That's why I like his bar. So, where do you want to eat."

"C&Js across the street? And no you can't do lines of coke there."

"How do you know I do coke."

"I saw you snorting shit up your nose before I came down the stairs." He said sounding like the ex-cop she didn't know he was."

"My hair is wet and stringy; and fuck you very much regarding your coke comment. Let's go to a pizza joint. How about Mario's?"

Tom handed her his navy watch cap. "Put this on. We'll look great. You're too pretty for them to throw us out."

Tom looked at her green eyes. Her whites were crisscrossed with steaks of red. His cop training kicked in. He bet she had more coke in her than the line he saw her snorting.

"I need to get around you?" He asked as he stepped around her to shut the safe.

He followed her up the stairs close enough to see her legs were bare and just as freckled as the rest of her.

He wanted to reach and touch her taut skin. But he'd been raised—like most men—to sneak a glance, then look away. He looked but didn't touch.

She stopped at the top of the stairs and disappeared into the women's toilet.

Tom decided she was going to be a pain no matter how good looking she happened to be. He found a barstool and motioned John over. "She's gorgeous and she was snorting cocaine downstairs."

"Too bad." John instantly judged her based on Tom's report. "Have you met a coker that wasn't trouble in the long run?"

"She's not my problem," Tom said. He looked around the bar. "Do you know her?"

"No. She said she was new to the city."

Tom gave him a tired smile. "I'm heading home. I'm not doing well with complicated women and your safe is safe."

John popped open a Heineken for him and resumed his bartending.

Tom felt a tap on his shoulder.

The stranger in the seersucker raincoat stared at him for a long time without saying anything. Something was different.

Then he figured it out; she looked like a different person with her wet strawberry-orange curls up in a ponytail. She had put on lipstick and a smile. He put the wool cap back in his hands. "Is dinner still on the table?"

John mouthed *thank you* to Tom as he and the mystery woman in seersucker walked out into the rain.

John was enjoying the rear view when she turned and flipped him a middle finger.

THE GENUINE ARTICLES

In the cantina trade, if you're a big dreamer—all smiles no collateral, or in over your head for a thousand reasons—all you need to do to make up for your shortcomings is to hire good people. One day, one good decision, is all you need to get your rocket off the pad.

Michael Cortland and Jimmy "Seamus" Doonan hired civil attorney Garrett Ellis to dot the proverbial i's and cross the t's. Thirty years as bartenders, they never owned a car much less a bar until they leased the recently shuttered Washington Square Bar & Grill at Powell and Union Streets.

The jovial ex-pat Irishmen from Dublin were Garrett's favorite clients. Garrett made it his mission to ensure that the amiable publicans would never lose their tip money.

The two ex-pat Dublin airport shoeshine boys were now among the city's roster of millionaires.

Cortland and James opened their eating and drinking establishment of the same name two years ago on June 16 on Dublin's annual Bloomsday. It sits catty corner from Powell's They took over what used to be last century's popular Washington Square Bar & Grill.

C&J laughed to each other knowing full well that they created a genteel establishment that their fathers would have been tossed from onto their immigrant asses.

They insisted on black-jacketed waiters with white aprons. Bartenders and waitresses wore white shirts with puffy casino-style gartered sleeves.

The narrow space resembled a train dinner car without the windows. With its tin roof and ancient circulating fans, it appeared more of a Manhattan-style bar ala Martell's or P.J. Clarke's.

The only tables were next to the main entry and a bigger room in the back. Space along the bar was reserved for stand-up drinking.

C&J was refloored in white octagon tile, the back-bar cabinetry was repurposed fire stove smoked black redwood from the Hudson Bay Saloon that someone took mercy upon and stored in a farmer's barn near St. Helena, where nineteenth-century scribe Jack London howled and prowled before it closed. It is the Hudson Bay Saloon that Jack London never wrote about. It was his secret.

But what almost broke the Cortland & James from day one was the shekels they spent to import a mahogany bar from Harold's Public House in the Temple, where it toiled hundreds of years serving the average Dubliner better than the governments ever did. At one end of the bar the initials JJ were carved into the auld wood. Native Irish wood was too soft for pub use and Harold's Bar was crafted from mahogany imported from Sweden. Cortland, with his most sincere look, insisted the initials were carved by James Joyce himself.

Then later, to anyone that was interested, Seamus Doonan would say his partner's bar tale was pure malarkey. James Joyce was so blind his hand had to be guided to his drink—carving initials took time away from downing a good Irish whiskey.

C&J was a better restaurant than it was a bar. It served two items on its menu: fish and chips and corned beef and cabbage. That's all, folks. Seven nights you won't find a seat until the kitchen closes at 2:00 a.m. The owners at one time turned down adding clam chowder soup to the menu. *Too much trouble*, they vetoed.

Ellis had the idea to limit the size of the Cortland and James menu at the beginning. Working in a campus restaurant as an undergrad, he saw first-hand the amount of waste that resulted from an "all things to all people" menu. He swore if he had a say he would create a very limited menu; work hard to deliver taste, quality, originality, and service orders with zest.

"People just want to get out and enjoy themselves. If they're picky, there are other places for them to go," Garrett said, and that convinced the Irish.

Originally, a bakery with two large Edwardian-era windows flanking an opaque crystal glass front door. The latter salvaged from Ye Auld Sod in Galway before sunny day lightning caused a massive fire—the largest ever on Eire's west coast.

Behind each window was a small deuce. No finer seats existed in North Beach.

Tom Gresham's choice of Cortland and James was as good as any. Annee liked it immediately because the eyes she saw glancing her way were friendly. And Tom was determined to show off his new friend to the fullest. It was not every night that he had a woman on his arm, but when he did, he enjoyed coming to the C&J to share her with the Irish.

Of course, he believed all were watching the couple's every step.

To Mike and Seamus's credit, they treated every woman, especially those who were regulars, like they were the Queen of England. Part Irish charm, part smart business. But because they were fond of Tom, they too enjoyed meeting who Tom brought in.

And in Tom's defense, he did not bring in a date every night. No one called him a womanizer, but that was only because he could not afford it. Also, he got used to being with Carly Martin, but they got tired of having to show up in public with a pretense they were on official business that required security for the mayor's daughter. If he could not be with Carly, he was content to stay home.

If he did show off a new woman like Annee, he seldom strayed from the C&J and Powell's.

John Wald, for one, wished he had a dollar for every time he heard, *Well, it's the only place we could find, but as soon as something opens up, we're moving there.*

Also, what Tom lacked in his wallet was made up because two of his best friends in the world, Garrett Ellis, and Mayor Joe Martin, had all the clout in town. And, lucky for Tom, those names were gold with management. He strolled in as one of the players in town. As a result, if Tommy wanted the table, he got the damn table.

The tables were allotted not by democracy or even royal decree or name droppers or cash cows like *Daily News* publisher John Bruce, whom Seamus called "his queenliness himself." In truth, it was Michael Cortland himself who personally approved the seating.

While the unknowing buttered up Seamus to wrangle the front window tables, Seamus knew his vote didn't count if Mike was in the house. Even if the bar was jammed and waiters begged for the tables, nothing was released until Mike would give a wink or nod to the maître d' after the host conferred with the owners. No one could tip high enough to grab one of the cabaret tables with green checked tablecloths by the front door until they received the "nod."

Tom smiled at Seamus's double-take—not because they were cads, but it had been the longest time since they had seen such green eyes, curly hair, and full facial freckles this far west of the Liffey River.

Gresham was in luck.

Michael Cortland motioned Tom front and center.

No matter the topic or the intimacy of the conversation, Cortland leaned forward toward his listener's face as if he were about to pass on atomic secrets before Ethel and Julius Rosenberg allegedly did back in the 1950s. If it was not a secret, it had to be juicy gossip or what horse was fixed to win at Golden Gate Fields, as an example only.

Cortland's eyes lifted. "Bollocks, where you been?" the bartender leaned over the bar and slapped a cocktail napkin in front of Tom. If Cortland were Stan Laurel, Seamus "Jimmy" Doonan would be Ollie Hardy. Cortland motioned to his partner as if to say, "Look what the cat dragged in."

Seamus, who spotted Tom talking with Cortland, walked down the planks to add his welcome. He went straight for Annee, wiped his hands on his apron and offered a handshake.

"Jesu, woman, I've been waiting all my life for you to come in."

Tom heard that line a lot from Seamus but always loved hearing it in a genuine Irish brogue. Like all good bartenders, it is not what they say but how they say it. With all bar stories, most of the time you had to be there to get it. And, if you can't be there in person, then, dammit, read about it.

He stuck his hand out: "James Doonan, pleased to meet you, lass, call me Seamus."

"Annee." She shook the bartender's hand.

"You got a last name, Lass?"

"No."

Tom feigned nonchalance. He was full of himself playing tonight's serendipity with Annee to the max. Life had improved dramatically by crossing Union Street. And even better when he heard, "The deuce table on the left is all yours."

He got the wink and the nod from Cortland, who was at the other end of the bar.

That was gold on a rainy evening.

* * *

Seamus came around the bar and followed them to their table. "Tommy, does she know she's sitting at the love bird's table?"

"No, tell me about it," she asked.

"Only the best of lovers sit here. You have to thank His Honor, Jr., here for your good luck."

"Please tell me he's a good man," she asked.

"One of the best. We think he comes from a line of Gresham's in Cork, who were escapees from Norfolk, England. But we don't hold that against him." Seamus put his hand on her shoulder.

She looked confused but said nothing.

Tom beamed at the attention Annee was getting.

"Are you new to North Beach," Seamus continued.

"Yes. A couple of days. I'm looking for a job."

"What are you drinking?"

"Stoli neat with a lime squeeze and a glass of water," she said.

"And for you, boy scout?"

Gresham smiled. "I'll have a Perrier."

"The hell you are. I dinna think you'll be drinking pussy water in my bar any time soon."

"I'll have a shot of Jameson."

"Damn straight," Doonan said. He walked away to fill the orders.

* * *

When a cocktail waiter brought over the drinks, Annee immediately reordered another round before excusing herself to the toilet.

Tom watched her stroll away. Ponytail and blue raincoat never looked better.

She had been gone enough time that Tom began to look around the room for her. He eventually spied her at the far end of the bar yakking with a rare collection late-staying softball players in team uniforms. They were the Lapin Savages, the team Mike Cortland sponsored. The dress code obviously had been lifted for them. Tom thought it odd that Cortland, who hated American sports, would sponsor a team. And, John, who had his bar TV permanently tuned to sports channel didn't care to sponsor a bar league team.

Seamus came over in the meantime. "Tommy, a quick word. I seen the lovely Annee come in yesterday with Mike Kinder, and I know you and Mike are water and grease. Kinder's been saying she's the new Mrs. Kinder."

Tom was surprised. "She's too classy for Kinder."

"Maybe so. But he told Cortland that he fucked the most expensive whore he's ever had. Said it cost him $2,000 and that night he took her to Reno to marry her on the spot."

"I don't know her, but I'd take her side any day over Kinder's bullshit. The only way Kinder would have two grand is for him to hold up a bank—and get away with it."

"Where did you meet her?"

Tom pointed a thumb over his shoulder, "At Powell's earlier and she's said nothing about being married or Mike Kinder."

Seamus asked, "You think she's a working girl?"

"Give me a break, I just met her."

"Don't worry, she's no hooker," Seamus said. "Trust me."

Annee returned to the table. "What? You guys staring holes in me."

"You're easy to look at," Seamus said and left the table.

"This is a fun place." She put on her Helen of Troy smile. "But getting to the toilets is a big deal."

"That end of the bar has always been its own subculture. Guys flock there because all the women gotta stand in line to use the toilet," Tom offered.

"Why they build restrooms in bars with only two stalls for women is stupid, especially on crowded nights like this," she said.

"I know what you mean," he said. "I live a block away and on weekends it's faster for me to go home to take a pee than stand in line."

"Two women waiting in line were sharing cocaine. Is coke easy to find here?"

"Not at C&J's, but on weekends when the yahoos invade North Beach, you can find it more easily. Depends on the crowd. During the week, it's not so blatant."

"Do you know where I can buy some coke?"

It's a human peculiarity to know how much thinking can be crammed into one pregnant pause.

Tom was disheartened by what Seamus told him and now she was showing signs of a very beautiful coke whore. But if she hung out with Kinder, what should he expect. He decided to play her as a one off for the evening because of her good looks.

Annee broke the silence. "I've only been here a couple of days and I've never seen so much coke on the streets. I'm not a junkie, I'm just curious."

Tom shrugged. "North Beach is one big party—you can find what you need if you look for it."

"Are you a native?"

"Yep. I grew up in North Beach. You can't see it from here but across the park is a boarding school run by Augustinian priests. I lived there until I went to the academy."

"Academy?"

"Police academy."

"That makes you a cop."

"I'm assigned to city hall. I run the mayor's security detail."

"Hoity-toity, where is His Honor, tonight?"

"He stayed home, tonight."

"Do you have a gun on you?"

"Yes, ma'am."

"Well, I feel like a fool asking if you had any coke."

He grinned. "It's a long story, but I do have a small jar in my kitchen pantry. It had been there for months."

"Really. Are you dealing on the side?"

"Believe it or not, I found it about a year ago. If I were dealing it would have been gone."

"Why isn't it?"

"Forgot about it."

She asked, "Where do you live, again?"

"Look out the window. I live two floors above Mario's Café."

"So far, this place and Mario's are my favorites."

Tom laughed. "Where are you from?"

"The South."

"You don't have an accent?"

"I was raised a Yankee. My parents have little use for Bubbas."

She glanced at the menu. "Not a lot of menu choices."

"True but look around. See any empty seats?"

"No, I guess less is more."

Tom smiled. "You told Seamus you were looking for work? Maybe I can give you some leads, especially if you're a cocktail waitress?"

"Do I look like a bar type?"

"I don't know you. I'm trying to be nice."

"I got fired tonight."

"Does that have anything to do with you showing up in a man's trench coat?"

Annie leaned back on her chair.

He figured he touched on a sore topic, but now he really didn't care."

More drinks arrived delivered by the frat boy blonde waiter, Seamus had assigned to their table.

She waited until the waiter left. "Let's make a deal," she said, "Let's finish these drinks and go over to your place so I can taste the coke you stole. I don't see anything on the menu I like here."

Tom's stomach flipped in anticipation. He went from zero to love in nanoseconds.

He waved to get the waiter's attention to pay the tab.

Annee used her index finger to push apart C&J's curtains at their table. After a moment gazing at the rain, she pulled her head back and stared at Tom.

She started her story about how a nice girl like her ended up naked in a wet raincoat in the basement of John Wald's saloon.

"The GM comes up to me and asks if I wanted to work another shift. He told me the catering staff could use another waitress for the black-tie party later in the evening.

"I said yes. When I got up to the penthouse floor, I saw there were only two doors. Of course, with my luck I knocked on the wrong door.

"Mr. McGrath answered the door. I didn't know what to say. He was standing there in his tuxedo. Biggest goddamned penguin I've ever seen. I told him I was looking for the catering crew.

He recognized me and asked him how I liked working in the hotel. I told him thanks for bailing me out of Clementine's"

"How long did you work at Clementine's?" he interrupted.

"One day. Don't interrupt me if you want the story. I'm not going to repeat it."

Tom put his hands up in surrender.

She continued, "He asked me inside. He was drinking Champagne and he asks me if I wanted a glass. I told him I was on duty. He said he makes the rules. I ended up taking a glass.

"Next thing I'm out in the kitchen eating pate and caviar and drinking more Champagne. Handed me a wad of money out of his wallet—he didn't even count it—and told me to get into the hot tub out on his terrace."

Gresham nodded, "that's the Wally I know. Did you take the money?"

She laughed. "I never thought growing up that I would ever have sex for money. That only happened in movies and books. I never knew anyone that did that until…

"Until?" Tom asked.

"Until a man I didn't know offered me $10,000 for one night in bed with him."

"That's a lot of money."

"Men, who have that kind of money and don't have a soul. They can do a lot of damage."

"Did that man damage you?"

"I figure for one time I'd do it with my eyes closed."

"Was he weird?"

"Harmless to the point of being boring. He was good looking. Arab in Western clothing, who had so much money."

"How old were you?"

"Nineteen."

"Ever see him again?"

"I googled him once. Read that he was dead. Got drunk and flew his Cessna into some utility wires in Saudi Arabia. Killed him and four of his wives."

"What was his name?" Tom asked.

"Stop with the questions. I'm trying to tell you how I ended up naked under Wally's trench coat."

"I'm all ears," Tom grinned.

"Wally said he'd match the $10,000 if I jumped into his hot tub out on the penthouse terrace."

"Did he?"

"He paid, cash. While he was at the cocktail party next door, I counted the money he gave me. It was ten grand—not a penny more. Mostly big bills. Real big bills. I stayed in the hot tub because he told me to because he said he'd be right back. And, besides it was colder than a ditch diggers ass if I got out. About half an hour later…here, I want you to picture this… a goddamned helicopter comes out of the clouds and shines it big ass spotlight on me. I thought it was going to land on me. Instead, it lands on the roof on the floor above. Next thing I know an old woman in a dark suit comes rushing toward me. Next to her is this huge guy with ugly cars on his face. It was a scene out of some horror flick. I start to scream, but the helicopter was making so much noise no one heard me.

"Next thing I know the dude pushes my head underwater. When he pulls me up out of the water by my hair he says if I scream one more time, he'd flip me over the side of the hotel and swear to the police that I jumped from the building across the way."

"So, you shut up."

"Sure did. Then I'm yanked out of the hot tub. The old bag wraps me into a tan trench coat that's five sizes too big for me. The dude picks me up off my feet and carries me over his shoulder to the kitchen service elevator. Next thing I know I'm in a laundry cart inside the elevator under a pile of sheets. The asshole tells me I'm dead if I make a peep. He rolls me out from the hotel basement into the garage and puts me in the back of the hotel limo and asks me where I want to go."

"Hell, you should have said Las Vegas."

"I didn't find it one bit funny. To put it bluntly, I was fucking scared shitless. So, I just said take me to Powell's. I figured if I made it that far I'd be safe."

"Did he say anything to you? Any threats to keep your mouth shut?'

"No. In fact, he ends up giving me a plastic hotel bag stuffed with my cocktail waitress uniform and the $10,000 bucks that Wally gave me, up in the penthouse. It's in the bag I've been carrying around."

"You're carrying it around? Ten grand? Christ, you're buying the drinks."

"Fine."

"Will there be anything else," the waiter approached the table.

"No, just the check," Gresham said without looking at frat boy.

"I'll take it," Annee said.

The check came to $75 for two rounds of drinks. She didn't flinch and placed two c-notes on the small tray. "Courtesy of Mr. Wally McGrath."

"Fine with me," Tom said.

Annee parted the café curtains a bit wider. "Tom, I just saw dessert. Wait here." Annie leaped from the table and hurried outside to the sidewalk.

Gresham stared over the half curtains. "Crap," he said aloud.

Annie greeted Junior DeLuca as he exited a taxi.

Tonight, Junior was a sight to behold. The smarmy owner of Clementine's and son to Larry DeLuca's, the owner of DeLuca's Italian restaurant was wearing his pimp deluxe: three quarter length camel coat with matching camel colored shirt and shiny almond-shaped leather shoes. The three-inch heels made Junior every bit of 5-7 and at 130 pounds he looked like the edge of a knife. But what put him over the top was his silk tuxedo pants in screaming magenta with the black strip down the leg that put the 30-year-old in the white guy pimp hall of fame.

Annie kissed Junior on the cheek, but he deftly moved his mouth on to hers and wouldn't release her from the long kiss. She pulled away. He smirked, shook the rain out of his curly black hair and stared over his shoulder at Gresham in the restaurant window.

"You prick," Gresham mumbled. His anger was rising. Junior, the punk. If there was coke around, Larry DeLuca's weasel son was right in the middle of it.

Annie rushed back into C&J's. "Tom, meet me at DeLuca's in half an hour. I got to talk to Junior for a second. You're a doll," she pressed against him and kissed him on the mouth. She intended the kiss to be brief. She tried to pull away. Gresham held her tight. He made the kiss linger. The gesture irritated Annie. She stared up at him. "DeLuca's in half an hour."

"I don't want you going anywhere with Junior. He's bad news." Gresham held on to her.

"Tom, I need to get my job back at Clementine's."

"No, you don't."

She shook her head. "Relax, he'll sell me some coke."

"Stay here. I told you I got maybe an ounce and you can have if for free. You can have it all."

She looked at him hard.

She glanced down at his hand on her arm. "Tom, I want to see him because tonight I lost my job at the hotel. I need a job."

"Doing what?"

"Dancing…serving cocktails."

"Stripping. Nothing good happens at Clementine's trust me. Everything Junior DeLuca touches is slimy…bad news."

"Why are you so uptight all of a sudden?"

"They will eat you up."

"It's easy work. I can have my days free to find a real job. I can handle Junior."

"He's Larry DeLuca's son. Both he and Larry will be climbing all over you. He loves to share his dancers with his best customers. He's done that since I've known him."

"I work for Junior."

"The hell you do."

"Tom, look at me. It's your lucky night. Let's have some fun. See you at DeLuca's. I can take care of myself, and I do need the job until I can find a better one."

"Annee, you can stay with me until you find a job. No rent. Think about it."

As Annie stepped into the taxi, Junior closed the door behind her and gave Gresham the lousy part of a one-finger salute.

In Gresham's book it was low class for a woman to go off with someone else in the middle of a date. It was fucking rude and not to mention he felt like a fool in front of Mike Cortland and Seamus Doonan.

The waiter returned with the change.

"It's all your."

"Thanks, man."

Gresham walked out in the rain and headed to his apartment to cool off.

WET CAT

When he was a cop, Ezra Ounce had made his wee hours round of the park benches at Washington Square to roust the winos and get them to move out of the rain. Once the bums hit the road, Ezra walked over to the middle of Washington Square to take his nightly piss on Benjamin Franklin's statue.

He always looked to see if the old priest watching him from the rectory window.

Now, jobless, bored, Ezra walked from his flat on Filbert Street on the East side of Columbus. He was heading to Dante's saloon to catch up with Mike Kinder. Even joining his roomie at Dante's was better than staring at the four walls.

As he approached the Southwest edge of Washington Square Park at Columbus and Union, he waited for the approaching Union 41 bus to pass in front of him.

He crossed Union in a southwardly direction and stopped a few feet from the front door of Mario's Café.

From the direction of Dante's bar and backlit by the streetlights along Columbus, Igoe transformed himself into a scene from Casablanca. Could it be Ilsa Lund in her famous trench coat languidly approaching him from out of 1942?

Mouth open, he paused and stared.

Within a few steps, it registered with Ezra that his Ilsa Lund was Annee Kinder. Her soaked red hair was splayed, abandoned around her ears and forehead. She held the collar of her plaid seersucker raincoat tight around her neck. The rain creeping down her neck was freezing cold.

What Ezra didn't know that his Ilsa from Casablanca was heading to Gresham's flat. He also didn't know Junior DeLuca tried to rape her in the Club Car Room inside his restaurant. Lucky for her she kneed him in his balls and made her escape. She wasn't in the mood for another bozo to cross her path.

Ezra on the other hand, had Annee in his sights. It was a sign from God. Meant to be. He figured he had a chance with her by sweet talking or giving her cash.

He was about to invite her out of the cold and into Mario's when she abruptly stepped inside the alcove of the apartment building next door.

"She did that on purpose," he said aloud. He took her sudden swerve as rudeness. It angered him that she avoided him. He was trying to be friendly.

Truth be told, she never saw the bowling ball.

Erza moved quickly into the alcove. He expected her to be hiding in a corner. He was wrong.

She was gone.

Ezra didn't recognize the building right away. Angrily checked the names on the door buzzer. At the top he read: Gresham. "Man, this sucks. Christ almighty," Ezra moaned. Already Tom Gresham had his paws on the blonde that Mike Kinder had told everyone at Dante's Saloon was Mikey's new Reno bride.

Ezra figured if anybody it was him or Mike Kinder who had rights to Annee. Of course, 99 percent of Dante's drinkers could care less what Kinder, or Ezra were up to.

Ezra was beside himself. He mumbled: "Fucking poacher. Why can't that be me? What's so fuckin' special about you, pretty boy? What's the uppity bitch see in him?

Ezra wanted to feel Annee's lips on his. "Just once," he groaned to no one. "Just once."

In all his life, he'd never been so close to a woman so good looking, and what he believed to be within his reach. Now she was heading up to meet a joker that wasn't half the cop he was.

When is it going to be my time? Why do I have to stand in line behind every pretty boy, and rich asshole to get my share?

Fuckin' Gresham is such a loser and yet there she is waltzing up to his flat.

"Come on? I don't get it?" he continued to rant into the wind.

Ezra stepped through the rain holding his umbrella and marched toward Dante's wearing his gloom like graffiti.

He wanted to tell Mike Kinder that Gresham was moving in on their turf. "Fuck that!" Ezra growled. He knew if he told Kinder about Annee that Kinder would undo the safety on his .38 Smith & Wesson and barge into Gresham's flat and put bullets into the sonofabitch.

He pushed into Dante's. The old bar was packed. "Is Mike Kinder here?"

THE SUITS

Carly took her second Uber of the night to Powell's. She was hoping she would run into Gresham somewhere in North Beach. Powell's was her first choice to look. She wanted to be with a man, now that Garrett had bailed for the evening—Tommy Gresham was on her radar. She'd had enough Champagne to reconsider seeing him again. And if she got drunk, she didn't have to report for work in the morning. Why not, she reasoned. Her career was stalled with her imposed stress-related sabbatical.

In Garrett's defense, Carly didn't know he had just received news from Victoria Martin that Joe had a urinary infection that turned to sepsis. He was in the ship's infirmary. Victoria said, "I've decided to fly us back home in the morning when the Coast Guard chopper gets here. Please, Garrett keep all this under your hat. Let me tell the girls once I learn Joe's condition."

* * *

As Carly entered Powell's, the foursome from Sonata's had arrived and waved for her to join them. They were surrounded by Mills College coeds eager for older men to buy them drinks and at the same time stay in a pack.

Carly called her Sonata posse grown up sophomores. She joined them. Horace was growing on her the more she drank and at lease in combo they kept her mind off Garrett.

Soon, Carly was up to date on the engineering history of fusion engines for mass-produced American cars. And how California would never have another drought because of the water pipeline they designed.

Good natured and oh, so touristy, she *rollez les bon temps* with her Midwest posse.

Carly managed to catch a second with Powell's owner John Wald, who was behind the bar. She asked if Tom had been in.

"He was here with a new blonde in town a couple of hours ago. I haven't seen him since."

Well, that was the end of the line for her. All dressed up and no man to impress, except a very married Horace, who despite swearing he was single was lying through his teeth.

Years later, Carly would say to her diary that if Horace had been given some ordinary name, he probably would have gotten laid that night. No way she wanted anyone named Horace on her horizontal dance card or in her diary—ever.

The evening ended when Carly came out of the toilets. She bumped into Horace, heading in the other direction. She tried to make herself heard that she was calling it a night, but was she drowned out by the ongoing din from the bar.

Carly's head was beginning to spin. She dodged into the jammed toilet to toss cold water on her face.

She felt a tap on her shoulder.

Carly turned to face an attractive brunette.

"Are you Carly. I'm a friend of John Wald's. Can I ask you a question?"

"I can't hear you," Carly said. The two women found an empty table in the restaurant part of Powell's, where they could hear each other.

"What's your name?" Carly asked.

"Shannon Reading. I want to report a crime."

Carly gave her a fake smile. "Did John give you my name?"

"No, but I know you're his friend. I know who you are and you're with the District Attorney's office."

"Shannon. I'm drunk on my ass. I seriously doubt I'll remember being in this bar tomorrow morning much less what you're about to tell me."

"It's serious."

"I'm not the police. My job is to take care of what the police and the courts send my way. If this is important go down to Vallejo Street station and speak to a nice man named Charley Nye. He runs the place. Tell him I said he should listen to you. It's two blocks away."

THE INFERNO

The difference between a dive and a saloon is simple. Saloons, like Powell's Bar & Grill, are clean, well-lit establishments with windows open to the world, a comfortable place where you can sit and read, watch sports on television, enjoy some good company and at the same time have a drink.

A dive bar is nothing more than a cave that is lit by the hue of small neon beer signs. They are windowless pits, where it is important to place your wallet in your front pocket before you enter.

People like Ezra Ounce slouch over their elbows in dives. They mumble and hold onto their booze with one hand and a cigarette with the other. Dives are where slobs like Mike Kinder can show off their ass cracks while at the same time bellying up to the bar.

Friendships only last a few steps beyond the front door, but inside each barstool is a rented throne. It is a filling station for a drive to nowhere, a peep show without walls and a place to play with chemical crayons.

Repeat. Dante's was a dive.

Bartender Guthrie "Gus" Oklahoma, who ran the joint for his late brother, the lost and gone forever Norman Oklahoma, walked out of St. Vincent's hospital a week earlier after surviving his second heart bypass operation.

Gus checked himself out of the hospital because he ran out of smokes. But for the past week, the seventy-something cut down to a pack a day and his booze to half pint a day.

But lately, he had picked up the classless habit of yanking his false teeth out of the cocktail ice bin and spraying them clean with the water gun beneath the bar.

Medical science was in awe of his industrial-strength liver. Gus had been abusing it for fifty-five years. How that poor organ had survived belonged on some unsolved mystery show.

Because he drank 100-proof off-brand-bourbon in tall tumblers with no ice or water, somewhere there's a very sad picture of Dorian Gray with jaundice.

Gus also defied city ordinances by allowing customers to smoke inside his dive.

You'd think a place that's filled with cops would follow the rules. Off duty cops could care less about city ordinances.

Smokers like Fat Larry DeLuca loved Dante's.

The inferno was an apt nickname.

Gus was working a full bar—full of empty seats. It was Unhappy Hour, a marketing gimmick that some out of work saloon marketing men came up with for the price of free drinks.

During unhappy hour, he doubled the price of his drinks between 6:00 a.m. and noon and again between midnight and 2:00 a.m.

The scheme worked. Dumbshits by the dozens came in regularly to pay the stiff tariff only to find out nothing happened during Unhappy Hour. Everyone left unhappy.

A downside to unhappy hour price hikes is the homeless drunks did not get the joke. Upside to the gimmick was the price hike also cleared out the riffraff.

Even Dante's had standards.

About a week later, the big homeless drinkers soon realized Dante's was the only place that would let them in regardless of the time.

One by one the bums came back.

Gus did not mind one bit soaking a drunk.

Ezra had stepped into Dante's wearing a longshoreman's jacket and wool cap. The tinny smell of wet beer on the floor marked a typical DeLuca-owned bar. Each bar had its own distinct aroma like cat spray on drapes. It did not take long for Gus to spot the aging cop.

"How's life?" Ezra asked. He had not seen Gus in a while because the barkeep worked the noon to 8:00 p.m. shift. Somehow, Ezra caught him working the wee hours.

"What did you say?" Gus cupped his good ear.

"I said someone's fucking your wife."

Gus offered a sour look. "That's a sick thought."

Ezra smiled. "Is she that bad looking?"

"No. Dead ten years." Gus shook his head. "Sicksonofabitch," he mumbled and stared into the mirror behind his cash register at the rain-covered cop. "It's not supposed to be this way; where's the fucking sanctity of marriage?"

Ezra shrugged and noticed there was not a filled seat in the pie-shaped corner bar.

"Who's in the back room?"

"Mike is passed out on top of a motorcycle crate. He was snoring so loud, no one wanted to play cards."

"Passed out. I just told him I was coming over to talk to him."

"You missed your chance."

Ezra checked out the back room.

Kinder was out cold.

"Damn it, Gus."

"If it's important, I'll tell him when he wakes up."

"Tell him I saw Annee go Tom Gresham's flat. They're fucking their brains out."

"So, what. Ain't nobody's business but hers and Tommy's."

"No way. Mike figures it another way. He says he saw Annee first and if she's gonna fuck anyone in North Beach, it's gonna be him. When he's coked up there's no reasoning with him. He thinks she's his property."

"Well, if you ask me that sounds like Mike's got a coke problem. Sounds he might be a bit paranoid."

Ezra sighed. "It used to be a lot easier when there was no coke to be had. Everyone just got drunk."

"Amen."

"Give me a shot and a beer," Ezra said while taking off his parka.

"I wanna buy your parka now that you ain't a cop anymore. I love the gang bang yellow color."

Ezra frowned. "What's yellow got to do with gang bangs?"

"You're too damn literal. It was a figure of speech. Sell me the goddamn raincoat."

"Just because I'm not a cop doesn't mean it'll never rain again. I'm keeping it."

Gus shrugged and went back to drying pilsner glasses from the below-bar washing machine. He looked back at Ezra. "How about a trade. You can have my gas guzzler Ford for the parka."

"What year is it, again?"

"Fucking old. It's illegal to drive on the road."

"Will it get me to Portland? I gotta sister up there I haven't seen in a while."

"No." Gus laughed. He whistled through his bad teeth. "Tell you what. Pay Mikey's bar tab and I'll give you the rust bucket for free."

"I could buy a new car for what he owes you."

"Fuck it, Ezra, here are the keys. It's yours for nothin', just pay the parking lot guy where I have it parked. Get it outta my sight."

"How long have you had it parked?"

"Since yesterday."

"If that's true, you got a deal," Ezra said. "I'm keeping the parka."

11.
SHEET MUSIC
Novella

Cantina Psalm:

"Everybody wants to get into the act!"
–Jimmy Durante's early 20th century vaudeville running gag

THE INAUGURAL BALL

Cold from the storm, Annee trailed rainwater up the flights of stairs to his flat.

Tom waited for her in the hallway outside the front door his flat.

"I'm sorry," she said after clearing her throat. "The sonofabitch tried to rape me in his fucking, stupid man cave."

Tom wrapped his arms around her. He felt her shivering under the drenched raincoat. "I'll take care of him in the morning. Let's get you dry." He marched with her to the rear of his flat, where that part of his world was colored in greenish gold from the naked bulb reflecting off vintage emerald-colored Catalina tile.

Tom led her to the shower. He reached in to turn on the water and stepped back. He wanted to kiss her, but this was not the time.

"I'm so cold," she stuttered.

He helped her climb out of the seersucker with one hand and adjusted the shower knob with the other. "This will warm you up fast. I'll find you some dry clothes."

At his feet was the plastic bag she'd been carrying like a purse since she left Powell's.

He picked it up and curiosity got the best of him. He looked inside to see the colorful colors of what he recognized as the cocktail uniform of a Klondike Room waitress, plus underwear and 100 loose $100 bills and a hard steel revolver. He put the safety back on.

He tossed the bag on the bathroom counter and went to retrieve a pair of gray Dior jogging sweats that Carly Martin left behind so long ago she forgot Tom had them.

He carried back the sweats and dropped them on the small tile counter next to the lavatory.

Now, he couldn't get out of his clothes fast enough to join her in the shower.

"What are you doing?" she asked.

He stood behind her. His male excitement pushed gently against the smooth folds of her ass.

Tom spun her around. They both felt the hot water on their heads. Their mouths met and they playfully danced around like schoolkids to feel the warmth over their skin.

He forced a kiss on her mouth.

Bold, but at the same time tender.

She accepted.

The kiss was intoxicating. They slipped into his bedroom. Wet. Passionate. He was now in bed with a woman he only met hours ago, and she was whispering in his ear in some primal language he had no clue to what she was saying. He pulled the puffed quilt over them.

* * *

Annee in her borrowed sweats sat cross-legged at the dinette table. She was credit card chopping the illicit powder Tom had promised her earlier into long lines on a jadeite plate. Using a rolled $20, she noisily sucked a five-inch-long line into her nose.

"Wow," she said softly. "Where did you get this?" she asked.

"I found it."

"I thought that's what you said, but I don't believe you."

He explained last summer across the street in the park there was a fight between two teenagers. Lots of screaming, clawing, and spitting. They were both teen girls in green and gray parochial school uniforms.

"I went downstairs into Washington Square and broke up the fight by walking toward them. They took off in opposite directions and left behind a brown bag with the coke inside. I ended up putting it in the pantry expecting I'd be contacted by someone from the precinct asking if I had seen a drug deal go down in the park. No one has called me to his day."

"And you never have been tempted to try it."

"Yes and no. I know what coke tastes like and what it does. It gives me a headache and I feel like crap for a couple of days. To be honest, I figured I'd sell it and keep the cash."

"From where I come, an ounce of coke goes for $6,000. For this, you could get $300 a gram. Why would they leave it behind?"

"Because one girl figured the other girl had the dope. And they probably blamed each other to their dealer."

"People have died for less."

"I wish I could say I cared."

"And you're willing to share it with me?"

"It's all yours."

"Just like that? Because we made love or you're being a nice guy?"

"I'm more than happy getting rid of it."

"That's too much money to give away. Thanks, but I can't take it all."

"I thought of selling it, but as much as I'd like the cash, I have a feeling something will go sideways. I never get away with anything. It would be really greasy for me to be accused of dealin' dope. I work at city hall. What I do reflects on everybody there, including the mayor." Tom stopped himself from preaching. "Is that holier than thou?"

"Yes." Annee inhaled the long second line, then put the lid back on the small peanut butter sized jar and left it on the coffee table. She dug into her purse and pulled out a 4x6 black and white snapshot.

She looked up at him. "Have you seen this guy around?"

He recognized the face in the image immediately. Caught by surprise, Tom took a bit longer staring at the picture. It was the photo Art Garcia showed him the night they had dinner on Angel Island. This was the case Art had brought him in on.

He decided to play dumb until he could talk to Art. Maybe she was one of Art's freelancers. Maybe not. "Not off the top of my head," Tom lied. "Who is he?"

"Alan Carter. I'm a friend of his family. His sister and I went to the same college back East. I wasn't doing anything back home, so I've decided to come out here to look for him."

"I'm guessing San Francisco was the last place you've heard from him?"

"Yes."

"Did anyone file a missing person report?"

"I've only been here a couple of days and you're one of the first I've shown Alan's photo. You're a cop. Tell me, does it do any good to file a report?"

"No bureau is perfect, but Missing Person's has a good reputation. I've heard good things about them."

"I'll do that."

"Are you a private eye?"

"No, just a friend."

"You're staring at me, again."

"Because you're very, very beautiful."

"Stop it before you gawk your way out of a good deal tonight. Let's let things happen."

He took her at her word. Tomorrow, he would tell Art he had competition to find Alan Carter.

* * *

Tom refused any coke, but to start his half of the party, he did open a bottle of red Salazar Wine. It was the last of a case he and Carly had purchased on a trip to the winery last summer.

She shifted next to him on his living room sofa.

He leaned over and nuzzled her neck. "I think you have the world's best collection of freckles."

Annee yawned. "Is this your first date *ever*?"

"What did I say?"

"I don't like pillow talk."

Tom decided not to ask any more questions. It was warm enough to begin taking off the dry clothes he'd given her a few minutes ago. He brought her into his arms.

She generous with her kisses.

He couldn't keep his hands off her body.

ONE BRUNETTE TOO MANY

A loud, unexpected knock on anyone's front door late at night is not good news. At best, it's a drunk pounding on the wrong apartment door. At its worst, the grim reaper is making a house call.

When tonight's knock came, time stood still.

Wide-eyed, Tom said, "I hope it's not your husband."

Annee whispered, "I don't have a husband. Don't answer. It's never good news this late. No law says you have to answer," she whispered.

"That's not the way I play," he said and jumped to his feet. He hurried to the hat rack by the front door, where his holstered service revolver hung on a hook next to his bulletproof vest.

Nothing like seeing Superman peeking through his front door spyhole holding a Glock 9mm behind his back with his ass hanging out below his cape.

* * *

Tom first opened the door as if he were cracking a safe. Then he shrugged, "My God, what are you doing here?"

Annee heard a woman's voice respond.

"I'm drunk, I'm wet, I'm pissed and I don't have any place fun to go that's warm."

"I have company."

"Good, let me join in." Carly Martin pushed the door wider and stepped into the flat. She saw Annee covering her nakedness with a throw pillow and smiled and put her finger up to her lips. "Shhh, it's OK, I'm not his wife or his girlfriend but we mess around when we're bored. Does that make sense?"

The strawberry blonde reached up to shake hands with the pixie haircut brunette. "I'm Annee."

"You're certainly pretty," Carly said and pulled off her wet raincoat to reveal her spaghetti strap dress. She reached down and touched Annee's bare knees. "Do you have to be naked to play?"

"Yes." Tom grinned. He knew Carly was blitzed. That was not something she would do or say sober. And because she was at his door, he knew something did not go well wherever she had been tonight.

Carly slid onto the sofa next to Annee. "Is that coke? Tom, you renegade. Since I got stood up. I deserve a line."

Tom rolled his eyes.

Annee put her fingers on his lips. She obliged and used the edge of a credit card to lay out a thick line of coke for Carly.

Tom came up behind Carly quickly pushed the silk straps off her shoulders. She felt her dress start to fall the floor. Now, she had a choice either catch the dress before it slipped to her waist revealing her breasts or she could ingest the line Carly had cut for her.

The coke won.

"Sounds delicious," Tom laughed at her noisy snort.

She immediately started coughing and ended up sneezing.

"God, I'm such an embarrassment. That's strong stuff."

"You'll have a nice buzz going for you in a few minutes," Annee warned.

"I've had too much Champagne," Carly said. She lay back on the sofa and closed her eyes.

Annee cupped Carly's breasts with her hands.

Startled, Carly immediately sat up.

"Relax," Annee cooed, "let's have some fun." Annee tugged the dress over Carly's hips.

Carly eased back on the sofa. "I had a boring date with Garrett," she said, looking at Tom, who took off his T-shirt. "He's so disorganized," she continued, "I don't want to see him anymore... I'm blabbing. Why am I telling you this?"

Annee kissed Carly, who pulled away. "Oh, Tom tell her I don't do girls."

"Too late," he said.

"Oh, what are you doing?" Carly asked Annee, who moved her tongue slowly down from her navel.

Tom came around behind where Annee was kneeling and inserted himself. He whispered. "What are we doing, Carly?"

Carly's breath became quicker. She answered softly, "Annee's sucking me and you're fucking her in front of me."

Tom reached across Annee's pink, freckled back to hold on to Carly's hands.

Carly's head was spinning. Oh, how she loved being on the carousel. She had never been so overwhelmed with cocaine or aroused by a woman and a man at the same time before.

Tom's hands explored both women. He had never made love to two women at once. Being the most sober, he was filming in his mind these two wonderful women. Something to savor some day in his old age.

The trio reversed positions. Tom was inside Carly and Carly's mouth found Annee's pussy.

Soon, he could tell them apart by just touching their skin. Annee was far more athletic. Her body was taut and smooth, while Carly was soft and easy to touch living velvet. And they were both his for tonight.

"This really can't be," he pulled his cock out of Carly before he ejaculated.

Annee found his penis and held on to it.

Tom closed his eyes as he continued to skyrocket wetting them both.

Carly stroked Annee's breasts, twisting nipples one after the other between her thumb and forefinger.

"You can do that all week," Annee laughed.

Carly slipped her hand into Anne's mons, "My turn, let me try that."

Annee whispered, "I can't move, Tom's inside me."

* * *

On then off the sofa, three consenting adults spent three hours in a pile of asses and elbows as some country western song so delicately blared.

Sometime during the night, Tom woke to their voices. They were in the middle of an existentialist coke conversation. Exploring. Whispering and asking silly, drunk questions.

By touch he knew he was spooning with Annee. He heard Carly and Annee giggle. Carly whispered, "Have you ever had a black cock in your mouth?"

"Lots of times," Annee whispered back.

"How is it? I've never had a black cock."

"If you close your eyes or turn out the lights at night, all cocks are black." Annee laughed.

Tom moved across from the sofa to his favorite overstuffed chair to sip his half full glass of wine.

The body heat and the radiator had made the small flat almost hot.

"Have some more coke." Annee pointed to the lines of powder on the coffee table.

Carly inhaled both lines. "This is it, no more."

Tom began to laugh. Annee was on her hands and knees crawling toward him.

Carly jumped to her feet. She ran ahead of Annee, grabbed Tom by the hand and led him into the bedroom.

"No, you don't." Annee chased and fell into bed with them.

THIS SHIT'S SO GOOD I CAN SEE MARS

Dawn revealed a rain-swept Friday—another in the endless parade of arriving Arctic storms drenching, depressing the Bay Area. Climate restorers had long given up trying to bring what used to be normalcy to the worldwide weather patterns. Instead, meteorologists worked on prediction models aimed at coping with Mother Earth's rage at what humans had done to her. Science forecast another month of rain. Now, they were seldom wrong.

Brain fogged, Annee barely slept. She felt miserable, nauseated from last night's coke fest. She'd enjoyed the coke; now she was paying for it.

She edged out of bed, covering her nakedness with Tom's blazer that until now lay on the floor. Annee was happy the flat was warm. Tom had left the ancient steam radiator on all night.

Moving to the living room, she sat on the sofa, crossing her bare legs, and lit one of Carly's filterless cigarettes from the pack of Lucky Strikes she found on the coffee table. Lighting it, taking a drag, she watched the smoke trail curl upward as if confined by some invisible straw. The flame end matched the colored tips of her manicured nails.

Among last night's cocaine addled conversations, Annee listened to Carly drone on about how the maker of Luckies had been resurrected by Big Ben Industries, a British conglomerate that has been buying up rights to names of deceased twentieth-century brands, especially those who fell victim to politically correct badmouthing.

Carly made a point to import such brands via Amazon. She hated the political correctness that had spilled from the previous century. It was all so hypocritical because it was a form of censorship imposed by those who supposedly championed civil liberties. Carly insisted she looked forward to when it would go away like fedora hats on men, which was a fad during the 1920s and lasted till the 1950s.

Annee decided the only way to stop her monologue was to walk over to her and begin kissing her. And that's what she did. The more Carly blabbed the more she got kissed.

Tom returned from the toilet with a beautiful erection. And, in slow motion, the menage a trois began all over again. In a flash of dexterity, Annee jumped into Tom's arms. They coupled instantly.

Carly followed Tom as he carried Annee to the sofa. She sat on Tom's chest, facing Annee. The women kissed while Tom exploded in passion inside Annee.

* * *

An hour later, fully awake, Annee stood and stretched. She rummaged on the floor for one of Tom's t-shirts that someone wore last night. Yawning, rubbing her eyes, she saw night fading into a gray dawn. She tiptoed across the worn carpet to the kitchen's linoleum tile. There she made coffee.

Waiting for the water to boil, she opened one of the casement windows facing the park. She hoped a jolt of cold air would dispel her nausea. The few wisps of rain that made it through the window felt good on her face.

Despite the early hour, North Beach smelled of garlic, bacon with a wave of coffee being fresh roasted. The aromas were distinctly those of North Beach.

The mix of fresh air and spits of rain did little to ebb her hangover. It was a lousy cycle.

Closing the window, she turned to the refrigerator, where Tom had a full quart of orange juice sitting next to a bottle of milk and four cans of Anchor Steam craft beer.

Annee alternated gulping the soothing juice and making coffee from freshly ground beans.

*　*　*

Carly was next to reach the kitchen, naked below the waist. She also had on a white t-shirt from Tom's chest of drawers. "You have such beautiful legs," Annee said and handed her a cup of hot coffee.

He was still in bed, snoring.

Carly welcomed the coffee.

Annee kept touching Carly's body. She couldn't resist; she playfully teased Carly about how the brunette announced every arriving orgasm like a train conductor calling off next stop: *I'm coming, coming: Wow* or *I'm coming, coming: Ouuuu* or *I'm coming, coming: God, don't stop.*

Carly, surprised by Annee's bluntness, caused an immediate unladylike snort that shot coffee up into her nose. Coughing, she hurried into the kitchen for a paper towel. "That was unnecessary," Carly breathed through her mouth.

"But funny," Annee added. "You were the belle of the ball. How much do you remember?"

"Too much. Don't ask, I'm still in a fog."

"Do you like girls?"

"Oh, God, I'm such a whore," Carly whispered and rubbed her hands into her face. "I was all over you, wasn't I?"

"Tom had to peel you off so he could take his turn with me. Was this the first time you tasted a vagina?"

"Stop being so graphic." Carly's eyes widened. "Remember I'm new at this."

"You had me fooled." Annee playfully pushed Carly's shoulder. "You're not married, are you?"

"No, far from it."

"Now you have a war story. Am I your first?"

"First what?" Carly rolled her head back and closed her eyes.

"Pussy. First pussy."

"Arrrrgggg, stop it."

"Well, am I?"

Carly tilted her head to the side and blew smoke at her, "No, not exactly. When I was in Manhattan last fall, I took on the entire line of Rockettes. Every single one of them."

Annee grinned. "I asked for that, sorry." She reached across the table to hold Carly's hand.

Carly did surprise herself by how casual the evening played out. Now, she was holding hands with a woman she had known for only a few hours. What she believed was taboo (threesomes) turned out to be normal. Kissing another woman was surprisingly easy. Touching her. Tasting nipples, thighs, other places became normal. Skin tasted like skin no matter the gender. What was the big deal? Erotic sensations were more intense with oral sex. She basked in the glow of one tongue after another stroking, nibbling, caressing her.

Where was the guilt, the sin that the polite society had raised her to dread?

Annee, by far, was more aggressive in her passion than Tom.

Annee reveled in oral sex. She was relentless, spending Tom then moving on to Carly.

Carly took turns with Tom to run tongues along Annee's freckled skin, tonguing her navel, her mouth, her delicious neck while Tom locked himself inside her strawberry-colored mons.

Carly's reverie recalled other moments when she lay passive, running her hands through her short hair, whispering to be touched. Lying on her back, moving her knees apart with each new partner, she could not tell what mouth brought her to such a rampant orgasm. Tom laughed and put his hand over her mouth to mute her loud ecstasies.

Now in the kitchen alone together, the two accidental lovers smiled at each other in an afterglow somewhere between peace and curiosity. Carly's skin was pink in blotches from head to toe.

Annee interrupted a Cheshire grin by sticking a Lucky Strike between her lips. She was able to light it on the old-fashioned gas stove.

"Let me have that," Carly asked, trading a lit smoke for an unlit one.

* * *

Carly finished her coffee and poured more into her cup. "How did you meet Tom?" She moved her feet on to the chair and bent her legs under the t-shirt.

Annee noticed Carly's feet. "Your toenails match your fingernails. Even naked you're so buttoned down."

"I don't know what to say to that?"

"I'm just blabbing," Annee said. "Hoping you-like me? Lift your t-shirt, let me see your breasts."

Carly obeyed, pulling off the shirt. She threw it, hitting Carly in the face.

Annee stripped.

Both naked, they embraced and kissed like teenagers on a wobbly dinette chair.

Finally, Carly pulled away. "I met him last night at Powell's. John introduced us. He bought me dinner. I thought he'd be a great one-off."

"Was he?"

"I'd see Tom again. Unless he's yours?"

"We're in a relationship that isn't a relationship. He works for my father, and I simply adore him, but I don't want to marry him. Maybe if a woman like you spirited him away, I'd hate myself. But at least I'd know he's happy, and we'd be able to finally shake loose of each other."

"Office romances are so hard to manage. Everyone who cares probably knows."

"Not in this city," Carly added quickly. "If they knew, it would be on the front page…"

"Would you be mad if I saw him again while I'm in town?"

"So, I wasn't enough for you?" Carly pretended to frown.

"It's always nice to hang out with someone you don't have to cut through the fog with every time. I'd like to do this again. Besides, I don't know how long I will stay in the city."

"Go for it. I told him a dozen times it was over between us."

"But you still showed up at his door last night—unannounced."

"I know, I know. I'm glad you want to see him again. I figured I messed up any chance he had with you by showing up last night."

"You made last night better," Annee said.

"I don't know what to think. And I can't believe the things you did last night in front of me. I'm thinking you must have been one nasty little girl."

"I like touching girls, especially myself. Here, give me your hand."

Carly slapped Annee's fingers away.

Annee laughed, "See what a whore I am?"

"Last night was fun. Not something I plan on repeating anytime soon but I will remember all this when I'm a little old lady, definitely."

"Good," Annee said. "Did you know Tom offered to let me stay with him until I find a job. Does that work for you?"

"It's his call. I want him to be happy. I want one of us to decide."

"I wasn't thinking of romance. I need a place to stay."

"He'll be a gentleman."

Annee had clearly excited herself with her fingers.

"Can you stop that, now?" Carly was looking away.

Annee continued. She gently held her tongue between her gapped front teeth. Her breathing grew deeper. "I'm really enjoying this. I won't be long."

Carly closed her eyes. "Why are you doing that?"

"Because you turn me on." With her free hand, Annee moved her hand between Carly's white thighs.

This time Carly didn't slap at Annee. Instead, she moved her knees apart and let Annee's arousal grow.

"You're going to make me explode," Annee said.

* * *

Tom walked into the living room to what had become a pornographer's set. He walked by Annee and Carly, who were lying on the sofa kissing while their hands explored each other. "Are we having fun?" he asked.

Each held Tom's hand. He pulled them up from the sofa and took his naked friends back to bed.

And so went the carousel, a night and a morning spinning that may or may never be repeated but while it happened it was pure joy.

* * *

Tom left them tangled in bed. Carly's white body was a rosy pink between her thighs and over her breasts.

Annee leaned into Carly and whispered. "When he wakes up what will we do with him?"

"I hear him in the shower," Carly said.

Annee giggled. "Let's go pee all over him."

"No. Stop it!" Carly insisted. "I really can't have any more sex or listen to your kinky mouth."

"Amateur."

"Yes, I am and count me out if you think peeing is sexy."

"He's really a good man," Annee finally said. "I could see it by the way he made love to you. Were you jealous?"

Carly wrinkled her nose. "A bit."

"I'd keep him."

"God, listen to us. We sound like we're talking about a car we're about to buy."

That made Annee laugh. "I need a shower."

Carly agreed, then asked "I just realized I know nothing about you."

"Let's keep it this way for now. We may never have a chance to do this so…so…comfortably."

"Like I said, this is enough for me," Carly said. "I'm not going to make a habit of this."

"Too bad, you're amazing."

They embraced; Carly sighed, "I can never say no. I'm just as bad as you."

"Now you are officially gay?" Annee announced.

"I wish all gay persons well. I'm not one of them. I like traditional love?"

"What the hell is that?" Annee asked. "Are we talking two and a half kids, a white picket fence and the PTA?"

"Something like that. Are you gay, Annee?"

"Sweetie, if it feels good, I'll fuck anyone or anything if they're cute. No toads for me."

"Then I'm a gay-in-training toad?" Carly held her hands out to her sides.

Annee had that look in her eyes. She wanted Carly in her arms, "You're gorgeous and especially with tits like yours and your face. Damn, your face is amazing."

"You're prettier than me," Carly offered.

"You're younger," Annee said, "but answer me this: have you had your heart broken? Yet?"

Carly didn't answer.

Annee pointed to her. "I'm taking that as a no. You must experience both the good and bad aspects of men. They're all jerks, but if you want a man for the rest of your life, you gotta find out what makes them tick."

"Who has the time for that?"

"If you want a man in your old age, then you'll have to make the time," Annee said.

"What if you have the right man now and then invest ten years fucking jerks. By then it's too late to go back to him."

"Hedge your bets. Find someone like me," Annee smiled.

"Sex is so political with me," Carly said, "like two lobbyists trying to get the last word in… I hope I'm wrong."

"If Tom made love to you the way he did to me last night, I'd reconsider," Annee said touching her lover's face.

"But we all know the honeymoon goes away."

"Not if you find the right man."

"Really?" Carly asked.

"Yes, really. I feel in my gut that I could trust a man like Tom the rest of my life and love him…love him. Lasting love." Annee added, "But for now, I have to ask what keeps you from committing to him?"

"Fear. I hope my parents won't think I'm marrying below my station."

"God, woman, how absolutely medieval. Marry him. Who cares how much you make? You're probably a very rich bitch, so who cares about money. You got plenty for both of you."

"How do you know I'm rich—if I am?"

"That little silk dress you tossed off last night like a paper towel cost you 1,500 new dollars."

"It was on sale."

"Not funny, I want to live in your shoes if all your men are like Tom. He fucked me blind, and I think you know that…no wonder you can't let him go."

Carly was embarrassed, scarlet. "Why don't we both marry him?"

Annee wasn't smiling. "You better hurry and decide."

Carly looked her in the eyes. "Who are you?"

"I'm your competition, if you don't want him."

They walked hand in hand into the shower.

Annee greeted him in the steaming shower by putting a hand on his cock.

Carly cooed into Tom's ear, "Lazarus is that you?"

Tom was very glad to see them. Two partners in a shower. It dawned on him how very lucky he was.

Until the hot water ran out.

* * *

Tom's phone rang at noon. It was from John Wald.

"What's up?"

Wald made no small talk. "Last night before closing I saw Carly Martin talking with Shannon Reading. I haven't seen her since."

"What's that got to do with me?"

"Tommy, I'm concerned. The world isn't just about you. I need you to find Carly for me. I want to know if Shannon told Carly where she was going?"

"Did you call the DA's office and ask to leave a message."

"I did. Someone there said she hadn't been picking up her phone messages since yesterday afternoon."

"I talked to Carly this morning. She's OK. I'll call her and tell her to call you."

Tom put the phone down. He was about to decide. He knew full well that if he relayed the message to her from John that the interlude—the menage would come to an end. Selfishly, he didn't want the bubble to burst.

Carly was a grown woman, he judged, when she wanted to retrieve her phone messages, she could do that. For now, he felt she deserved some time off from the office.

He turned to see two women staring at him. It made him laugh, "What?"

"Are you taking us for breakfast?" Carly asked.

"Too late. How about lunch," Annee said.

By noon, they cleaned up nicely and the trio walked down the block into C&Js for something to eat.

Michael Cortland put his hand on his partner's shoulder. "Look what the cat dragged in."

Seamus said, "For the love of God, he's got two of them. He should've been born with four hands and two dicks."

Cortland shook his head. "Now there's a man not wasting his youth."

* * *

The trio split up after lunch. Carly took a SuperUber back to her Russian Hill aerie while Tom and Annee walked back to Tom's flat.

It was still raining. It was probably going to rain forever.

No one could remember what day it was.

They spent the entire day in bed ignoring one phone call after another.

One of the calls was from Art Garcia. When Tom resurfaced, he heard, "Tommy, It's Art. I just found out you know an old squeeze of mine Carla Boris. Her stage name is Carol Law. You heard her sing when we met over on Angel Island. Speaking of small world, she told me you have the shortest dick she's ever seen—alive or dead." Art laughed and hung up.

12.

MEA CULPA HALL OF FAME
High-Rent District

Cantina Psalm:
Armageddon tonight at 10 pm,
details on the 11 o'clock news

THE KING OF GREASE

Wally McGrath was a big deal in San Francisco. A fucking big deal if you considered that he was president of the Board of Supervisors, the panel that oversaw the city and county of San Francisco. He was the fourth-generation owner of McGrath International, the world's largest engineering firm, and owner of a string of hotels around the world—all having names of Alaskan cities. And, most dangerous of all, he was a serial adulterer, who believed if he fell from a high rise unlike his mother that he would be shatterproof.

In San Francisco, it is the penthouse of the Fairbanks Hotel where Wally and his wife, 39-year-old Jennifer dwell.

The pair—she as the only heiress of Hawthorn Oil and her husband—could have bought or built the most outrageous mansion in the West.

But they chose to live in a two-level penthouse atop his hotel because it provided him an address in the city. That was a requirement of being an elected supervisor.

Jennifer was the 10 p.m. news anchor for KNUZ TV, a station where she was a 49 percent owner. It kept her busy and gave her media clout, which was golden in this town.

The other 51 percent of the TV station was owned by John Bruce of Bruce Communications.

The McGraths came by their ownership share by bailing John Bruce out from his most recent bout with bankruptcy, which was aided and abetted by the broadcaster being a chronic loser at a certain Chinatown casino.

That is a story for another day.

Two nights ago, Jennifer surprised Wally by coming home early.

Her husband was sitting in the hot tub on the terrace outside the master suite. Even in the cozy candlelight she had no trouble seeing the brown-haired, white-shouldered young woman, who had her arms around Wally's neck.

Jennifer flashed on the overhead patio lights.

At that moment, Wally experienced the stomach-churning horror of being caught by his wife with a younger woman—never mind it was the second time in the past year.

The embarrassing revelation showed on Jennifer McGrath's face. To use an old-fashioned word, she was flabbergasted—not at the bare-ass adultery being committed in front of her eyes and in her own house, but by the fact that the woman was not a lioness but merely a bar maid. For that insult Wally would pay dearly.

Jennifer grabbed the hotel phone on the living room end table. She was able to reach Ruth Dolan, the McGrath's long time butler on first ring. "Bring Vanchester to our suite. I need both of you to take the trash out."

Within minutes, the in-house duo took care of Wally's situation.

Wally stared at his pregnant wife and displayed his total command of the obvious: "I didn't expect you home early."

She had been at a broadcaster's convention in Denver. "I came down with a cold."

"Of course, I remember you telling me that," he added quickly. "I'm off to Paris in the morning for a meeting of McGrath Hotel managers," he said, then took a sip of Champagne. "We can discuss this when I return."

"Not much to talk about. I'm fed up with you. End of story."

"I will apologize if it does any good."

"That's not important anymore. This is the second marriage contract you just blew through. I got you by the balls, Wally. How does it feel not to be a billionaire anymore?"

MEA CULPA HALL OF FAME

"Perhaps Mrs. McGrath would like to come in for a sizing," the Union Square Tiffany's & Co. jeweler said as she presented the diamond choker to Wally McGrath.

"I like it, and please wrap in a bigger box. I'm going to surprise her by putting it inside one of those big chocolate Easter eggs." He smiled and handled her a credit card.

"Would this be a surprise?" asked the jeweler, a remarkable-looking fifty-something brunette who was wearing a blue silk suit.

"Probably."

"This will look splendid on her, especially in black." She smiled. "She's a very lucky lady."

"I'm lucky." McGrath was wearing a custom-tailored Brioni silk suit by Cesaro Callivano and a matching lightweight raincoat.

"Would you like this delivered?"

"No, I'll take it with me. We're having lunch."

"Maybe a message in a card to go along?" she asked.

He didn't hesitate, "How about something that says, 'Sorry, I was a raving asshole, sweetheart.'"

"We send a lot of those."

"Really? Who to?"

"Mainly from politicians."

McGrath looked at his one hundred six-year-old Rolex wristwatch. It was 1 p.m. He had enough time to walk six blocks from his office at the Fairbanks, down Nob Hill to Le Central Restaurant to meet his wife for lunch.

LIGHTWEIGHT CHAMPIONSHIP OF THE WORLD

Childless and ensconced in San Francisco, Jennifer was fond of her prime-time 10 p.m. news anchor post with KNUZ-TV. The McGraths owned 51 percent of all John Bruce's Bruce Communications stock. She insisted her motherhood would not harm her career.

Today was different. No longer could she hide from the truth. Wally was not as faithful as the next dawn. Yet, times were good, and she loved being belle of the ball; besides, who has time for a messy divorce when you own the city.

But when someone slaps you hard across the face, one must deal with the situation. Flee or stand your ground and fight.

Jennifer Hawthorn McGrath arrived at Le Central fully armed to launch a marital Armageddon. She was not in the mood to lose.

* * *

Wally McGrath seldom entered Le Central, the brasserie of choice for Financial District powerbrokers, the media, and politicos, always remembering his father and grandfather saying the bistro was the best in the city.

Jennifer McGrath had bittersweet feelings for the Parisian-style eatery. Located in her favorite part of downtown, she loved the area between Nob Hill, where she lived, and the fashion district surrounding nearby Union Square.

If she had a favorite perch in the bistro, it was the window table with provincial-style curtains. From there she could see busy Bush Street and the ornate gate into Chinatown. But she seldom returned to Le Central, after hearing Garrett Ellis report that Wally loved to show off his *femmes au moment* to the silk suits that packed the bistro's lunch trade. Garrett was on retainer with McGrath International despite being the attorney of record representing her in the negotiations following Wally's first infidelity. And, most likely the second.

Hard as she tried to ignore the whispers—*Oh, that's his wife*—she could still feel a chilliness from the staff. They knew he'd be more subdued on visits with her in attendance. Wally tipped better when he was being the freewheeling raconteur with the other women at the table.

Jennifer forced herself to dwell on how much she loved the history of Le Central's cassoulet, which was first put on the stove in 1994 by the long-ago original owners, Pierre and Claude. The duck, beef shoulder, and the veggie stew had been simmering a bit longer than she.

Marital small talk proceeded. She unconsciously twisted her wedding ring around her finger while she waited for an opening to stab him in the balls.

* * *

Jennifer, in her second trimester, refused to look at the small package wrapped in baby blue paper with a white bow that was sitting on the edge of their restaurant table. She smiled at her husband but refused to open it.

Because she'd called ahead and used her media clout, they'd arrived at the last empty table.

Dressed in their power suits, Jennifer wore a silk pink blazer, a loose white Emilia George blouse, and maternity chic stretch-waist stove-pipe pink pants with white low heel mules from Prada.

Wally was impeccable in his bespoke three-piece Brioni.

Wally and Jennifer sat at the same window table where years earlier a magazine photographer had snapped a black-and-white image of *San Francisco Chronicle* columnist Herb Caen having lunch with politico and future Mayor Willie Brown and haberdasher Wilkes Bashford. In the 1970s, the photo was framed behind the main door next to Le Central's coat rack, where it remains decades later

"Here we are—on a date." He smiled and ordered a bottle of San Pellegrino water. "Impressive pinks today. Is that a hint? Can we expect a baby girl?"

"No, I could have worn le bleu just as easily…flip of a coin… nothing more." Gender was a closely held secret with Jennifer.

She lifted the lapel of her blazer. "I bought this in Paris when we were exploring sites for your new hotel."

"That was a great trip, I remember we stayed at the Georges V," he said.

She reminded him her outfit was created by the owner of a just-opened boutique on Rue Jean Goujon. "I remember it because there was a cute brasserie across the street from Georges V."

Wally glanced around the restaurant. "I do like you in pink," he added.

"Let's get down to business." She stared at him over her hands clasped in front of her face. Her elbows were on the table.

Wally's smile got wider. "How about if I tell you I love you more than anything and I'm looking forward to the baby?"

"My opening line is not quite so endearing. Another of your bimbos left something in the guest powder room last night."

"Didn't Ruth Dolan talk to you about that?"

"It's not Mrs. Dolan's purse."

"John's party next door was so crowded, and it went on for hours, that Mrs. Dolan asked if some of the waitstaff could take a break in our kitchen and use the front bathroom. Since you were in Denver, I figured that wouldn't be a problem."

"No, I'll speak to her to make sure her staffer gets her purse back."

"Are you feeling better?"

"I have the flu, Wally. I feel like crap."

"You should be in bed," he offered.

"It doesn't matter. I've asked Garrett Ellis to file for a divorce. I'm fed up, Wally. We're done."

McGrath flinched. "Is he the only lawyer in this burg?" He was starting to feel the weight of the bricks she was loading onto his back.

Her hands unfolded. "Good. I'm glad he upsets you. I'm winning already."

McGrath stared. It was his no-nonsense take my deal or die look. "Shouldn't we talk about this in private?"

She returned a mock smile. "We have no privacy. There hasn't been a moment in our marriage where there has been privacy."

"You exaggerate."

"Wally, I picked this restaurant because it wasn't in North Beach. But it might as well be C&J's or DeLuca's or Fior D'Italia or some other North Beach diner. It doesn't matter. You spend all your time away from our marriage and city hall in these bars. Why?"

"Nice places. I'm the duly elected supervisor—North Beach and this part of town is in my district."

"I don't see you out in Polk Gulch or Union Square or down at Fisherman's Wharf. When was the last time you were in the other parts of your district? What is it with you and North Beach?"

"Your point?"

"You've got a death wish for your reputation. You're crawling the sewers with bimbos and your sleazy friend Larry DeLuca. None of them are in your class. And that's not even considering what kind of diseases you're exposing us to.

"And Wally no matter how hard you try; you will never be like them. You've got too much friggin' money. No matter how much you try to be cool and be one of the boys at DeLuca's or Cortland & James or Le Central behind my back, you'll never be one of them. Trust me."

He offered, "I am one of them. I went to school with all of them. That's why I go there—because it's the only place I can be normal. They don't care about the money. I'm Wally and that's it." He glanced around and smiled for the sake of the unabashed stares from other patrons.

Jennifer twisted her napkin in a knot.

He reached across the table and put his hand over hers. "I am very sorry for the way I treated you last summer. I was wrong then. You are very important to me. You're my wife, and nothing has changed how much I love you." McGrath spoke softly and, as he did, he kept edging the small package toward his wife's side of the table. "Last night was a staffing problem. Check with Mrs. Dolan. It was not an infidelity."

"Christ, Wally! A staffing problem. How stupid do you think I am? I'm not a wide-eyed twenty-two-year-old."

"I know you're upset. I don't go out plotting how I can make you miserable."

"But Wally, your other women make me miserable. This is not a marriage. If you love me, how can you keep rubbing my face in the garbage?"

"Mea Culpa."

"Don't say that. Asshole lawyers use that phrase to cute their way out of lousy situations. Say it in English."

"I'm sorry," he said softly. "If you still think I have a problem with women, I'll get some professional help. You've suggested that before. OK, last night was a misunderstanding. But, if you're so quick to judge me—then I'm prepared to do anything you want. I've been committed to you since we were married."

"Good, I'm glad you believe that—because I don't believe you. To me, there hasn't been a really good day since Havana."

Puzzled, Wally asked, "Why? What happened in Cuba?"

She rolled her eyes. "That was where we had our honeymoon."

A woman at the next table gasped. Her lunch partner snickered.

Wally's face turned red. "Why can't you believe me about last night? What do you want me to do? I don't want us to fail."

"For how long? A week? I believed you the first million times. Right now, you're laughable. I can't tell you how hurtful it is to me knowing you're taking so many other women to bed with you."

"Jennifer, I've always had women friends. I don't love them."

Jennifer tossed the twisted napkin in his face. "What a load of crap. Pardon me, Wally, but this is me over here on this side of the table. Plain and simple, I don't feel very loved by you. As a husband, you're bankrupt. No, worse than bankrupt—you're an unrecoverable loss."

Wally looked at the little box on the table. "Do you love me?" he asked in a tone he hadn't heard from himself since he uttered his schoolboy prayers.

"Yes, Wally. I have since the moment I met you. I sacrificed a lot to become your wife. I ruined a perfectly good marriage to be your wife."

He ran his hand through his hair. "You were too young to call that a marriage."

"It was a marriage. It says so in our prenuptial."

"Look," he insisted, "I know I never really had a mother growing up. I might have been a different person. All I've known is a certain commodity attitude toward women. I saw that in my father and John Bruce. I swore and Mrs. Dolan made me swear that I would be a gentleman to women."

"Being a gentleman is owning up to responsibilities. Marriage is not a piece of property that you fix up and sell off at a profit."

"Mea culpa," he said again, "I'm sorry. I'm sorry. I have taken you for granted, but that doesn't mean I've stopped loving you. Growing up after my mother died, I was raised by aunts, au pairs, my father's girlfriends. Maybe there was too much. Maybe because it was always there, I never stopped to check out the quality of that love."

Jennifer had heard this before. But she wasn't sure what direction he was headed this time. She reached over and placed her hand on his.

"Let me finish it for you," she said. "Sons who don't have a mother's love or affection are doomed to search the planet looking for it," Jennifer said slowly. "But guess what, Wally. She's dead. She was dead before you were two years old. She jumped off the top of the Fairbanks Hotel because your father was going to divorce her. Wally. No one will replace her, so don't confuse that need with the desire for other women."

McGrath slumped in his seat. "So, what do you want from me?"

"You need a new writer, Wally. Remember that I'm the one you live with. Bimbos hearing this crap for the first time may jump out of their pantyhose but not me. After our little financial adios, I'm going to leave you and San Francisco. I'm selling my interest in the station and I've decided to take an anchor job in Washington, DC."

"Really? See that's what I love about you. You reach out for what you want. I saw that the day I first met you. What station?"

"WWW."

"Clever."

"They're a new all news, sports, and C-SPAN type of station. They're cable but they're kicking ass. I'll start as an entry-level owner—maybe anchor the news, but I doubt that. Covering news in DC is a very tough gig."

Wally reached for her hands. "What can I do to talk you out of this? I feel helpless because I have been trying—last night is simply the appearance of impropriety. Nothing happened. Look, she's new. She came up to our floor and knocked on our door by mistake. She was delivering a bottle of booze for John's cocktail party next door. She asked to use the powder room. I haven't seen her since."

"Wally, listen to yourself. Even so, if she knocked on the wrong door, employees are trained not to use the toilet in our suite."

"She is new."

"You're brain dead, Wally."

"One more chance. If I fuck up, again, you can have it all."

"Are you admitting you fucked her?"

"I'll admit to anything to end this torture. If you want me to play guilty I will, but I'm not. I don't need to win this debate, but it is obvious to you that it is important that you do."

"This is not about money or property, Wally. Between our families, we have more money than we deserve. You piss away more money on booze than a convention of drunks."

"Jennifer. I have never faced losing you. I am sorry. I will change. One more chance."

"Wally, I see you heading into a downward spiral. You're drinking too much and you're probably doing drugs."

"Don't say that. I've never done drugs."

"Maybe so. Booze is a drug. Women are a drug. I just want you to realize how much good you could accomplish in this world if you used your skills. John wants you to be president. Hell, you could be mayor or governor just with your smile. Use that silver spoon you inherited to be a man."

"My father has ruined me in politics."

"No, he hasn't. The public forgets. Politicians today are shatterproof. The new political mantra is to apologize, and you'll bounce back to the top. No one remembers he was jailed for contempt of Congress. All you must do is face the truth that your father was a right-wing toady who used his company planes to run guns during the Iran Contra era. Be honest with the public. Don't hide anything. Tell the truth and they'll get bored. Don't let them find dirty secrets because if they do, they'll never give up."

"If you leave me, I will kill myself."

She gave him a sardonic smile. "Green Street Mortuary is across the street from DeLuca's. Shall I call them that you're on the way?"

The restaurant burst into laughter for a split second—then went silent.

Jennifer leaned forward. "I'm leaving, so deal with it." She put her hands on top of his. "Aren't you going to ask me what I did in Denver?"

"I'm afraid to ask."

"I spent the night with a man."

For the first time in their marriage, she saw sadness on his face. He looked around the restaurant as if he was stumbling for something to say. He seemed to have little experience with that emotion. For a fleeting moment, he looked helpless. Vulnerable. Sad. Defeated. "I don't know what to say?" he said. "Did he make love to you?"

"Wally, he fucked me until I was blind."

"Did you suck his cock?"

More gasps from the diners, who were now riveted on every word.

"For an hour. Then he did me for another hour in the ass, and when it was over, we did it again, out in the hotel elevator."

"Was he anybody I know?"

"Do you want to know? Because I'm not joking about what I did."

"No. I don't want to know. But I'm disappointed you didn't invite me to join in."

More howls of laughter.

Jennifer couldn't believe what she had heard coming out of his mouth. It took everything she had to remain in her chair.

By this time, she realized Wally was playing to an audience. "Wally, do you realize how God damned serious all of this is?"

"I know, I know. I want you to stay. I'll do whatever you say."

"Say goodbye because it's over between us."

"Jennifer, honest to God, I'm sorry. Do you want me to beg? Do you want me to get down on my knees in this restaurant and beg you not to leave me? I will do it."

For the longest time, she stared into his eyes. He'd never said he would beg before. Did he finally get it? Had she brought this huge and powerful man to his knees?

"No—you won't. You'll end up saying another smart-ass remark and spoil it and then it would be final—I'm gone." She stared.

He said nothing. He was afraid to move because suddenly, he was in Sister Cyrilla's office. She was the only nun/teacher/woman he truly feared as a teenager.

He had tossed a cherry bomb firecracker into the faculty toilet at school. The janitor caught him. He sat in her office waiting for his punishment. Until this moment, he had not realized that the waiting was the punishment. Dealing with the uncertainty—dealing with the consequences of his actions, was thoroughly painful.

Finally, Jennifer spoke: "It's up to you, Wally. It boils down to them or me. What's it going to be?"

"Maybe I do need some help."

"You need a lot of help," she laughed. "If you don't get help, then there's no hope for us."

"I don't do shrinks. I don't live in Marin County suburbs."

"Well, you certainly fuck in Marin County."

"I love you, Jennifer. You're my strength. Help me through this. I want to change. I want the chance to be a good father."

"Poor baby, you must be exhausted."

"Don't make fun of me. I'm serious. I don't want to destroy each other."

"Wally, I'm sitting here like I'm at the stage of a Shakespearean play, wondering if it is a comedy or a tragedy. I'm wondering about my future. It's serious for me, too. I still have a lot to offer. I have my looks. I got a career. What I don't have is a faithful husband. I can't spend the rest of my life looking over my shoulder and checking the god-damned toilet in my own home."

"I'll do whatever you want."

"What I want and what you're willing to do—" Jennifer interrupted herself. "I can't even think about it."

"What do you want me to do?"

"Let me go."

"Give me some options. If there is one last prayer for us—what are the terms?"

"OK, for laughs, here goes: No nooners, quickies, or other women. That means no more booze unless you're with me. No more DeLuca's restaurant, and that includes his new Club Car room."

"How about chopping off my dick?"

"That too, and I want you to take six months off and attend a clinic that specializes in controlling addictive personality disorders. I'll help you. In the meantime, we'll both get some private counseling. I know of a compulsive treatment program a woman doctor runs at Jenner Hospital in Sonoma County. I did a KNUZ white paper report on her clinic and hospital. I want you to go there. Maybe we can find a program that we can do together in private. Are you willing to meet me halfway?"

"I don't have a booze problem."

"Yes, you do."

"I understand where you're coming from, but I really don't have issues with drinking."

"Then we're back where we started," she said.

"Let me think about it."

"Wally, I want to be more important than John Bruce, or Larry DeLuca, or whatever bimbo is sucking you off."

"Fine." He slumped in his chair. "Fine. Whatever makes you happy."

"One more thing," she said. "I want a promise from you. I don't want John Bruce living next door to us. Fuck, I don't want him in the same building. I don't give a shit if your father promised him he could live there for life. Get rid of him. Him or me, Wally!" It's not like we need him to cover the mortgage. I hate him. I want him and that old woman butler to go, but most of all, I want a husband."

"Is that all?" he murmured.

"My way or the highway."

"I don't want to live in this city without you." He was serious. She saw it in his eyes. Her index finger caught a tear before it ran down her cheek.

Wallace McGrath leaned across the table and surprised his wife with a kiss. It was a passionate kiss on the mouth.

The kiss lingered.

The small gift box fell off the table.

A waiter rushed over and retrieved the package to the applause of the dozen diners that had been listening to the live soap opera.

Jennifer gave her mock Hollywood wave before staring at the gift.

A murmur of curiosity went around the tables.

A waitress and the woman bartender started a chant that brought on laughter: "Open, open, open, open."

Jennifer lifted the two-inch wide diamond choker out of the box. The restaurant was stunned into silence until someone at the far end of the bar whistled: "Put it on, put it on, put it on."

Was it the most expensive gift he had ever bought for her? It didn't matter. Maybe it was a bargain. She had him cornered—a cool $50 billion or more for each testicle.

She wasn't going to put it on until the chant from the restaurant kept up. "Put it on, put it on, put it on."

Jennifer let Wally do the snaps. He pumped his fist in the air. It was political theater. But for the next hour, Wally enjoyed lunch followed by a walk around Chinatown holding hands. At a curbside flower shop, he bought her a fragrant gardenia and pinned it on her lapel.

For one hour as they strolled, there was a serene calmness.

She had hope.

Wally promised.

And he had never promised before.

She sat back and let out her breath. For the first time in a long time, there might be hope for them as a couple. And that would please her because she knew she loved him and she was aware of the cost she paid having given up a man who loved her deeply. Or at least did so at one time.

"Let's see how long this will last," she mumbled before a delivery truck honked at them jaywalking across Chinatown's tiny Grant Avenue toward the parked Fairbanks Hotel limo that was waiting for them.

Jennifer was quiet for most of the time it took the limo to climb the steep hill from Chinatown to Nob Hill. For the most part, Wally's grandiose display at Le Central didn't sway her disappointment.

Wally figured as much. That's why he put his fortune on the line in the form of another gift-wrapped package that sat on the mantel in their penthouse living room.

Red foil wrapping paper was accented with a gold ribbon. The square foot package sat between a third-century statue head of a terra cotta soldier excavated from China's tomb of Emperor Xinzhuang and the original sepia-colored photograph of Abraham Lincoln taken by Matthew Brady in 1860. The latter in a pure gold frame from Marie Antoinette's boudoir.

Jennifer unwrapped it slowly, carefully opened the lid and peeked in.

Astonished, she pushed the top back in place. "Wally, my God, they're looking all over the world for this."

"You recognize it, then?"

"Of course? How did you…? It can't be real. Can it?"

She reopened the box and for the longest time stared at an original Faberge egg that was now hers.

"This is real?" she asked. "How did you get it?"

"Yes, its genuine. I have friend in Russia. After Russia was humiliated in its last war—security has gone to hell. It wasn't hard as I thought to get this into my hands."

"It's stolen?"

"Call it revenge for the Russians bombing my hotel in Luiv. Remember the Leninist Communists stole it from the Czar. I had a Russian don steal it from the Kremlin and I bought it from him.

I had some help from a friend who brokered the deal. He made the introductions with the black marketeers. They owed him a favor."

"I don't want you to go to jail for this, but I absolutely love it. My heart's pumping like I was in on the job."

"I'll hire your attorney if it comes to that."

"We can't leave it on the shelf out in the open."

"Of course, we can. Tell everyone it's a remarkable duplicate. Who will know? It's our secret."

13. HEAVYWEIGHT CHAMPIONSHIP OF THE WORLD

Snippet

Cantina Psalm:

What the fuck?

RETURN TO REALITY

Clueless as to the time, it took every bit of energy for Annee to open her eyes after crashing all night entwined with Tom on the old bed. *You play, you pay,* she mumbled.

Splashing cold water on her face didn't chase the nausea.

She borrowed a pair of his matching sweats and a baseball cap from his closet. She had accepted Tom's offer to move her stuff into his place until she found somewhere else to stay.

She was up only because she knew she had to get to Mike Kinder's apartment to grab her backpack and computer. She hoped he'd be gone.

It was now or never.

* * *

Each step down the two flights of stairs was brain agony. Stepping out into a blustery wind and pelting rain was no cakewalk.

Miserable as she was—it only got worse. An unseen hand grabbed her upper arm from behind.

She spun around.

She didn't see it but she more than felt the fist slam into her stomach.

Two pedestrians stopped to see what was going on.

She was now face to face with Mike Kinder. Finding some breath, she gasped: "Let go of me."

"Police business—move along," Kinder shouted. The onlookers scurried away.

She saw immediately that he was in a cocaine fog. He was grinding his teeth in anger. They were the couple of the year.

"Mike, let go of me, I don't have time to talk." She pulled her arm away, but he held it tight.

"Are you fucking Gresham?" He had her arm in a vice grip.

Agonized to the point of being blinded by the pain, Annee gave an elbow to his thigh.

She recognized the clenched jaw and the strained wild-eyed stare. Why she ever moved in with Kinder was beyond her now.

She pulled away.

"Answer me, are you fucking Gresham?" He now had her a choke hold on her.

Gasping, she squirmed away. "It's none of your business. What gives you the right to touch me? Let go, Mike."

"You're nothing but a whore." He moved his face an inch away from hers.

"Listen to yourself. It's your dream. I'm not your wife or your girlfriend. Now stop it," she growled. "Let go of me. I'm moving my stuff out of your apartment."

"You can't without permission. I'm your husband."

"Husband? Are you nuts? What are you talking about? I just met you. Fantasyland is closed. Forever."

"Not until I say so."

She pulled at his hand. "What a disaster you are."

He squeezed harder. "You got my name. You're my wife!"

"You're hurting me."

"Good." He pushed the index finger of his free hand hard into her throat.

"Mike, stop it," she gagged. The finger pressure was painful. His nail dug into her flesh.

"Call a cop, bitch!"

Her anger flashed. She raked her fingernails across his cheek and the bridge of his nose.

The slash hurt. He backed off, releasing his grip.

She tripped into the news rack in front of Mario's and went down on one knee on the wet sidewalk. Pain tore into her hip and head. The metal rack had cut into her forehead.

She never saw the blow to her face coming. She dropped into the icy water flowing fast along the curb.

The world was still spinning when he yanked her to her feet.

His gloved fist slammed into her ribs. She gasped. No breath came to her. No scream of pain. Her feet tangled. Her knees caught the brunt of her fall onto the sidewalk.

The ex-cop straddled her. He reached to pull her up.

"That's enough!" Father MacDonald's voice bellowed. Crossing Union Street against the traffic light, the priest had just stepped off the thirty Stockton bus stop when Kinder's first blow struck her.

He spun around. "Stay out of this!" The ex-cop was in no mood for interruptions.

"Stop it, Mike. Leave her alone. She's hurt." Father Mac had his arm extended and pointed an index finger direct at Kinder's face.

Annee rose to her hands and knees; her vision spun in circles.

The cop slapped the priest's hand away, then turned to level an uppercut into the woman's shoulder that deflected against her jaw.

She went down hard.

Father MacDonald spun Kinder away from her.

Kinder pushed both hands into Father Mac's chest. The blow sent him backward into the arms of Pauley Carbone, who had roared out of his café.

Two male customers, one a Latino and a much taller linebacker-sized African American had followed Pauley.

The smaller man, using a sweeping soccer kick, knocked Kinder's feet from under him. The cop landed flat on his back, revealing he was fumbling for the snap on his holster.

"You touch that gun, and you lose your arm," the Black man shouted into Kinder's face.

Pauley dropped his knees on the cop's chest. "Someone call 9-1-1, she's fallen on her head."

Prone next to the curb on her back, Annee gasped for breath.

Someone had ripped off Kinder's yellow parka and held it over her.

She blacked out.

"Don't be dead," Pauley yelled. He started pumping her chest with both hands.

Tom burst through his apartment door. He ran to her side.

Seeing that she was in Father Mac's care, he turned toward where Mike was rising to his feet.

Tom unleashed a wild uppercut with his right hand. The blow missed, but the left hook did not. It landed solid in Kinder's face, causing him to fall to his knees.

Tom's next punch to Kinder's right ear put him down on the sidewalk.

Pauley Carbone and the linebacker-sized Black American came up to Tom. "No more. He's not worth killing."

Tom looked at his friend, "Did someone call an ambulance?"

"I did," Pauley said.

Kinder wobbled to his feet. He steadied himself on the traffic signal post.

Father Mac came up to Kinder. "Go home, Mikey, there's nothing here for you to prove. Go."

Kinder stumbled a few steps before righting himself. He leaned once more on the traffic signal post to orient himself. His forehead was on the post he was hugging.

HARD PLACE

Pauley Carbone bent over Annee placing a bar towel from his café under the back of her head. He stopped the bleeding.

Annee manage to open her eyes. She didn't know where she was. Blood was in her mouth. "I'm OK," she managed to say. "Pauley, what are you doing here?" She tried to sit up. "I'm freezing."

Father Mac whispered words of thanks. "She's aware. We still need the ambulance. Where's the ambulance?"

She said barely audible, "I'm so cold."

* * *

Amid the melee no one noticed Gus Oklahoma's rusting Ford had skidded to a stop in front of Mario's Café.

Ezra Ounce flung open the driver's side door.

A voice shouted. "He has a gun!"

Ezra rested his elbows on the roof of the beige Ford to steady his aim at a blur of people standing over who he believed was Annee.

Sound from three shots echoed off the buildings and down Columbus.

People screamed.

Father Mac picked up Kinder's service revolver that had been yanked from the ex-cop's holster and lay on the sidewalk. His intention was to slide the weapon across the sidewalk to Tom.

But it was too late, Tom had been hit by two bullets, one in his upper torso and another entered full force through his flesh, ricocheted off his hip bone and lodged in his upper thigh.

Another shot ripped into Pauley Carbone's temple. Lifeless, his body crumbled on top of Annee. In death, he shielded her from more harm. Father Mac shouted, "Someone go put pressure on Pauley's head. Help stop the bleeding. Oh, merciful God, Anyone, call an ambulance!" Other screams and the calamity of café patrons clamoring over fallen chairs and tables—some wanting to help, others to run for their lives.

The huge African American, who had tripped over a fallen chair rose to his knees and howled, "Everybody GET DOWN!" The linebacker grabbed the chair.

Seeing that Father Mac had Kinder's gun. Ezra aimed toward the priest just as a fold-up chair bounced off the hood, a metal leg hit him in the mouth. Ezra flung the chair away and shouted to Mike Kinder, "Mikey, get into the car, now!"

Only a few seconds passed as Kinder stumbled forward and clamored into the Ford. Ezra stomped on the gas pedal and roared down Columbus toward Fisherman's Wharf. The passenger door was still open. Mike was vainly trying to shut it.

* * *

Ezra ran several traffic lights. He did so with ease, almost as if he was enjoying himself.

Kinder's face was in anguish bordering on horror. Finally, he brought himself to yell, "Stop the car, Ezra. Let me out."

"What for? We got to get across the bay." Two lanes of backed-up traffic at Bay Street and Van Ness slowed the Ford to a crawl. "I figure if we drive all night that could put us in Oregon. We can ditch the car and fade into the forest."

"Let me out, I ain't going nowhere with you."

"Mikey, it's too late, we're in this together. I gotta cabin in Bolinas where we can wait it out. No one asks questions up there."

"Fuck no, Ezra, you just can't shoot people."

"They were beating you. I should have shot all of them. Something I should have done a long time ago."

Gus's Ford idled roughly. "This piece of shit won't make it across the bridge," Kinder said and opened the passenger door.

Ezra screamed, "MIKE, STOP!"

Kinder turned to face his old friend. "Why do I want to run? I didn't shoot anyone. Why should I run?"

Ezra's face contorted "I love you like a brother. Yuz can't leave me. Yuz can't turn on me now. I've always had your back. DON'T GO ON ME NOW!". Tears flooded his eyes. He fired two rounds into Kinder's forehead. Mike's body melted into the rain-swollen gutter. His armed twitched. It was his first second of eternity.

Ezra jammed the barrel of his gun into his mouth and pulled the trigger several times. No explosion. He was out of bullets.

Ezra threw the weapon out into the rain. He punched the accelerator, steering the old car over the curb and onto the sidewalk. He circled around the cars backed up at the intersection, then slammed on the brakes to avoid hitting crossing traffic. The move forced the passenger door to slam shut.

Drivers around him realizing he was a madman at the wheel stopped in all directions. Ezra squealed the tires making a left turn on Van Ness and gunned it south to Lombard Avenue.

There, Ezra made a right turn onto Lombard instead, where he decided to blend in with the traffic flow and stay within the speed limit toward and across the Golden Gate.

* * *

The bullet that went through Pauley had enough remaining velocity to enter Tom's right lung.

Tom had fallen to his knees. Father Mac rushed to grab Tom from falling on to his face.

The bullet's damage sucked the air from Tom's lungs, leaving him gasping.

He slipped through the priest's grip and hit the side of his head hard on the sidewalk. His vision doubled then blurred. He reached for Father Mac's hand. The cleric pressed his hands hard on Tom's wounds.

"EVERYONE TO THE GROUND. GET DOWN!" Tom heard himself yell yet no sound came out of his mouth. *What the fuck!* He could not move. *What the fuck!*

From where he lay, Tom stared at the old Ford as it roared away. The next moment brought a knifing spasm of searing heat to his chest. Immense pain caused his eyes to roll and shut. He felt his hand in front of his face. *What am I doing lying down on the sidewalk?*

The picture faded to black, yet he could still hear the traffic along Columbus Avenue until someone flipped the sound to mute.

* * *

At last, the gurney burst through the St. Augustine carrier ER doors from the arriving ambulance. Paramedics Draper Webster and Paul Gallagher refused to hand over the victim to St. Augustine Hospital's triage team because they did not want to release applying pressure on the ripped flesh until they reached the main operating table. Only then did the arriving ER team take over from the veteran ambulance team.

"We got him, we got him," yelled a nurse donned in military camouflage. Every Friday was Veterans Day and any staffer who wanted could dress up in camo.

Wrapping up her third overdose emergency of the morning, Dr. Victoria Martin stood waiting for the new arrival. Tired from her tenth hour of a twelve-hour shift, she pulled herself to attention. She was ready for battle like she had been for a generation.

She glanced at the victim and let out a cry, a heartbreaking whimper. Her mouth trembled, "Oh, my God. Oh, my God. Oh, Tommy, what have they done to you?"

To be continued.

[Sequel to be published early 2023]

EPILOG
CAST OF CHARACTERS
(main characters in all caps)

1.
ART OF THE DEAL

ART GARCIA—Retired special agent U.S. Customs and soldier of fortune. Grad of Sts. Peter & Paul School for Boys.

Jonna Berk Art Garcia Investigations [AGI] co-partner and chief logistics officer.

TOM GRESHAM—divorced, ex-San Francisco Police Officer before becoming an independent security agent (top bodyguard) for Mayor Joe Martin's city hall security detail. Youngest peer group grad of Sts. Peter and Paul School.

Carol Law—torch singer, who plays hotel bar venues throughout the Bay Area.

JOE MARTIN—Two term Mayor of San Francisco after serving as District Attorney for the City and County of San Francisco, the only California city and county sharing the same boundaries. Oldest graduate of Sts. Peter and Paul School for Boys (K-12) on Filbert Street, North Beach.

CARLY MARTIN—deputy district attorney, single, eldest daughter of Joe and Victoria Martin. Tom Gresham love interest.

EDUARDO AYUNAR—Man of mystery in Madrid, who meets with Art Garcia to warn him he was being watched.

THE BRUNETTE IN THE BAR—Garcia love interest who eventually surfaces as Doria Ziti

JOHN WALD—Owner of Powell's Saloon, North Beach; ex-San Francisco Fire Dept. firefighter. Graduate of Sts. Peter & Paul School.

Fred Pontchatrain—A.K.A. Art Garcia.

Fernando Abba—A.K.A. Tom Gresham

Concierge—Hotel Attu, Madrid.

Santiago—bartender at Hotel Attu.

Olivia—cocktail waitress at Hotel Attu.

King and Queen of Spain—as themselves.

2.

APPEARANCE OF IMPROPRIETY

Anthony Guereca—discoverer and subsequent billionaire of permanent charge batteries for cars, phones and public vehicles.

GARRETT ELLIS—prominent civil attorney, acting chief of staff, second term, Martin Administration, sports attorney, member of City Black Caucus. Graduate of Sts. Peter and Paul School.

VICTORIA CARLING MARTIN—Doc Martin, wife of Mayor Joe Martin, chief of staff and head emergency room surgeon, St. Vincent's Hospital, Tenderloin District.

Pauley Carbone—Owner, Mario's Bohemian Café.

EZRA OUNCE—Ex-policeman, San Francisco PD.

MIKE KINDER—Ex-policeman, San Francisco Police Department, once SFPD partner with Ezra Ounce.

MELISSA 'MISSY' MARTIN—teen second daughter of Joe and Victoria Martin. High school volleyball phenom.

Carla Boris—County of San Francisco, medical examiner, assistance coroner.

3.

THE DENIZENS

Cat—Halloween day customer at Powell's

Rabbit—Cat's co-worker at Clementine's strip joint, North Beach.

SHANNON REDDING—dancer at Clementine's who left to work at Powell's. Love interest of John Wald.

Eddie Peabody--a City of San Francisco parking enforcement officer.

FATHER MAC—A.K.A.--**FR. RONALD MACDONALD,** Order of St. Augustine, founder and headmaster of Sts. Peter and Paul Catholic School for Orphan Boys, North Beach.

4.

COY POND

Zorenzo Ziti—Acquaintance of Joe and Victoria Martin, editor of *Il Edifico* architectural magazine, Milan.

DORIA ZITI--Russian agent attached to Spain's Interpol bureau, wife of Zorenzo Ziti and clandestine love interest of Art Garcia in Madrid.

Andrew Roehr--Chief of Police, San Francisco, member of the city's Black Caucus

HARRE LING--District Attorney, alum of Sts. Peter and Paul School and best man at Joe and Victoria Martin's wedding.

WALLACE 'WALLY' MCGRATH—scion to Oakland-based McGrath International, a fourth-generation scion to McGrath International, a multi-national engineering and hotel conglomerate. Builders of hydroelectric plants, dams, airports most recently in Rio Huego, Peru. Head of McGrath Hotels, a chain of ten 5-star hotels. McGrath Aviation, aviation and supply carriers for McGrath International. Elected to the San Francisco Board of Supervisors; then became Mayor after Joe Martin termed out.

Dr. Amanda Ruiz—Chief of Staff at Jenner-by-the-sea Rehab hospital, Sonoma County.

Ben Adams—partygoer at Martin wedding anniversary soiree. Husband of Karen Adams.

EUGENE CARLING—Father of Victoria Martin, retired editor in chief of the San Francisco Daily News; and part owner of Salazar Winery in Healdsburg, Sonoma County. Earned a Pulitzer Prize for investigative journalism while he was editor of the Lee County Traveler, a daily newspaper serving the Ft. Myers, Florida region of Southwest Florida.

Archibald McGrath--founder of the McGrath Empire beginning with a mercantile operation during the Alaska Gold Rush, circa 1890s.

Thomas McGrath, Sr.-- son of Archibald, expanded the McGrath holdings.

Thomas McGrath, Jr--grandson of Archibald, who diversified the McGrath brand. Father of Wallace "Wally" McGrath. Iran-Contra figure 1980s.

Ille Druck--the late architect of the Russian Hill Bauhaus residence owned by Eugene Carling and used as the Martin home, except during Joe Martin's stint as Mayor. Current home of Carly Martin.

5.

HEMOPHILIAC OF LOVE

C.J. Frank Barnett--KNUZ-TV news helicopter pilot.

JENNIFER HAWTHORNE MCGRATH—Sole heiress to Hawthorn Oil Corporation, a privately held oil exploration company and second wife of Wally McGrath, majority owner of KNUZ-TV, a 24-hour all-news station, who enjoys being the stations's prime time Anchorwoman for its 10 O'clock news segment.

6.

ROUGHER PART OF TOWN

Nearly Normal Norman Oklahoma—former owner of Clementine's, a strip joint on Broadway, across the street from Leon Lee's Broadway café.

Juicy Lucy--stripper, moll, mistress to Norman Oklahoma. Silent business partner with John Wald, owner of Powell's Saloon.

Charley Nye—Policeman, San Francisco PD later Captain, head of Green Street (North Beach) precinct, SFPD.

MAX WAX—ex reporter *San Francisco Daily News* and losing end of a libel action brought forward by plaintiff Carly Martin. Wax, a wannabe Jack Kerouac era writer, who leaves North Beach with his tail between his legs.

Scott Keating--on-air reporter, KQED, public radio.

Ray Potter—managing editor, *San Francisco Daily News*.

Alan Carter—Missing person, heir to Carter Pharmaceuticals, and dead body washed up off the Farallon Islands.

Angelina—76 ft. seiner, sole fishing boat of DeLuca Wholesale Fish., Fisherman's Wharf.

Kerouac's Bookstore—used bookstore next door to Clementine's, where Max Wax lived in a back room.

LARRY DELUCA—Owner of DeLuca's Restaurant at Grant and Columbus Avenue; owner of Clementine's strip joint and owner of DeLuca's Wholesale fish and trawler *Angelina*.

LI-YUAN "LEON" LEE— owner of Broadway Café and Pacifica (24-7 underground) Mall; Chinatown and Central Officer New Chinatown Businessmen's Association (Tong).

Lyn Lee--soldier of fortune working as waitress at Broadway Cafe, niece of Li-Yuan Lee.

Junior DeLuca—son of Larry DeLuca, GM of family-owned Clementine's, a long-time strip joint near Broadway and Columbus. Head of operations for DeLuca's Fresh Fish trawler berth at Fisherman's Wharf.

Don Vanchester—ex soldier of fortune, captain, ret. US Navy PT and river craft, head of Fairbanks Hotel Security; Chauffeur and pilot of the DeLuca's trawler, the *Angelina*.

Jazzy Montgomery—homeless resident of Fisherman's Wharf, one-time popular jazz singer.

Jerry Longstreet—former band leader turned homeless. Married to Jazzy Montgomery, his lead singer.

Ebony Williams—A.K.A. "X," Xandy, stripper at Clementine's.

Cilla Davis—Filipina nurse at St. Vincent's Hospital, Tenderloin District.

7.

WHO KNOCKED UP BABY CAKES?

Frank Salazar, patriarch of Salazar wine family, first client of Joe Martin.

Ted Salazar—son of Frank Salazar and current owner of the winery.

Sebastian Salazar, grandson of Frank.

8.
ODD DUCK SEASON

ANNEE KINDER—new call girl in town, ex-Clementine's dancer, ex-Klondike Room (Fairbanks Hotel) cocktail waitress one-woman tough crowd, fake wife of North Beach police patrolman, Mike Kinder; Love interest to Wally McGrath and others.

9.
EX, X

Melody D'amour—Stripper, Clementine's.
Mambo Morretti—head waiter DeLuca's, part time love interest of Angela DeLula.
Dennis Rath—County Medical Examiner

10.
THE PUBLICANS

Michael Cortland—Co-owner of Cortland and James, Public House, North Beach.
Seamus Doonan (aka. Jimmy)—Co-owner of Cortland and James, Public House, North Beach.
Alexander Duvee—co-owner, Sonata's Restaurant, Nob Hill.
Horace Smith—Engineer McGrath Corporation, Pipeline Division.
Gus Oklahoma—younger brother of Clementine's founder, the late Norman Oklahoma. Gus sold Clementine's to the DeLuca's and later became the hired GM of Dante's Saloon, across Grant Avenue from DeLuca's Restaurant.

11.

SHEET MUSIC

Carol Law—torch singer, love interest of Art Garcia and Tom Gresham.

12.

MEA CULPA HALL OF FAME

Ruth Dolan—Fairbanks Hotel, Butler to the McGrath and John Bruce penthouses.

13.

ANNEE BEATEN

Draper Webster and Paul Gallagher—Ambulance drivers.

ABOUT THE AUTHOR

Thomas Shess is a former reporter with the *San Francisco Examiner*, editor in chief of *San Francisco Magazine* and *PSA Magazine* and executive editor with *San Diego Magazine* and *San Diego Home/Garden Lifestyles Magazine*. He is an award-winning prolific freelance writer specializing in travel, food and current and vintage arts & crafts and midcentury architecture. His wife, Phyllis, is a retired homicide and sex crimes prosecutor for the San Diego District Attorney's office. Sons Zac and Mike live in northern and southern California, where the family gathers often.

The author at Sirkeci Terminal Railway Station, Istanbul, Turkey
Photo by Phyllis Shess